1936

Printed in Australia
First Printing: October 2022
Shawline Publishing Group Pty Ltd
www.shawlinepublishing.com.au

Paperback ISBN 978-1-9228-5027-0
eBook ISBN 978-1-9228-5036-2

A catalogue record for this
work is available from the
National Library of Australia

1936

BRUCE RYAN

For Hirell and Janet

FOREWORD

This book is fiction and any resemblance of the Australian Olympic team members or the support staff is purely accidental.

I fashioned the story after reading about the terrible treatment of the Sinti and Roma people which started long before the Nazi machine came to power.

The violence against the so-called 'Gypsies' had started in the 1800s, perhaps earlier, but became even more prevalent and fervent after New Year's Day, 1934, when the 'Law for the Prevention of Genetically Diseased Offspring' was put into effect.

People were dragged off the street if they were thought to have had two or more grandparents of 'Gypsy' origin and forcibly sterilised. If there was too much public protestation, people were 'disappeared' or imprisoned.

Terrible experiments were already being conducted on members of both communities' children, under the guise of racial preservation. Such extreme and cruel treatments included attempts to dye children's eyes blue and blood replacements to name but two – these treatments often saw the victims blinded or worse, and deaths were not uncommon.

Those with a disability and homosexuals were also among those targeted by these evils which were forerunners, a practice if you will, for the holocaust perpetrated on the wider community. Those seen as impediments to the progression of the Nazi credo, and the Jewish communities of Germany and many other countries in Europe in the 1930s and 1940s, were targets of this attempted genocide.

I had not previously heard about this early 'Law for the Prevention of Genetically Diseased Offspring' and wanted to shine a light on its terrible consequences.

I hope you enjoy the book.

Bruce Ryan

CHAPTER 1

No one was more surprised than I was when I received the letter stating that I had been appointed as one of the team doctors.

I was told that I had been selected from a long list of doctors who applied to care for our athletes at the Olympic Games in two years' time.

Yes, I had treated several athletes over the last year since gaining my qualifications and setting up practice in Sydney. Yes, I had been accepted in to the prestigious Baltimore Practitioners firm in Macquarie Street in the central business district. I had been very surprised – I had not applied for the position.

I had also not applied for the position on the Olympic team.

Growing up I had learned to speak fairly fluent German from my best friend Peter Nagel

The Nagel's lived next door to us all of my life in Wollongong and Peter, the eldest of three sons, and I were of the same age. I thought that may be the reason I was picked. But how did they even know about me?

I wondered if there was some mysterious benefactor helping me along.

I attended the first day at Baltimore's as instructed and was ushered past several other people waiting in the outer office and into the presence of Archibald Baltimore himself.

He rushed to take my hand and offered me refreshments, tea coffee and even brandy, all of which I declined. I felt embarrassed; I had only come twelfth in a class of 26. I was certainly not one of the better candidates from my class and the offer, which had come by mail, was the greatest opportunity any of my class could have hoped for. To put it bluntly, I felt like a charlatan. I didn't deserve to be there.

My professor at university had been the renowned Mordechai Abraham Hochberg. When addressing him, we were expected to use his full name as he often did when speaking his own name in the third person.

Professor Mordechai Abraham Hochberg had taken a liking to me from day one. I was not sure why. At first, I thought he had singled me out as a possible 'close acquaintance'. His approaches had seemed almost propositional. I later learned that he was a happily married man with three daughters.

I simply didn't like dead bodies. Dead bodies we were to deal with on a daily basis. We would have a body delivered from the mortuary, usually that of an unnamed street person, too many of whom there were in Sydney in the early 1930s. We would each be given a part of the body to dissect. I was fairly handy with a scalpel but I simply didn't like doing the task. I knew full well that it was a necessary part of medicine I knew I had to know the inside as well as the outside if I wanted to be a doctor. If I wanted to be a doctor?

The first week at Baltimore Practitioners, was given several young athletes to do medicals for few other members of the public, each of whom were young. I liked the work, to my surprise, and thought that if I only had to see young people, it was less likely that I would have to deal with corpses.

I had been afforded a luxurious, large office which I felt guilty using – every time I walked through the door I felt like an imposter.

During one of these first week visits I met a young boxer named Graeme Weathers who I became quite friendly with. It seemed we had been friends for years when he visited for the second time. I had been instructed, from on high, to keep him fit. He had rather rough hands and had, on several occasions, broken bones around his knuckles. At 20 he was already showing advanced signs of arthritis. Weathers had fought in pain since his first bout and was undefeated in his six fights to date.

He invited me to attend his next bout and to sit in his corner. Because I liked him and was at least a little interested in boxing, I agreed, and watched him TKO his opponent in only the second round. After the fight, I also treated the vanquished fighter for a severe cut over his right eye.

Over the next few months, I watched two more victories and in one, he never had one blow landed by his opposition, knocking the young man down in the first encounter of the first round.

We spent quite a bit of time together during the weekends I had off, and he even convinced me to spar with him one afternoon when I went to pick him up from his training gymnasium, it was a debacle. I could not land a punch as he danced around the ring. He gave me a couple of taps to keep me interested but made sure he didn't hurt me.

About a month or so into my work at the practice, I was asked to care for a stunning young lady who was training for the New South Wales Athletics championships. Berta Smith was tall, blond and quite beautiful. She had strained a calf muscle, and though I examined the sore area, I could actually not find the slightest thing wrong with her leg, or any other part of her person. She was, simply put, a beauty. Her laugh was engaging and her eyes twinkled with the excitement of youth. There was little I could do for the injury but suggest that she rest for several days and then resume training slowly to build back to peak fitness.

I saw Berta once more before the championships. She attended the practice to make sure that the wound had healed and I informed her and her coach that there seemed to be no further problem. This was a very beautiful and alluring young lady and when I examined her for the second time, I found myself blushing. I was still learning how to remove personality from my bedside manner. There really was no need for a physical once she informed me that she was in no further pain. She was, the first beautiful young lady whom I had had to treat, and I had always been clumsy and a little tongue tied around young ladies. That is not to say I had never gone out with one. I had spent some time in my late teens dating Sharon Green back in Wollongong, even then she had actually asked me out to the local dance because I was too shy to ask her.

At the conclusion of the appointment, I shook hands with Berta and her coach and said 'Please come back if there are any further problems.' I couldn't believe how I stumbled over the words. How unprofessional.

The coach gave me a knowing look and hurried the wonderful Berta out of the room. I was somewhat embarrassed again and vowed never to be such a jackass in the future.

Later, I followed Berta Smith's progress as she won first the New South Wales State championships over 400 yards, then the Australian championship over the same distance.

In early 1935 it was announced that Australia were going to compete in the Berlin Olympic Games, despite the voices of many renowned people who thought that Hitler's rise to power and the violence surrounding his becoming first Chancellor and then Führer was not worthy of Germany retaining the status of host.

The decision had been made in 1931 and it was thought that Germany's hosting of the games would bring them back into the fold, so to speak, as a peaceful member of the world community. It was therefore decided that Germany would continue to work toward the world visiting in 1936. Many countries voiced their mistrust of Hitler, and black athletes from around the world spoke of boycotting the games because of his 'pure Aryan' beliefs.

Australia followed Britain and other leading countries in choosing to believe that this may help to bring the disgraced country back from the shame of the First World War. Australia therefore looked to their athletic bodies to provide the members of the proposed team.

I was pleased to hear that both Weathers and Berta Smith were selected in the team.

A few days later, I was invited into the office of Archibald Baltimore. I was surprised to see all of the practices' doctors present and was even more surprised when they began to clap on my entry.

Baltimore came forward, shook my hand warmly and started a speech which was only unexpected by me.

'We are lucky,' he began in a loud voice, 'to have within our midst one of the doctors who will be caring for the Australian Olympic team in Germany.' He handed me a piece of paper with an Australian Government insignia at the head of the page. Quickly, I read the statement that I had been appointed to the role as one of the two team doctors.

I blushed and looked self consciously down at the ground; not only had I not known that the team had traveling doctors, but I had not even applied for the position.

I looked up. Now I really felt like a complete imposter and I knew that if I didn't say anything, at some stage I would be found out. 'But I didn't—'

My voice was drowned out by Baltimore who said loudly, 'Now put your hands together for Olympic Doctor Robert O'Calahan, then get back to work.'

He leaned close to me and said quietly, 'Don't look a gift horse in the mouth, boy.'

I had no intention of looking said gift horse in the mouth. The appointment was strange, but intended to accept the position by return post as was instructed in the letter. How terrible it would be if, in the next few days, the team officialdom realised that the Dr Robert O'Calahan they had appointed was not the correct Dr Robert O'Calahan.

To my surprise, that didn't eventuate and the next I heard about myself was the appointment of the team's officials in the Sydney Morning Herald three weeks later.

I rang home and spoke to my parents. I had not wanted them to get their hopes up only to have them dashed if it was discovered who I really was. My mother was all a-buzz when I told her the news. She ranted and raved of how proud she was, and then handed the phone to father who listened as I told him the news.

His reaction was not at all what I expected. He said simply, 'I thought this may happen. When will you be able to come and see us at home? I have a lot to tell you.'

I paused for a moment, unsure what he meant, thinking how to answer the question. 'Well, I could come home for a few days next week after they fit us for our team uniforms.'

'That will be good. We will see you on Friday then?' he agreed and put the receiver down. I had no idea what was on his mind. He had asked to see me and then hung up; that was so strange and usually Mother would have talked again. She would be the one to say goodbye usually.

I thought perhaps he hadn't understood what I had told him, but how strange. I wondered about what he had said. I went through several scenarios as I wrung my hands and paced up and down trying to make sense of things.

Eventually, I walked back to the phone and re-rang my family's home number.

I received the engaged signal.

Oh well. Mother must've been ringing friends and family. I tried an hour later and again received the same signal. I thought I would ring later in the day. Weathers had asked me to pick him up from the gymnasium at three o'clock so we could go out on the town and celebrate. I arrived around 15 minutes early and was surprised to find Weathers on the footpath in the rather rundown looking rough part of the city. As he neared the car, I could see that his hand had a large towel wrapped around it. There was just the outline of something larger than a hand.

'What's going on?' I asked,

'Bloody hand,' he said and started to unwrap the towel, revealing an ice pack. He sat next to me so I reached over and took the slab of defrosting ice away to reveal a large swelling over the three middle metacarpal bones.

'Oh God, what bad luck,' I said, knowing instinctively that at least one of the bones was broken.

'You have to do something,' he said, looking as though he may cry. I knew it was not the pain; he had had much worse injuries and was usually very stoic. No, this was about his position in the team.

'I will take you to casualty,' I told him.

'No, there will be people there who will report it, and if this gets back to the doctors …' He paused as though he was going to say something more, but didn't.

'Don't forget, I *am* one of the doctors,' I reminded him.

'I know, but you won't let them know, will you?' he asked. There was a pause. 'I will treat it, but if it isn't better in a few days—'

'No, you can't bloody tell anyone. This is my only chance. I can't do anything else – I can't even read and write properly. I have only one way out of the gutter,' he said.

I thought for a while again. 'Let's go to the surgery, and check out how bad it is.'

I drove back into the central part of the city. I thought that few people would still be at the surgery and was surprised when Baltimore himself met us at the front door.

'You took your time getting here,' he said, and proceeded to take Weathers by his good hand and led him into the number one consulting room. I followed in what seemed to be a regular state for me: the state of confusion.

'Sit,' Baltimore said pointing toward the patient's chair. Like my room, this one seemed to be oversized, but it differed by being even more richly appointed. Now I understood why the room never seemed to be used; it was the old man's personal place of consultation.

Weathers obeyed, looking quizzically at me. I nodded and then raised my shoulders to signify that I didn't know how the old man knew we were coming. He sat.

Baltimore glanced over his glasses at me. 'The treatment tray, man,' he snapped. I was bumbling around, still shocked by the whole thing, and he added, 'Well, hurry up.'

I nodded and moved to the trolley which was situated in one corner. I wheeled it over to where my boss was now seated in front of the injured hand. He grasped the injury and started to feel the swollen parts.

'What do you think, Doctor?' he asked me, and I thought I would be finally found out for the imposter I really was.

'Well, broken metacarpal?' I questioned back.

'Yes, and what else?' he continued.

'I'm not sure,' I said honestly.

'We don't usually admit that in front of a patient,' he said, glowering at me, then he broke his gaze and added in a friendlier voice, 'We do always admit that to a superior if it is true though.' His face had an almost paternal quality when he was teaching.

'Yes, sorry, sir,' I said.

'No need to be sorry. I practiced for twenty-five years to be the top-hand man in this country. You're not expected to know what I know.'

Weathers looked at me and gave a small smile of reassurance, then he looked back to the real professional in the room.

'Yes, sir.' How in the hell did I get a Guernsey from the Olympic team, in front of this man, or any other doctor for that matter?

I was thinking of resigning at the next possible point from the team. How could I treat our athletes when I couldn't even diagnose a broken hand properly?

'He has a broken metacarpal as you said, but he also has a piece of floating bone. Come here and feel it,' he instructed. I felt where he indicated he added, 'Can you feel what I am talking about?'

'Yes, yes I can,' I answered, obviously sounding surprised, as he continued my lesson.

'It is quite easy to diagnose when you know what you are looking for,' he said in a somewhat condescending tone, then added, 'We all have to learn, don't beat yourself up.'

I felt a little relieved but only nodded as I could not think of anything sensible to say.

'You have two main choices, young man. I operate now here or you go to the hospital and the team finds a new middleweight.' The old man explained to Weathers who looked shocked and unsure how to answer at first.

'Please do whatever you can, sir,' he pleaded and then added, 'I don't really have any money though.'

'We are here to assist Doctor O'Calahan in his education – that can't possibly cost you anything,' Baltimore said. 'Your coach is an old friend. He rang and said he thought you would be in needing help.'

There was a pause as both the patient and I got our heads around the statement. How on Earth would a top specialist doctor like Baltimore be an old friend of a pugilist coach?

With great dexterity, my teacher took a syringe, filled it with anaesthetic of a kind I was not yet acquainted with, and injected the back of Weathers' hand.

He gave seven small injections and then waited for several seconds, then again entered the needle in what looked like the sorest part of the hand. 'Can you feel that?' he asked.

'No,' answered Weathers, though the grimace on his face put lie to the words.

'Good, good, now you might want to look away for this,' Baltimore said as he deftly took a scalpel from the table. He poured some alcohol over it and then over his hands. He rubbed the liquid thoroughly into every crevice and then handed the bottle to me. I did the same and then placed the bottle back on the tray.

'Right, now,' he said, and made a small incision in the gap between the index and forefinger, and immediately extended it when he didn't see what he was looking for. This time he could see the offending broken piece of bone.

'Tweezers,' he demanded and I complied, handing them to him. 'Is there a smaller pair?' he questioned.

'No, not here,' I answered, scouring the tray and each of the two drawers.

'Well, find one. There is usually one in the glass cabinet,' he said, somewhat impatiently pointing at a glass-doored wall cabinet at the far end of the room. I moved quickly and gained the instrument he had requested and handed it to him.

'Sterilise it,' he ordered and I quickly poured it with the liquid and then handed it on.

'Yes, this will do nicely,' he said and began to extract the piece of bone which was no more than a quarter of an inch long and quite thin. It came away quickly and then he handed me the tweezers back.

'Wait,' he said. 'I think we have another piece.'

He took the tweezers back and extracted another smaller piece of bone.

'The break is pretty clean, but I will need to reset it.' He said, taking a small hooked instrument which he manoeuvred into the incision and then turned it to go under the bone of the middle finger.

Weathers had not been watching but turned as he could obviously feel the pressure. 'Oh God!' he exclaimed, looking quite pale.

'As I said, it would be better if you look away,' the old man instructed him. Boxer or not, it did look somewhat gruesome and Weathers turned his head.

Once the hook was in place, Baltimore said 'here,' nodding toward the instrument, and handed it over when I complied. I could feel the tightness of the tool in the wound.

'Can you feel the bone lift as you draw the hook toward you?' he questioned.

'Yes, sir.' I answered.

'Now, take the finger with your other hand and extend it till you feel a click,' he instructed and I began to pull the finger gently. 'You will have to give it a bit more than that,' he said. 'Patients suffer less and are more settled if you are confident in what you are doing. When you have the finger extended fully you need only pull up a little and the bone will go into place.'

I was a little scared of hurting my friend but did as he instructed and the bone actually meshed back into place without me even lifting the hook.

'There you go. You have done your first metacarpal relocation,' Baltimore said in a slightly condescending but fatherly way. 'I think I better do the stitches though,' he added.

I nodded agreement and handed him the suture he had pointed to on the tray. With great dexterity of hand, he began to stitch the wound, and in only a few seconds he had four stitches in place. I admired the work as the usual pulling at each knot was not evident; the skin sat over the wound as if it had never been disturbed.

'Now you can do the bandaging,' he said in a triumphant voice.

Weathers looked around to see how things had gone and raised his eyes in surprise.

The old man recovered, put on his suit jacket and, looking quite composed, said, 'Now, I have cards at the club, so I will let you lock up.'

He turned to leave and Weathers said, 'Thank you, sir. I can never repay your kindness.'

'No need. Win that bloody medal and tell Bolt he owes me one.' The old man said, smiling, and left.

'Well, what do you think of that?' Weathers said, giving a little whistle.

'Yes, he is quite a man, isn't he?' I said.

My friend nodded and then asked, 'When do you think I will be able to use this?' He nodded toward the hand.

'Well, usually we say two weeks, but for such a used part of the body it may take longer,' I answered, not really having any idea but trying to sound as though I did.

'Bloody hell, I have the medical to go through in less than that,' he said.

'Don't worry, I know one of the doctors,' I said tapping the side of my nose with innuendo intended.

'Thanks, mate,' he said, extending his good hand which I took and shook warmly.

'At the end of this week, I have arranged to take a few days down home to Wollongong, you know, before I get into the medicals, and then we go into a week of meetings to learn just what is needed from us in Germany,' I told him Do you want to come down with me?'

'It would be easier than explaining what has happened to the hand,' he confided.

'Yes, well we can leave early and be gone for four nights if you like.'

'I only need to grab a few things from home and then go and see Coach Bolt.'

'Tomorrow afternoon then, and perhaps you can wear a pair of gloves over this,' I said, finishing what was, I thought, quite a good bandage.

He nodded and said, 'I can't thank you enough.'

'You can thank me by being my bodyguard on the Olympic trip,' I answered, laughing, and little did I know how prophetic the pun would be.

CHAPTER 2

Two days later we arrived home in my somewhat battered old Ford. Actually, the car was less than two years old but had been in a major accident and had been written-off. Father had acquired it and handed the keys over on my leaving for university. The front panels on both sides were beaten out by hand and it looked pretty poor, but the interior was as-new and it ran like a beauty.

I walked quickly up the front garden path and knocked on the door which I had expected to be open, with my mother standing in the gap, expectantly, as she usually did.

No one answered.

I knew where the spare key was kept so I recovered it and, joined by Weathers, entered shouting, 'We are here,' louder than I thought was really necessary, in what was quite a small house. There came no answer and I walked quickly to the kitchen and, seeing a note on the middle of the table where we always left notes, unfolded it and read aloud.

'Father has been in an accident gone to the hospital.' It was simply signed Mother.

'Oh crap,' I said, startled, and then turned to Weathers. 'I better make my way there, you can stay here if you like.'

'Not likely,' he said, putting his hand on my shoulder. 'Bodyguard, remember?' He pointed to himself. I nodded and we headed off to the local hospital.

Once there, we parked, entered the main front doors and came face-to-face with Peter Nagel, my best mate from childhood.

'G'day. It's pretty bad,' he said as we shook hands. I introduced him to Weathers.

'I saw it happen,' he said.

'Saw what happen?' I questioned.

'Oh, you haven't talked to anyone then?' he asked, and as I shook my head, he continued, 'Your father was crossing the street to go and get the papers as he does each day and he was hit by a car. I got to him first but he was unconscious. The bastard didn't even stop.'

'Where are they?' I asked.

'My parents are with your mother down in emergency. I'll take you down,' he answered.

When I got to my mother's side, as she saw me, she started to cry. It was obvious that she had already been crying for some time.

'What's going on?' I asked. She could only shrug her shoulders in answer.

Mr Nagel took my hand. 'He was pretty smashed up but he is in surgery, and now we just have to wait,' he explained.

'How the hell did it happen? Our street is so quiet. No one goes over about fifteen miles an hour,' I said.

The old man shrugged. 'We will talk later after we find out how the surgery goes.' Heave me a little nod as if I should know what he was talking about.

'Okay,' I answered and gave him a little nod. He still had hold of my hand and gave it a hard squeeze then let go and returned to his wife's side as she comforted my mother. I gave mother a hug and sat down next to her for a moment. I suppose I just wanted her to know I was with her. Then I quickly got up and walked over to the nursing station to try to find out what was actually happening. The young lady sitting at the desk nodded as I approached.

'Oh, sorry to interrupt, but my father is Brin O'Calahan. I am Robert O'Calahan.'

'I really can't tell you much, sir. He has gone into surgery.'

'Yes, I understand, but I am a doctor,' I said, placing my accreditation on the table in front of her. She read the document, then looked back at me.

'Well, I still have nothing to tell you, sorry,' she answered in a slightly more consoling voice.

'Could I gown up and go in?' I asked.

'I don't think that is a good idea, sir,' she answered shaking her head.

'I do,' I said in my most stern voice.

'I will get Sister,' she said and bustled off into an adjoining room.

After a short while, she came back with the rotund old biddy who had been the sister here for as long as I could remember.

'Can I help?' she said in her lyrical Welch accent.

'Yes, well, my father is in surgery and I am a doctor I would like to go in to see what is happening,' I answered again, flashing my qualifications.

'That would be improper, and would distract the doctor from what he is doing,' she answered forcefully.

I was losing patience, and getting a little angry, though I knew what she said was technically correct.

'Please let the doctor know I am here,' I said, trying not to show my ire.

'Please take a seat with your mother, Mr O'Calahan,' she said and walked off toward the operating theatre. I did as instructed, knowing there was no bluffing this woman with any sort of angry outburst.

I was just sitting down when she came back and said loudly, 'The doctor is almost finished and will be with you in just a few minutes.'

I nodded, understanding, and stayed where I was, not thinking I could do anything else.

Ten minutes went by and it seemed like eternity. I was just

getting up the strength to tackle the old sister again, when the doctor came into the hall and walked down to us. He looked very sombre.

'Robert,' he said in a professional voice as he reached for my hand. I took the offer and he, in turn, nodded to Mother and the others who now were all clustered around a bench seat where my mother sat with my younger sister Lilly.

'Brin is in a bad way,' he said earnestly. He allowed us a moment to take in what he was saying. 'He has a fractured skull and several other injuries. He lost a lot of blood, having broken his femur. He is still unconscious. I have placed a drain into his skull to take away the blood.' He took Mother's hand and added, 'Everything I can do has been done, now we just have to wait.' He reassured her.

He began to walk toward the nurse's station and nodded for me to follow him. He walked into an adjoining room ushered me in closing the door.

'I didn't want to worry your mother further, but he *is* in a bad way,' he said in a soft voice as if someone was going to hear. 'I think he may live, but he may also have some brain damage. It is hard to know just how he will recover, if he does recover.'

'Should I try to get a top surgeon to come and see him?' I said, and immediately realised how rude I was being.

'Oh, sorry, I know you have done everything you can.' I apologised.

'No need to be sorry, lad. I would be delighted if you can get a specialist to come.'

'I am working at the Baltimore Practice in Sydney. I will ring Baltimore and see who he suggests,' I said.

The doctor nodded.

'You can use this phone. Just tell the girl on the switch that I have ratified the call,' he said and left me, pulling the door closed. I composed myself and took the receiver and dialled nine.

'Hello, this is Dr. O'Calahan, I need to get the Baltimore

surgery in Sydney. The doctor here has approved the call,' I said to the girl who answered.

'Yes, sir, do you have the number?' she asked and I relayed the number to her.

'Please hold the line. The number is not answering. I think I have another number here, would you like me to try that?' she asked, and soon the second number in Sydney was ringing.

Baltimore himself answered the phone and asked, 'How can I help?'

I was a bit taken a back at the boss answering, and at him being there on a weekend.

'Oh, sorry, sir. Um, I am in Wollongong. My father has been in an accident and I – I think he needs to have a brain injury specialist see him.'

'Yes, I heard. I'm sorry, boy.' He paused and then added, 'Leave it to me,' then he rang off without allowing me to thank him.

After a short time, I was allowed with Mother to enter and see Father. He was not conscious. His head was heavily bandaged and only one eye was visible. Major bandaging was covering both of his legs and his right arm and hand were covered and splinted.

He looked terrible. His face was, from what we could see, extremely swollen.

My mother broke down and kissed the back of his hand, saying, 'I'm here, darling. Now you must get well.'

She sobbed and I placed my arm around her shoulders to show my support. It was more than I could bare to see her weeping. I had seldom witnessed this from her, and supressed some tears myself. My parents had always been in love; they were like a young couple, and they showed their affection openly. This was unusual for the day and I thought it must be the Irish heritage.

Soon we were ushered out of the room and into a waiting room where the doctor came to speak to us again.

'Did you get onto Baltimore?' he asked.

'Yes, he said he would handle it,' I answered.

Baltimore, true to his word, arrived with another man later in the afternoon. They spoke briefly with the local doctor and then, signalling to me to follow, they entered the room in which father had been placed. I followed as did the local doctor.

'I will need the x-rays and get a nurse in here to remove the bandages,' the man with Baltimore ordered.

'This is Professor Steiger, Robert O'Calahan,' he said to introduce us.

'Thank you for coming, sir, and you, Professor,' I said.

I had heard of Steiger – his reputation was that of a trail blazer in Australia for his treatment of brain injury patients. His credentials were bolstered by the fact that he had been called to England to treat Queen Victoria in her final year 1901.

I knew that Father was in the best hands in the country and I felt that he would surely therefore pull through. That belief was sorely tested when the bandages were removed and I saw the extent of my father's injuries.

He had an open wound over his right temple and though an attempt had been made to control the bleeding, it was still oozing blood. His right eye was swollen closed and a deep gash showed the bone in his lower jaw extended through his top lip and on to his left cheek. Though this had been stitched the swelling allowed one to see into his mouth and the upper teeth were visible.

I could see where the local doctor had drilled a hole to place the shunt.

'Yes, this is very well done,' Steiger said in his strong German accent.

The x-rays were handed to him and he said, 'I don't like this piece of bone here.' He pointed to a fragment which had become detached from the main body of the skull and was floating just above the right frontal lobe of the brain.

'What can you tell me?' he asked.

'The piece didn't look very involved, but had pierced the outer covering of the brain – more like a graze than an incision.'

Steiger nodded. 'I think we need to remove that and see if it causes more bleeding. It will only slow the recovery if we have to open and remove it later,' he said.

The doctor and Baltimore nodded their agreement and I, not knowing what to think, also nodded my head, though no one was in the slightest way interested in what I thought.

We, all scrubbed and walked into the small operating theatre and waited for a thickset wards man to push Father's bed in through the double swinging doors.

Steiger was in charge and it was obvious how much regard the other two men had for his skill. Baltimore assisted and I and the local GP stood to one side watching and marvelling at the expert's dexterity.

The scalp was quickly peeled back and the two stitches closing the wound gently removed. Soon, the piece of offending bone was removed and though there was a little bleeding, a small amount of swabbing quickly saw the area of exposed brain looking fairly clean and undamaged.

'I think we have it, and it looks, remarkably, not too bad. There is a little bit of swelling, but I think things will be alright,' Steiger assured me and turned and left the room.

Baltimore then placed a few stitches to secure the scalp and cleaned the outer edges of the wound, then with the doctor's help, he bandaged Father's head in almost the same way it had been when I first saw him.

I stayed with my father in theatre until the wardsman returned to take him back to his room.

Baltimore and the GP had left, following Steiger.

I was in kind of a daze, I followed the procession back to the ward and found Mother waiting there with my younger sister, Lilly.

Lil, as we all called her, was red eyed and was comforting

mother with her arms about her shoulders. She watched the bed being positioned and then came and hugged me, asking, 'How did it go?'

'Well, quite well, I think,' I answered, sounding very unsure.

She looked into my eyes; she had always had the ability to tell if I was lying. I must have looked so unsure that she started to cry again. I didn't know what to say. One is given some lessons on how to let members of a family know the condition of the patient, but not your own family.

We stayed with father for several hours until the sister on evening shift asked if we could leave as the visiting hours were over and there was work to do. She was really quite rude. She would have also been given many lessons in their training but obviously not one on tact.

We left through the front door and found Weathers and Peter in the entrance waiting area. It had become too 'family' for them both to stay at the bedside.

It appeared as though they had been friends for years as they sat quietly, both smoking Weathers' roll-your-own cigarettes. They quickly put them out, looking guilty.

'Father is in the car,' Peter said 'He would like to speak with you briefly, if that is okay?'

I helped Mother into Lil's car, an old Zephyr, then walked over to the Nagel car. It was also an old Zephyr even older than Lil's; it still had broad running boards.

Peter stayed where he was, and Weathers stayed with him. It seemed to me that they felt they would be intruding if they had followed me.

Old Mr Nagel sat in the passenger's seat and wound the window down as I approached.

'How is he?' he asked.

'We will know more tomorrow, when he wakes. If he wakes,' I said and thought how flippant that had sounded.

He nodded and then said, 'I have known your father all of his life. There are many things to tell you. Make time tomorrow,' he said, then having a second thought. 'Look over your shoulder. This was not an accident.' He paused again and then continued, 'I will tell you all tomorrow.'

I nodded and he raised the window. Once Weathers and I had boarded my car I began to think what the old man had told me. I was thinking that his mind must have been wandering. This was an accident, plain and simple.

The sun had made the car very hot inside even though the front windows had been wound down and I let out a whistle to indicate that it was warmer than I had expected.

'I thought Nagel was hinting at something, but I couldn't make him out,' I said to Weathers when I had repeated the conversation.

'Well, there is one thing which makes it unusual: the car didn't stop. Young Nagel said it had to alter direction to hit your father on the wrong side of the road. He also said that it tore away at breakneck speed.'

'Yeah, you would have too if you were going to get into trouble. I don't think he has an enemy in the world,' I reasoned and Weathers shrugged his shoulders, showing his lack of understanding.

❧

The next morning when I walked into the family kitchen, Lil was at the stove preparing breakfast. Mother sat at the table, which was set in its usual formal way. Mother always liked to have a neat and inviting table. Obviously she had had little sleep. Likewise, I had tossed and turned and not slept well, with the words of warning given by old Mr. Nagel running through my head.

I thought I would have to wake Weathers who slept in the next bed in my boyhood room. When I had risen, I saw that he was not in bed and wondered where he might be. It was a few minutes until he came in from outside. Lil had told him to prepare for breakfast and he was well groomed and dressed in a pair of dress pants and a plain, if a little bright, green shirt.

'Morning,' he said and I replied the same.

I walked over to my mother and gave her a kiss on the cheek and sat down beside her, asking, 'How are you?'

'Oh, I'm all right,' she said in her most stoic voice. 'Will you take us up to the hospital at nine?'

I consented and when Lil had dished out all the food she had been cooking, we all sat and ate quietly.

Upon finishing, I helped my sister to clear away and we stood together; her washing the plates and me drying them. Mother excused herself and left to prepare for the day. This gave Lil the chance she was waiting for.

'If Father doesn't get better, Mother must come and live with us,' she said, meaning her and her husband and the two children, Paul and Susan.

The children were six and seven respectively, though Father used to say Sue was 'seven going on twenty-one.'

Paul was the apple of his eye; he would play for hours in the garden with the 'little man,' as he called him.

As I finished my second cup of tea, Peter arrived at the back door and I admitted him. We shook hands and he repeated the greeting with Weathers.

'Morning, Lil,' he said.

Lil replied simply, 'Morning.'

Barely a word had passed between them since they had been boyfriend and girlfriend at high school. Lil had gone her own way but I thought Peter never did. Both of our fathers had forbidden the relationship and though I had never understood why two great friends should not wish their children to date, I never thought to question Father's motives. It was, after all, none of my business.

Peter turned back to me and said, 'Father wishes to see you.'

'What, now?' I asked.

'Yes, before you go to the hospital,' he answered.

I was a little surprised but consented then walked out the back door through our mutual gate in the side fence and entered the back veranda where I knocked on the main door.

'Come in,' said Mrs Nagel and I greeted her with a small peck on the cheek. 'He is waiting for you in his office,' she said.

I had been there many times but it almost seemed like going before the principal at school when you were summoned to his office.

I walked down the hall and knocked on the half-open door. Mr Nagel was in view but facing away from me.

'Come in, Bobby,' he said. He had always called me Bobby even though no one else did. Without looking up from the papers he was studying, he added, 'Take a seat.'

I obeyed and sat at the only other seat in the sparsely decorated room.

'I have the need to give you a deal of information, and I am not sure how you will take it,' he said. I simply nodded, not really understanding what he was on about.

'You know your parents came here from Ireland, and I and Ingrid, from Germany?' he said in what was meant to be a rhetorical question. I nodded again.

'Well, all that is true, but it is less than half the story.' He paused to make sure I was listening clearly. He looked into my eyes deeply and then said, 'Your father and I are more than close friends. We are brothers.'

I nodded again, assuming that he meant the statement metaphorically.

'Our parents were Romani. "Gypsy," they used to call us. We were both from Munich, Germany.'

'But Father came from Ireland,' I said, frowning as I thought the old man had gone off his rocker.

'Here are our birth certificates,' he said, reaching for some papers on his desk. He handed them to me. I read the first: it was the certificate of one Durril Heam and the second was for a Bereli Heam. I looked up questioningly but said nothing.

He continued, 'We were, in our childhood, used like slaves by the German elite. They called us Zigeuner. They treated us terribly – our families were persecuted. We lost our parents. We don't know what happened to them. Many were killed and we came home one day to find our caravans all gone. The family where we worked took us in, in a way – they allowed us to live in the cellar. We had little to eat and would literally lick the dishes after the family ate. We were there for two years until I reached ten and your father was eight.'

He paused to take a breath and tears fell from his eyes. I thought he had lost his mind. Father had never mentioned Germany, though he had never mentioned Ireland either.

I must have been looking very doubtingly at him because he said, 'You think I am mad, but here – look at this,' he said and handed me a creased photograph. It was a family photo and though the three boys in the shot with their parents were very young, there was no doubt that one was my father and one was Mr Nagel.

I looked with eyes wide opened.

'Ah, now you believe,' he said, smiling knowingly.

I was shocked, to say the least, and I thought how strange it was, that the whole of the time they had lived next to us he had been my uncle.

I wanted to say, 'What the hell is all this about?' but before I could, he started a long diatribe which must have taken some hours of practice.

'Our family, Heam, were considered to be royal by the early Romani families who came to Germany from Transylvania.' He took a deep breath. 'Our mother's family were Cioaba. The highest of high. We were tolerated in Germany, though we were never popular. In the late 1890s, our people were set upon by the German public.'

He took another long break and studied me to make sure I understood.

'We had been Christian for hundreds of years, but that did not stop them – the mostly Christian populous – from passing laws that gave the authorities the power to detain anyone with two or more "Gypsy" grandparents and to sterilise them.' He nodded knowingly.

'They were doing this long before the word genocide was used. They saw us as "undesirables" and they wanted rid of us.'

A tear crossed his cheek; his memory drifted to a terrible time.

'In around 1899, they started breaking up our camps and killing anyone who dared to try to stop them. None of the Christian churches spoke out in our favour. In that same year, the German Jews became ill-disposed to the action, many disgusted that their leaders had not protested more strongly to these terrible deeds. Many spoke out, openly saying that the treatment of the Gypsies and the Sinti was unholy and should stop. This caused distrust and the hatred of the money lenders, as they were often known.

'Even the richest of the Jews refused to have their name linked with the awful deeds being committed. It was a Jewish family who took your father and me from the place of servitude we had wallowed in, for more than two years. The Rabien family found us in the forest, starving, after taking a terrible beating from our "Employer".

'They took us to their home and fed and clothed us. Then they left the area and moved back to their family home in outer Berlin. There it was thought that we were just part of the Rabien family. They took a holiday to Holland where we became separated accidentally for almost a year. Your father had been taken to Ireland, and though I had been taken in by a friendly family in Badhoevedorp, I had continued to search for him. He too was always looking for me and through the families of the Dutch who had moved to England and later Ireland, he was able to contact me, we made a pact to find each other.

'In 1901 I made my way as a seventeen-year-old to Ireland and we met and planned to move to the Americas. My visa was not going to allow me to stay any longer in Ireland and people were trying to get out of the bitterly impoverished country.

'Your father was only fifteen but we lied about our ages and tried to gain passage on boats to the United States. We had no luck, but were eventually accepted as stokers on a steam ship to Australia. We didn't even know where that was, but thought that anywhere was better than where we were.

'We arrived in Sydney in 1903 and sought to stay. The Australian government had only been formed a couple of years earlier and the settlement was screaming for more British subjects for the very quickly growing young Democracy.'

He paused again and smiled when he saw the shocked look etched on my face. I could find no words. I wanted to ask a million questions but could not articulate even one.

He continued. 'Neither of us had papers which would see us called British but we both said we had lost our parents to consumption which was taking many at that time. I continued to use my Dutch family name, and your father the name of the people who had taken him in: the O'Calahans. The Australian officials didn't seem to know one accent from another and accepted us on our tickets from Ireland as Irish Nationals.'

He paused again and then looking worried, said, 'Oh, I have forgotten to say that we both met our wives on the boat on the journey here. I was old enough to marry but your father and mother, actually announced first that they were getting married. He was really only sixteen, but we had celebrated his nineteenth birthday on board. We had a joint wedding six months after we were accepted into Australia, and we eventually became citizens.

'It is a great country and we learned to call it home. We decided that no one should know that we were brothers and that we came from Germany originally. During the Great War, we both joined up, but when we arrived in France, almost all of the fighting was over. We saw action only once in skirmishes in France as we found some retreating German soldiers. That is where your father gained the shrapnel wound in his back.'

He looked at me to see if I was taking all of the information in.

I was, to be truthful, not really taking it all in.

'But why keep it secret?' I asked.

'The Germans are not regarded well here in Australia and we knew that if the wrong people found out who we were, and where we were, that we could be at risk. We wanted to stay here. We loved the land and that is why we bought our second piece of land at Wollongong. We raised vegetables and sold them running up to the war, and then, though they worked incredibly hard, your mother and my wife were forced to sell the land and move out. This sale was done through the Australian Government and we were paid a portion of the money that the land was worth and were given a promissory note for the estimated two thousand pounds still to be paid.'

Just as he finished the sentence, Peter entered and, knocking on the open door, said, 'Your mother is waiting to be taken to the hospital.'

'You go and tell her that Bobby will be with her in a minute,' his father instructed, and Peter, as he always did, obeyed immediately.

'I will not detain you anymore but I ask you to not tell Peter or Lil what I have told you. Your father and I made a pact that if one of us were gone, the other would tell the family the truth. I have fulfilled my promise even though your father is alive, because I believe we have been detected. I think your father was run down deliberately.'

He paused briefly and then said, 'We will speak more tomorrow, and please remember me to your father if he comes around.'

He stood and ushered me out of the room and then shut the door at my back.

My head was reeling; I felt sick in the stomach, I didn't know what to think or what to do.

I met my mother in the front hall where she had obviously been waiting for some time. Lil joined us, and we left Peter and Weathers sitting in the lounge room reading newspapers.

CHAPTER 3

We arrived at the hospital a few minutes later, it being so close, and were admitted by a nurse. The front doors had not yet been opened to the public.

Father had been moved to a smaller room and we were led there, and entered to see the doctor taking his temperature.

'He seems a little better today,' he said as he noticed us. 'He has not regained consciousness yet though,' he concluded, and then as he left the room, he said, 'We should know more late this afternoon or tomorrow.' He nodded to my mother and walked out.

I knew that he was just guessing and would have no real idea when, or if, Father would regain consciousness. It was as we had been told at college: 'If you can't give an answer you are certain of, reassure the family without making promises.'

I knew what he was saying but Mother looked a little less worried and I thought it better to say nothing. Mother sat on the chair at the right side of the bed and Lil walked around the other side and took fathers hand and began to shed a few tears; this was the first time she had seen him since the accident.

We stayed with Father in the room for several hours until the gruff old Sister entered to tell us that visiting hour was over, and that they were about to feed the other patients. There always seemed to be a veiled threat when this dilatant spoke.

I had been sitting in a chair at the far side of the room for some time and could see well that Father had not stirred even a little in the hours we were present. I rose and neared Mother who kissed Father and I took her hand and Lil followed us out of the room.

Once in the car, Mother asked if we could possibly do a little shopping. She said that there would not be enough food now that we had extra mouths to feed. I drove to the small corner shop at the end of Main Street and Lil took the shopping list Mother had prepared and left us in the car.

I felt awkward; I had had all this new information dumped on me earlier in the morning and now wondered if I should tell Mother anything.

As if she had read my mind, she said, 'You had a long talk with Nagel then?'

But before I could answer, she added, 'You will have a lot of questions. He *is* your uncle.' She took my hand. 'This was not information you were to have while your father is alive. Say no more now and talk with him again.'

I nodded and then began to ask a question, which she raised her hand to deflect as Lil returned to the car.

The question I was about to ask was, 'Who are we really?'

We arrived home and I went in search of Weathers and Peter; I could find neither of them. I nodded to Mother as I walked through the kitchen where she and Lil were preparing a light, though late, lunch. She nodded back knowingly and I continued on through the back door and went to the Nagel house. The doors were locked and I turned to go home when Nagel himself opened the door and ushered me inside.

I had never seen the doors in either house locked and was surprised when he locked it again after we entered.

I followed him dutifully into his office and sat as I was instructed in the same chair as my previous visit.

'How is your father?' he asked, and I answered that Father was still in a coma but may have improved a little.

'He is a fighter. I think it is not his time yet,' he tried to reassure me, though it sounded as if he did not believe his own words.

'You have had some time to think about what I have told you?' he asked.

I nodded.

'And what do you think?'

'I am not sure what it is all about. Mother tells me that you *are* my uncle, but would say no more. I don't feel I know who I am – who we all are?' I said, sounding somewhat despondent.

He took a long pause, and then took a cigar from his top drawer and prepared to light it. He offered me one, but I declined, never having liked either the taste or smell of tobacco.

'I know exactly who I am and who we all are,' he said, slowly lighting a match and, placing it at the end of the cheroot, took several strong if short puffs to light it.

'You are an Australian. You need not fear – you were born here. You, and your generation of our children, are all Australians. Your parents are, as I and my wife are, all Australian citizens, and proud of it. But there is a past which we carefully hid from you and from everyone. I mentioned how poorly we were treated in our own country. It should be obvious why we have done so?' He paused; this was a rhetorical question and he continued. I still had nothing to say.

'In Germany, our people were being sterilised and even killed. Men were taken off the street and castrated without any type of aesthetic. We feared being caught and often went hungry rather than going out into the street. We were considered to be untermenschen – "inferior people". This did not start, as many in the world believe, just last year when it was written into law by this terrible new leader. Oh no, it started much earlier and was covered up. There are many of our relatives today in German internment camps, and the Germans have people who have migrated around the world who report back on us expatriate Germans.'

He gain and took another large drag on the vile-smelling cigar. I sat quietly like a ten-year-old in a class at school.

'They have never detected us before. We have remained undiscovered, until now,' he concluded.

'And you think you are discovered now?' I asked.

'Yes, I fear we are.' He paused and then continued. 'Look at this photograph. It is your father. What do you think?' he asked and handed me the picture which I had never seen before. It was in a very expensive-looking silver frame. I saw my father as a newly landed fresh-faced youth, and Nagel was standing next to him.

'I am so like him, it is uncanny,' I said, not thinking much else.

'Yes, here is the picture of you in the local paper just a short time ago, on your selection as a doctor for the Olympics in Germany. You will notice the likeness even more.' He said holding the two photos alongside each other.

I did. I had never seen a picture of my father when he was so young. I had seen only the staged pictures of my parents wedding, and in these, they were in a larger group. These wedding photos were hand coloured, and though it was obvious that I was my father's son, the likeness was not as noticeable.

'So, you think someone had seen this and—'

He interrupted me and said, leaning forward, 'I know they have. Two days after this was in the paper, your father had a visitor. Your mother answered the door and the man with a German accent asked to see your father. Your mother asked him to come in but he declined, so she called your father. When he came to the door, the other man said simply that he was mistaken, that he was sorry he had been looking for a Mr Heam. Then he just walked off, not saying anything else, though he turned and gave a knowing sneer as he exited the gate. Your mother said he drove off in a large green car with another man. The car that hit your father was a large green car.'

He made these statements with complete belief in his voice and I could see no reason to disavow him of his belief. My head was still spinning.

'You look as though you don't believe what I am telling you?' he said, almost as a statement, though I took it as a question.

'Well, err. Sir – I'm not even sure what I should call you?' I said.

He smiled and looked hard into my eyes. 'Call me what is easiest for you, but remember that other people don't know what you know,' he answered.

I thought of a passage in the Bible which says, 'I speak in parables lest they understand me.' Or something to that effect. I held my tongue; it would do me no good to antagonise him and sound like a smart-alec.

'Now, as we are all in danger, I must tell you a few things: there are still many thousands of us in Germany – we live hidden in full sight, and we are many in Australia also. Baltimore is one of us. Professor Mordechai Abraham Hochberg is a German Jew but has always supported us, and though your friend Weathers does not know it, he is Romani.'

I stared, open-mouthed. Could all this have been around me all my life, and could I have been oblivious to it? It seemed impossible; it seemed far-fetched, but somehow, I knew it to be true.

'Then I did not earn the benevolence of either Baltimore or Hochberg?' I reasoned more to myself than to him.

'You were fated to meet both of them, but they would not have given you the chances you have received if they thought you were not worthy,' he answered, seeing that I was losing confidence, doubting myself because of what he was telling me.

'Well, what is this all about?' I asked, shrugging my shoulders.

'You are our chosen one. Oh no, not in some religious sense, but chosen to do our people a great service. In recent years there has been a powerful lobby working against our people. Since the turn of the century, they have been trying to eradicate us. It is no less than genocide. Your position on the Olympic team is the only thing you did not earn.' He paused, looking at me and I thought he was sizing me up somehow.

'You are to go to Germany and bring back evidence of what is being done. An evil man – a scientist, if he can be called a scientist – has been working for the German government for some years under their cover. His name is Dr Robert Ritter. Ritter became the director of the Centre for Research on Racial Hygiene and Demographic Biology in the Ministry of Health recently.'

'He began locating Roma and Sinti who were still living in Germany, classifying them as inferior racial types. He performs so-called medical and anthropological examinations in an attempt to classify us. They are interviewing Roma to determine and record their genealogy, establishing a register of almost all Roma and Sinti, living in Germany. When they are done with these "interviews", they are often never seen again by friends and family.'

He took one of his long pauses and puffed on his cigar, looking as though he was remembering the worst of times.

'We have a large body of people who are looking to support you on your quest. There are some thousands of us still in Germany, many Jews may also be your tools and protectors. They fear that they will be next to meet with this regime's displeasure.'

'Who is driving this?" I asked.

Looking surprised at the question, he frowned and said slowly, 'Adolf Hitler.'

He paused, watching me as I raised my eyebrows and realised what a stupid question I had asked. Of course, that was who he was talking about.

'But how am I to be involved? I am just a team doctor. I have no political standing. How can I help?' I asked and I thought how pathetic and feeble I sounded, even to myself.

'We need you to bring back proof of what we are saying. You will be under the protection of the Olympic countries, and you will seem to be going about your business, sightseeing, having the time of your life. But you will be documenting and photographing everything you see. That will prove to the world what an evil threat this man is to all people.'

He paused for some time. 'You were picked for a task just like this, when you were still in high school. That is why your father has had you trained in speaking German fluently, in the medical profession, and in many other ways. For instance, you have trained with your father to be a code breaker. You have spent many hundreds of hours from a young age learning the art of writing and deciphering code. You can write in several languages: English of course, German, Latin and French. You are trained in locks and escapology in a way. No these were not just games you were playing,' he said, seeing my doubt and took a deep breath and continued, 'You have been groomed. You are calm, usually, when things go wrong. You have been taught not to panic and you will need all of your talent if you are to succeed.'

He took another long meditative draw on his cigar and then, judging that I was struggling, spoke slowly and deliberately. 'This is your time to shine. You are our best hope. We believe in you; your father has trained you well. What will you say to your people now they ask for your help?' he asked.

I thought for a moment, and then said in a very uncertain and doubtful voice, 'I will do what you ask of me, but I feel that there must be better people to do this?'

'You will need to believe in yourself and in the people around you. You will have many thousands of helpers as I said, but you will have many more trying to stop you in your tracks. Now there are only a few months until you leave, and you and several of the people who go with you will have some special training. It is due to start tomorrow, and all of our operatives will be going to a meeting at the Museum of Sydney.' He paused again and looked me up and down.

'Many, like you, do not know what is happening, and many are still unaware of who their real families are. Some of the families have planned this as a family trip and many will be amazed when they are told their true story.'

He sat, watching me squirm for a short time, then said, 'Your father will see you if he regains consciousness before tomorrow, and I know that you will not want to leave tomorrow. But that is not negotiable. Your father has worked all of your life for this, and for his sake, and for all the members of your race, you must attend. Your mother has always known about this and will understand.'

Again, he watched me. I shifted uneasily in my seat.

'What about these mongrels who have attacked father? Won't they know we are coming?' I enquired.

'They are but a handful and though they don't know it yet, their communications have been being intercepted. They will be dealt with by our operatives,' he answered without even batting an eyelid.

I wondered what this meant; did he mean these people were going to be killed? Well, yes, that is exactly what he had inferred, but could I be a party to that?

'Do you mean they will be killed?' I asked. I had to know what he really meant, to be certain.

'Though it is not for you to know, nor to worry about – yes. It will be some terrible accident at the hostel where they stay,' he answered, and seeing the look of despair on my face, he added, 'You are soft on the enemies of your people but, as Thomas Jefferson said, "Our enemies have found that we can reason like men, so now let us show them we can fight like men also."'

His brilliance with words had always seemed to come easily, though with a great deal of learning. He often delivered, like this, in the words of men he thought to have been great.

I could think of nothing to say and so I did just that: said nothing.

'I will be accompanying you and Weathers tomorrow. We will need to leave at around five in the morning,' he said, standing.

He ushered me out of the room like a young boy, and at that

moment, that is exactly how I felt. A wide-eyed young child with a newborn distrust in the world.

I returned home and found that lunch was waiting on the table. Peter and Weathers were eating, but the women had retired to the lounge. I sat and looked at the food but did not begin to eat; I felt so totally lost and no food was going to help.

Both of my friends ate and talked of trivial things. They could see that I was suffering and tried to take my mind off the accident and my father's condition, neither knowing what the real worry in my mind was about.

I tried to be jovial but there was little humour in me. Eventually, when my mother re-entered with the plates on which they had taken their sandwiches, I began to eat. She insisted that I needed to keep up my strength.

I knew I would have to talk to her about leaving in the morning and so I signalled to Peter to take Weathers and go outside.

They obeyed and after a moment, to make sure we were alone, I said, 'Nagel wants me to go to a meeting in Sydney tomorrow.'

'Yes, you must go,' she answered with her back to me.

She walked to the great old marble-look sink and turned on the tap. There was no hot water tap in the kitchen, so she filled the large kettle and placed it on the gas stove top to boil for washing-up.

'But what about you, and what about Father?' I asked feebly.

'Something like this has been feared by your father for many years. I always thought it to be a little paranoid, but he would want you to go.' She paused and though she had her back to me, I could tell that she was crying.

I walked over to her and gave her a hug. She nodded but didn't look around.

'I will have all of the news when you ring, and if things work out, you will be able to come and see us next week,' she said reassuringly.

I held her for a moment longer, then understanding that she wanted to be alone, I joined my two friends in the backyard.

They had taken up residency in the back shed, and were polishing off another of the bottles of home brew. I joined them, and as I could think of nothing to say, I just sat there as they babbled inanely. I was not even registering what they were saying.

I could hear only my uncle's voice saying those words: 'now let us show them we can fight like men also.'

CHAPTER 4

In the morning I walked to the car with Weathers. He had earlier said that he would take a train home if I needed to stay. I'm sure he thought I needed to stay.

Already sitting in the front passenger seat was Nagel and in the back seat was Peter. I was not expecting to see him.

'I didn't know you were coming?' I said, smiling. He nodded back at me with a sort of a half-smile.

Mother and Lil were still in bed but Mrs Nagel was at her front gate looking gaunt. She waved goodbye. Tears brimmed in her eyes.

Very little was said on the way along the coast road to Sydney, but as I drove in to the southern suburbs I said to Weathers over the seat, 'We are going to a meeting at the museum. Will you come with us?'

'Sure, I have an uncle who works there. I can call in on him,' he answered, and nothing more was said until I had parked the car near Hyde Park.

'This should do. We only have a couple of hundred yards to go,' I said, trying to sound flippant.

We entered the grand front doors of the great museum. I had been brought here many times as a child and remembered how grand I had thought the entrance.

Once inside, a short officious-looking man in a drab but neat suit, was waiting for us.

'Good to see you,' he said, shaking my uncle's hand and nodding to the rest of us.

Another man came from a large group who were standing near the hat stall. It became evident very quickly – he was Weathers' uncle.

They embraced and the man said, 'Good to see you, my boy.'

He was introduced by Weathers as his uncle, Joshua Weathers.

'I am the senior archivist here,' he said as he shook each of our hands. 'Now, do you have a little time for your old uncle?' he added.

'Yes, my friends have a meeting and I am free for a while,' Weathers answered and they began to walk toward what was Joshua's office.

Weathers turned and said, 'I will come and find you before you leave.'

We all nodded knowing that he was likely to see us sooner than he thought.

Entering the main hall, Peter said that he needed to use the facilities, and as it had been quite a long trip, I walked to the door with the silhouette of a Victorian Gentlemen on the ancient-looking door. The word 'Gentlemen' on the sign seemed redundant.

We entered and, seeing that no one was in the room, Peter immediately asked, 'How long have you known about all this?'

'Only for a couple of days. What do you make of it?' I enquired.

'Well, I was told last night. At first I thought he was joking,' he said, referring to his father, then he continued, 'I never had any former information but he had banned me from going out with your sister and she was also banned by your father. I always thought it strange, but now I understand. We are first cousins,' he concluded and moved to the nearest urinal.

I walked to another where our backs were to each other.

'I always thought it strange too, as I knew they were best of friends, and I knew father liked you. I just thought it was because he thought you were both too young,' I answered.

'Well, it seems I am to accompany you to the Games. We have some business to settle when we get there,' he said.

I just made a sound of agreement and when I had reclothed myself, I walked to the large marble-looking sinks and washed my hands.

Peter soon joined me and said jovially, 'Well, it seems as though it won't be boring.'

He watched me nod agreement. I was unsure what he had been told and wanted to let all of the information we needed be conveyed to us by the people in charge.

We exited the restroom and were immediately accosted by Nagel.

'Come, we are expected upstairs,' he said and hurried off up the grand stairs. Walking along the gallery, we noticed Weathers, looking very unsure of himself as he entered a side room with his uncle.

Soon, we were taken into the same room and found it to be almost full of elderly men sitting around a very beautiful hand-carved table. It looked to be made from fiddle back maple and was very highly polished and extremely large. About 50 people were in the room and more than half were seated in the matching carved chairs.

Uncle ushered us to the far side of the table and sat in a chair. His name was emblazoned on a small plaque in front of him; to my surprise my name was next to it and then Peter's. We sat.

Shortly, Weathers came to the opposite side of the table with his uncle, almost opposite to me. He raised his eyes as he noticed his name, and then to me as if asking what the hell was going on. I just nodded and shrugged my shoulders. He sat.

Soon, a very short man entered, followed by several men I had seen at the Baltimore Practice. Baltimore was the fourth to enter. I was naturally surprised to see him and he nodded to me as he moved to the head of the table.

The other four men sat, two to his right and two to his left. These, I thought, must be the boffins in charge. The short man stood at the opposite end of the table to Baltimore and said a few words in a language I thought to be Latin. I did not know what he said, but the other people at the table stood and the man tapped a small gavel on a wooden block positioned in front of him for just that reason. We all stood dutifully. He called us to order and stated that two women would be joining us shortly as they had interest in these proceedings. He then opened a separate door from the one we had entered through, and an older lady was followed into our presence by Berta Smith, my other Olympic athlete. She looked even more beautiful than when I last saw her, if that was possible.

She nodded uncertainly to me and I returned the gesture. The two women sat on the opposite side of the table to the short man's right.

The pomp and pageantry over Baltimore stood and said what seemed to be a prayer, though I did not understand the language – again it sounded like Latin.

'I call this meeting to order and ask that all draw near who wish to be heard.' He paused for a moment for effect and then continued:

'It is with great pleasure I welcome the many new members to this meeting. We are at a high stage of alertness; there have been more of our operatives silenced. There are said to be many who have been dragged from the street and sterilised. In short, the Germans are trying to eradicate the Roma and Sinti people of Europe. Thousands of our brothers and sisters are being "disappeared." They go out for any reason and are never seen again. Some are taken off the street as the world watches on and does nothing. These Olympic games are a great opportunity for us to prove these atrocities to the rest of the world.' He cleared his throat and, taking a deep breath, continued.

'We must not allow this to continue unchallenged; recently,

Jewish leaders have spoken out against these vile acts. They are, silently, backing us to get proof and put it on the world stage. Many of you have been trained to conduct this kind of operation. We have six people with us who will be traveling as part of the Australian Team – they will have in their possession the best miniature equipment for photographing, and they will also have some other secret tools with which they will be able to gather information.'

He paused and looked around the room.

'This is the time when we need to stand up, and, with the German-Jewish community, expose these evil men for what they are. Gentlemen, I would like to introduce to you, Vadoma Codona, she is Sinti–Australian and will be one of the team throwing athletes in the javelin and shot.'

Codona stood. Her features were strong and she looked to very formidable in her grey suit-like outfit.

He continued. 'She is to collate any information gained and bring it, on her person, home to Australia.'

There was a short and quiet round of polite applause.

'Next it is Berta Smith. Berta has gained a position on the running and track team and will be a general operative. She has been in the field before in both Romania and Germany.'

The clapping came again.

'Next, we have Peter Nagel. His father you will all know. He will be traveling as a team assistant.'

Peter was proffered the loudest support as he too stood.

'Shipton Graeme Weathers has earned his position on the boxing team and will be our muscle if we need him.'

Weathers stood still, looking surprised but seemingly resigned to his fate. He hated his first name 'Shipton' and would usually threaten violence if someone used it in his presence. The applause grew louder as he and his deeds were well known.

'Last, I give you the head of the operation, Robert O'Calahan.

He will, we hope, have the opportunity to visit and investigate hospitals and asylum in and around the capital. Robert will be traveling as one of the team's doctors.'

I trembled from head to toe as I stood and looked around the room. The clapping was now booming as the rest of the people in the room stood and gave us a standing ovation. I felt confused, and a little embarrassed as I took the accolades I believed to be unwarranted.

Baltimore signalled the room for silence and was soon obeyed. The meeting then moved into the introductions of the man who was providing the equipment we were going to take with us, Mose Patinkin.

Patinkin was already standing and continued to clap. He was a weedy little man with mouse-like features and a nose which simply looked too big for his face – well, for any face, really. The five of us, 'The Chosen Few', were then conducted to another room and the meeting went back to ritual, to which we were not witness.

I squinted as we entered the new room as it was bathed in a very bright light. It seemed that this may be a room used for embalming or other tasks that required extra light.

He walked to a table where several gadgets sat, 'We have made many different cameras for you to take which will remain inconspicuous,' he said On the table there were several large cameras, several matchboxes, a cigarette lighter, two wrist watches, four men's rings and a pair of rather gaudy broaches.

'Everything you see before you is a camera,' he said, and continued handing each of us one of the items to inspect. Mine was the matchbox. I looked at it then handed it back. I didn't really smoke, occasionally taking one when offered at a party, and I thought that it may be more believable that someone who did should take the box.

I was given one of the rings and a watch. Each ring was different in design but each had a slightly thicker than normal stone set in its surface; these we were shown swivelled to one side when pushed to reveal a tiny lens. I still had a smoke lighting device in the cigarette lighter but it was obvious that we were to take what we were given. All of the little gadgets were explained and operated to show every detail of use.

'Ladies, the broaches will take up to five photographs to miniature film; in fact, each device has a miniature film inside. The rings will take only one shot each, so use them wisely. The matchboxes have the ability to take five shots and the wrist watches, five. The lighter will take up to twelve. The actual cameras have a film of twenty-four frames, which you can buy from any chemist – it is normal film.'

He continued as each of us toyed with one of the objects.

'It would be wise to use the cameras a lot as that will detract from your real purpose. Freely show your camera to any official who asks for it and have spare film available.' He paused for a moment and then added, 'Be real tourists, take lots of shots and make sure you are observed.'

We were each handed a brown paper bag which contained our objects and he instructed us to rid ourselves of the bag, and to wear or carry each item, so we were not noticed carrying a bag.

'Two of you should take some shots of the museum exhibits as you exit to justify the large cameras. You will now have an instructor who will show you what is expected of you.'

He said, pressing a button on the wall which obviously summonsed three men who entered from a door which was opposite the one we had entered by. The men carried large rolled paper sheets, some notepads and several large piles of typed paper.

Patinkin excused himself and returned to the meeting. The three men unrolled one of the sheets and it was immediately apparent that it was a detailed map of Berlin; two others were opened and revealed a less detailed map of Germany and the other, a map of the surrounding countries to the west of Germany. This map included all obvious border crossings from Germany into to other countries.

'You each have an area to cover. It will be very unlikely that you will all get in and out and get all of the information we wish you to get. In short, we need proof of the terrible way the German government is treating our people.'

One of the three, a short round man, said and continued, 'Sachsenhausen is an internment camp only twenty miles from the centre of Berlin. There they are sterilising and killing thousands of people: many Romani, Sinti and Jews who are called Untermenschen. This means, err, sub-human.'

He paused and looked around the wide-eyed group.

He nodded as if agreeing with himself and continued, 'Yes, they wish to get rid of all of these people and more. Somehow, you are to get information on the camp and other oppressive behaviours, err, for the world to see. These atrocities are happening right now and they are only set to get worse as the Nazis get more and more power.'

He paused for a moment and then nodded to another of the instructors who turned the lights off and then turned a projector at the far end of the room on, and began to flick through slides with the first man narrating. The first was a picture of a sign saying 'Sachsenhausen'.

He made no comment but when the second slide was displayed, he began a long narrative about the people who have tried to get other photographs and information out of the camp.

'Three of our operatives have been killed and several are missing. These are good people – people who were trained to find information, to take photographs and to get them out of the country and into the safety of our organisation. We have people in many countries around the world, but the most involved here are the Americans, English, French and us here in Australia. The people in Germany who we are in contact with are fighting the good fight, but they are being overrun by these evil men, the Nazi.

We, the Australians, are in charge of this effort to gain information. The other three countries are seen to be hostile to the behaviour of the Nazi and we are a much smaller group, being only twenty-two hundred or so in Australia. You have each, in turn, been brought up without being taught of your heritage, without your real names. This was done very deliberately. Our many older people have been training you to speak fluent German and to understand certain customs, preparing you each for a use, a purpose, in the fight for our very existence.'

Everyone in our group looked at each other, raised eyes in disbelief, shrugged and generally looked bewildered.

The little man, still standing, noticed our discomfort and said, 'Sit. I can see I have to do more convincing.'

We all sat and he assumed a position on the opposite side of the table which was the centre point of the room.

'We have been persecuted for many centuries; there is no homeland, you see,' he said and continued in a quiet calm but instructive voice.

'There are few photographs and the few we have of Sachsenhausen and the many other camps do not show what is happening there. The numbers of people just going missing is not any proof of what is happening to them. They are just gone. We need to show the world what they are doing to us and to the Jews and any other being who gets in their way.'

I felt that I must say something, but I stumbled so badly over my first few words that I felt like a fool. 'What, um, what do you expect us to do exactly?'

'We are asking you to take on the plight of the people, of your people, and find information and get proof of the crimes which are being committed.' He paused looking deeply into my eyes, reading me, I think, then added, 'You will not be alone; our people know you, Robert, and you, Berta, are coming. The rest of you are going in support. No one knows you are part of what is planned. I am sure you have all been introduced to Vadoma Codona. She has contacts in the existing Sinti community in Berlin, if any of them still exist. Vadoma has been in Australia for more than twenty years, but visited Berlin with her parents for twelve months in 1930. She will work with the Sinti directly as they do not know she is coming and they will not accept outsiders into their confidence. Any information which is gained by any of you should go to Vadoma. She is able to transport it,' he said and nodded to the woman who looked to be around 50, though could've only been 30 or so.

'You, Mr Weathers are to be a personal bodyguard for Miss Smith and you, Mr Nagel, for O'Calahan here. You both have been chosen for your fighting ability and the training you have both received, all through your lives, will be vital if something goes wrong.' The little man finished and walked back to the projector and again nodded to one of the other men to turn the lights down.

The next projection was a man standing in a white coat. He was a stout man with white and somewhat receding hair.

'This is Dr Robert Ritter. He is the architect of this insidious hatred of the Roma, Sinti and to a lesser extent the Jews. He, as the head of the Racial Hygiene and Demographic Biology Research Unit puts forward the preposterous claim that inheritability of criminality is inevitable in the Roma and Sinti.' He moved to the next slide.

'Dr Adolph Würth, an anthropologist, of sorts, is his colleague.' He flicked to the next slide.

'Eva Justin, Sophie Ehrhardt, and Ruth Kellermann – these women all work with and for Ritter. They are dangerous they are complete zealots. Even children are not safe around this group.' His voice cracked as he said these last few words.

'O'Calahan, you will be introduced to Eva Justin in the hope that you are able, by this means, to infiltrate their collective and their work. She is a beautiful woman but do not be taken in; she is as evil as they come,' he said, pointing to me.

I just shrugged my shoulders. I really didn't think I was up to this level of deception.

He again flicked to the next slide that of a very surly looking tall man whose eyes seemed to be too close together.

'This is SS Oberführer Oskar Dirlewanger. He is the man in charge of all of the camps and the Ritter group. He will not hesitate to destroy anyone who gets in his way. If you see this man, try to seem insignificant, unimportant. He is known as a psychopathic killer and child molester. We know these claims to be true from his actions in the Great War and the Spanish Civil War, where he committed some of the most heinous crimes possible.'

He swallowed and then said in a wavering voice, 'He executed my parents and grandmother without trial in a mass killing in Romania in 1916. My brother and I had been secreted away from the home in an underground bunker my father had built because we lived near the border.'

He took a deep breath and then in a stronger voice said, 'They lined up the people of our small village and his machine gun troop opened fire. No one survived. For this, and other actions where he was wounded, he was awarded the Iron Cross second class.'

His eyes looked down and he sat for a moment before saying, 'Our people will kill him, even if I have to travel to Germany myself to do the job.' He took a long moment to calm himself.

'You should not try to be involved in this man's world. You have other, pressing tasks and they are imperative to our success.'

His voice trailed off a little and he did not look up.

One of the other men in the room, realising that he could not continue, stepped forward and said, 'Your real training will start in three days. I suggest you go home and practice as much German as you can.'

He turned the lights on but left the grim figure of Dirlewanger projected on the wall. Leading us back to the main area of the museum, through a different door to the one we had entered by, he left us without saying another word.

Vadoma nodded to me and left, walking quickly to the front staircase.

Berta said quietly, 'I will make an appointment to see you later in the week, Doctor.' She bowed her head slightly and then said, 'Until then.'

I, in turn, bowed my head, and felt a little foolish as this was not one of my inherit traits.

I was left standing with my two friends.

'Better take a couple of snaps,' Nagel said and wandered off, trying to look as if he were interested in the large dinosaur skeleton in the display gallery to our left.

Weathers and I just stood and waited for Nagel senior or someone else who would come and tell us what to do next.

'What do you make of all this?' he asked.

Noticing that a tall thin man was standing within ear shot, I said, 'Well, I'm not that interested in dinosaurs or any of the long dead animals in this place,'

Weathers looked up at me. He realised he could have compromised our position almost immediately after being warned about being careful.

'No, I don't find them very interesting either.' His voice sounded uncertain and it was obvious to me that he was not going to be very good at any kind of deception; he was such an honest man. He usually said what he thought, rarely thinking before saying it.

'I wouldn't mind going down stairs and waiting,' I said and he nodded.

We walked to the top of the stairs and I said, 'I wonder where Nagel is?' and turned, using this slight deception to see where the tailing man was.

He was, it seemed, certainly following us as he stood only a few feet away, looking into a glass case displaying many brightly coloured butterflies.

I had no doubt that he was following us, even though his eyes never turned in our direction.

'I suppose he will catch up,' I said, turning and re-joining Weathers.

We walked slowly down the sweeping staircase, but the man I thought to be following us did not.

I smiled as I glanced back up the stairwell, thinking how paranoid I was being. However, as we neared the lift doors, they opened and the man stepped out, almost knocking Weathers over.

So, he was following us.

He apologised and moved to the hat stall and recovered a rather dapper-looking trilby hat, and moved to the notice board on the outside of the main doors. I quickly darted back around the nearest corner and beckoned Weathers to follow. He dutifully followed and soon we walked into a small room, obviously not meant for the public.

'What's your problem?' Weathers asked.

'We were being followed by the man on the lift,' I answered.

'I didn't even notice. What makes you think he was following us?' he queried.

'When I first noticed him, he was looking at us and the hairs on the back of my neck stood up, so I watched him and where we moved, he followed. At the stairs, our eyes met and he knew I had caught him out. We moved down the stairs and he mysteriously met us from the lift,' I explained.

'Are you sure?' he queried.

'I am,' I answered vehemently.

'Well, let's try him out. I'll go out and walk around the block and we'll see if he follows me.'

I nodded my agreement and he left the room. For a few moments I looked around the room, wishing I had another mode of exit, but there was none and I began to wonder where I was, and in whose office I stood.

I moved to the desk and noticed that the name of Weathers' uncle was on the plaque with the many letters following his name, signifying that he owned the room.

I decided to sit, knowing that if I were discovered I could just say that I was waiting for Weathers who had gone to look for his uncle.

After a few minutes, becoming bored, I began to scan the papers on the desk and small side table which stood to its left. They were mostly run-of-the-mill papers, and I was not really reading the titles, but I became more interested as I noticed one document which bore my name.

'What on Earth would he have an interest in my information for?' I thought. The folder was near the top of a group of the files on the chosen five and though I was a little taken aback, there could be a perfectly plausible reason for their presence.

I turned the file bearing my name and quickly opened it. There were my personal details and the details of my family, and, included in these, was our real family name.

The words 'A threat, silenced' were handwritten in the border next to my father's name. Suddenly, I heard someone walking down the hall to the office. I closed the file and quickly sat down in the guest's chair, trying to look relaxed.

Weathers entered and said, 'He didn't follow me.'

I was about to respond when the door opened and Weathers' uncle entered.

He looked a little put out that we were in his room but quickly he seemed to calm himself and then asked, 'Finished your tour?'

'Yes, I just thought I should come and say goodbye,' Weathers answered then added, 'What about all of this? I'm more than a bit surprised. Why has no one ever told any of us that we are Gypsies?'

'We are Roma, not Gypsy and not Sinti,' his uncle corrected, sounding slightly angry. He looked at us both and added, 'Gypsy is what our enemies call us. It is just one of the insulting names we have been called. Make sure you don't use it again.'

Showing his surprise Weathers said, 'Oh, I'm sorry. I am a little mystified about all of it, and as I have no information, I might be expected to make at least a few mistakes.'

'Yes, I understand, but you must be careful,' the older man said in a more conciliatory tone. 'These are dangerous times.'

He walked to his seat and looked at the papers on his desk. He seemed not to notice anything had moved but shot a quick glance at me which I met, trying to seem uninterested.

'And you, Mr O'Calahan, what do you make of all of this?' he asked.

'Well, sir, it all seems a bit of a farce at the moment – secret whispers, hidden facts about everyone, and frankly, I would just rather go home and look after my father, and the family, after what has happened,' I answered, also trying to sound a little displeased.

'Yes, your father. I heard about that – a good man. Pity. Pity he was not more careful. We all need to be more careful,' he said, sounding unsure of himself.

My mind was reeling, what did the writing next to my father's name mean? A threat silenced?

'I was very sorry to hear about his accident,' he added and sounded sincere.

'Thank you, sir,' I said and stood to leave.

Weathers moved to his uncle and shook his hand.

Once outside, he said, 'He is always a little grumpy, but he doesn't mean anything by it.'

I nodded but had nothing to say. We walked back into the main foyer, and I noticed that the 'Tail' was nowhere to be seen. I smiled again, thinking that I had imagined the whole thing.

We waited around for another 15 minutes or so and then Nagel met us and started toward the front doors saying, 'I have taken the liberty to have Peter bring the car to the front of the building. I hope that is alright?'

I nodded, Peter often drove my vehicles.

From a young age, I had had a car of one sort or another, and I always left a spare key in the glove compartment.

We exited and saw that the car was the second in line to pull up in the queue of around half a dozen vehicles. We followed the bustling, elderly Nagel, and boarded. Peter went to hop out of the driver's seat, but I suggested he may like to drive for a time and he agreed.

As he pulled away from the kerb, I suddenly noticed the man who I thought had been tailing us getting into a car on the opposite side of the road. He still seemed to be watching us.

As we drove away, the car opposite did a U-turn and followed us. I had turned to watch it, having sat in the front passenger seat, and Nagel noticed my interest.

'Yes, they are following us,' he said, smiling, then added, 'Well done for spotting them. They have been set the task of making sure you three are safe.'

I raised my eyebrows, glancing at Weathers. He gave that unsurprised look of knowing.

'Ah, so you both clocked them?' the old man questioned. Weathers nodded.

'You will need to keep your wits about you at all times. There are dangerous men out there,' Nagel said and Peter looked around, trying to see what we were talking about.

'They are in your mirrors, boy – in the green coupe,' his father said.

Peter looked up at the mirror and nodded. We then travelled almost half an hour before any one spoke.

Nagel broke the silence, no doubt we were all still trying to take in the information we had only so recently received.

'I presume you all have questions?' he asked.

All three of us nodded and Peter asked, 'Why keep this all from us? Shouldn't we have been better prepared if we had known?'

'Not at all – as teenagers you were each being trained in the things you would need to know. The old saying "loose lips sink ships" applies – if you knew nothing you could let nothing slip. You have each been brought up as Christians as that is our religion. Most of us are Catholic, some are Presbyterian, but we are all Christians.' He paused for a moment then asked, 'Are there any other pressing questions?'

'I have many,' I said and began with 'How did you know we would be needed as, err, well, spies for a start?'

'The people who would harm you – us, have been persecuting Roma and Sinti for hundreds of years. We are seen to be a lesser race across much of Europe, all criminals. This is of course a fabrication. Any crimes we have committed as a people have been because we were treated so badly. We often would not be given work and therefore had to rely on stealing or begging to make ends meet.'

A knot formed in the pit of my stomach. I just couldn't understand how one race could be so cruel to another. I exchanged a glance with Weathers – he too looked astonished.

Nagel seemed to be enjoying his own flow and continued. 'In some countries we have a bad reputation and are banned from working. In Germany we were used as ostlers and blacksmiths, and many of the bakers are Roma. There, we were settled and important – in fact, your grandfather was an ostler.'

'Forgive me, but what is an ostler?' Weathers asked, sounding very uncertain and a bit embarrassed.

'Oh yes. In many large towns there are inns and hostels – each hires an ostler to look after visitors' horses. They usually have a blacksmith and they sometimes have a fettler as well. These people were often from one family and though the women worked as hard as the men, they were not allowed to earn a wage,' he answered and continued. 'The children were put to work as well. They would wash and groom the horses and even feed them, round them up if they had been put out to the fields. Things like that.'

He paused and took his glasses off and cleaned them on the front of his jumper, as I had seen him do many times before. The three of us just sat and listened, bewildered, fascinated and frustrated all at once.

'I took on the leadership of what we call "The People" in 1921 and spent several years building the numbers and bringing them together when needed here in Australia. We have few problems here but we do seek out, and deal with, those who persecuted us, who have come here to live,' he added.

'Deal with? What exactly does that mean?' I asked.

'We usually try to have them disgraced in some way. We have people in the emigration department, and if we can we find some inconsistency in their paperwork and send them back to Europe. In other cases, we have to be a little more decisive.' His answer left the question still hanging, on an unexplained word: decisive.

'And that means?' I pushed.

'Well, we do not like to see people have accidents. But sometimes it is necessary,' he answered, still not saying what I needed to hear.

'You mean they are killed?' I continued.

'Yes, don't be naïve. If it is us or them, we do what is necessary.' He sounded annoyed at the question but I felt I could not leave it there.

'Have you been involved on these occasions?' I blurted.

'We are all involved on these occasions,' he answered and after settling down a little, added, 'You want me to say they are killed? You want me to say I have killed? Well, yes, they are killed. I have not done the task here in Australia myself, but I have ordered such actions and would have done it myself, if it were to protect my family, my people.'

Put like that, I felt I could go no further. My mouth gaped and I saw Peter glance disbelievingly at his father. None of us had any more questions at that time. None that we felt needed answering anyway.

Arriving at our home in the early evening twilight, I said to Peter and Weathers that I needed to speak briefly with my uncle so they left us.

I moved to the back seat and spoke directly, 'We ended up in the office of Weathers' uncle today and there were files of each of us who are to go to Germany on his desk. I should not have mentioned it to you, only for the words I saw written next to my father's name: "A threat, silenced." I didn't—'

He interrupted me and asked, 'What exactly did it say?'

'That is it. "A threat, silenced,"' I answered.

He looked a little unsettled and then said, 'I will look into it. I am no longer the leader of the group, getting a little old, but I am still in the hierarchy.'

He then leaned a little closer to me and whispered, 'Don't trust anyone, not even your friend Weathers, until I can prove their position.'

He frowned and shifted his gaze to the green car which had followed us all the way home. 'The two men in that car were hired by Weathers senior. Keep an eye on them. This may not be anything but just the same,' he paused, drawing a pistol from his inner vest pocket. 'You may need this,' he said.

'Oh, I don't think so,' I said, shocked.

'This is the safety,' he said, persisting and showing me the catch operated by his thumb.

'I have never used a pistol,' I said, and did not take the gun as he handed it to me.

'You have been trained with a pellet gun and a .22 and are, I think, an exceptional shot,' he said and re-offered the pistol again.

It was a U.S. Colt and bore the date 1911. I took it in my hand and was surprised that it felt as light as it did.

'It will make me feel more secure if you take it. I will get it back before you step foot on the boat,' he said.

I relented and stuffed it into my pants pocket. He turned his back and got out of the car and as he walked away, he murmured, 'Come and see me first thing in the morning.'

I just sat there for a moment, thinking. Was all this real? Was I now some kind of a spy, or operative, as they called it?

This all seemed like a bad dream and one I hoped, soon, to wake from.

CHAPTER 5

The next morning, I rose early. I had not slept well, and at 5am, I could stand it no more, and rose trying not to wake Weathers in the next bedroom. I walked out into the kitchen, thinking to make a cup of tea, and sitting at the table was my sister.

'Morning. Couldn't sleep either?' I asked.

She nodded and then said, 'What do you make of all this?'

Here I was with my own sister and I wasn't sure how to answer the question.

'All what?' I asked.

'Father's being run down, this Roma stuff and all that it entails?' she answered.

'Oh, you know about that, do you?' I asked in a surprised voice.

'Yes, I have known for a long time. Since Peter and I were told, you know, when we were going out. Father and Nagel sat us down and explained why we were not to become involved, being first cousins' she answered.

'Oh, for God's sake, I seem to be the last to know everything around here,' I muttered with a few choice expletives.

She could see that I was annoyed and tried to placate me.

'I was sworn to secrecy, as was Peter. They would never have told me if they hadn't had to,' she said. She waited for me to get a grip, so to speak, and then added, 'Well, what do you think?'

'I'm not really sure. It all seems like some ridiculous melodrama. What do you think?' I asked, and as she had always seemed to be a confidant in my life, she began to tell me what she knew.

'When I was told all of this, I didn't believe it. I thought, unkindly, that father and Nagel were just not happy that their children were getting together. You know, too young, not sensible enough, too close to home. I went to Mother and asked her and when she confirmed the story, I felt betrayed. Why were we not told, why was everything so secretive?'

'I know. That is why I am a bit put out. Were we not trusted? Could we not cope with the information?' I asked rhetorically.

'Yes, all of that, but then I decided to go and find out more at the library. More real information, and there wasn't a lot. The Sinti and Roma migrations are listed in some books, but the attempts at annihilation, sterilisation, are not spoken of. So, I went back to Mother and asked questions, questions she had no answer for. She sent me in to see Mrs Nagel and *she* provided me with everything I needed to know. Her brother and sister were both killed in Germany. Did you know? Then her family ended up in Ireland,' she explained and I, dumbfounded, just shrugged my shoulders.

'They have always been persecuted. They first came from India, which is why we have skin darker than normal. The Roma who migrated received some help from the Travellers of Ireland. They are a group of roving people as well.'

'Our father spent time with them but they were very different to what he was used to.' She nodded then went on, 'But about Father's being run down, what do you think?'

I was still dumb and shrugged my shoulders again.

'You must have an opinion?' she asked.

'Well, I'm not sure that I do,' I murmured, then thinking better of it, continued, 'I suppose I have to believe it, with all of the people and organisation I saw in Sydney yesterday.'

'Yes. It does seem strange, though, that they would hit at Father. He is no risk to anyone.'

I nodded and then paused when Weathers entered the room.

'I heard you speaking. I thought I better come clean,' he said and added, 'I knew we were Roma – that is, *my* family. Father and Mother explained where we came from when I was first beginning to fight at a representative level. They thought someone may ask questions about my family and that is why I have never given an interview to the papers,' he said.

'Does everyone but me know what the hell is going on around here?' I asked, feeling very unsure of everything. Who the hell was I, even?

'Sorry, I didn't know you were Roma as well.' Weathers apologised.

'Oh, sorry. I am just finding it hard to get my head around it all,' I said.

We all just sat there for a while then Weathers asked, 'What news of your father?'

'He is at least a little better. Still in a coma, though.' I answered.

The coma lasted another three days and I had to return to work in Sydney. I returned as soon as I could, hoping that father would be able to confirm all of this strange information.

When I entered his room, he was asleep and he did not wake while I was there. The next day when I entered, he was awake but not very lucid. There were worries that he had received irreversible brain damage. I spent some more time with Nagel and he tried to answer any queries I had.

The following Thursday, I received a phone call from my mother at the clinic.

'I have your father for you. I will put him on but don't ask questions. He just wants to let you know a few things, and he's not very well.'

'Hello, Robert?'

I answered, 'Yes.'

'You must take heed of your uncle. Trust everything he has to say as if it came from me,' he said slowly and breathing heavily.

'Yes, sir,' I answered and then Mother's voice said, 'I will tell him.'

'What are the doctors saying?' I asked.

'Not on the phone,' she answered shortly and then hung up.

That afternoon I saw Baltimore and asked if I may have the next day to go to Father's bedside.

'You must take two. Settle all of your family commitments as you are going into camp next week with the team,' he ordered.

It seemed to me that every time I opened my mouth, I had something more to think about.

I had been avoiding Weathers. I was not feeling sure of his uncle's allegiance, but that afternoon while I was packing, he arrived at my door and he looked terrible. I asked him in and as he sat on the couch in the lounge room, he blurted, 'My uncle is dead. They found him stabbed to death in his office.' He paused and, shedding a few tears added, 'No one was seen going in or out, but I can't believe he did it to himself.'

'What?' I asked stunned.

'Yes, they are saying suicide. But how and why?' he answered, looking at the ground.

'I'm sure he was happy; he had no reason …' He broke off mid-sentence.

'Oh, God,' I said, thinking what if this was all my fault? Was he done in by our side or their side? Who was their side?

I only found the words 'oh God!' again, and then gained my composure a little. 'I'm so sorry, mate.'

I rested my hand on his shoulder and gave him a moment.

'Could you take a look at him, and tell me if he did it himself?' he asked.

'I could try, but I have no real knowledge about that sort of thing.' Then I had a second thought. 'Wait here and I will see if Baltimore will see us.'

He nodded and I left the room. Crossing the waiting room, I knocked on the boss's door.

He said 'enter' and I obeyed.

'I thought it may be you,' he said, taking my hand. 'Your question is, was it us? No, it was not. He took his own life. He got there first. It has been released that he had terminal cancer and that is the story you need to follow.'

'Weathers is in my office. He wants to have me see the body. *He* wants to see the body?' I asked uncertainly.

'I can organise that,' he answered. 'But I would like to see him first. He is in your office?'

'Yes.'

'Give me just a minute to ring the city morgue and I will come in,' he ordered.

I nodded and crossed to my room again.

'Baltimore is organising things. He will be with us shortly.'

We both waited in silence and when there was a knock on the door, I gratefully answered it.

'Come in.'

Baltimore entered and moved directly to Weathers, taking him by the hand.

'Terrible business, this,' he said. 'I knew your uncle had an aggressive form of cancer but I had no idea he was that low.' He continued to hold the younger man's hand.

'But he never said anything, and he didn't look sick,' Weathers mused.

'Yes, yes, he was a very private man, as many of us are who got out of Europe. I have arrived for you both to see the body, err, but I would advise you not to,' Baltimore said and released his grip.

'Thank you, sir, but I feel I must.'

'I thought you would say that. Now I know your parents and grandparents are all gone, but you have an aunt?' Baltimore asked.

'Yes, I have let her know. I had to send a telegram as she lives out in the country and has no phone,' Weathers answered.

'Where does she live? I could send my car with a driver to pick her up?' Baltimore offered.

'Well, she lives near Galore, a little place called, err, Collin Gully, I think,' Weathers answered and then added, 'I couldn't ask you to do that, sir.'

'You didn't ask and as I have offered, I would be insulted if you refused,' the old man said sounding very sincere. He paused for a moment and then said, 'Would you like it if my wife arranged the funeral? She works as a beautician for one of the leading undertakers.'

Weathers opened his mouth to protest but the old man saw his intent and said simply, 'That is arranged then. I will let her know. And when would you like it to occur?'

'Oh, I have no idea. Perhaps early next week. Oh no, I forgot. We have the team camp next Monday and Tuesday,' he answered.

'Well then, shall we say Wednesday or Thursday?' Baltimore suggested and lifted the phone. 'I will let my wife know.'

'I can't begin to thank you enough, sir,' the young man said in a very uncertain, youthful voice.

'Your uncle was quite a wealthy man, but I will guarantee the bill until his lawyers are in the loop.' Baltimore changed his voice as he responded to the answering phone. 'Hello dear, I need you to organise a funeral for me.'

He placed his hand over the receiver and said, 'You should both go then. I will see you on Friday, Mr O'Calahan.'

He did not wait for an answer and turned his back to us and continued his conversation with his wife. I took my coat from the hat stand in the corner and we left without saying another word.

Once in the street, we both looked up and down. I suppose we were both being a little paranoid, but I don't think that was very surprising considering all that had happened in just a few short days. The street was almost empty – only one car was parked a few houses down on the same side we were on.

'I'm sorry to put you out, but I didn't know where else to turn,' Weathers said.

I slapped him on the back and said, 'Not at all, not at all.'

We left for the morgue.

Around an hour later, we were presented with the body of his uncle, still on the post-mortem table. The face was uncovered and Weathers looked at it, then lowered his gaze.

'I will have a look at things. Wait for me outside,' I said and he left with a sullen look on his face.

I lifted the sheet which covered the abdomen. The organs were all removed. I moved to the side table and uncovered the trays which contained them, and inspected that which was present.

The liver was very large and necrotic. I was surprised by the look of everything. The lungs, the left of which had been transected, were obviously diseased but size-wise, they bore no resemblance to each other. In short, these were not the organs from this body. I was certain of that.

I quickly left the cadaverous room. Weathers had waited for me.

'What do you think?' he asked.

'There was cancer in many of the organs,' I said.

'And what or how did he kill himself?' He pushed.

'Well, it seems to me that he placed a knife against his heart and drove it straight in,' I answered and then added in hindsight, 'I'm sorry. He would have died almost instantly.'

'Isn't that a strange way to commit suicide?' he asked as though he smelt a rat.

'Well, for an average man, yes, but your uncle was far from being an average man.'

'What do you mean?' he fired back.

'Well, he was a trained veterinarian, taxidermist and anthropologist. He knew that there was no chance that he would live once the knife entered his heart,' I explained. I felt terrible not telling him my suspicions. I hated all of this, the falsity, even to one's best friends.

'But wouldn't it have been much easier to take a drug overdose or something like that?' he continued, perhaps seeing the real uncertainty in my expression.

'Well, one has to be in a terrible state to take one's own life, but there is one thing for sure: he would not have suffered,' I answered, trying to convince myself.

He shed a tear and nodded. I felt distraught for my friend and would have liked to tell him the truth as I understood it, but knew that doing so would only have made him feel much worse.

'He never seemed to be sick for even one day,' he uttered in a still unconvinced voice.

'With enough pain medication it can seem as though there is little wrong. The lungs were very badly affected. He would have had only months, perhaps weeks, to live,' I said, patting his shoulder.

I sat down next to him and just sat for a while.

Sometimes, I had been told, there was a time to say nothing to bereaving relatives. But just be there for them.

∾

That afternoon, I went to see Baltimore in his office. I needed to get his take on the death of Weathers' uncle.

'What did you make of the corpse?' he asked as I closed the door to his office behind me.

Baltimore sat behind his grand desk, a cigar in the corner of his mouth. It was unlighted, and this was not unusual as he often held one there, not smoking, when he was inside a building. I think it was almost used as a sign of his status, him thumbing his nose at the world and the rules that didn't apply to him.

'Altered, to say the least,' I answered.

'Yes, that was necessary,' he answered, studying my face.

'Why?' I asked.

'He did take his own life. He was given that choice,' he answered.

'Not much of a choice,' I said a little flippantly.

'Don't be naive. What did you think would happen?' he said, looking a bit disgusted.

'Well, not that,' I answered.

'He had betrayed us. When you reported what you saw in his office, I and some of our operatives moved. We confronted him after intercepting his mail. He was sending all of you to your deaths. Yes, even his nephew,' he answered and then added, 'We gave him the chance to deny it but he did not. He took poison and was dead in seconds. The knife wound was an afterthought to cover up our presence and the thought of anyone finding the poison in his system. It was our coroner who did the autopsy.'

'This is all a bit too much,' I said, I had never been more unsure of myself – suicide, murder? Whatever it was, it was not a normal way of living. I was not sure if I could even go ahead with the trip.

'You should now arrive without anyone knowing you are working for us, I hope,' he said.

The next day I left to visit my father for the last time before traveling to Berlin.

This time he was much more lucid, and after asking Mother and Mrs Nagel, who had accompanied her, to leave us alone for a short time, he got me to come very close to him so he could be heard in a whisper.

'I am very proud of you, Robert, but you will need to have your wits about you when you get to Germany,' he said in a very low voice. I nodded.

'You now know why you are going and how important your actions are to me – to all Roma.' He said the word 'Roma' in an even quieter whisper.

I nodded, understanding.

'You will not know who to trust, so trust no one, until you have to.' He took a long breath and added, 'Young Nagel was a last-minute inclusion. Him you know well, at least. Watch your back and you should be alright.'

He took a long, slow deep breath. This talking was taxing him greatly.

'You need say no more, Father. I am well informed, now.' I interjected with a little barb in the word 'now'.

'Yes, yes, but you had to be raised in secret. You all had to be raised in secret.' He coughed and it obviously hurt his chest. 'There are too many enemies.'

He gasped and lay back and closed his eyes. I had that terrible thought for a moment that he was going to pass away.

There was a pause, then he opened his eyes again and mouthed the words 'be safe,' though there was no sound, and he drifted off into a quiet sleep.

After a short time, I checked his pulse and it seemed to be a little raised but strong. I went out to the waiting room and found Mother, Mrs Nagel and another woman I didn't know, seated, having a sullen conversation. I waited a moment until Mother realised I was standing just to her left.

'Oh, you are finished?' she said, sounding a little surprised.

'Yes, he said what he had to say, and has gone to sleep. He seems quite a bit better,' I reassured her.

I had arranged for Mother to come with Mrs Nagel, as I intended to leave from the hospital for Sydney.

She stood gave me a kiss and strong hug and said loudly, 'Have a wonderful time.'

But as she kissed my cheek, she whispered, 'Be careful.'

When on the road, I kept thinking of both of my parents' last words, 'Be careful.'

So many times in my life I had heard this from them both that I had almost always taken the sensible path – the safe path, thus I had achieved nothing. I had risked nothing.

I vowed to myself on that trip home that I would change all of that. This journey to Germany was an opportunity to do something – for me to be somebody, not to take the road most travelled. I was going to embrace the chance.

'Be careful' be damned.

CHAPTER 6

Several weeks passed and the Olympic team was finally, officially, announced. There were to be 34 competitors, and the New South Wales police eight-oared rowing team (nine members, the eight top rowers, and the coxswain.) They would also attend if sufficient funds could be raised.

This team had been all but decided for months but was only now made official and public through the press. This was in case a late exclusion needed to be made through injury or some other unforeseen problem.

The team were to travel on the ship Mongolia, which was to leave Melbourne in May. The New Zealand team were also traveling on the Mongolia though their quarters, and the Australian teams were distinctly separated. Six weeks' training was planned in Berlin before the games began.

I, Peter, Weathers, Berta Smith and Vadoma Codona, along with the NSW police rowing team, joined the ship, SS Mongolia, in Sydney. The other members of the team and the New Zealand team had joined in Hobart and Melbourne. The 37-day voyage would end in Marseilles in France.

The trip into Circular Quay was slow as the streets were filled with over 5,000 well-wishers. They had broken down the barriers police had erected to keep them off the actual wharf. People were now blocking our luggage from being loaded and the gangway was continually being cleared so we could board.

I was not delighted with the size of the crowd. I did not like that amount of people in one place.

The only other time I had been in such a huge throng of people was four years earlier when the Great Harbour Bridge was opened. On that day my family and I were positioned close to where Francis de Groot was arrested after cutting the ribbon with his sword. We saw a commotion and him being led away but did not witness the actual incident.

This crowd was much unrulier. A fight even broke out among a small group of people who obviously thought we should not be going to the Olympics in the Nazi-driven country.

Many obviously remembered the Great War and thought that we should not be giving 'The Enemy' the chance to get back into the world community. Several were carted away by police but later released far enough away from the Quay that they would not be able to get back in time to be any more of a problem to the launch.

We wore our green Olympic team blazers and, I thought, looked every bit the part, though I did think at one stage, 'Like lambs to the slaughter.'

The accommodation was a little cramped. Our section had four births in each cabin. I, Weathers, Peter and a young man called Jake Pankhurst were put together.

Pankhurst was to act as a general 'dog's body' to the management and athletes. He was a very personable young man and soon became good friends with Weathers.

Once out of the immediate mid-harbour area, our entertainment on board started for real, as one of the athletes stripped to his running kit and started running laps around the deck. Each time he passed us, there was a loud cheer from everyone on board. Soon, we were shown the makeshift training facilities which had been cobbled together by the crew.

They had created a small swimming pool, where, if one dived in, serious injury would result.

There was a very rough wrestling mat made up of multiple mattresses covered by a large sheet of canvas and bed sheets.

Adding to the high quality of the equipment was something, we later learned, was brought on board by one of the cyclers: a homemade bicycle cradle, which allowed one to ride without actually moving. It consisted of two pieces of water pipe in a support which allowed a rider to place his bicycle's rear wheel on the pipes and ride – that is if the rider was very careful. That was not the case when one of the rowing team members decided to take a turn, and, putting too much pressure on the front wheel, he found himself propelled forward at a great rate and he crashed into a group of unsuspecting passengers. Luckily no one was injured, but the man's pride and bicycling prowess took a beating.

❧

As the days started to run into one another, as they do at sea, I found myself spending most of my time with Weathers, Peter and Jake Pankhurst, trying to impress Berta Smith. She was, it seemed, most amused by our antics and would laugh and shake her head every time one of us did something stupid. Unlike her, Vadoma Codona was aloof. It was as if she had never met one of us before and didn't want to now.

I tried to engage her in conversation several times but she would make some excuse and quickly move away. She even kept her distance when we sat down to meals, making sure she never sat at the same table as any of us, and unlike all other passengers, she made it perfectly clear to the purser that she did not want to take her turn at the captain's table.

Eventually each of us gave up trying, except Jake, who would walk up to her every morning when she took the air on the main deck. He eventually gained her confidence and she would walk with him, briskly, around the ship. I couldn't help thinking that it reminded me of a crow being pestered by a peewee at nesting time. They did, however, strike up a sort of friendship.

At the docks in Marseilles, the greeting was far less heralded than our departure. There were a couple of banners welcoming Australia, and the Australian Ambassador to France met and shook hands with the team long enough to get the photo opportunity and then departed as quickly as he could.

We had little time to think of looking around as we were briskly marched to taxis and then placed on a luxury train, the likes of which we had never seen in Australia. We were not allowed to take any of our luggage with us and were told that it would be loaded on the train and things needed would be handed out as needed on the train.

Everyone had spent time on deck as we arrived, and then in lines at the taxi rank, and again at the station and there were, when we finally boarded the train, long queues at all the toilets.

Eventually, we moved away from the station and settled into the trip. We were all delighted to be off the ship as it had become a little hum-drum and boring, being confined to such a small area. Though most of the voyage had been on very calm seas, there were those of us who were still a little seasick.

'Maladie de la mer' is what the French call it, and for me and several others in the team, it did not let up once on the train.

I was forced into my bunk and stayed there for almost two days, being tended to by another of the team's doctors, Dr Best, and Berta Smith.

What a pity, I had thought, that she was seeing me at my worst. She did, however, like many women, enjoy the opportunity to care for someone in their 'hour of need,' so to speak.

On the second evening, she came and hand fed me a bowl of broth which was the first thing I was able to keep down on the train and the next morning I felt much better and was able to rise and take a short walk without the thought of embarrassing myself by having to run to a safe place to throw up. I was still 'green around the gills' according to Weathers who also jibed me about doing anything to get Berta's affections.

When we arrived in Berlin, we were all heartily sick of the train – it seemed to me that no matter how luxuriant they make a train it was still just a box on wheels bouncing me around as if for its own amusement.

I took another day to rest when we were eventually placed into an army camp where the men athletes were to stay during the games.

The camp was, though not very luxurious, extremely clean. One could almost have eaten off the mess room floor.

We were bussed into the main part of Berlin daily and would meet the three female competitors and four female officials before going to a training facility, or on guided sightseeing jaunts around the great city.

The German people were extremely friendly and eager to help in any way they could. The city was magnificent and no expense had been spared in the decorations on the streets. It was, however, very noticeable that there were many more swastika flags than Olympic flags.

On day three, I decided that I must go to training if only to show the façade of being a studious team doctor. As usual, the athletes separated into their individual sports and began to train in their own groups; though, at the end of the day, all would gather and go for a one- or two-mile slow run around the area.

All officials joined in this activity to ensure that they were seen to be part of the team.

On the run, Berta sought me out and running both forward and backwards, she ran rings around me. I must admit that like most of the team members on the Mongolia, I had lost any semblance of fitness I may have had. I was puffing like an old man and she had hardly raised the pink glow of her cheeks.

We laughed as Jake ran past us, being pursued by one of the boxing team who had taken a dislike to something he had said.

We heard later that he had told the other that, 'You may be a light middle weight but your brain is more like a paper weight.'

All was in good humour and the team was, to all intents and purposes, a united one.

The next day we were given a day to go sightseeing. This was the first real freedom we had been given and most of the team, after meeting at our usual meeting place, stepped out together. That was except the police rowing team who had increasingly become almost a team unto themselves.

They had stayed on the bus we had come from the men's camp on and we did not see them again for several hours.

One of the major places people wanted to visit was the German Nationalgalerie – the national art gallery which was a part of the Berlin State Museums.

We – Berta, Peter, Weathers and I – had decided to use this time to explore the less-frequented parts of the city, the 'underbelly' if you like.

Berta and Peter were wearing the large cameras and both began to snap photos even before getting off the bus. The four of us walked around, fairly oblivious of anyone else. We were not expecting to have any chance to take the type of pictures like those we had been sent to procure, but we did hope to meet some of the members of the Roma or Sinti population, or at least the ones who knew we were coming.

Walking up a rather new-looking flight of marble stairs which seemed to go to nowhere, we suddenly heard a loud commotion which seemed to be coming from the area at the top and to the left of the staircase. We increased our pace and as we neared the top of the flight, we were confronted by a falling woman. She crashed heavily to the ground only a few feet in front of us.

The woman looked fairly young, perhaps 25 or 26. Blood was

streaming from her face and she didn't move. We heard words in a cruel voice shouting insults at her in German and as I moved quickly to her side, I noticed several uniformed German soldiers who had been obscured by the large wall which enclosed the area and shielded it from view.

One man, an officer, was obviously the one screaming the insults and it was also obvious that he was acting in an almost unhinged way.

I bent to the injured young lady and began to help her to her feet. Berta began to take photos, especially of the perpetrator of the violence.

Here was the kind of thing we were hoping to get on film, the Nazis treating the poor and defenceless with violence.

'What the hell do you think you are doing?' I yelled.

The officer took his pistol from its holster and pointed it at Berta. 'Detain her,' he ordered.

His subordinates and two of the three moved and took Berta by the arms.

I'm not a particularly brave man but the actions of this animal were more than I could stomach, and I rushed to Berta's side and began to grapple with one of the soldiers. The other struck me in the side of the head, though it was only a glancing blow.

Before he could take a second swing, he had been flattened by a blow from Weathers.

Peter rushed between us, and the man holding the pistol, and started shouting, 'Help, Australian Olympic team. Australians, Australia, Australia.'

Before we knew it, four members of our Olympic rowing team entered the area from the direction we had come, and shouldered up to Peter and stood as a wall all shouting, 'Australian Olympic team, Australia.'

Obviously fearing to cause a diplomatic incident, the officer recalled his men and said in very clear, if somewhat basic English,

'This is none of your affair.'

'Beating an unarmed woman is everyone's affair,' Peter shouted back.

After making sure Berta was alright, I moved back to the young woman on the ground and began to treat her. The officer re-holstered his pistol and moved to where I was kneeling and I stood and looked into what I thought was a very unappealing face. Thin, almost gaunt and not of normal proportions.

'You misunderstand. We were helping this woman, she fell,' he said in broken but quite passable English.

Weathers bristled and I thought he would run at the German officer. He restrained himself, though it was marginal.

'Well, now we are helping her,' I said, holding my ground. He smiled, and stepping a little closer, he brushed some imagined dirt from my shoulder and then leaning in even closer he whispered, 'Be very careful Mr O'Calahan.'

I felt a shiver go down my spine. I pretended not to take any notice to him using my name, and re-knelt to continue helping the girl.

He turned and blurted at his men, 'Come with me, you fools.' And they left quickly, seeing that a number of other members of the public had arrived and seen what was happening.

The girl was conscious but still bleeding from the nose and she was obviously very frightened.

'You are safe,' I said and she shook her head a little.

'Oh, no English?' I asked and she shook her head.

'You are safe now,' I said in German.

Her eyes had been downcast but now she looked up into my face. 'I will never be safe again.'

She began to regain her feet. I stood also and Berta quickly helped the girl straighten her clothes and gave her a handkerchief to hold to her nose.

'What was that all about?' asked one of the rowers.

'He was beating her as we came up and Robert got between them,' Peter said.

'Either brave or foolhardy?' the man said, but held out his hand and shook mine warmly. 'Sergeant John Cain.'

There was plenty of backslapping and hand-shaking as each of the four rowers in turn came and introduced themselves. We had seen each other on the voyage but had never really spoken.

Cain helped me collect the groceries which had fallen from a package the girl had been carrying.

Berta assisted the girl to a nearby bench seat and they sat down.

I joined them, asking, 'Where is your home? Can we take you there?'

'I am homeless. They have taken everything,' she answered, wiping more blood from her nose.

'What do you mean?' Berta asked.

'My father was a professor at the university and he spoke out against the Nazi party. He was found shot dead in his office. They said it was suicide, but he didn't even own a gun.'

She wept a little as she spoke but was obviously desperate to get her story out.

'The next day when I went to arrange his funeral, they came and took possession of the house and threw all of our belongings into the street.'

Now she sobbed and Berta put her arm around her, trying to comfort her.

'Have you any friends or relatives you can go to?' I asked.

'It seems that all of our friends are too frightened to help. I have been walking from home to home but none of them will open their doors,' she answered, still trying to stem the blood trickling from her nose.

'Can you think of no one who will help?' I asked, not knowing how to help.

'My uncle and aunt, my mother's brother, would help, I am

sure, but they live in Dresden and I have no way of getting there,' she answered, dropping her eyes again.

'You must come with us, let the team diplomats work this out,' suggested Weathers, trying to be supportive.

I was unsure if that would make the girls position better or worse and put my hand to my forehead to try to think.

'Whatever you decide, I think we should move from here to a place more public,' Cain said and though I had no idea what we were going to do, I agreed we needed to be more visible to the public at large and so we helped the girl to her feet and down the stairs we had arrived by, and back into the square immediately in front of the university steps.

Our bus had been left in a side street just a few hundred yards away from where we now were. I had no idea if it would be there still but we made our way slowly in that general direction. On reaching the corner, we could see that the bus had stayed where we had left it, though as we neared, we could not see the driver.

Cain directed two of his men to find the driver and they ran ahead, going in and out of the four or five small shops on the street adjacent to the vehicle. Each time they exited the shop they would look back to us and signal with thumbs down to say they had not had any luck.

We reached the vehicle and I tried the door and it was locked. I gave it a soft hit with the side of my hand out of frustration and said, 'Damn it.'

The second of the police rowers came out of the last shop and hurried over to us.

'No, he's not in any of the shops,' he said and Cain, deciding it was imprudent for us to stay where we were, gave the door an even harder shake than I had previously.

With that, a head popped up from around three seats back from the door. It was the driver who had decided that the hours he was going to have to wait were a good time to have a nap.

Looking dishevelled and a little put out, he came to the door and opened it.

'What is the problem?' he asked, scanning all of us.

Cain answered him before I could think.

'One of our women has taken ill and we need to take her back to the camp,' he explained.

'No, but she must go on the other bus to the women's camp,' the driver answered.

'I am the doctor here, and I will need my equipment which is in my room,' I insisted.

Cain pushed past the man and started to help the girl up the stairs. The driver stood, looking very unhappy about the situation but said nothing until Berta tried to enter.

'No, no more women,' he protested.

'I am to chaperone my friend,' Berta said indignantly and pushed past the man who threw up his hands in despair. He had very good English, but now muttered in German, 'Damn foreigners.'

I had just passed him, and turned and said quietly in German, 'Be careful my friend, I understand every word you say.'

His eyes widened and he quickly retorted, 'This woman is not dressed like the rest of the team.'

'No, we were buying clothes she has her uniform in this bag,' Berta answered.

The man threw his hands up again and moved to the driver's seat, muttering, 'Someone else can work this out.'

He started the motor and soon we were traveling back through the square the way we had come.

Luckily, we had laid the girl on the back seat and Berta sat with her. There she was not visible to the many people in the area, and suddenly among those people I noticed the form of the German officer and his men. They would have had a difficult time stopping the bus as they were just arriving at the corner of a street and we passed, moving quite quickly.

The officer pointed at me and sneered but did not direct his men to do anything. He could not have seen the girl and I thought he would probably think she had gone about her business and we were just going back to our camp.

I felt very uncomfortable and Peter, who had sat alongside me, noticed.

'What did he say to you?' he asked quietly.

'He warned me to be careful and, Peter, he knew my name,' I answered.

'Oh shit!' he exclaimed.

Cain had sat down directly behind us and had obviously heard our conversation.

'That man is Oberführer Dirlewanger,' he said.

Shocked that he would know that, I looked around, and seeing my face, he added, 'Yes, Mr O'Calahan, we are here to protect you and the rest of the, um, *team,*' he explained.

My eyes obviously gave me away further, and he added, 'Our rowing squad needed to get together enough money to come to the Olympics, donations, you know, and who stumped up the cash?'

He waited for a response and when I just shrugged my shoulders he smiled and concluded, 'A man named Baltimore.'

CHAPTER 7

Our very first sojourn into Berlin had given me real surprise. They knew we were here. How?

The rowing team were here to help us, and we had already met one of the architects of the onslaught on the Roma, Sinti and now even on the Jews: Oskar Dirlewanger.

I had already heard the terrible things this creature was capable of, but now I had seen this psychopath in action, I thought it would be far fairer if Ritter and his cronies were cutting into his amygdala, instead of those of the unprotected and tortured souls they took captive.

I sat at the end of the bed in which we had placed the young girl who we now knew to be Ronja von Esser. She slept and Berta sat quietly, attentively, at her side.

We had decided to wait for the management of our Olympic team to send someone to take things in hand. Cain had taken it upon himself to represent us and ask their indulgence. I was very uncertain that this was the correct decision but he had argued that too many people knew about the girl and the fact that she was in our camp.

He had also added that there was no way for us to get her out of the camp and that we would need help with the fall out surrounding our actions. He was, of course, correct, but the words of both Baltimore and my uncle echoed in my mind: 'Don't trust anyone.'

Actually, I didn't trust anyone, outside of Berta, Peter and Weathers. Even Cain and his men were outside my full trust as they had not been mentioned to any of us prior to the trip and they had not been present at the meeting at the museum, which seemed like a lifetime ago.

'Don't trust anyone.'

It kept running through my mind like a popular song that you just can't get out of your head.

'Don't trust anyone.'

What a terrible way to live. This was not what I thought I would be doing with my life, though I was sure that whatever else I had done would have been of much less importance. Funny how quickly one can begin to have self-doubt when placed in a new and stressful situation.

'Don't trust anyone.'

If Cain was to be trusted, it would take a lot of pressure off my shoulders. Why was I to be the leader of this desperate crowd?

Perhaps seeing the doubt in my expression, Berta said, turning away from me, 'You acted properly, bravely, even if you were a bit reckless.' She turned back to me and smiled reassuringly.

'It may have been reckless but it was not brave. I just did it; I didn't think. If the truth be known, when I saw that evil man, gun drawn, I was as frightened as I have ever been,' I admitted in an unsure voice.

'You defended me,' she said and smiled again.

'Well, everyone defended you, but, yes – I was just so angry that that bastard would put his hands on Ronja and have his men accost you, or any woman for that matter.' I confirmed what she had asserted and it gave me a little more confidence.

'Yes,' I thought. 'I have done the right thing, though it may not have been the most prudent action.'

'What do you think of him knowing who I was? Do you think the whole thing was staged?' I asked after a short moment of thought.

'I can't see how. We only decided to go that way on the spur of the moment, but we will have to be even more vigilant. He obviously has an insider working within our ranks to know as much as he does,' she answered.

I admired her more every time she opened her mouth to speak. I was a bit smitten. She could have said practically anything and I would have believed her.

'Yes,' I thought to myself. 'I am falling for her, if I hadn't fallen for her months before.'

How wise was that, and was it in any way reciprocal? God, I was in a state, unsure about everything.

I had little time to worry any further as an official I knew to be one of the team managers entered, wearing his team blazer and looking very official.

'Well, what is your take on this, Doctor?' he asked in a brusque manner.

Cain, who had entered with him, said, 'I told Mr Armetage what happened and that there was no other action than the one we—'

Armetage interrupted him and said curtly, 'I was talking to the butcher not the block.'

He was obviously annoyed and meant to say his piece but I was not about to have anyone treat another member of the team in such a discourteous way.

'You need not be rude, Mr Armetage. Cain was the man who kept us from being shot,' I said, standing.

I wanted this bullying bureaucrat to realise that he was not going to push me around.

'Do you realise what this could do? This could cause a political incident. Things are uneasy enough here without you bumbling around making things worse,' he was obviously annoyed that I would be anything other than subservient.

'And what would you have had us do? Let that animal kill a woman in front of us and just go on with our sightseeing?' I answered, surprised at my own eloquence.

'Don't be flippant, O'Calahan. You know exactly what I am saying,' he fired back.

I thought better of enraging him any further and though I thought of him as nothing more than a bully, I stilled my tongue.

He paused for a moment and then realising that I was toeing the line, he asked, 'What is her condition?' and nodded to the girl.

'Well, considering she has been through a lot, she is surprisingly not seriously injured, as far as I can tell. She has a badly bruised face and bruising to her right side – ah, ribs. At this stage there seems to be no internal damage but we won't know that for a few hours. Perhaps a day,' I answered.

'A day? She can't stay here for a day,' he blurted.

'I do understand the difficulty but no one knows she is here but us and we can't just throw her out. We are a long way from anywhere,' I conceded, thinking that he would take the chance to sound like a human.

'No, no, can't stay here,' he exclaimed and seemed to be dithering over what was to be done.

'Well, if I may make a suggestion?' I asked and he nodded. 'The women's camp would be a more appropriate place for her and we could arrange for her and Miss Smith and I to be transferred there. We told the bus driver and the guards at the gate that she was one of the team members and had taken ill.'

'That is just passing the buck. She can't stay there either,' he said in a condescending tone.

'Yes, I understand, but she is closer there to the city and we would be able to arrange to take her to her people when she is well enough,' I suggested, trying to be as conciliatory as possible.

'No, no, it won't do!' he scolded.

Suddenly Weathers, who had been in the corner of the room listening to everything, walked right up to the man and said very close to his face, 'Why don't you just shut up?'

The reaction of the man was quite comical. He backed away, wide-eyed, surprised and perhaps even a little scared.

'I'm just trying to solve this problem,' he spluttered uncertainly.

'O'Calahan has already solved it. Now go and make it happen.' Weathers snarled, taking another step forward, threateningly.

The man bustled out of the room without saying another word.

I smiled at Weathers who nodded back and said, 'Like most bullies, if you give their nose a tweak, they usually back down.'

He smiled widely and I was as impressed with him then as much as in any of the fights I had seen him contest.

⸙

Later in the evening, we were transferred to the women's accommodation. I was surprised how much more salubrious it was than our area.

The men were basically in an army barracks style of building; the women were in what seemed to be a health spa. The rooms were much nicer and more richly appointed. I whistled as we were taken into the large eatery where a table had been prepared for Berta and our guest, as in all the excitement we had missed the regular meal time at both camps.

The tables were quite well dressed with a small vase of flowers adorning each. They were all covered in a flower motif, that of rambling non-descript blooms in red and pink.

Berta said to the serving girl, who curtsied as we entered, and we noticed the table, 'There will be three of us for dinner if that is possible?'

The girl nodded and quickly left the room, going to the kitchen, and returned with extra cutlery crockery and an extra bread roll.

We were seated, and Ronja, who had been breathing heavily as I helped her from the vehicle and into the building, sat down giving a quite loud groan.

'Are you alright, my dear?' Berta asked, taking her hand and sitting down next to her.

'Yes, just a bit sore,' she answered, putting her hand to her side. Berta flashed me a look of concern.

'Well, I could arrange a room for you and have the food brought there?' I proposed.

She shook her head. 'No, I need to be as inconspicuous as I can,' she answered.

I nodded and then said, 'Yes, I forgot to mention that, um, don't speak in German. People will know you are a local.'

She nodded but added, 'But I have not, err, much English.'

'Then Berta and I must speak for you,' I concluded, thinking out loud.

She nodded her understanding.

We ate the meal which was cobbled together by the kitchen staff, and though these were only left-overs, we ate heartily. It had been a long hard day.

I was surprised that we had not seen any team officials. I thought the pompous little man from our camp would have set up quite a greeting party.

We ate our meal fairly quickly and Ronja ate hungrily but tired before finishing what was on her plate.

'Do you feel unwell?' Berta asked, noticing that the girl had stopped eating and sat back in her chair.

The serving girl was quite close, having just removed some of the plates and so Ronja just shook her head in answer. Berta sat back in her chair and raised her eyes at me, realising her mistake in asking the girl to speak.

I just smiled back. After today, there was nothing Berta could do that was wrong, in my eyes.

I thought to leave but didn't know where we were to go, so we just sat there for a few minutes. Then, two men in our team blazer entered, and quickly noticing that we had finished eating, signalled for us to follow them. We obeyed and after helping Ronja to her feet, followed them down a long hall and into a dimly lit office.

As we entered, one of the men lit another lamp, an oil lamp, on the desk and pointed to the three seats on the entry side of the large wooden desk. The taller of the two sat down opposite to us in a large comfortable leather chair.

Leaning forward, he wrote on a piece of paper and then held the paper up so we could read what was written:

'We are probably being listened to.'

I read and it nodded my understanding. Then I whispered to Ronja, telling her not to speak.

The man raised his eyes toward Berta to assure she was in understanding; she nodded back and he said, 'Now, Miss Smith, you were taken ill today and fell and hit your head?'

'Yes, sir,' Berta answered and our charade was under way.

'Doctor, how is Miss Smith now?' the man continued and I answered.

'She is not that well. A slight concussion and some sore ribs where she fell, you know.' I paused and he signalled for me to continue.

'Yes. She seems to be over whatever upset her stomach,' he said.

'The food here is richer than what we have at home, what with the depression and everything,' I answered while he wrote another note.

'There are lots of pickled things here, cabbage and what not. Miss Smith, did you eat the preserved cabbage or anything like that?' he asked.

I bumbled through the sentence and passed on to Berta as I could not think of anything further to ramble about.

'Yes, I fear I did, and it did taste a bit strange, but I just thought that was because I had never tried Sauerkraut before,' she answered, playing her part much more convincingly than I was doing.

'That must be it then,' the man said and held up the note, reading: 'You will stay in the team manager's apartment tonight. There are two bedrooms. We will get the girl out on the bus in the morning.'

I read the note and he raised his eyes to solicit a response. I nodded and Berta quickly did the same as he turned to her.

'Doctor, I think you should stay here tonight with your patient. The other young lady, Miss Johnstone, isn't it?' he said, pointing to Berta, who answered 'yes, sir' in a slightly changed voice.

'Yes, you will stay in the bedroom with Miss Smith to act as chaperone, do you understand?' he added and again waited for a response.

'Yes, sir,' Berta answered and the man added, 'If Miss Smith is not well, in the morning I will have her transported to the hospital.'

There was a slight pause and he turned and pointed to me, and I, having forgotten myself for a moment, mumbled, 'Yes, that seems best.'

The man stood. 'Oh, by the way, I am Jones, and I am the head of the management team,' he said, shaking my hand and then added, 'I will show you your rooms.'

Then he placed his finger to his lips to signify to all of us not to speak further.

Leading us from the room, he walked down the hall a little further and turned into the so-called apartment.

It was obviously a suite of offices which had been hurriedly converted to three major rooms. In the main area there was a sink and a couple of roughly placed but new-looking couches and a large arm chair. At the furthest end of the large room, a table had been placed with two chairs.

'There is a bathroom over there and if it is acceptable, I will quickly use it. All a bit of a rush. We have been busy getting things together since you came, you know.'

I nodded and he signalled for me to follow him. Entering the bathroom, he signalled for me to follow and leaving the door open, he quickly flushed the toilet and turned the tap over the basin on full.

'There isn't much time,' he whispered, the running water covering his voice. He continued, 'I am Major Alexander Jones. I was in intelligence in the war. That is why I was given this job. I know this Dirlewanger – a very dangerous man. I have connections and will get the girl away in the morning,' he concluded and nodded to me as he pushed me back out the door.

'Ah, well, I will get out of your way. I and Jeffries here are just in the next room. Please call us if you need anything,' he said loudly and he and his assistant left, closing the door behind them.

I walked to the first door at the side of the room and opened it and found that it was furnished with a large bed and little else other than a single-doored cupboard.

I moved to the second door and could see that there were two smaller beds positioned alongside each other.

'Well, it looks like this will be your room,' I said, turning to Berta and Ronja.

'Thank you,' Berta said and headed through the door.

'Please let me know if I am needed through the night. I am in this room,' I said and nodded my head toward the other door.

I was confident that I would not sleep well. I often had that terrible problem of tossing and turning when I couldn't turn my brain off.

This did not prove to be the case, and indeed I awoke to a loud knocking on the door of my room and in inviting the knocker to enter, I was surprised to see Jones.

'You have overslept. We need to be moving. I have had breakfast served in the other room,' he said and walked out.

I hurriedly dressed, having slept in my underwear, and rushed into the main area to find the two girls eating a very hearty meal.

I quickly joined them, saying, 'Why didn't someone wake me?'

This sounded as if I were blaming someone and I added, 'Sorry, I never sleep in. I am always up and about before six o'clock.'

'We didn't exactly sleep well. We have only just got up ourselves,' Berta answered, nodding toward Ronja.

'Oh, of course. I didn't think I would sleep but as soon as I hit the sheets, I was sound,' I said.

I took up a piece of toast and after swallowing a mouthful, I questioned Ronja very quietly in German, 'Are you well?'

She, taking no chances, nodded.

Jones re-entered the room and nodded toward the toilet again and I followed him, thinking, 'Isn't there anybody here who isn't a spy or operative or something?'

'The driver will be distracted and you three will get on the bus, just in case he counts,' he whispered with the water he had turned on, almost making it inaudible even to me.

I nodded and we re-entered the breakfast area.

'Now, I will have to ask you to get ready quickly as the rest of the team is on the bus, or almost all,' Jones said.

Quickly, we readied ourselves and as we exited the front door, where the driver had brought and loaded the bus, I noticed that he and two of the rowers were inspecting the rear of the vehicle.

We bustled Ronja on board. She had a silk scarf tied over her head and was looking down so that no one would notice her. Everyone on board was looking toward the back of the vehicle where Jake was preparing to do a back flip and making quite a fuss, a perfect distraction.

We rushed Ronja into the third seat and she positioned herself with her face lowered and Berta sat next to her with a large-brimmed hat that hid Ronja's face.

Cain had assumed the fourth seat directly behind the girls, and I took the seat next to him but did not sit. I stood, turned toward the play-acting Jake.

'I don't think that is wise, Mr Pankhurst,' I shouted in a disapproving voice as the other members of the team chanted a countdown from ten prompted by Jake as he teetered on the edge of the seat.

Unusually for Jake, he took notice to what I said and stepped down from the seat to a loud 'boo!' from the crowd.

He hurriedly jumped back up and did the much-vaunted vault. Landing perfectly to the delight of the cheering onlookers, he turned and took a deep obeisance and then was jostled back into his seat. The driver, now sure that the tail-light was indeed working perfectly well, mounted the steps to see what the cheering was all about, and muttered something under his breath which sounded like 'stupid people'.

He climbed into his seat and after the last of the rowing team members who had been with him entered, he slammed the door shut and the bus began to move. To his surprise, Jones came out of the building carrying a large net full of training equipment and tapped on the glass panel of the door.

The driver let him in and room was made for him on a seat on the other side of the aisle.

'Thought I might come and see if the training is going as well as it should be,' he said and a more sombre tone gripped the team. He was revered and feared by the members from the youngest to the oldest and this quieter tone stayed in vogue until we reached the street outside the training stadium.

As we approached, we noticed Oberführer Dirlewanger and two of his men waiting for us.

'Oh shit,' Cain said quietly.

Jones leaned across to Berta and I, and whispered,

'Miss Smith, put on the head scarf and as soon as the bus stops, you two jump off and run to the corner and into the café just a few doors down. The troupers are likely to follow you and I will get the girl away and then come and make sure you are safe.'

Berta nodded and I, a bit slower in understanding, followed suit. The two girls quickly swapped head gear.

Berta said 'good luck' as she and I got to the door. As the vehicle stopped, we disembarked and hit the ground running. This was obviously not what Dirlewanger was expecting and for a moment he and his men just stood, then he ordered 'follow them,' and 'halt!' to us.

We, of course, did nothing of the sort and ran into the café as the chasers followed by Dirlewanger rounded the corner. No sooner had we entered when the door burst open and the evil bastard charged in, snorting.

'I called halt!' he yelled as his men joined him. Berta and II ignored him with our faces pressed up against the beautifully stocked pastry counter glass.

A small man, perhaps the concierge, perhaps the manager, came from a doorway behind a counter. 'Who is yelling?' he asked.

Now that he noticed who had burst in, he began to backpedal, saying, 'Oh, I beg your pardon, Oberführer.'

He bowed almost double and backed away as Dirlewanger glared at him.

'I ordered you to halt!' he again roared and I turned to face him.

'Oh, were you talking to us? We are not used to being bellowed at like someone calling cattle in from the fields,' I said, trying to provoke him.

The customers at the nearest tables got up and cowered to the back of the eatery. Berta continued to look in the opposite direction as if hiding who she was.

Dirlewanger's already-red face turned positively crimson as he roared, 'Show your face, Jewess.'

Berta did not turn and he began to rush in her direction.

I stepped between them and as he pushed me aside, Jones burst into the room and roared, 'Halt!'

Dirlewanger turned outraged that anyone would address him this way.

'What the hell do you think you are doing?' Jones said.

The guards grabbed him and held him while Dirlewanger moved back toward him. 'And who the hell do you think you are?' he said in English.

'I am the manager of the Australian Olympic team and I demand you unhand my team members,' Jones said forcefully without taking a step backward.

The enraged Dirlewanger got very close to him and said, still in quite a loud voice, 'You don't demand here!'

He pushed Jones in the chest and the smaller man did not give way even slightly, snarling back at him. 'Who is your superior?'

Dirlewanger gave him another push and turned back to Berta and I, roaring, 'I said show your face, Jew!' and he moved to rip the silk from Berta's head.

I stepped between them again and Berta slowly turned and, looking him directly in the face, reached up and untied the scarf. She did this slowly but deliberately and then put her head forward, lifting it from the back so her long hair was freed, and then lifted her head again to stare him down.

'Were you speaking to me?' she said, calmly.

He looked surprised and turned his stare to me and I unfortunately smiled. This enraged him even further and he made to strike me with the back of his hand.

Jones grabbed his hand and shouted, 'Now see here. We won't be having any of that.'

Dirlewanger drew away from him and took a step backward. His face was almost purple.

Jones stepped forward again, making it understood that he held the upper hand. There were witnesses and it had been impressed upon everyone in Berlin that the world was to be shown as a modern, forward-looking country, at least while the Games were on.

Dirlewanger changed tactics.

'Oh, excuse me. I must have mistaken you for someone else,' he said and bowed, as if humbly, then, lifting his head, he said to me, 'I'm sure we will have the chance to meet again, Mr O'Calahan.'

I gave him one nod of my head and thought what a pitiful

excuse he was for the supposedly pure Aryan race. He turned and left with his men.

After they had walked out, the few people in the café gave a quiet clap and I took Jones's hand and shook it warmly.

'Well done, mate,' I blurted and then thought I had sounded too familiar and corrected myself. 'I mean sir.'

He raised his eyebrows and signalled with a head gesture for us to leave.

We followed him out and as we neared the corner he said, 'I will see you in the bus before you go into training.'

We walked to the bus and he said to the driver, 'Please step out. I am about to discipline these two and I wish some privacy.'

The driver smiled and slowly exited. Jones shut the door behind him and led us half way down the bus.

'Sit down,' he roared, obviously so the driver and anyone else who may be listening in would hear. Then he leaned in close to us and whispered, 'Who the hell are you, and what the hell are you doing here?'

Then, as if some strange secondary personality had gripped him, he yelled, 'I won't have this kind of behaviour!'

I whispered back, 'I am one of the team doctors.'

He again raised his voice and said, 'That is not acceptable.' Then he whispered, 'Don't play games and how did Dirlewanger know who you were?'

'I really don't know how he knew who I am, but he knew even the other day,' I whispered.

'Oh God. You aren't Jewish, are you?' he gasped.

'No, far worse than that,' I said quietly.

'What?' he yelled, keeping up the charade.

'I am Roma,' I stated quietly.

His eyes raised and he gave a little whistle and looked at Berta. 'You too?' he asked.

Berta nodded proudly.

'How the hell did this happen?' he again roared, then whispered, 'What are you doing here?'

'I have been training for this all of my life,' Berta said loudly and proudly.

'And you?' Jones said in a normal voice, forgetting himself for a moment.

'I am here to protect her,' I said quietly, looking into his eyes, hoping to see if he was going to help or hinder us.

He paused for a moment and then said, 'We will talk more of this. In the meantime, I will try to keep you safe.'

I looked down as I did the only thing I could: I nodded my agreement. I still wasn't sure of his intentions, and where this was going, but I felt we had little choice other than doing exactly what he said.

He looked back and forward at each of us searchingly.

'The management team will meet tonight, and you will be brought before them, and if there is any more of this kind of behaviour I will have you both sent home. Do you understand me?' he shouted.

'Yes, sir,' we both answered penitently.

'Now get into training,' he roared and followed us to the front of the bus and opened the door and let us out.

We reached the door at the front of the building; we had to go through to get into the training ground. He came down the steps and shake his head to the driver who also shook his head knowingly and said in English, 'Silly young people.'

Jones nodded and followed us into the building. I had held the door opened and as he came through, I noticed, standing on the opposite side of the road, a sneering Oberführer Dirlewanger.

CHAPTER 8

Training that day and the next was extreme. So many of the athletes had lost their fitness on the voyage and needed to be pushed to find their best before the games started in just three weeks.

Many strained muscles and several had falls. I spent both days administering to their needs and though Jones had threatened us with having to go before a committee, he did not even approach me until the second afternoon. He waited until the last of the boxers, who had strained a back muscle, was treated and left the small room I was using for a treatment centre. He walked in and after taking off his shoe, he raised his foot and put it on the table top.

'If you will be so kind, Doctor, I need this toenail to be treated.'

I could see that he had a very red and swollen big toe. It was obvious that he was in discomfort. Ingrown toenails were so very painful.

As I began to examine it, he said quietly, 'I told the management team that I had put the fear of God into you and Miss Smith about jumping off the bus and running to a café, and that it had not been approved of first. I told them I had you on a short leash and would like to handle it in my own way at the moment.'

He paused for a moment as he was want to do and then continued, 'There were a couple of dissenters who thought you should be brought before them but I was able to shut them down. I have the numbers – at the moment, anyway.'

One of the rowers appeared at the door and Jones said curtly, 'I am having some treatment. You will wait outside.'

The man nodded and walked out, smiling.

'This will need to be removed,' I said to him loudly.

'Yes, well, get on with it,' Jones answered, steeling himself for the pain. I had seen the removal of an ingrown nail a couple of times but had never actually done the operation.

'I will give you a shot to deaden the pain,' I said and reached for my bag.

'No, no, not needed. I will bare up,' he said.

'But there will be quite a lot of discomfort. I think you should have a shot,' I concluded but he shook his head.

'You need to visit me in my room tonight and we will have a long talk. you can say you are dressing my toe,' he said and then I, taking a pair of forceps, took the nail and knowing that it had to be quite a violent pull to remove it this way, pulled. Jones scrunched up his face but didn't omit a sound. The nail came away easier than I had expected but quite a bit of blood followed and I took a large bandage and held it tightly, directly onto the injured toe to stem the flow.

He nodded. 'You were right – it did hurt. But wrap it up and I can get out of here,' he said through clenched teeth.

I admired his strength of character. I was certain I would have cried out if that had been my toe. I held it for a couple more minutes and then placed a dressing over it and began to bandage it, individually at first and then I wrapped around the next toe and then the rest of the foot.

'I need to be able to get my bloody shoe on, you know,' he said indignantly.

'I know, but if you don't have the bandage, it will be just that: a bloody shoe,' I said.

'Just get the shoe back on, funny man,' he said and then I added, 'Well, I was not really joking. It will bleed a lot and I don't want it to get infected,' I reassured him.

'You will come to see me tonight to make sure the dressing is alright then?' he asked and I realised that there was much more talking to do than bandaging. I nodded my assent.

Having treated the other few minor ailments of the team members, I packed my bag and walked to the bus. I arrived last and received a jeering for my tardiness. I knew it to be in good spirit and gave a little bow before taking my seat next to Weathers.

As the vehicle did a U-turn in the wide street to return to our accommodations, I noticed Dirlewanger standing in a doorway. He nodded, the sneer on his face no more pleasant than the last time I saw it. I pretended not to notice his presence, but I knew he saw me.

'That bastard again,' said Weathers.

'Yes, he seems to have my page marked,' I said.

Cain, who sat in front of us as usual, turned and warned, 'I wouldn't take it lightly, he looks like a dangerous man.' I always admired the way Cain spoke, he was an orator of sorts – always calm and seemingly in control.

'What the hell am I supposed to do about it?' I shrugged, asking rhetorically. He shrugged back and Weathers said, 'I'd like to get him in the ring. One round would do.'

We all smiled knowing that was highly unlikely to happen.

Once we had delivered the women back to their camp, and on arriving at ours, I noticed that there appeared to be more guards at the gates and that they were in different uniforms.

'More of Dirlewanger's work,' I thought.

Noticing the difference, Peter, Weathers and Cain all turned and looked to see if I had noticed. I just nodded and we all left the bus and headed directly to the mess where we knew there would not be food being served for some time; we thought this would allow us to talk things over.

'We need to watch our backs even more now. They are

Schutzstaffel. The same as Dirlewanger,' Cain said quietly as we sat down at a middle table. I could think of nothing to say but I nodded.

He continued, 'We were warned about these mad bastards.'

'Who warned you?' I asked.

'One of our own first, and then Baltimore,' he answered.

'Is there anything he doesn't have a hand in?' I questioned rhetorically, and Cain shrugged his shoulders.

'For Dirlewanger to know about you, well, there must be an informant in our own camp,' Cain reasoned.

'I was wondering about that, but he must have been warned in advance. There were no real chances for a member of the team to warn him before our first meeting,' I answered.

'Yes, that seems right,' Peter said then added, 'What are we going to be able to do with him watching you like a hawk?'

'Well, it may work in our favour, that is, if you and, err, Weathers were to lead him a merry dance each time we go into Berlin, then the rest of us can do the work you came here for,' Cain suggested.

'Yes, I see what you mean, but that puts much more pressure on the rest of you,' I answered.

'My men and I have seen our share of danger. We were part of the teams who handled Tilly Devine's razor gangs. But what about Berta? She will be at great risk too, and you don't want that,' he said with a knowing smile.

'What do you mean?' I asked, a little flustered.

'Oh, good God, man – anyone with a pair of eyes can see you have fallen for her.'

I felt my face blush red and then answered, 'Am I that transparent?'

The three of them laughed quietly and Peter said in a good-natured way, 'Who wouldn't fall for her? But you are the only one she has eyes for.'

'Oh, I don't think so. She has never said anything,' I answered, still blushing and a little displeased that my proposed love life was the topic of conversation.

'Ha, give me a break. She glows every time you speak to her.' Weathers laughed.

'You're the man. She's expecting you to say something.'

I hoped they were correct, but I said, 'Well, there is little chance of me saying anything while we are here. That would only put her in a worse position. 'Can we talk about more important things?'

All three laughed again. It seemed that they each thought my painfully clumsy dealings with Berta were hilarious.

'The day after tomorrow is Sunday and nothing is scheduled for the team. It is a rest day of sorts. We could all go into the city together and split up if Dirlewanger shows his ugly face,' Cain suggested.

I thought for a moment and then said, 'Do you really want to get this involved? After all, this is not your fight.'

'Criminals are criminals wherever you find them, and bastards like this man need to be stopped no matter who he is targeting. If I got the chance, I would take him out,' Cain answered.

'Kill him, you mean?' I asked, shocked.

'From what Baltimore has said, killing him is exactly what should happen. Don't look so shocked. I have never killed anyone, and I won't get the chance with him, but I think I could do it if I had the chance,' he answered.

'Bloody hell, that's not part of our instructions,' Peter said.

'Maybe not, but I'd like a chance at him,' Weathers said, and somehow that didn't surprise me as much as it had when Cain had suggested the same thing.

'I know I'm not the boss here, but I don't think that sort of thing will help our cause. No doubt the Nazi propaganda machine would have a field day if one of their pinup boys was murdered,' I said pointedly.

'Yes, yes. We need not to break cover, I know,' Cain said

repentantly. 'He has done some pretty bad things, though, and the world would be a better place without him.'

We all nodded.

'Oh God, I wish he were a boxer,' Weathers concluded.

'I was just thinking – what if I were to ask to see some of their medical institutions? They would probably want to show off their superiority in such things and that might take Dirlewanger's attention for the day. What do you all think?' I suggested and thought to myself that I was getting better at devising a plan.

'Sounds good. Do you think you could take Dr Best with you? I don't trust him at all. He always seems to be sticking his nose into other people's business.' Cain agreed with my suggestion, but I was not too delighted with his.

Best was a real pain, and had so much more experience than I had. He looked down on everything I did as if I were a first-year intern. But I could see the sense in his suggestion: I didn't trust Best either. I couldn't put my finger on why exactly but I just didn't like the man.

'I'll see if Jones will help me set it up,' I suggested and the three of them nodded.

We all stood to leave and Cain said, 'All of you keep your heads down.' And we all nodded and left to go to our respective rooms.

Later in the evening, I went to see Jones as he had instructed. I changed the dressing on his foot and noticed that it was more inflamed than I would have expected.

'I think we should have you wear shoes a couple of sizes too big over the next few days, then I can wrap the toe tighter and pack the shoe.'

I covered the wound with a thick layer of the powder we had been given to use on open wounds. I had never used it before but it seemed to help, as after I placed a pad cover, and then wrapped the toe, and then the whole foot, Jones seemed to be able to walk more freely.

'What size shoe do you wear?' I asked.

'Size seven to eight usually.'

'I may have some to fit in my case,' I mused and then left the room returning with a pair of my size tens and, packing the toe-end with a halved roll of bandage, I helped him to fit the shoe. It was certainly too large so I added some more packing and soon Jones was walking around the room, looking like he might be able to run if needed.

Then he tried on the other shoe and it flapped around as he walked, so we in turn packed the rest of the roll of bandage into the heel and he again tried walking.

Deciding that this was in no way practical, he put his own shoe back on and though he looked ridiculous, with one black and one brown shoe, he decided that this was the most comfortable.

Having rid myself of the physical reason for my visit, I asked quietly, 'On our rest day, do you think I could be shown around some of the Berlin medical facilities? There are a couple of hospitals I would like to see, and a teaching facility at the university.'

Jones sat down next to me and said, 'Surely there are better things to do on your day off?'

'Well, I'm not really a tourist type and I thought there might be some new advances I could take in. I hear there is a world-leading unit which treats burn victims, at Totgeschwlegen, I think, and I have an interest in that field,' I said, stumbling over the hospital name.

I really was interested in the treatment of burns, so I had a bit of knowledge of the work being done and though this was not the hospital I wanted to gain access to, I thought I might be able to work the university into the tour.

We had been told that Dr Robert Ritter worked there with his collaborators, Eva Justin and Sophie Ehrhardt.

I think Jones realised that I had an ulterior motive for the request but he nodded and then said, 'I could see the people in charge of our movements tomorrow. Do you think Dr Best would be interested in accompanying you?'

It was a fortuitous thought from him, and saved me from having to suggest the same.

'Yes. I don't think he likes me very much but you could ask him if you like.'

The next day at the end of the training outing, Jones and Dr Best attended my treatment room. Best had his room on the far side of the long passage which led through the ground floor of the facility. He was the senior doctor and was treating all of the women and the more serious injuries of some of the men. He was a pompous-looking man full of self-importance. I took an immediate dislike to him.

'I have set up the tour of the hospitals for tomorrow, and Best here, would like to accompany you,' Jones said.

'Good, thank you, sir,' I said and continued to pack my equipment into my treatment bag.

'I thought you would be out running around the town,' Best said in a surly condescending voice.

'What better time to learn a few new skills?' I answered.

'Yes, there are a few world-leading practitioners here in Berlin,' he said in a slightly less gruff tone.

'You will need to be about early as they are going to pick the two of you up at seven in the morning,' Jones told us and we both nodded.

Best then left the room.

'I have set this up through the Reich Minister of Propaganda, Goebbels. He seems to be another unsavoury character, but he was keen to see people interested in the great German medical system.

'There will be several minders and one of their photographers traveling with you. Don't cause an incident – just learn what you need to and don't provoke them,' Jones said to me quietly as if he thought someone might be listening.

'I'm just going there as an interested student of medicine,' I assured him.

'A student?' he said in a slightly bemused tone.

'Yes, we always need to be learning in medicine,' I answered.

'Well, learn what you like, but keep out of trouble,' he reinforced.

CHAPTER 9

The next morning, we were picked up in a sleek black staff car with dual swastika flags mounted on either side of the bonnet.

The driver, obviously a Nazi officer, greeted us and opened the door for us to enter. Best was his usual self, and had not spoken to me, having had his head buried in what seemed to be some medical papers. Now, he grunted a 'morning' greeting and pushed past me to enter the car. I stood my ground and though he passed, he would have felt the resistance.

'Yes,' I grunted back.

The driver did not speak at all on the trip to a large building on the outskirts of Berlin, where we picked up two other officers and a young lady with a very large camera. She took the front passenger seat and the two men bundled themselves in to the back seat with us. It was actually quite uncomfortable.

I had, of course, been in a squashy situation before but usually when you pile into a car to go somewhere, one knows the other passengers.

Neither of the men introduced themselves until we were alighting the vehicle, then the senior man, though I didn't know his rank, introduced himself in English.

'I am Joseph Berchtold, writer for Völkischer Beobachter Newspaper and this is Helene Riefenstahl, who is here to photograph your visit.'

The woman stepped forward and said in strongly accented

English, 'My friends call me Leni.'

She shook hands with Best and then myself.

The other two men hovered around behind us and at no time spoke. It was very uncomfortable to find oneself being shadowed everywhere, but it was nothing more than I had expected.

Riefenstahl was a striking young woman and though her hair was tied under a bright red scarf, one could tell that its colour was out of a bottle.

'Miss Riefenstahl is a very famous German director, actress and photographer. "Triumph of the Will" Is one of her movies you may have heard of?' Berchtold said in a triumphant voice.

Best answered, 'Delighted to meet someone so famous.' And he bowed his head slightly.

I had to admit that I had never heard of Riefenstahl.

I copied Best and said, 'Delighted to meet you, Miss Riefenstahl.'

'Leni, please,' she said and gave me a flirting look, lowering the right side of her face and closing her eyes a little. I smiled back, though I was certainly not flirting.

Though she was quite pretty, I somehow disliked her already. There was no reason for it and I thought how ridiculous it was. Perhaps I felt that she was a part of the pure Aryan race, as proposed by Hitler – but I had no such feelings for Berchtold. He seemed perfectly reasonable and his allegiances were on his sleeve.

Though I didn't see the name of the huge building we were led into, it was quickly obvious that it was a hospital. Though I thought it may have been attached to the university.

The main foyer was full of people in queues and many administrative staff were attending to their enquiries.

Several men in white coats were moving around from one hallway to another. The large directional board was informative; there were several teaching units and on the second floor, the Racial Hygiene and Demographic Biology Research Unit was mentioned.

This unit, I knew, was that run by the infamous Robert Ritter.

This seemed too good to be true: here was the exact thing I had come to try to investigate.

On the same floor, I noticed there was an optical treatment laboratory and when asked what we would like to see, I suggested the same.

Best said he would like to see the experimental Radiology Unit. He mentioned that he had read about it, and knew it was dedicated to 'Wilhelm Conrad Roentgen: the man who discovered x-rays in the late 1800s.'

Berchtold seemed delighted with the suggestion and led the way to a different wing –the one I wished to visit. When we arrived in the new department, some time was spent having the equipment explained to us and I must say I was impressed with the expenditure, which must have been limitless, on every last little item. The beds were all seemingly brand new and each had a small treatment table fitted as part of the head board. The room was spacious for the time; indeed, I had never seen such a perfectly dedicated ward.

Riefenstahl had taken the opportunity to photograph every move we made, looking for the most publishable photo for her newspaper.

When we had had our fill of x-rays, I again asked to see the optical treatment laboratory. Best said he would like to see the x-ray equipment in operation and Riefenstahl suggested that she could show me to the other wing, and Berchtold agreed, pointing to one of his shadowing men to go with us.

As we walked back to the main foyer, Riefenstahl asked, 'What do you think of our facility, Mr O'Calahan?'

'It truly is a wonderful place,' I answered, and added, 'I must admit, though, I am most interested in seeing the optical unit and the burns treatment area.'

'Yes, I'm told that they are both the best of their kind,' she answered proudly.

I could still not warm to this woman. She may have been the

best photographer in the world but she had eyes which seemed to look right through you – cold eyes, almost mad eyes.

As we neared the lift which was to take us up to the floor which I had asked to visit, I noticed a woman approaching from the other end of the corridor. I knew the face and as she stopped and pressed the button for the elevator, her profile told me that this was the henchwoman of Robert Ritter.

It was *the* Eva Justin.

She did not look in our direction, and when Riefenstahl said 'good morning,' she nodded but still did not turn in our direction. This was another hard face, a somewhat unpleasant face, which a mother may or may not love.

'This is one of our visitors for the Olympics, Mr Robert O'Calahan. Mr O'Calahan, please meet Eva Justin. She works in the scientific racism field under Dr Robert Ritter,' Riefenstahl said.

Justin turned to face me and attempting to be polite, I offered my hand. She did not take it.

'Ah, yes,' she said as if knowingly.

'Pleased to meet you,' I said in German.

She gave no answer and after the lift arrived, she stepped in, obviously hoping we would not do the same. We did.

'Pleased to meet you,' I said in very poor German, deliberately. 'Am I saying that correctly?'

I looked to Riefenstahl for confirmation.

Justin answered indignantly, 'Yes, I can understand you.'

I paused and looked at the side of her head and realised that she was still not looking at me.

As we reached our floor, she stepped from the lift and I, not wishing to miss the opportunity, said, 'I would like to discuss your work with you some time.'

She flashed a nasty glance in my direction and said, 'I think not.'

She turned on her heels and quickly disappeared through the double doors which were marked with the words 'Eintritt verboten'.

I made to follow her but Riefenstahl stepped in my path, explaining, 'entrance forbidden'.

She thought for a moment and added, 'I'm sorry, that may have seemed a little rude, but she is a very busy, and, I'm told, a most brilliant woman in her field.'

She paused again and then asked what I'm sure was meant to be a loaded question. 'Do you have many women doctors and scientists in your country?' There was a snootiness to her tone.

Lying, I answered, 'Oh yes, our medical system is built on the wonderful women who chose to work in the field.'

I was sure she knew I was lying. The women I spoke of were mostly nurses and though there were women doctors in Australia, it was seldom that they were advanced appropriately in their fields. Things had improved a little since the declaration in Great War newspapers which read, 'The War Office regrets it cannot utilise the services of women doctors.'

I had always thought that to be ridiculous. Many excellent women enrolled to be trained at the university I was trained at, but in my year, only two were accepted. They were made to feel so unwelcome that one left after only two months and the other was dismissed after her first year on some trumped-up charge about an affair with a married professor or something of that nature. It was all hushed up at the time, and I thought it very unfair.

Riefenstahl smiled back at me condescendingly.

'Oh, I see,' she said and smiled again.

Leading me past the doors Justin had taken, she brought me to a desk where a very pretty young lady was stationed. She had a slim face and figure to match. Her hair was tied in a tight blond bun with a red ribbon.

'Oh, Miss Riefenstahl. How may I assist you?' she gushed eagerly.

'I am here with Mr O'Calahan and a delegation from the Australian Olympic team,' Riefenstahl answered proudly.

I must admit I thought it a bit of a stretch to call Best and I a delegation but it obviously impressed the girl who stood and gave a slight bow.

'How may I assist?' she repeated as keenly as had been the first time around.

'We wish to see the unit in action and I will be taking some photographs – for publication, you understand,' the girl's idol answered, enjoying her notoriety.

'Yes, I will assist you in any way I can,' the girl answered, placing a 'temporarily closed' notice at the desk. She led the way into the optical unit.

I followed, clinically examining every tool and machine as if enthralled; truthfully, I was quite bored. Most of the things I was seeing were available in any teaching facility in Australia. Perhaps there were a few innovations, but I really was not interested.

I racked my brain as to how I could get through the doors which had taken Justin. I could think of nothing and the man who followed us, though at a respectable distance, never let us get out of his sight.

The tour, which seemed to go on for ever, finished with one of the optical surgeons bidding us farewell with the young office girl. Riefenstahl positioned us and took her photograph as I shook the man's hand, smiling diligently; the other two positively beamed. Being included in one of Riefenstahl's photos in the newspaper would be the highlight of their lives.

Somehow that made me like her even less.

On the landing, I glanced at the other doors and wished I could enter, but our guard was standing in the way and there was simply no way I could think of to make it possible. The lift duly opened as we neared and Best and Berchtold stepped into view. Their guard arrived at the top of the staircase opposite and soon we were heading down in the lift again with the two guards again meeting us at the bottom of the stairs.

'Seen enough?' Best asked, though he seemed rather disinterested in my answer.

I nodded as if disinterested in the question.

'I think we should move onto the next facility,' Berchtold suggested.

I had in my mind that to keep up the pretence I should ask about the burns treatment unit, but before I could say a word Best chimed in with, 'Perhaps a short tour of the burns clinic?'

Neither Berchtold nor Riefenstahl answered the query but she said, 'I will need to leave you now. I have much to do for the filming of the Games.'

She nodded and walked off. I would not have been unhappy if that was the last time I would ever see her.

Berchtold stood for a moment and then said, 'I do think we should leave now.'

It was a fait accompli, I'm sure, and Best and I just accepted that we were moving on.

We spent the rest of the day mindlessly trudging through boring, uninspiring facilities and a little before five in the afternoon we returned to the camp.

I went straight to my room and Best, too, walked in that direction. He did not proffer a single word and I had no interest in conversation with him either.

I found my bed and slept for around an hour and a half and, waking, realised that it was time for dinner. I redressed, as the day clothes I had been wearing looked more dishevelled than my usual attire. On reaching the mess, I looked for the trio I most wanted to see but only saw Peter.

On approaching him, I asked, 'Where are Weathers and Cain?'

Peter signalled with his eyes for me to sit down and I complied.

I realised his cautiousness, as a man who was sitting behind a newspaper at the next table lowered it to the surface.

It was Oberführer Dirlewanger.

His eyes met mine and the usual sneer appeared on his face. I sat.

'Oh God, what a day I have had,' I said.

Peter answered, 'Not me. I don't think this bloody German food sits well in my stomach. I spent the day very near the gents.'

'Oh, that's no good. I went on a tour of the great Berlin hospitals. Quite eye opening,' I said.

'Couldn't think of anything less interesting, though I thought I may be going there at one stage,' he answered as we were approached by the waiter – a man, not the usual woman we had become used to in the first days of our stay.

I ordered some lamb cutlets and a pot of tea and when the man turned to Peter and raised his eyes enquiringly, Peter answered, 'No food, just water and another pot of tea, thank you.'

He did look green around the gills, so to speak.

I quickly ate my meal and we both knocked back several cups of tea, all the time keeping our conversation to the uninteresting, and non-committal events of the day.

At no time when I looked up were Dirlewanger's eyes directed in any other direction than mine.

We stood to leave and as we exited the main double doors, we both noticed that the surly looking sod rose and followed us. We entered my room without saying anything and I turned on the light

I gave the door a little slam and turned to see Peter had been joined by Weathers and Cain. Both had a finger to their mouths to signify that they didn't want me to speak.

'Oh God, I'm going to need the toilet again,' Peter said and rushed to the bathroom, signalling me to follow.

Once inside, he whispered directly into my ear, 'They got out of here while I stayed. When I spotted Dirlewanger at the side of the bus, I pretended to be sick and he followed me back into the camp, watching my every move. Jones came to find me and said he had found the bastard hanging around my door, listening. I told Jones I would stay in my room and he left to go on the bus.'

We exited the bathroom, turning the taps off, and Peter said loudly, 'Can you give me something for this stomach upset?' and nodded and then realised that nodding would not be heard outside or on any listening device.

'Yes, I'm sure I can find something,' I said and then we gathered on the couch.

Cain had a writing pad on his lap and a pencil in his hand. He had written, 'We got away from the main party and found some of the contacts you were expecting to meet. They have given us a film and we need to keep it safe until we can get it to Vadoma.'

He patted his chest to show that is where the said film resided.

I took the pen and pad and wrote, 'What is on it?'

Taking the paper back, he produced another pencil and answered, 'It is a film of atrocities from one of the sterilisation units.' I nodded.

His dark brow creased as he scratched the pencil to the pad, writing his next sentence. 'We were shown a lot of terrible things and it seems people are disappearing without anyone knowing they are even picked up. Many are just gone. No one knows where.' I read what he had scribbled across the page in a quick but intelligible hand. 'Yes, we have known this for some time.'

'I hadn't.' He scrawled on page without taking it back.

He sat next to me so all four of us could read the page. I had forgotten that he and his men had not gone through the process of enlightenment the rest of us had. There must have been so many things they had not been told.

I was sure of Cain. I felt that he was true to his word and so I determined to, at a more advantageous and private time, give him much more information.

I nodded and he took the pad and wrote, 'Who do these bastards think they are?'

I nodded and we all just sat there for a few minutes until I thought to add, 'How did you get back into the camp?'

Weathers took the pad and wrote, 'The people we met brought us to a field and we simply walked into the rear of the camp.

I was surprised at the speed Weathers wrote and even more at the beautiful handwriting he possessed. This was my friend the boxer, I thought.

I nodded and he continued, 'They want to meet you.'

I nodded again then Cain took the paper and wrote, 'I don't know how that is going to be possible?'

I instinctively put my hand up to my face and felt both temples, one with fingers, the other with my thumb.

Peter took the pad for the first time and wrote, 'We could meet them where you were dropped off?'

We all thought for a moment and then he added, 'But how do we contact them to set it up?'

Again, we all thought, then as if hit by a flash of inspiration, Cain took back the pad and wrote, 'They are contacting us, and told us that that was easier.'

I nodded, then I thought about our current position. No doubt Dirlewanger was listening into some sort of earpiece somewhere, and he only knew that there were two of us in the room. How were we going to get the others back to their rooms?

I took the pad and started to write 'how are we' … then I rethought, and scribbled over the line and started again. 'How did you guys get into this room?'

Weathers wrote, 'I had to pick the lock, but we were not seen.'

I thought again for a moment and then answered, 'But how do we get you out of here?'

Peter intercepted the pad and suggested, 'I will check the hall and then if there is no one out there, you can both knock and pretend to be arriving.'

We all nodded and Peter walked to the door and started to step out, then he backed into the room.

'Dirlewanger,' he said quietly.

We all looked at each other and I sat back down.

'We will just have to wait,' I said and then realised that I had spoken out of turn.

The other three just raised their eyes and trying to think on my feet, so to speak, I added, 'We will have to wait until tomorrow to know if the medicine works for you.'

I opened both of my palms to the ceiling and shook my head. I really wasn't very good at this.

'Well, I am starting to feel a little better already,' Peter said.

Cain had written on his pad: 'We will leave it for 15 minutes.'

We waited, all sitting back on the couch. After about the arranged time, Peter again moved to the door and after opening it, he stuck his head into the hallway.

Turning back to the other two, he nodded and they quickly left the room and then knocked on the door, pretending to have just arrived.

Peter swung the door open widely and said, 'What are you two doing here?'

Cain said, entering the room, 'Young Weathers here is feeling a bit under the weather. Sick in the stomach, you know.'

I called from across the room, 'Come and let me take a look at you.'

Weathers duly came over to me and I stood and took his wrist as if monitoring his pulse.

Cain had deliberately left the door open and in just a few moments Dirlewanger's unpleasant face appeared at the opening.

'May I be of assistance?' he said in a mocking voice.

'I'm sure I can care for a case or two of food poisoning,' I returned in as churlish a voice as I could muster.

'As you will,' he answered and walked away.

I raised my eyebrows; the pretence was at an end for the day.

CHAPTER 10

The following day, having returned to the training facility, I went to my treatment room and seeing that there were no athletes lined up to see me, I laid down on the treatment table. I had been so tired the previous night but had one of those nights where one just tosses and turns. I was tired and meant to get as much shut-eye as I could during the day.

I dropped off almost immediately and after what seemed to be around an hour, I had that half-slumbering feeling that someone else was in the room. I just lay on my right side and turned away from the brightness emitted through the glass panel at the top of the door.

After a moment more, my curiosity got the better and I rolled over to see a stranger standing, staring at me. I was a little surprised. I had locked the door when I had entered.

The man put his pointer finger up to his lips. I obeyed and said nothing. He pointed to the desk and I walked over to it and sat down. He took a pen from the stand on the desk and began to write on an open pad. This was all getting a bit much. I had seen no glimpse of any kind of recording equipment in any of the areas where people had warned me to remain quiet.

'I am known as Mazarin,' he wrote in English. 'Our people are keen to meet with you.'

I nodded then, taking the pen, I answered, 'How do I know you are who you say you are?'

As I turned the paper around to him, being left-handed, I smudged the last word.

'Your father is Bereli Heam?' the man wrote in answer and question.

I nodded and he continued writing. 'Tonight at 11pm meet us at the place where we dropped your men off last night.'

I nodded and he left through the unlocked door. I locked it and resumed my slumber.

෮

On our arrival back at the camp, we found that each of the rooms had had a guard posted at the door, sitting at a small desk.

We simply would not have been able to cause a diversion big enough slip out to meet our friends. There was no way of letting them know that we were not going to be at the rendezvous. I puzzled over the possibilities – were we being held captive?

After eating in the mess with my three most trusted confidantes, I thought I would make a bit of noise about the guards at the doors.

'What on Earth are these Germans doing, putting guards on each of our team doors?' I asked, deliberately soliciting a loud response.

'What a bloody joke. One of them asked me my name when entering my own room,' Weathers said loudly, glaring at one of Dirlewanger's men who was stationed at the door of the eatery.

'Well, it doesn't really matter, does it?' questioned Cain, playing the devil's advocate.

'Just a bit rude. People keeping tabs on every move we make' Peter added.

'Oh well. I don't really care. Having a bit of extra security won't do any harm.' Cain again dismissed the objections.

I took the chance to put Cain under a cloud in our external display. I could see how this would work in our favour.

'What, are you one of them?' I fired at him in a savage tone and shot him a wink on the blind side.

'Oh, well. I don't think they are so bad,' he quipped.

'Not so bad?' Weathers roared, realising what we were doing. 'You have to be kidding.'

'Well, I'm not saying I agree with their politics, but you have to agree that the people have been very welcoming.'

'Don't forget these were the Hun in the Great War, and I had an uncle killed in that,' Peter said,

We were all on the same wavelength.

'But look how they have rebuilt the place and how clean it seems. I know they were ruthless bastards in the war but so were we.' Cain proffered and continued, 'Millions lay dead because of them, and now they want to be leaders in the world. I'm not saying I back them, I don't, but they should be admired for the good things they have done since 1918,'

Peter and Weathers got up and started to walk out, and Cain got to his feet saying, 'Let's not fall out over this.'

Peter flashed him a bitter glance and said, 'too late,' and the two left.

'I suppose I should go as well, but I do admire the German people. They are not all bad and we are no longer at war with them,' I said, trying to sound unsure of myself.

'Exactly what I was saying. It's not the people we have to fear, it's the bloody politicians,' Cain answered.

'Well, I think I would keep that information to myself if I were you. Feelings are pretty high. There are many people back home who thought we shouldn't even be here in Germany,' I advised.

'Yes, I understand that and I have some real misgivings about the hierarchy. Not only in their country, but the German people have been so welcoming,' he reasoned.

I noted that no one was within hearing distance but still kept up the charade. 'They have built some impressive buildings. I would love to go through the art galleries,' I said.

I looked at the vase on the middle of our table, trying to see if there was some sort of listening device and then decided to tie my shoe and look under the table for a microphone or a tell-tale wire of some kind, but I could see nothing.

Cain sat, watching me, and then raised his eyes enquiringly. I shook my head in the negative.

He shrugged his shoulders and said, 'Well, how about a game of cards or something?'

'No, I don't think so. I need to get some good sleep. I have been finding it hard to settle at night.'

He nodded and returned, 'Okay, I will see you in the morning then.'

I got up and left him there still musing over his cup of tea.

On reaching my room I found Peter and Weathers waiting outside my door. Peter was leaning against the wall and Weathers was sitting on the ground with his back to the door.

'We thought we had better come in for a talk after that,' the former said.

Weathers, getting up, said, 'Yes, the bloody cheek of the man.'

I made no comment but unlocked the door and the three of us entered.

'I can't believe you agreed with him?' Weathers said incredulously.

'Well, if you noticed, I didn't agree with him, but I thought it prudent to stay on his good side. We don't need enemies here,' I answered and smiled widely to show that I was playing along.

'I don't bloody care about that; I could have flattened his nose,' Weathers continued.

'There is something to be said for keeping your friends close and your enemies even closer,' Peter said.

'I kind of liked the fellow, but now, I'm not so sure,' I said.

'No, he can't be trusted, but we should still let him think we are the best of friends,' Peter suggested, but Weathers was not to be placated and continued his rant as if it had been rehearsed.

'I don't think I can bring myself to even talk to the bastard,' he blurted and then shrugging his shoulders, he added, 'What possible use could we have for him?'

'I'm not sure, but he helped us get out of the scrape with the girl,' I said and Peter added, 'There is strength in numbers.'

'Alright. If you want me to pretend he didn't say what he said, then I will, but if he starts again, you better move him along or he might get a black eye,' Weathers said.

The time was about 10pm and I knew I was supposed to meet the local Roma at the back of the camp. I could think of no way to make that appointment and therefore dismissed it from my mind.

Over the next few days, we found ourselves watched carefully most of the time. Dirlewanger was not there himself, it seemed, but one of his people tailed us wherever we went.

Meeting Berta and Vadoma in a coffee house near the training ground on our next day off, Peter, Weathers and I sat quietly with them and talked about things as they stood.

We had seen several things which hinted at the terrible sterilisation program and other crimes against humanity which were being perpetrated under Robert Ritter and his cohort, but to date we had not been in a position to get absolute proof of anything.

The local Roma movement had as yet not tried to contact me following the missed meeting. Clearly it was their intention to work out a way for us to meet.

One of the waitresses working at our end of the busy, if fairly small, eatery, placed a piece of paper into my hand when I was paying the bill.

I excused myself and asked if they had a convenience I might use. The waitress led me back to the customer toilet and I entered and proceeded to the first cubical. I noted that the second was in use.

I took the note from the pocket where I had secreted it and read. 'I will meet you in the male toilets.'

I placed the note on the floor so if anyone saw it, they may know it was me.

Soon, a hand reached under the wall with another note, I took it and read, 'We saw the increased security and understand why you could not meet the other night. It is now very dangerous to even get a note to you. We have decided that the best place to meet would be at the practice of the opening of the Games. There should be plenty of chances to get away and meet us. That is in two days. Just head toward the under-stage area and we will find you. PS. here is another roll of film to be sent out.'

While I finished reading the note, the toilet flushed and I could hear the man exiting. I waited for what I thought would be a prudent amount of time and then on leaving my stall, I washed my hands and walked through the door. I was in the small vestibule which blocked the patrons from seeing the doors to the two conveniences. At the end of the area to the rear of the building, I could see another postern door.

I quickly moved toward it and opening it, I could see that it led to a narrow alleyway. I stood, looking to see what it was used for, and decided that it was there for deliveries. This gave me an idea. I would be able to enter the eatery with my friends and make a discreet exit unseen by our guard who had stayed near the front doors of the building but had, as yet, not come into the building. He was just there to follow us and note everything we did.

I was not sure if I would ever need to use the escape plan but thought it prudent to have an exit strategy.

As we left the shop about an hour later, I noticed that our guard had crossed the road and was sitting on an outdoor seat, just pretending to read the open paper he was nursing on his lap.

As we wandered along the street, we noticed that the guard rose and followed, but remained on the other side of the street to us.

I quietly said to the others, 'you make a diversion to the right at the next corner,' and I crossed toward the area where the bus had left us earlier.

I noted that the guard followed me and the others were on their own. I quickly walked past the bus and to the next corner left and walked as quickly as I could to see how closely our German friend would follow. I almost ran to the next left and saw a reflection of him following me getting a little closer. I got to the next left corner and turned and began to jog. On reaching the next left, I saw that the man was now following at a full run.

I reached the next left and turned it; there was the bus and my friends, and they were mounting, having seen that our 'tail' was obviously there to watch me.

I quickly got on the vehicle and sat near the front door. The man came running around the corner and seeing I had loaded, he went back to reading his paper while leaning against a shop front. Inconspicuous? I didn't think so.

Once I sat down in the usual seat, Peter came and sat with me.

'So, he chased you then?' he said, meaning to be rhetorical.

'I just gave him a bit of an outing. I'm sure he didn't mind stretching his legs,' I answered, and we both smiled.

There was still two weeks until the Games opening, and I decided to go out with my friends and have dinner one night at the coffee establishment we had visited each day when on our own time.

We decided that a dinner would be the best plan as there was much more the chance for me to slip out the back door and disappear for as much as an hour or so. The night came, and we had informed the team officials that we would like to dine out. The excursion was approved by Jones and Berta, and Vadoma had also been allowed to accompany us.

We met in the usual parking place for the bus and walked cordially to the café, watching at all times for anyone who may be following us. We noticed no one.

Entering the shop, we were ushered to a table which had been prepared for our benefit. It had four small Australian flags in glasses at each end and five larger swastikas in individual little stands in the centre of the table.

Berta took my arm as we were led to our seats and I found myself serendipitously at the head of the table, nearest to the toilets.

After initial drinks, around 20 minutes having elapsed, I excused myself and left to the gentlemen's convenience. I walked right past the door, with the head of a man on it, and continued out the postern door.

Once in the alley, I quickly strolled to the next cross alley and turned, taking it to the main street on the left. There were no signs and I also had no idea where I was going. I just wanted to test the idea of getting into the city without being noticed.

I walked a couple of blocks and then heard a disturbance, which I recognised was emanating from the next street. I walked to that corner and, peering around, saw several people being bundled roughly into a small truck. The last of the men gave a good account of himself but two of the four soldiers, who were forcing them on board the covered tray, knocked him down, and threw him in.

Now things were much quieter as the soldiers stopped and surveyed the street to see if there were any witnesses to their actions. One looked in my direction and I feared he may have seen me so I moved quickly to the nearest alley and ducked around the corner. In but a few minutes the vehicle with its human cargo rushed along the street and passed the area where I was secreted, having hunched behind what I thought to be a coal shoot attached to the side of the building.

I was not seen – apparently the troopers had secured the freight they were looking for. I had one of the small cameras with me but never thought to use it, and if I had I am sure it would have shown little more than a van being loaded, from the distance I was from the action.

I cursed myself for not being more prepared. From my position, I then noticed another vehicle heading in my general direction so I hunkered down even further. This car, I saw, was an open-topped staff car and it carried the obligatory swastika flags on both sides of the bonnet.

Passing by to my left hand, I felt sure that someone must've seen me but it continued on, not pausing even slightly. As it was moving so slowly, I determined to follow and see exactly where it was headed.

Two alleys down, the car turned into another major street and as I neared the corner, I heard the slow screech of breaks and a door of the car opening. I peered around the end of the sandstone block wall and saw that two people were alighting the car. I had no doubt that they were none other than Dr Robert Ritter and Eva Justin.

As I watched, determined to get a picture of their entrance into the building, I felt a crashing pain on the back of my head, and then no more.

CHAPTER 11

I awakened but felt such pain in my head that I again passed out.

I had no idea of time but when I did start to come around again, I could tell I was bound and in the back of a truck of some kind. It was almost completely dark but by the flashes of the corner street lamps as we passed them, I could make out the form of another, sitting near the cabin end of the truck. Perhaps there were two men there. I passed out again.

The next time I awoke there was a damp door under me and though it was very dark, I could tell that I was now in a building of some kind.

I heard a noise in what seemed to be a distant corner and tried to call out. My gag was secure but the mumbling noise I made was answered by a similar incoherent sound.

I stopped for a moment and tried to understand the other person. I was not successful. Having been positioned on my left side, I attempted to roll into a position where I could start to work on the ropes which secured my hands and feet. I had no luck. I was well trussed and could not even get into a sitting or kneeling position no matter which way I attempted.

After three or four attempts I gave it up as a bad joke and resigned myself to my captivity.

After about half an hour, my eyes having adjusted to the light, or lack of light, I was able to see that the silhouette at the far corner of the room was indeed a chair and table.

There seemed to be no other furniture in the room and I could still not even sit up or roll over. I continually tried the ropes but could not budge them even a small amount. They continued to cut into my arms connecting through a knot to the ankle ties.

Soon, I heard some yelling in another room, which must, I thought, have been in the same building, though it was a fair distance away.

I listened intently and though I tried, I could not make out any of the words being said. A few more screeches came from what seemed to be a male voice. It was very high pitched and obviously in pain.

Then there was a knock. It was much closer than the screams and I could hear footsteps approaching.

The outside door was opened and I heard two distinctive thuds and the sound of something falling to the ground. Then there was a call from the further end of the building and another three thuds. Then silence; it was earth shattering silence, and though it seemed to last for a long time, it was perhaps only a few minutes.

Footsteps in the hall again. My door was being opened and I steeled myself for the terror which was coming.

The light of a torch traced the room's walls until it fell on me. I wriggled trying to free my hands still in a last-ditch effort to at least land a few blows before whatever was my fate.

A voice spoke. 'Calm. I am here to help.'

It was a woman's voice and I thought I recognised it. It was a German voice and as I could simply do nothing, I stopped struggling and felt my tethers being cut.

'Can you stand?' The voice came again and I answered with a nod as I still had my mouth muzzled.

Realising that I could not answer, hands removed the putrid cloth from my mouth and repeated the question, 'Can you walk?'

'I think so,' I said,

Two sets of hands took my arms and assisted me to get up from the floor.

'We must hurry,' said the woman's voice and I began to walk, obviously in the wrong direction as I was turned bodily and helped from the room.

Though the hall outside the room was not well lit, I could see the female to my right – it was none other than Ronja von Esser, the girl we had saved from Dirlewanger.

'How—' I started to ask.

'Don't make a sound,' she said and continued to bustle me out of the building and into a car.

She got into the rear seat with me and then another man was carried to the vehicle and put on the other side of her.

He was wrapped in a blanket and seemed to be unconscious.

Another two men joined the driver in the front seat and we moved away quietly, not lighting our headlights until we found the next street.

I decided to speak in German as I needed to understand what the hell was happening.

'How are you here?' I asked Ronja, my voice breaking.

'I am one of the underground's operatives. We are trying to get people out of the country. You were just a lucky recovery – we were following this man when he was taken, and then they took you.'

She paused for a moment and then added, 'You really should not have been out in the city without someone backing you up. Where were you going?'

'I, well, I really wasn't going anywhere. I was following Ritter and one of his women – I think it was Eva Justin.'

'Did you see where they went?' she asked urgently.

'Yes, I saw them enter a terrace building.'

'Do you know where it was?' She gasped.

'Well, no, I didn't see any street signs, but better than that, I took a photo,' I answered proudly.

She took the camera from me after I fumbled in my pocket to find it, and said, 'I will get this developed and get you the negatives.'

'There is no need for that as I got nothing which would help us with our mission. Just a few shots of a group rounding up people in a truck, but I didn't even get their faces or anything, as they were too far away.'

'I understand, but I'll get them to you anyway,' she said.

I was, however, not listening as I had had to break away from those holding me up to vomit in the corner.

'Oh God. Sorry,' I blurted between wretches.

I stood there for just a few more seconds and then the hands were again leading me to safety.

I had little time to settle and we were back again in the toilet area of the restaurant.

They left me sitting on one of the toilets in a very small cubical. The walls seemed to be closing in on me. I was sick again in the bowl.

Soon after, Peter entered the bathroom and found me seated.

'What's going on?' he queried and then seeing my face and how sick I must have looked, helped me to my feet and led me to the basin where he cupped his hands and filled them with water. He splashed them in my face and went for another lot. I shook my head and, cupping my own hands, splashed my face.

Standing for a few moments, I stared into the mirror and realised that I looked as bad as I felt. I brushed back my hair with my hand and, feeling the moisture at the back of my head, I brought my hand back to the basin covered in blood. The blood was not flowing but there was still an amount in my hair.

'What the hell happened?' he asked, seeing the blood wash from my hands.

'I found where Robert Ritter and his cronies were, and one of the street patrols found me,' I informed him, again feeling sick.

'How the hell did you get away?' he asked doubtingly.

'Members of the underground rescued me and Ronja was with them. I think she is the leader of the group.'

'Hell, I wouldn't have thought that,' he said, surprised, then thinking, he added, 'We must get you back to the camp, I will tell everyone that you drank too much and had a fall in the bathroom.'

'No, that would raise too many suspicions as I really wasn't drinking.'

He nodded and then as a thought flashed through his mind, he said, 'Food poisoning – so many of us have had food poisoning. Yes, you have food poisoning and fell.'

'Yes, I think that sounds feasible. I can say I felt sick on the way here,' I answered, thinking that no one would know any different.

Peter helped me back to the table and as I sat down, he said, 'I thought something was wrong. He thinks he has food poisoning, and he got dizzy and fell. He has a cut on the back of his head.'

Berta and Weathers, who were on the same side of the table as me, got up and took a look at the wound.

'Mate, that looks pretty bad,' said Weathers.

Berta, taking a napkin, held it over the wound.

Seeing the kerfuffle, the concierge made his way to the table and asked what had happened.

I answered in very poor German. 'I am fine. I just slipped in the bathroom and hit my head.'

'I will call for a doctor,' he said and turned to walk away.

'I am a doctor,' I said and added 'I will be fine if I can just get back to the camp.'

'But, sir, you should have that cleaned and dressed,' he protested and again turned. He obviously wasn't going to take no for an answer.

'Help me to the bus,' I said to Berta and she and Weathers helped me to stand and walked me out the front door and after stopping at the gutter to once again be sick, we made our way to the vehicle.

Our driver was sound asleep again and it took several loud bangs on the door to rouse him.

He came to the door and, opening it, said, 'What has happened?'

'He has had a fall and we need to take him back to camp as soon as possible,' Berta answered and she and Weathers helped me to a chair.

'Of course, whatever you need. There is a hospital just around the corner,' he added.

'No, I don't need stitches or anything. I just want a shower and a good sleep,' I answered

Everyone in our group was located and loaded back onto the bus and the terrible evening was over. Berta asked me a few questions on the way to the women's camp but quickly realised that I was not in any condition to answer her. She sat next to me and allowed my head to rest on her shoulder.

After the women were dropped off, Peter sat alongside me, realising that I needed the support.

Though I could walk unassisted, Peter and Weathers insisted on taking one of my arms each and walking me to my room. They lay me on my bed and I slept almost immediately.

The next morning, I woke with quite a headache. Nothing seemed to be silent – even the antique, though very simple, mantel clock seemed to roar at me. I realised that I was suffering from a concussion and though I had to get up to use the bathroom, I quickly settled down again and slept again.

The next thing I knew, I felt someone sponging the wound on the back of my head. It took a few moments to adjust my eyes to the light, then I could see that it was Dr Best. The light shining in the window seemed very bright and, squinting and covering my face, I realised that it was early morning.

'Ah, good, you have decided to wake up,' Best said and added, 'Twenty-four hours should be more than enough recovery time.'

'Twenty-four hours?' I queried, somewhat groggily.

'Yes, I stayed with you overnight,' Cain said, though I could not see him. He was positioned behind Best sitting on the chair at the head end of the bed.

I attempted to turn my head but it caused considerable pain and Best said, 'Just rest. I have nearly finished.'

He had indeed stitched the wound and I took the instruction he gave and tried not to move at all. I just had to place a hand to shield my eyes and seeing this, Cain walked over to the window and closed the blind. The effort was somewhat successful as there were no curtains.

I just lay there, my head aching. As soon as Best completed his task, he stood and walked out. I thanked him but he didn't even reply. I couldn't help thinking, not for the first time, what a strange man he was as the door closed behind him.

Cain brought his chair to the right side of my bed and said quietly, 'Was it worth the risk?'

'Yes, yes. I think it was,' I answered in slightly more than a whisper.

'Can you tell me?' he asked, and though I shook my head, I indicated that I needed a pen.

Once it was retrieved from the table along with a notepad, I began to write what had occurred on the dark streets of Berlin. He took the pad and raised his eyebrows as he read the full but concise story.

'Ronja? I would never have guessed that,' he whispered.

'No, nor would I. She hid that from us when we first met, not knowing if we were to be trusted. They were going to "visit" the house where I was held, I showed them,' I whispered back, putting my finger to my mouth

He had slipped using a person's name; we usually only whispered names in the bathroom with the door shut and the water running.

'When you say "visit", you mean?' he continued to whisper and I answered by nodding. He understood the inference and gave a little whistle.

We moved to the bathroom where our conversation could be masked by the flushing toilet.

'You must have had quite a night,' he said and I nodded agreement.

'I stayed with you, not knowing if you would speak while you were in your stupor,' he said and then after a short pause, added, 'You never said a single word, but I am glad I stayed. I don't trust that Best. He is far too smug and is interested in every detail about the night out.'

'Peter said the same thing,' I answered, wondering if I had just been under the care of a Nazi sympathiser.

'I may go and take a couple of hours sleep when Weathers and Nagel come. They have been in every couple of hours,' he said.

'You can go now if you want to,' I assured him.

'Are you sure?' he asked. I nodded and then wished I had not as the pain in my head rushed back at me like a wave.

I lay back down, having been up on one elbow, and said,

'Yes, I think I will go back to sleep.'

I closed my eyes and soon after heard him leave and close the door. I drifted off quietly and I think a very short time later heard footsteps which awakened me. Standing next to the bed was Dirlewanger. He held a pillow and I tried to sit up as he neared. He had a surly sneer on his face and his eyes were like glass, and gleamed coldly.

As he took another step, the voice of Peter broke the silence.

'I see you have a visitor,' he said, and then as Dirlewanger spun around to look at him, he added, 'How nice.'

'I was just going to see if the gentleman needed another pillow,' the Nazi quipped, though I had no doubt of his real intentions.

'I will take care of him now,' Peter reassured him, winning the staring competition as the villain glanced in my direction.

'Yes, I will be perfectly alright now, thank you,' I said.

Obviously disappointed, Dirlewanger turned, passed the pillow to Peter and beat a hasty retreat. Peter closed the door behind him as he left.

'What the hell is he about?' Peter said as he offered me the pillow.

I shook my head to decline the offer and said, 'Well, I guess he thought it was a perfect chance to finish me off.'

'We will need to have someone stay with you day and night,' Peter said, nodding as if to solicit my approval.

I shrugged. If the truth be known, I had been startled by the Nazi's presence and feeling as weak as I did, I couldn't say that I would have been able to fight him off.

Peter sat down beside me on the edge of the bed and we talked briefly before there was a knock at the door.

'Come in,' we both said in unison.

Weathers entered and, walking over to the bed and sitting on the chair to my right, he asked, 'Morning. How did you sleep?'

'Almost permanently,' Peter answered and added, 'When I came in, that bastard Dirlewanger was about to smother him with a pillow.'

'Really?' Weathers asked as if he didn't believe what he was being told.

'Yes, I think that was his intention,' I confirmed.

'This is all getting a bit too dangerous for you, don't you think?' he asked, looking into my eyes, perhaps to see how I would react.

'It is no more dangerous than the first day of the trip, or when we were in Sydney for that matter,' I answered, and though it may have sounded as though I was not worried, nothing could have been further from the truth.

'Perhaps we would be less watched as a group if you were to go home,' he suggested, though I'm quite sure he knew what I would say to that.

'No, I'm not going anywhere,' I confirmed.

'Then at least we have to go everywhere in groups, and you will need to have someone stay here with you at night,' he ordered.

'That is what I have just proposed,' Peter interjected, and continued, 'We won't give the bastard a second chance.'

The way we would work, the movement of each of us, was

agreed and I decided to give a show of strength and get up and go to breakfast with the two of them.

After a very small omelette and a cup of extraordinarily poor-tasting coffee, we went back to our rooms and readied ourselves for the day of training.

Peter accompanied me and when I had my things together, we moved to his room.

When he in turn was ready, we walked slowly to the bus departure area. We were too early and the bus had not yet arrived.

I still felt somewhat unwell and took a seat on the edge of the lawned area at the front right of the building. After a short wait, Cain and the other members of his team of rowers, arrived and he quickly walked over to where I was sitting.

'I thought you were not coming today. Best said you needed several days bed rest?' he enquired.

'Better to be where I can be seen at the moment,' I confided quietly.

'What do you mean?' he asked and sat down beside me.

I recounted the happenings of the previous night and, shaking his head, he said, 'We had better have someone stay with you at night.'

'Weathers and I have already decided that. I stayed in his room after that bastard's *visit* last night and Weathers is staying tonight,' Peter informed him.

'Good. Well, let me do one night as well. Perhaps tomorrow. We have only a few days until the opening of the Games, and then Dirlewanger and his cronies will be busy with security. That should get him out of our hair,' Cain said.

Peter nodded and I said, 'Thank you. It probably shouldn't be necessary, but I think we should all stay in groups, or at least in pairs.'

They both nodded.

When the transport arrived, we found that it was driven by yet another driver – a thick set balding man who I immediately took for a soldier.

'One of Dirlewanger's men, probably,' I thought.

The many athletes and assistants began to load, but we saw no Weathers. I didn't think much of it but I should have. He was simply never late; he was a stickler for promptness.

Just before the bus door was closed, we noticed Weathers striding quickly toward us. As he stepped into the vehicle, I could see that he looked quite unwell. He came along and sat down on the opposite side of the aisle.

'What's going on? It's not like you to cut it this fine,' I asked.

'Oh God. I think I've been poisoned,' he answered, then continued after wiping his brow, 'I have been in the bathroom for most of the night.'

'What are your symptoms?' I asked.

'I just haven't been able to keep anything down since last night, not even water,' he answered.

'You better spend the day with me then,' I suggested and he nodded and laid back on the seat.

There was little more conversation as the bus wended through the streets and I began to feel as though I would be sick again. Weathers also looked green around the gills.

The trip was uncomfortable for both of us as he struggled not to vomit, pressing his face into his rolled-up jacket, and my stomach churned.

Once the bus trundled into the parking area, I helped him to the footpath where he moved to the gutter and emptied the small amount of contents he still contained. For a while he dry-retched and I fought hard not to join him.

We spent the day together in the room provided as a treatment room and took turns napping on the treatment table.

We were both happy to see the bus arrive to return home in the afternoon. Berta had come in to see me at around lunch time and we had shared a sandwich she had brought from the women's accommodation canteen.

Weathers had only awakened when she was leaving and though there were provisions for food in the main part of the stadium, neither he nor I were interested in food. Shortly after our visit from Berta, we received a second from Best who seemed a little more pleasant than usual and offered his services to us both.

'I've started to feel a little better. I will just take an aspirin when we get back to camp,' I said, and Weathers refused any medication, saying that he would be fine.

Best seemed a little put out at this and simply closed his bag and walked out, not even saying another word.

We retired to my room once we arrived home and Cain, who had decided he would stay overnight with me, came with us. A few minutes later, Weathers was asleep on the couch and I was laying on the bed while Cain plied a pack of cards, trying to gain a victory in a game of clock patients.

I almost dropped off to sleep but my head was still worrying me a little, so I rose and took the medication satchel from my medical bag.

After taking the bottle of aspirin out, I went to open it and I realised that the bag had been tampered with. I knew things were in a different order. I was surprised – the only time it had been out of my sight was when it had been carried from the bus to the treatment room early in the day by one of Cain's men.

I took the whole bag and signalled to Cain to follow me into the bathroom where we went through the regular process of turning the water on so it was making a loud noise to cover our lowered voices.

'My bag has been tampered with,' I told him quietly.

'How can you tell?' he asked in a whisper.

'I always have the medication satchel in this inside compartment,' I answered, showing him the position I was talking about.

'Perhaps you forgot, being that you are unwell yourself,' he suggested.

'No, there is no way. One of the things I learnt from our professor at college was the absolute need to know at all times – where the medications are kept. Not just for ease of access in an emergency, but also to know that I was the only one who had touched them. A pill in a wrong bottle can be lethal. I'm not happy about this. It is not my doing – I'm not sure I will be able to use any of this,' I said, holding up the satchel.

'Is there any way of telling if the bottles have been opened?' he asked.

'Some pills have identification markings but even that is not enough to make me feel comfortable,' I said, beginning to rummage through the pills, pulling out one bottle after another and looking to see if there were more or less than I expected in any of them.

'Which of your men carried them in?' I asked.

'Jarvis. But you can't suspect him – we have been friends for years,' Cain answered.

'Well, you better ask him to come in and we can see if he saw anything,' I said, beginning to feel very uncomfortable about the whole thing.

Cain left and soon returned with Jarvis.

'You brought the doctors case to the bus this morning?' he questioned as soon as he had closed the door.

'Yes,' the man answered, looking a little bemused.

'Did you see anyone near the case?' Cain continued.

'Ah, yes. I had put the case down to pack the rear compartment. The other doctor handed it to me so I could place in the back of the bus,' the man answered.

'Do you think he would have had time to open it without you seeing?' Cain probed further.

'I don't think so,' Jarvis answered then added, 'I think he had it handed to him by Jake Pankhurst.'

CHAPTER 12

Suspecting Jake, that was not what I expected to be doing at all. He always seemed to be the life of the party. He had never asked any questions and I found it hard to imagine he even knew a few words of German, let alone him being a German.

No, no, it just wasn't possible. It must have been someone else, perhaps the driver. He had packed the bags on to the rear of the bus and helped the ladies load their luggage when they were picked up in the morning, as was now the custom.

I had asked Berta, as soon as we were seated on the bus the next morning, if she had seen anyone near the bag the previous day. She told me that Vadoma had put her own bag and Berta's on to the rear of the bus when it was being loaded at pick up.

'That was an everyday thing. She always carries our bags around to the driver to be packed,' Berta said, looking a little confused by the question until I told her of my suspicions that the bag had been tampered with prior to arriving in the room at the training stadium.

'I have flushed all of the opened pills and tested several of the tincture lids and got rid of any that were opened,' I said.

She raised her eyes and whispered back, 'Who do you suspect?'

'Unfortunately, just about everyone,' I confirmed quietly.

She thought for a moment and then suggested, 'Not Vadoma?'

'Well, no, not really, but Jake and her and the driver were the only people we have been able to say that they were alone with the case. Oh, and Jarvis – one of Cain's men,' I answered.

'I don't think Vadoma would have had enough time to do much. She walked to the rear of the bus and then straight back to me.' She paused a moment and then asked, 'What do you know about Jarvis?'

'Only what Cain tells me and that is that he has known the man for many years. He thinks Jarvis is above reproach.'

'I think the same of Vadoma, don't you?' she asked.

I paused and then said uncertainly, 'I think so, but who knows – who can we trust?'

We mused for a little while longer until Cain brought Jarvis forward with him. The young man was a towering brute, over 6'4" and the one team member I would least like to have a conflict with.

'We watched the bags being loaded this morning. Jarvis placed the bag as he had done yesterday and we watched. There simply wasn't time for anyone to get at it,' Cain said and Jarvis nodded his agreement.

'I understand, but it was tampered with. Jarvis, we don't suspect you nor do we think the driver of Vadoma had time to open it. Jake had it in his hands for only a few seconds. I don't understand,' I said, realising I was rambling a bit.

'I can pretty-well say that it wasn't opened from your room to the bus or from the bus to the medical room at the stadium,' Jarvis said and I believed him.

Weathers had been sitting nearby and had heard the whispers.

'I was in your bedroom when you were having your shower and then you were in there when I was showering,' he said.

'I don't understand it, but one thing is for sure: I will be more watchful, and we all should be. I am sure of most of us and even though I don't really like Best, I can't imagine he would be stupid enough to think I wouldn't notice the difference,' I said.

'Perhaps you should talk to him when we get to the stadium,' Jarvis suggested.

I thought for a moment and then nodded.

'I will have to borrow some things from him if he has spares anyway,' I agreed.

We reached the place where the bus was parked each day with little other discussion. It was a burden on each of us to be suspecting one of our own.

Cain and Jarvis moved quickly to the rear of the bus as soon as the door was opened. Both were determined that no one was going to touch the bag without them seeing. Cain carried it in and I walked just behind him and Jarvis with Berta.

Just behind us, Weathers and Peter carried several other bags of training equipment and behind them I noticed Best, carrying his own bag. I resolved to wait for him and discuss the incident with him in his room. He turned to the left side of the hallway and I waited for him with Peter and followed him into his treatment room.

'Good, I wanted to speak to you,' he said as we entered and I closed the door behind me. I waited for him to start the dialogue.

After a couple of moments, he placed his bag on the table and opening it, he said, 'Did you borrow any medications for my bag?'

His mood seemed wary and a little disconcerted.

'Well, no. I was about to ask you the same question,' I answered.

'What do you mean?' he asked, frowning.

'My bag was opened yesterday morning and a number of bottles were opened and, I think, tampered with,' I answered.

He paused for a moment, as he was want to do on occasions where he felt less than in control or bewildered.

'My bag has been riffled through and everything opened. I can't, in good conscience, treat anyone, being unsure of what I am dispensing,' he concluded.

'I feel the same way. What do you think we should do then?' I asked.

He paused again and in a measured way, he offered an opinion.

'I think we will have to get all new drugs and keep everything under lock and key.'

I thought about this for a moment and raised my head to meet his gaze.

I asked, 'And where do you think we will be able to get the drugs and know that they are above suspicion?'

'I think you and I should go to a nearby drug store and buy the things we need most, and then we can know what we are getting,' he answered.

I was still looking at him, trying to gauge what he thought had happened, why indeed both of our bags were even touched. I could think of no real reason other than to do some harm. Had the pills been substituted with something dangerous? Had the bags been opened by one of our own looking for something they needed? Was there someone addicted to something we didn't know about?

'I wondered if some of our things had been substituted so our athletes would perform less than well,' he said, obviously trying to see if I had had the same thought.

'Do you really think someone would be that blatant? It must have been one of our own,' I reasoned.

'I wouldn't put anything past this mob,' he said, pointing at one of the several swastikas on flags which adorned every wall. I was surprised by the comment.

'Oh, I thought you were impressed by the Germans, especially when we were at the hospitals?' I queried.

'One can be impressed with the great strides they've made, but I can't see past the people they have stepped on along the way.' He said this while looking back into his opened bag which sat on the table in front of him.

I was so surprised that I could find nothing to say and stood just looking at him.

After a moment he lifted his head and seeing that I was staring, said, 'Any fool can see what they are like. You are not the only one with a set of morals you know.'

I simply nodded and then thought how strange it was to be seeing him as anything other than a pompous wind bag. Perhaps I had been misjudging him from the start.

'Well, are we going to replace these drugs or not?' he questioned and the rude way that he phrased the question reminded me why I had thought him unpleasant.

'I think I saw a chemist a couple of streets down,' I informed him and we determined to go in that direction.

Cain, who had still been with us, indicated that he should go and do some training and left us as we exited Best's treatment room.

We walked for about 15 minutes and finally came to a small shop with a large sign pronouncing 'Apotheke' in bold letters. The sign was almost as big as the shop front. A little old man sat in the corner of the customer area on a stool and after looking us up and down, he asked in German, 'What is it that you need?'

Best replied in English. 'Do you speak any English?'

The man shook his head.

I knew that Best spoke a classroom-learned brand of German and he started to put it to the test.

'We are from Australia,' he said the word 'Australia' in a strange accent.

As usual I thought what a pretentious man he was. It seemed that no matter how many times I thought I liked him, he would dispel that feeling with his next sentence.

The man shouted something and a grumbling, equally old woman came from behind a partition and breasted the counter saying, 'What?' in accusing German.

Best began to fumble with the things we required and the woman became a little more interested when she realised that we were 'serious customers' – the kind who may well spend quite a bit of money. She scurried about, seeming to get faster with every request. I thought the scene to be very humorous.

I was standing, observing with a smile on my face, and this evidently annoyed Best, who now scowled at me and said, 'Well are you going to say anything, or just stand there looking like a fool?'

I smirked even more broadly when I realised that it annoyed him.

'I thought you were doing a wonderful job,' I said and gave a little laugh.

He mumbled 'idiot' and went back to the order, the old woman hanging on his every word.

Best had been ordering everything in double the quantity he thought he would need to cover my requirements and when he asked for two aspirin, meaning two boxes, the woman glared at him, muttering something about only selling medications by the bottle.

I laughed and Best, beginning to get really angry, repeated her last words 'bottles, bottles, two bottles,' and returned her glare.

I was now trying not to laugh, but this farce was beyond many of the radio comedy productions I had heard. She turned away and placed her hands on the two bottles and returned them to the counter with a deliberate 'bang' to show her displeasure. Best snatched the bottles and started to read the labels as if he didn't trust what the woman had placed before us. In fairly fluent German, I thanked her and asked her what we owed.

The old man laughed, hearing that I had a strong ability to converse, and said, 'Very good.' He gave another laugh.

If Best hadn't already been enraged, he now certainly was. He went to his pocket for money but I had already taken the money from my wallet and passed it over to the woman. I thanked her and though she could not see the humour in the event, she showed a forced smile. This brought another chuckle from the man but he stopped briskly when the woman shot a withering look in his direction.

Between us, we gathered the bottles, stuffing them into our pockets so we could carry them all. It was obvious that the woman was not going to offer a receptacle of any kind in which to carry away our bounty. I opened the door for Best and as I left, I again thanked the hosts. The woman turned her back and the man gave another chuckle. Just as the door was about to close, I heard the woman telling her husband that he was as bad as the fools she had to serve.

'Bloody people,' Best muttered once outside and walked off as fast as his legs would carry him without running.

I wasn't sure if he was referring to chemists, the German people or the Jewish race to which, it was obvious, the couple belonged. It didn't matter to me which he was talking about, I liked him even less, if that were possible.

Best was pushing to get back to the stadium as quickly as he could. I decided to have a languid walk, thus taking away his feeling of being in charge and giving him the exalted feeling of winning the race.

I saw him bustle around the corner and into the main entrance to the ground. I was not going to give him the satisfaction of saying something to me about being 'slow or lazy' so I stopped near the end of the building, and just stood around for another five minutes or so knowing he would be ensconced in his own room. Then I walked to my room and unlocked the door.

As it opened, I was confronted by Dirlewanger. He was just standing there with a smug smile on his face.

'What the hell are you doing in this room?' I said loudly, hoping someone would hear. Then I added, 'Where did you get the key?'

I blurted these questions in English and was more than a little surprised when he fired back at me, in English, 'Locks are of no concern to me.'

'What the hell do you want?' I scowled at him and he just stood there with that stupid smile.

Then after a moment which seemed an hour, he said sneeringly, 'Just making sure you are safe.'

He leered at me and raised his eyebrows in an even more smug expression.

I was trying to think of something clever to say but only found 'get out.'

He raised his eyebrows even higher and smiled even wider as he moved to the door.

Looking back, he said in just as smug a manner, 'I am going. I have what I came for.'

I walked to the door and slammed it behind him.

'Have what I came for, have what I came for.' What was that supposed to mean? I never left anything worth taking in the room and I had little or nothing in the medical bag which I noticed was on the table, opened. I moved over to the bag and glanced inside. Nothing seemed to be out of place and I could see nothing new or extra inside.

'Have what I came for.'

I paced around the room, looking in every nook and cranny. Nothing seemed different and I finally concluded that he was playing mind games, just trying to unsettle me. It was working, as I started to run my hands over everything, trying to find a possible bug or something of that kind. I didn't know what I would do with it if I did find one; I didn't even know if I would recognise one if indeed there *was* one.

I resigned myself to the fact that I would not be able to speak to anyone about anything secret in that room again. I couldn't find anything, but felt less than comfortable and less than trusting.

⌘

The day was spent quietly. Weathers came in around mid-day and said that he simply wanted to sleep, and took up residence in a short couch which had been pushed into one corner of the room.

Around an hour later Berta entered, but quietly exited followed by me after I put a finger up to my lips and indicated to Weathers, who was, by this time, snoring quite loudly.

We walked out into the field area. I had never seen fit to go through the boundary fence before and was surprised how good the little grandstand looked from the centre. Several people waved or gave us a greeting as we walked right to the far side and sat on a bench, obviously provided for athletes to use when not engaged in the thick of battle.

As we sat down, I related to her the surprise visitor I had had in the morning. She was surprised and asked what I thought he was doing there.

As I had no real idea, I shrugged and said, 'Probably just trying to make me uneasy, or placing a bug or something like that?'

I was very uncertain of his reasoning but felt sure he was not there to enquire as to my good health.

'It is all very strange; how do you think he even knows who you are?' Berta asked and as I had little or no idea, I again shrugged but added, 'Someone must be feeding him information.'

'Oh, I find that hard to believe. Who would have knowledge of why we are here and is not to be trusted?' she asked.

'Yes, well, Cain Peter and I have been musing on that for several days. I mean, Cain and his men know who we are, but they are policemen back home and have all been in Australia all of their lives. Of the women, only you and Vadoma know who or what we are and you are both above suspicion, as far as I am concerned.'

I tried to think, then added, 'I don't see Vadoma being an informant for the bastards who killed her family. There is Best, but he seems to hate the Germans, the Jews and anyone else he comes in contact with. Obviously, it is not Peter of Weathers, and I think the only other person who is in close contact with us is Jake, but I feel loath to suspect him.'

I paused again and then said, 'I can't think of anyone else really.'

'There is Jones?' Berta said questioningly.

'I don't think so, he is ex-secret service,' I answered.

'We only have his word for that,' she said, raising her eyebrows questioningly.

'Well, yes, I suppose you are right. I should try to enquire about his bona fides. Perhaps I should try to contact Baltimore?' I mused uncertainly.

'If you do that, the Germans would find out immediately. There is no way to contact home that they wouldn't see,' Berta cautioned.

I didn't answer, lost in my own thoughts.

Soon after this, Peter wandered over from one end of the running track and struck up a conversation with us, and Berta excused herself and ran off to do several laps.

'What are you doing out here? I've never seen you on the field before,' he questioned.

'Yes, well, I had a visitor this morning when we got back from the chemist. Dirlewanger,' I answered, watching his face to see his reaction.

He looked unsure. I knew him so well and yet I didn't think I could even trust him. I hated this uncertainty.

He frowned then asked, 'What do you mean by visit?'

'When I came back with Best, the bastard was in my room, making himself at home,' I answered and seeing the frown turn a little more quizzical, I added, 'He said he didn't need a key when I asked how he had got in and what he was doing there.'

Peter thought for a minute and then said, 'I don't suppose he told you why he was there?'

'Yes, he said that he was there to enquire about my health. I'm sure he knows everything, about my mission and the "loss" of the medicines in both of our bags,' I answered.

We both paused for quite a while and then I said, 'I wondered if he was planting a listening device or something?'

Peter nodded and said, 'More than likely I should think.'

Again, we both wandered off in our minds, thinking what Dirlewanger could have been up to.

Finally, he broke the silence, saying, 'What do you want to do?'

'Well, I don't think there is anything to do. If there is a bug I couldn't see it, and even if we did find one, what would we do? Hit it?' I asked rhetorically. We were both at a loss.

℘

The next day was the grand opening of the Games. I sat in the stand nearest to where the teams entered and had quite a good vantage point. Everything was an exultation of the greatness of Germany and her infallible leader.

The stands were a sea of swastikas that flowed in waves of red, black and white, leaving the Olympic flags looking like small islands. The fact that I felt somewhat impressed made me feel sick. This cult of one man showing the world how great they were.

Peter, Best and another official from our team sat with me and we applauded appropriately as each country's team were announced, and then entered. When it was the Australian's turn, we stood and cheered, waving to the many team members we knew. I have to say it made me feel proud and patriotic, even though my real interest was in Berta.

She looked wonderful in her Australian uniform and looked for me and eventually found me through my frantic waving.

Weathers, who walked in with the first of our athletes, also saw and acknowledged Peter and I, pointing and then waving to us.

I have to admit it was a wonderful spectacle, the best I had ever witnessed, to say the least, and a credit to the hosts. A German athlete ran into the stadium carrying a lit torch and climbed the stairs of the main grandstand and lit a large cauldron. This was the first time this was done at an Olympic Games, and it was very symbolic, and very impressive.

The other thing which put a dampener on the event for me was when the crowd and the athletes all stood cheering and giving, as was expected, the salute to the Führer. This had been a point of contention among many athletes and some did not perform the act.

How embarrassed I was that I did as I was asked, and my hand joined the thousands of hands in a terrible salute.

A great cheer met the return of the salute, though I could actually not see Hitler from where I stood; he was obscured from view by the thousands of people between us. Later when the crowd sat for further events, speeches and the like, I did see the man. Even though I was a long way away, he looked small and insignificant, this fact didn't seem to affect the crowd as they gushed, cheered and grovelled all at once.

I had saluted him. Was I so weak that I had become one of the fawning masses? Yes, I was so ashamed I wanted to walk out, I wanted to show my disgust but I did nothing.

The great success of the event was captured on film by cameras directed by none other than Leni Riefenstahl. She had done a very impressive job with the propaganda; still, I found her a person impossible to like.

The event took hours and that night we were fairly boisterous, driven back to our respective camps. The bus slowed to a walking pace as it tried to wend its way through the thousands of people who packed the streets of Berlin.

In another place and time, I would have been keen to join the revellers, but here and now it seemed like supporting the regime and that was something I was not willing to do. The salute gave me enough of a feeling of regret that I could never have forgiven myself.

When we arrived back at the camp, I met with Weathers and Peter in the dining room and had a late cup of coffee and we were also offered some toast. I declined the bounty offered, but Peter and Weathers ate the two pieces issued to them and went back for more.

After a short time, we began to talk quietly about our predicament.

✿

The next day, we were back at the training facility and Peter joined me, sitting on the fence at the far side of the oval. We just sat there for a few minutes until I noticed a melee near the long jump pit. It seemed as if someone had taken a fall.

I got up and started to walk over to the area, and on arrival with Peter by my side, I could see that one of the police rowing team members was on his back on the grass, unconscious. I quickly moved in to examine him and found that it was Jack Merrick.

I had not had very much to do with Jack; he had only been with the party, and I couldn't remember even speaking to him after our initial meeting on the ship.

I asked everyone to move back and give him some space. Everyone moved, and I could see that he was indeed breathing, and taking quite deep breaths.

I got to his side and knelt, asking him if he could hear me. He gave a little nod though his eyes didn't open.

'What's going on?' I asked and he spoke almost in a whisper, 'I have been feeling unwell all day—'

He was interrupted by the urgent need to vomit; he did, raising himself on one arm and heaving, though there was little result.

'Can you walk?' I asked.

He just sat there, dry-retching several more times. I looked around and noticed that Cain was not to be seen. Best now appeared and took it on his own authority to take control.

'Get a stretcher, and hurry up about it,' he said to several of the bystanders and soon after Merrick was being carried off to Best's treatment room.

On arrival there, the usual investigative questions were asked and soon Best had provided Merrick with some medication and a glass of water with which to swallow it.

Merrick looked very poor and almost brought the water and pills back up.

After a few minutes Best turned to me and said, 'I will look after him. You should go back out and see if anyone else has any complaints that are similar.'

I nodded. Some other doctors may have taken umbrage at being pushed aside, but I was really a very junior practitioner, and I felt no difficulty in handing up the responsibility.

Once outside, I walked over to the rowing team who had convened near where their comrade had fallen. I noticed that Cain was still nowhere to be seen.

'Where is Cain?' I asked and only received shrugs in answer.

Finally, one of them answered. 'He went to the change rooms about an hour ago.'

Thinking that we had been at the ground little more than an hour, I asked Peter, who had stayed with me, to go and find where Cain was. He headed off to the main building and after a few minutes, he came back and said that Cain was nowhere to be found.

I thought this to be very strange. He had not said anything to anyone about leaving the facility – his men were training, he was not.

I joined the rowers in sitting on the grass as they took stock.

'If Merrick can't row, we will have to pull out,' one said.

There was a long pause and then he added, 'There is nothing else for it.' He sounded despondent.

'It's a bit soon for that kind of talk,' I said but only received blank looks from the team. I realised that I was an outsider; they regarded my opinion as irrelevant.

Peter walked away a few yards and gestured for me to follow.

'This is bloody strange. Did you leave your door locked when we came out? I knew you closed it,' he asked.

'Yes, after yesterday's debacle I was very careful to lock it after me,' I answered.

'It was wide open when I walked in,' he concluded.

This gave me pause; I knew what I said was true. I had been more than diligent.

'What the hell is going on and where is Cain?' I asked rhetorically. Peter shrugged his shoulders,

I thought for a while and then asked, 'Was Best in his room?'

'Couldn't tell. His door was closed,' was his answer.

This was strange also. Why would he have the door closed?

'We better go and find out what is going on,' I said and we headed toward the building again.

On our arrival at Best's door, we found it locked and I knocked. There was no answer so I knocked again.

We stood there knocking for a few minutes but still received no answer.

Knowing how strange it was for all of these people to be missing at the same time, I decided to walk to the main entrance where we entered each day. Peter followed, but having nothing sensible to say, we both remained mute.

Several cars were parked on the same side of the road as our bus and there was a truck moving away from us, heading in the direction of the main part of the city. I stood, taking things in — this didn't help in any way. I wondered where our team managers were. We hadn't seen any of them since we left the bus.

This was all too strange.

A few minutes more elapsed, then a large Nazi staff car entered the road and made its way to where we were standing. Quickly, the rear door opened and Jones stepped out. Behind him, still sitting in the vehicle, was Dirlewanger.

CHAPTER 13

Jones thanked Dirlewanger and hurried to where we were standing. The door of the vehicle closed and as it did, I could see the detestable smirk on Dirlewanger's face. The car drove away.

'What the hell is going on?' I questioned.

'Not here,' Jones answered and hurried inside followed by both Peter and I, bewildered.

What was Jones doing with Dirlewanger and where were our missing comrades?

We entered the hall which ran down to the front of the grandstand. About halfway down Jones stopped and swung around, placing a finger to his lips to silence us.

He then whispered, 'Strange things are happening this morning. I came back to the building and found your door locked. I looked through the glass in the door and could see someone laying on the floor. I knocked louder and the body moved, just a little. I could tell something was wrong, so I put my shoulder to the door. It didn't give even a little. My second attempt saw the door unmoved, and I was just about to try to find something to prise it open when Dirlewanger rounded the corner and asked what I was doing.

'I pointed out the body laying inside and he produced a key. The body was Cain. He had collapsed, and as we tried to get some sense out of him, we heard Best ordering people around outside.

'I sang out to him and he entered and started to examine Cain. Cain was sort of babbling – he was incoherent and had vomited quite a bit. There was a terrible smell in the room and we opened the two outside windows. Best said he thought it was food poisoning and that he had just placed another of the rowers on a table in his room. Dirlewanger offered to take us all to the hospital and two of his men were brought in from out in the street to help carry the sick men out.'

Jones was full of explanations. He had blurted all of this, almost without taking a breath; now, he paused and then started again.

'Best thought it most important that he go. I decided to go with them as one of the managers. So, we left and when the two were admitted to a treatment ward I asked to come back to let you know what was happening.'

He took another breath and continued, 'Oh, and to see if there were any other members of the team feeling sick.'

'What do they think it is, food poisoning?' I asked but Jones just shrugged.

'Well, no one else has reported in sick yet,' I reassured him.

We walked out to the training fields and headed toward the rowing team, where I noticed Peter training with them. They were doing fast sit ups with each man and a partner interlocking ankles and counting as they each came to the sitting position. As we neared, the closest pair stopped and as the other pairs noticed they also stopped.

'I'm afraid we have bad news. Cain and Merrick are in the hospital. They are both very ill. Is anyone else feeling unwell?' Jones asked.

As usual, he spoke quickly and didn't allow people to gather the first point before asking the question.

'What is wrong with them?' one of the rowers asked, looking toward me for the medical prognosis.

'Well, I only just heard about Cain, but it appears that the most likely diagnosis is food poisoning,' I answered him in as truthful a manner as I could, with the limited information I had.

Jones waited for me to finish my answer, then he continued, 'We don't know very much at this stage. It is likely that they will be in the hospital for at least twenty-four hours.'

'But we race in the repechage in two days,' another of the worried-looking group offered.

'Yes, I have taken that into account. We will need to find you two stand-ins until they are well enough to take their place in the team,' Jones said and then seeing the outraged looks on the faces in front of him, he continued.

'This is how things are. We will need to practice on the river this afternoon and if we can get through that, and tomorrow's session, we will be ready – if they are back for the first race or not.'

'You can't be serious. We have trained for more than three years. You can't just row at an elite level with no practice,' the same man said.

It seemed that the group were allowing him to be their spokesman.

'I understand your concerns, but it is either that, or we go to the Germans and pull the eights out,' Jones answered.

There was a short silence while the stunned party looked at each other, shaking heads and shrugging as each weighed up the situation.

'Who did you have in mind to take the two places?' the man who had so far spoken for the group asked, standing, as if to take control.

'That is up to you, but Nagel here seems to be a logical candidate,' Jones proffered.

The man turned to Peter and asked, 'Would you give it a go?'

Peter, shocked, said, 'I have no training, but if you really need an extra weight I will try.'

Comments rang out congratulating Peter for his pluck and then Nesbitt turned in my direction.

'And what about you, Doc'?' he asked.

I had not for a moment thought of myself as a possible replacement. I was somewhat fit, but being far too fond of an evening glass of wine and having such a consuming practice, I had, for nearly a year, led quite a sedentary life.

'Oh, I don't think that's a good idea. I wouldn't be fit enough, and I have never rowed,' I answered, feeling quite embarrassed.

'We just need the practice with eight men in the boat,' Nesbitt suggested though I was still feeling embarrassed, I nodded, saying, 'Just for practice, then.'

I was very unsure about this but felt I could not let the team down.

'That's it then. We better spend some time teaching you what you need to know,' Nesbitt said, shaking first Peter's and then my hand. The other members of the team stood and followed his lead, several patting both of us on the back.

That afternoon, armed with just enough information to actually step into the scull, Peter and I were placed on board in second and third positions from the back of the shell.

Peter, I had no doubt, would pick this up fairly quickly as he seemed to be a natural at anything he ever tried in the way of sport. I, on the other hand, had to work hard just to become anything other than a laughing stock at every sport I had tried.

Soon we were moving across the water. The hardest thing, in my mind, was just keeping in rhythm, though the coxswain was calling us to keep time. It was certainly not as easy as the rest of the rowers made it look.

After a couple of hundred yards, I was struggling and Peter, who was in front of me, was sweating so much that his shirt had stuck to his body.

After about 500 yards the team, called by the coxswain, stopped rowing and I lay back as far as it was possible, exhausted.

I felt like I had run a marathon. The real rowers turned to see the two of us ready to collapse. They all laughed, and gave us another ten minutes rest, then started again.

Peter and I clashed oars after a short distance and this put everyone out of rhythm and we were forced to stop again.

The rower directly in front of Peter turned to face us and said in a fatherly tone, 'If you get out of time, don't panic. Just pick up on the next call.'

We now turned and began a third sprint upstream.

After this, I had to tell the team that I could not go on. I simply was not fit enough. I was very down-hearted, and though I think Peter was just about finished as well, he said nothing.

On our return to the small dock which we had departed from, we had to wait for a short time on the water as two teams were loading, ready to train. They were the favourites for the event: the USA and, relatively unknown, the team from Brazil.

The Americans looked amazing, and it was intimidating just being in their presence, even more so for Peter and I who were beginners to say the least.

The South Americans looked more at our team's level, but had had months of practice as a team.

When we had stowed the shell in the boat shed provided, we straggled toward the bus which was waiting to take us back to our camp. We were in position to see the team from the USA start their first sprint and were even more intimidated. I even heard Nesbitt say to one of his compatriots, 'Bloody hell, they are inhuman.'

Gaining our seats, we were addressed by Jones who had taken time to come and see if it was even going to be worth his while to apply for the two new rowers to be allowed to replace our fallen comrades.

'I know it is hard to go out and not perform as well as you would have as a complete team, but I think we owe Nagel and the doctor here our thanks for their efforts,' Jones said, waving his hand toward Peter and me, who had sat a distance from the other rowers. The team gave a more than generous round of applause.

'Now, if you are to get through the first heat, you will need to beat either Brazil, Canada, Hungary or Italy. It would be hard for us to beat Italy, if we were at full strength, and we don't really know the strength of Brazil or Hungary. The other alternative is that we forfeit the event.' He paused for effect, then continued in a slightly quieter voice.

'There would be no shame in forfeiting, nor in being beaten fair and square by Italy. They are known to be one of the best teams in Europe. For my part, I think you should take the challenge. If you can beat just one of the weaker teams, you go through to the repechage and perhaps the ill men would be well enough to take their place in two days' time.'

He paused again. He had worded the advice well, giving the team little chance of agreeing to forfeit. This he saw as a kind of cowardice; he would not like to have to go to the official Olympic hosts and withdraw the team.

Every member of the team spoke as one, saying they were not going to come all this way and withdraw, and so it was decided that we would, the next day, front up for the first heat.

CHAPTER 14

The rowing team dined together that night and were a very sombre party. Peter and I felt completely overwhelmed and the rest of the team, I'm sure, felt that it was unlikely that we could beat another team with two of our most talented rowers and indeed our captain, Cain, unavailable.

We again met for breakfast and ate as heartily as we could in the circumstances. Peter seemed to be quite happy to be going into battle, so to speak, but I had great misgivings. Were we just going to let our country down, or worse, would we be a laughingstock?

Overnight, a few of the team members had got together to discuss tactics and Nesbitt announced in a fairly honest way what had been decided.

'We realise that you are both beginners, and are probably not fit enough to give everything over the whole race. We think you, Nagel, should dummy row for the first half of the race and you, Doctor, the second half.'

I was unfamiliar with the term dummy row, but thought I understood what was meant. Both Peter and I looked uncertain, so Nesbitt explained.

'You will give it your all in the first half of the race, Doc, and Peter just needs to keep their oars in time with the rest of us, then you cut in and have a real go at the end.' Saying this, he nodded to Peter.

We turned and looked at each other and nodded. I, for one,

thought it a good compromise. I was certain I could give it everything for half the distance and I knew Peter was more than fit enough to finish hard.

After breakfast I had a flighty stomach, so to speak. I spent quite some time getting ready but when the knock on the door summonsed me, I answered.

Peter and I made our way to the bus and were met by almost all of the team, there to give us a cheerful send off.

Getting on board, I noticed that a few of the women were on board, having been picked up earlier. They were keen to watch our events, not having any of their own scheduled for that day. Peter and I sat in our usual position and soon Berta came and sat in the seat behind us. It was obvious that she wanted to talk.

I greeted her and she leaned forward and said very quietly, 'My room and several others were searched and things moved around yesterday, while we were at training.'

'Anything taken?' I whispered back.

'No, nothing,' she answered. 'I can't help but think that they are looking for something, or someone?'

I nodded, not having anything to say that I thought relevant.

'Are you both ready for the big race?' she asked and Peter quickly answered, 'Oh God, I hope we don't make fools of ourselves.'

I nodded resignedly. I was certain we would be laughing stocks by the end of the day.

'Oh, I'm sure you will get through it okay,' she answered, trying to sound positive and not really convincing anyone even herself.

At the docking point of our boat, we were given a rousing speech by Jones. I am sure it was very passionate and that he said all the usual positives, but I was in a world of my own and didn't even hear one comment.

Just prior to the call up to the starting line, Nesbitt said loudly, 'Keep in time and we will do the rest.'

Peter and I knew that he was directing this at us and though I felt unprepared and overawed, I resolved to give it my best shot. I took a deep breath and tried to slow the pounding in my chest and in my head. Surely what they say about the big moments in sport was proven to me there and then.

The starting pistol sounded and we broke the line. Within a few strokes I had got out of rhythm and had to stop and catch the right call of 'stroke' from our coxswain.

That little mistake took us back to last of the four boats, and it seemed as if we were almost half a length behind them as I regathered myself. Now I felt I had let everyone down and, if anything, started to try too hard and began to go slightly faster than the rate. After a couple more strokes I calmed and things fell into a good rhythm and we were moving smoothly across the almost pond-like surface of the river.

I think I was running on adrenaline alone by the halfway point and as Peter really put his efforts forward, I could feel the shell accelerate. I was still feeling a little exhilarated, and so kept rowing and soon we had passed the Brazilian and Canadian teams. We only needed to beat one team home to get into the repechage and with about 200 yards to go, it seemed as though we were going to do it. Now the build-up of lactic acid hit me like a brick and it was all I could do to keep in time let alone actually dragging any water.

The Canadians passed us as if we were standing still and the Brazilians came back to being almost level with us to our left. I tried to lift and as we could not see the finish, I thought we must have quite a way to go, but actually it was only a few strokes and then we were signalled to slow down.

I had no idea if we had come third or last and I was really too exhausted to think about the result. Indeed, everyone in the shell lolled about and the boat continued on, fuelled by the momentum which had been built up.

Eventually Nesbitt asked, 'Did they get us?' and the coxswain answered, 'Not sure, it's close.'

For a few moments, we continued to drift as everyone looked toward the score board where the names of the winning teams were displayed. Quickly, the Hungarian team was pushed into the frame. They had won handsomely and though the Italians were nowhere near them, they were easily second and their name was positioned.

A few interminable minutes passed and we turned the shell and headed back in. This put our backs to the crowd and the scoreboard and we actually learned our fate when the coxswain announced 'Bloody hell, we got there.'

The crew almost tipped us over as we all swivelled to see the name 'Australia' in the third position.

Peter collapsed backwards on top of me, letting out a loud shout of relief. I reached down into the river and scooped some water which I threw over him. He returned the favour, but it was the rest of the real crew who knew how to celebrate and each in turn splashed us with their oars.

It was such a feeling of relief, almost like being let off the hook to some extent. We all let out cheers of delight; a passer-by may have thought we had won the race.

Normally the heats would have been followed by the repechage on the same day, but the German committee had given the next day up to the repechages in the morning and the final in the afternoon. This, we had been told, was so that important members of the ruling party could attend.

It was even rumoured that Hitler himself could be there to reward the winning crew. This may have been the case if the Germans had not been well-beaten in their heat. It seemed that the supposedly great man was only interested in first place and this was born out several times over the course of the Games.

As we arrived back on land, our greeting party welcomed us with three cheers. Scenes like this were unheard of for the mere survivors of a heat.

Berta ran up with several of the girls and grabbed and hugged me and though I could only just stand, I felt like I was on top of the world. She then hugged Peter, something I was not quite so delighted about. In turn, each of the team members received this embrace as should have always been the case.

We positioned ourselves on the back of the bus and sang rousing songs and cheered and laughed virtually all of the way to the women's camp and then things settled down a little on the way back to our own as the gravity of the situation hit, each of us realising that we were going to have to do even better the next day if our two team mates were still unavailable.

As it happened, this was not the case as, though they were still in the hospital, one of our solo rowers was defeated early the next morning and eliminated from his competition. This let me off the hook and only Peter had to front up in the repechage.

Nesbitt announced this after he had spoken to the defeated man and he asked if that was okay with me.

I was bloody delighted. I felt I had almost cost them their shot at a medal and this would give them a far better chance.

Peter turned to me and said, 'Damn, that leaves me all alone out there.'

I gave him a shove and laughed, as did the rest of the team, one saying, 'What are we, pork chops?'

I don't think I had ever felt more relieved as the starting shot was fired and our boys blasted out of the stocks, so to speak. They sped out to a slight lead at the first 100 yard mark. In fact, needing to win this time, our crew led for most of the race, by almost a length at one stage, but in the last two hundred yards or so the Germans seemed to switch into a different gear and flew away to a very convincing win.

Though disappointed when the men came back, Nesbitt was soon on his feet leading a round of applause for the two team non-members, concluding, 'We would never have beaten the Germans today even with our full team.'

All applauded his comments and showed the great Australian trait of being good sports as our men quickly walked over to the Germans shaking hands and congratulating them heartily.

We got back on our bus to return home and though the men were all exhausted, they agreed that we should go and support the women at the Olympic stadium, where the track and field events for women had commenced.

We spent the rest of the day watching throwing events and saw some heats of the longer distance runs.

We had missed Berta coming a creditable second in her heat and though she waved to us when she realised we were in the stands, she stayed with her teammates; in particular Vadoma, who was performing at an incredible standard.

I took stock of the day's happenings and wondered how we were going to get through the next day. We sat there without shade for most of three hours and had less than enough to drink. At one time, Jake and one of the other men disappeared and arrived back with several large bottles of drink which they began to share around the team. Naturally, they needed to rehydrate, but Best and I both stepped in and told the team that there should be no sharing of bottles or glasses until the reason for our ill comrades being hospitalised was known.

Soon, several men pooled money and left, returning with enough bottled drinks to sate all of us including Best and myself. I gave thanks to the group as it was a very kind gesture and I needed fluid, perhaps even more than they did.

In the last hour of events, Peter, Jake and I left and went to the shop across from where our bus had parked, and I paid for drinks for everyone. We bought two wooden crates with eight bottles in each and carried them back with Jake, insisting he be the middle man holding the end of both, while Peter and I took one end each.

Berta took my arm as we left the stadium at end of the events for the day. Our entire team took the bus and headed home to our respective camps. I felt a pang of disappointment as I waved to Berta, Vadoma and all the other women – the pang, though, was at seeing Berta waving until we turned the first corner in the road and were out of sight.

Jake had loaded the two wooden boxes, saying that he would take them back to the shop the next day and keep them full so that we would not need to continually go to and from the shops.

⁊

The next day, several men were not around when the bus was ready to leave for the stadium, and as we had not heard from any of them, I was sent to see where the five were. On the way down the entrance hall, I was passed by two of the missing and, knowing that the other three were from the rowing team, I walked to their room to enquire if everything was alright.

I knocked and the door was opened by Nesbitt.

'Oh, I just came to see if you were all well,' I said, looking past him at the other two men who were sitting at a table, playing cards.

'Yes, we are going to stay here and lick our wounds. We'll come out later in the day if we can get transport.'

I nodded and said, 'We'll see you out there, then,' and hurried back to the waiting bus.

I had not seen Jones this morning and wondered where he was, but knew that I couldn't hold the transport up any longer.

We left for the women's camp and after they had all boarded, headed to the stadium. On arrival, I wished Berta and all of the women who had events good luck, thinking I would help Jake go and get the drinks.

I walked to the back of the bus and noticed that he and another man were already headed to the shop.

Thinking that the two crates they carried would be difficult for only two, I followed, though I was a good 50 yards behind them.

They entered the shop and a few moments later I entered behind them.

Initially, I could not see either of them and then noticed that there was an open door near the rear of the shop front. I looked around and could see no one so I walked through the door and almost bumped into Dirlewanger. Jake and his friend were standing just near the rear wall and looked surprised to see me.

'Lovely to see you, Mr Heam,' Dirlewanger said in his usual surly tone.

'Mr O'Calahan,' I shot back, surprised that he had used my father's real name.

'Oh yes, of course. My mistake,' he said sarcastically. He pushed past me and exited.

'What the hell did he want with you guys?' I asked Jake, trying not to seem too suspicious.

'I don't really know. He was here and the shopkeeper led us in here to get our drinks and he was watching our every move,' Jake answered. It seemed to me that he was a little flustered.

'I don't trust that man,' I said and the two of them nodded. The shopkeeper then came from the far end of the room with the two crates of drinks on a trolley and reached his hand out for payment.

Jake paid him and then we departed, Jake again in the middle using both hands, while I and the other man, whom I suddenly remembered as Simons, at either end.

We walked through the front door and saw the German staff car carrying Dirlewanger pull away. I could not see him, and was surprised that I had not noticed the car on entering.

I said nothing on the way back to the stadium. My mind was racing with thoughts of treachery. Was Jake in contact with that bastard Dirlewanger?

Was it Simons? I didn't really know him. What the hell was I doing? I was like a fish out of water.

I had no idea who I could trust, who I could even talk to.

Naturally I trusted Peter – I had grown up with him, he was probably my best friend. I knew I had to get him alone to air my thoughts, my fears.

On the way back to the camp, I sat with Peter and when I found a moment where everyone was engaged in their own discussions, I said quietly, 'Come to my room when we get back.'

He nodded his understanding without comment and around an hour later we sat together at the table. I wrote a note and handed it to him. He read quietly.

'I don't know who we can trust any more. Jake and that Simons were in a back room at the shop with Dirlewanger this morning when I walked in.'

Comprehending, he raised his eyebrows and wrote, 'I didn't expect that; did they give any excuse?'

'None, none at all. I also saw Dirlewanger with Jones, when he brought Jones back from the hospital. They looked pretty friendly.'

Reading, Peter nodded his head. 'I understand, but what are we to do about it?' he wrote.

I shrugged my shoulders. 'I wish Cain was back. I pretty well trust him.'

'Yes, we should be able to trust Nesbitt as well, but there is something about him.'

I nodded while reading this. 'Wouldn't trust Best for a moment, and even Vadoma worries me.'

After reading this Peter looked up and nodded knowingly.

We sat for a while and passed the time of day commenting on how well the team was competing and on general things that we thought those on the other side of the bug would be expecting us to discuss.

After about ten minutes of this, Peter wrote, 'Would you rather I stay here on the couch for the night?'

I took the page and though I may have felt more comfortable if he did stay, I wrote back, 'No, I don't think I am at risk here. Too public. Too many ways they could be found out or seen if they did anything.'

Peter nodded and then said, 'I'll go and get dressed for dinner. I'm starved. I'll come and get you on the way.'

'Sounds good. I will have a quick shower,' I answered and after he left, I locked the door and placed a chair against it with the back pushed up under the handle. Probably more cautious than was needed but I was feeling a distinct lack of confidence. I also took the sheets of paper we had used and placed them in an ashtray and burned them. I was certainly not going to make the job of spying on us that simple. I decided to always do this – previously I had flushed the notes but I wasn't even sure that was enough.

I stood with my head bowed, the water trained on the back of it, just thinking of the predicament I was in. I felt sure that Dirlewanger would love to bump me off if the chance presented itself. I knew that I was unable to trust Best or Jones.

I had never really liked Vadoma, for no reason at all, and now there was Jake and Simons to think about.

Really, I was having a crisis of confidence. Was I the wrong person to be involved in all of this?

I just stood there and time passed quickly. I heard a knock on my door and realised the water was nearly cold.

I hurriedly threw a towel around myself and bustled to the door, answering it with my head leaning around it to see who was coming to annoy me now.

Beaming in front of me was Cain. I was stunned and said nothing.

'What sort of greeting do you call that?' he said in his usual jovial manner.

'Oh, sorry. I was just surprised to see you. How the hell are you?' I said, stepping aside to allow him to enter the room.

Seeing my state of undress, he said, 'Would you like me to come back?'

'No, I am delighted to see you,' I answered and rushed into the bathroom and quickly put on some undergarments and carried my other clothes back into the main room.

Cain had seated himself on the couch, and as I dressed, he told me what he had heard about the 'goings on' since his return. He was careful not to mention anything we didn't want others to hear.

There were a few things I had to correct in his delivery but, essentially, he knew most of the mundane things. What he didn't know was the state I had worked myself into, regards all of the people around me.

I took a pad and started the usual process.

'Dirlewanger has been behind everything. He was there "mysteriously" when you got sick. I found him talking to Jake and Simons in a shop, in a back room.'

'Well, nice to see you too,' Cain said with a slightly less jubilant expression on his face.

'Oh, I have never been so happy to see anyone,' I answered and thought how stupid and inarticulate I sounded.

'Well, happy to be back. The food in that bloody hospital was nearly inedible,' he replied. Then, looking at me questioningly, he added, 'What do you think that was all about? Food poisoning?'

I went back to writing 'I don't have any proof, but I think it was probably not an accident. We all, pretty well, had the same food you guys had,'

'I wondered about that, but what had they to gain?' he said out loud.

I was a little surprised that he asked that, knowing what we were doing there, outside of the Olympics.

'Dirlewanger wanted you out of the way, or it could have been just making sure you weren't a threat with rowing team,' I continued to write and he realised his slip.

'It would be nice to think the great German rowing team were worried about us, but I don't think so.'

We both smiled knowing full well that we had never been a threat to the German team.

'How did you enjoy getting on the water?' he asked.

'I was nowhere near fit enough, but it was something to write home about: halfway around the world and filling in for the Australian team,' I answered and he smiled broadly back at me and said more than generously, 'You probably did as well as we would have done anyway.'

'I don't bloody think so,' I said, looking past the obvious compliment.

'I appreciated you both stepping up, though,' he added, and trying to change the subject, I asked, 'What have you been told?' I sat next to him and we continued in whispers.

'Nothing. None of my men would say anything except that they were obviously delighted to see me back,' he answered, still smiling widely.

'Yes, well, it was a strange time for them. They have not usually been involved in the planning of anything so far. Regular meetings have gone out the door as did any real discussion about what had happened to you. They are an amazing group of men, your blokes. Nesbitt stepped up and they backed him and just got the job done,' I answered quietly.

'Yes, well, they are police. They are used to a command structure and getting on with things when there is a problem,' he commented.

I paused, then asked, 'What do you know about Simons? I found him to be very positive but I was surprised when I found him and Jake with Dirlewanger. It almost seemed like an organised rendezvous.' I had leaned in to be heard.

He looked at me, surprised that I would question one of his men's motives. I could tell he felt a little disappointed.

'I'm sorry. I have ended up suspecting everyone of something.' I tried to reassure him.

He frowned and then said, 'No, I can understand your feelings.

I have had a few difficulties with the way I deal with Best for instance.' He paused for a moment and then continued, 'I would trust my life to Simons. He has been in the force for many years and so he is not a newcomer. I will ask him about the meeting with Jake and Dirlewanger.'

I nodded solemnly and he continued.

'Neither of us really know Jake, though.'

'No, that is right, but I think he comes across as the life of the party and he was with us that first day when Dirlewanger was throwing his weight around in the square and he bounced to my defence along with your guys,' I concluded.

'Well, how about going for some food?' he said, aloud.

I knew he was thinking things over as I had been doing since his falling ill.

I finished tying my shoes and followed him out the door. In the hallway, we met up with Peter, who was obviously coming to get me.

Peter looked a bit surprised and then said, 'Good to see you back, mate.'

The two shook hands and exchanged pleasantries as we walked to the eatery. I didn't really hear anything they were saying. I was thinking how good it was to have Cain back, but that it also gave me another person to worry about, not that I suspected him of anything. Nothing could be further from the truth, but he was another person at risk because of his association with me.

❧

Another day of competition at the Olympic stadium and in her next event, Berta was eliminated from the competition. I was very proud of her when she came back to sit with me in the middle of the seated area we had been allotted. The crowds were building up each day and now we had to fit into this area or stay away. Regularly, Peter or Cain came to sit with us and Vadoma came and sat next to Berta and me in the afternoon session. This was a much mellower day than we had been experiencing, there being no sightings of Dirlewanger or his band of thugs. By the last session I was feeling far better about the world than I had for weeks.

To the usual cat calls, Berta planted a small kiss on my cheek as she stood to leave the bus at the women's camp. Yes, the world was back in focus. I felt settled and vowed to myself that I would ask Berta to marry me on our return to Australia.

I felt that I could not confide in anyone about this as propriety dictated that I speak to her and gain permission before telling the world. I walked to my room, and on returning home, settled into the lounge chair. I could hardly wipe the smile off my face.

Soon after, I fell asleep and though I was in a chair, I slept for what must have been several hours. When I awoke, I had a crick in my neck from where my head had been lolling.

Standing, I looked at the wall clock and realised that it was almost nine o'clock. I had slept right through the evening meal and as I had not taken a meal at lunch, I was quite hungry. I knew that the meal area would be long closed and no food was ever left out.

I had a small bowl of fruit on the table in the room which I had replenished and took an apple and bit into it. A slightly bitter taste surprised. I spat the mouthful into my hand and then tossed the whole thing into the waste paper bin in the corner of the bathroom. I swilled some water around in my mouth to get rid of the taste and then spat into the sink. I decided I would have to give food a miss until the next day.

I slept well and was awakened the following morning by knocking on my door. It was Peter – he had volunteered to follow who ever went for drinks the previous day. He had not spent much time with me as he wanted to give me time with Berta. Now it was time to tell me all he had seen.

'I followed Simons and Jake who again went for the drinks at our usual shop. The staff car was outside as it had been previously. I walked right in and found our two men in some sort of conversation with the shopkeeper. There was no sign of Dirlewanger and though I thought it strange, there were no other people inside. I knew there was a second room and walked in there and found it empty also. I picked up some envelopes and brought them back to the counter to pay. Jake had not seen me enter and he and Simons were ahead of me, paying for the crate of drinks they had picked out,' he reported, and as I did not interrupt with any questions he continued.

'Jake said that I could have asked him to get the envelopes for me. I replied that I had not immediately thought of them and remembered that I had run out the previous night. As we left with them in front, I said that I had forgotten something and went back into the shop. Dirlewanger and two plain-clothed men were, it seemed, questioning the old man behind the counter. I was surprised as I knew they had not been in the shop just minutes before. They stopped speaking and waited as I asked for two stamps. I got them and walked out,' he concluded.

'Well, what do you make of that?' I asked.

'I don't think they had time to talk to either of our men, but what other reason could they have been there for?' he answered.

I pondered for a short time then mused, 'You may have interrupted a possible meeting.'

He shrugged his shoulders and then shook his head.

'We have to run this past Cain, I think,' I said and we left together to search him out.

❧

After very quietly telling Cain our news, the three of us sat at his table. None of us saying anything – we were all trying to make head or tail out of Dirlewanger's actions, nor could we see anything in the actions of Jake or Simons which would lead us to suspect them of collusion with the Nazi.

At length, Cain whispered that he trusted Simons with his life and Peter commented that 'it may just be what you are doing.'

'I have no preference for either being a collaborator. I like them both and neither seems to be working against us. What can we do?' I said.

Cain lent forward and whispered, 'We will have to set each up then see what happens.'

He produced a writing pad and a couple of lead pencils and started to write.

'What if I call Simons out and have a discussion with him about the presence of Dirlewanger, and you come over and let slip that something is happening? If Dirlewanger turns up we will know we can't trust Simons. If no one turns up we will try the next night with Jake.'

His writing was fairly untidy; I had trouble reading several words at first, but realising he wrote with his 'r's and 'e's looking almost identical, I was able to work out what he was suggesting.

Peter took one of the pencils and wrote, 'What will we tell him is happening?'

Cain paused for a moment then wrote, 'What if we tell him that there is a meeting with the Roma resistance tonight and then we can keep watch, concealed, and see who turns up?'

I nodded, taking the pen, and wrote, 'Sounds fine but no one else can know anything about this.'

We all nodded.

'After dinner I will ask Simons back to my room to get a full report on how things went while I was away.'

We all nodded again and he concluded, 'Then you turn up and let the supposed meeting slip and then we will know where we stand.'

Peter, taking the piece of paper, asked, 'Where would you say the meeting was being held? Obviously we don't want them to know about the real hole in the rear fence where we have got out before?'

'If I mention I am meeting Ronja at the side fence near the old tennis courts, it would be easy for a few of you to secrete yourselves near the garbage bins at the end of the building,' I suggested.

'I don't think it should be you. You are too important to things, and have had several run ins with Dirlewanger already. What if one of us goes?' Peter wrote.

Spinning the pad around again, Cain wrote, 'That could be your reason for coming to give me the news.'

We all nodded then Peter added, 'What if it were me? I haven't had any real part to play and so no one would expect my involvement – the Germans I mean.'

Cain again took the pad and wrote, 'Perhaps that would be a good idea. You could both come over to my room and I will say that you can tell me what is planned in front of Simons as he has my full trust, which he does by the way.'

We all nodded and Cain tore the sheets of paper we had been using from the book and after placing them into an ash tray, set them alight. We had always done this so they could not get into the wrong hands.

'Shall we go down for dinner?' Cain asked loudly.

'Okay. We are a few minutes early but it's better to be at the front of the line that the back,' Peter answered and we got up and left the room.

Cain went to eat with his men and Peter and I caught up with Weathers and sat at the end of a long table with our meals. We talked about the day generally and Peter asked when Weathers was to start bouts in the boxing. Weathers seemed a little surprised that Peter had not remembered that the next day was his most important.

'I've been preparing for this for more than a year and I really want to put up a good show,' he said.

'Oh yes, that's right. I couldn't remember if it was tomorrow or the next day. I'm bloody sure you will KO the first bloke – he's from New Zealand, isn't he?' Peter asked, realising that he had not given him enough support by not remembering.

'Yes, and he has been chirping about how good he is,' Weathers answered.

Our next bus trip was to Deutschlandhalle Stadium. From the outside looked rather plain but when we entered, it became obvious that this was one of the world's greatest indoor arenas. The size and amount of seating were larger than I think I had ever seen, and though we were one of the first teams to arrive, the seating was already filling with the paying public.

Only a few of our team members had events in other areas and they had been taken there by individual vehicles, as we had taken the bus. It was a very happy ride to the event, everyone enthusiastically encouraging the fighters. The excitement was palpable, perhaps more so than any other events we had visited. I think this was because the team only had four fighters and therefore there were more of us who were just going to spectate.

Weathers had been quiet and pensive. He had his game face on. I had seen him prior to other bouts but this time there seemed to be something different, something even more impressive than usual. He seemed as if he were almost glowing with the excitement.

❧

Several bouts were scheduled prior to our first fighter who was to take the ring, two of the three were won by Polish fighters. Their team was one of the largest, and they were both very dominant. Henry Cooper was our first contestant and though he fought with great tenacity, he was beaten by another Pole. It seemed as though we were destined to be just a footnote in the boxing events as the next fighter, another Pole, started with an incredible flourish against our man, Leonard Cook.

Cook, however, weathered the storm and in the second the second round, it became evident that he was taking the bout on points. His footwork was superior and as his opponents punching power began to wane, there was no doubt in anyone's mind that he had shown that he was a far superior pugilist.

We stood and cheered wildly, perhaps a little over the top, but this was a moment for us to dismiss all of the disappointments experienced in other events. Cookie, as we had affectionately named him, was obviously delighted and kissed his glove and pointed to our raucous rabble. We were to the right of the Polish supporters and they were obviously not as excited, as this was their first defeat and it was very unexpected. Pisarski had been the favourite for the event, not just for this bout.

There were two more bouts prior to our next fighter: a popular lad called Leslie Harley. Les had come to my attention first onboard the ship on the way to Europe. He was tall, considering his weight class was light heavyweight. These men were usually stocky and solid but his extra reach proved to be a bonus as he took on his much stockier Swiss opponent. His superior reach was the telling factor in the eyes of the judges as he took a narrow but decisive decision.

Another three bouts were scheduled prior to Weathers and I took the opportunity to go to the far side of the arena, to where the changing rooms were and, after showing my credentials, entered and found Weathers nervously having the hand bandages fitted prior to the gloves. He still had some discomfort in his hand from the previous injury and had the strapper and one of our trainers paying attention to getting the hand as protected as was possible while still fitting his gloves on.

'Hey, mate. How do you feel?' I asked, patting him on the shoulder.

'I'm ready, but bloody nervous,' he answered as the second glove went on and was laced.

'You have been training for this all of your life. You'll knock him down, no problems,' I prophesised.

'We'll see. These Poles are all fighting well,' he said, though he didn't look worried in any way.

'We will all be in your corner,' I assured him and then added, 'Give him your best, that will be good enough. I'll see you out there.'

I gave him another slap on the shoulder and as he nodded, looking fairly confident, I turned and made my way back to my seat.

The bout in progress soon finished and an announcer broadcasted the name of the winner, and then the names of the next two fighters. These men proceeded from the dressing room, met by cheers from their respective teams, and entered the square circle.

There was always a lot of, what I thought, unnecessary palaver to go through prior to each fight and it seemed that the announcer would never shut up. We had little or no interest in this fight; the majority of the crowd, on the other hand, stood almost as one to cheer the first fighter, a German, as he was introduced.

Through the masses of people in front of us, I spied Dirlewanger on the far side of the ring. He was standing, cheering with several other high-ranking Nazi leaders. I knew one of these to be Hermann Göring who was one of the Nazis' inner circle.

I learned later that he was the head of the Luftwaffe, having been a pilot in the Great War. He was dressed differently to all those around him and I thought he looked rather ridiculous in his uniform covered in medals, some of which may have been real honours.

Dirlewanger noticed me and stopped clapping. He glared at me, and though I felt intimidated, I glared right back.

After a moment he gave that wide all-knowing smile he used when he was wanting to portray his superiority. I held his gaze but did not return the smile.

The fight started and midway through the first round, the German knocked his opponent to the ground and the crowd erupted. The challenger bounced back to his feet and unfortunately, I noticed Dirlewanger again, smirking as the obviously superior master race fighter took full control.

He chased his opponent around the ring, not allowing him to get on to his front foot for a moment. Covering up, the Canadian fighter held on to the end of the round and both men collapsed onto their respective corner stools. There was no doubt that the German was stronger, but his opponent was a true boxer and in the early part of the second round, he danced gracefully around the German and eventually landed a right hook which caught the German off balance, and he fell to his knees. I stood and cheered, as did all of the teams and that part of the crowd who were not German. The Nazi leadership stayed seated and glowered as one. Again, I fixed eyes on Dirlewanger, and this time I smiled. He sneered back.

The German fighter was knocked down again in the final round of the fight and though a decision was pending, the group of Nazis in the front row stood, and walked out, certain, as the rest of us were, that the Canadian had done enough. The bout was declared and the house erupted as the hosts slunk from the scene. Dirlewanger certainly did not lock eyes.

Eventually Weathers' bout came with the two men called by the ringside announcer and we again stood and cheered as our man entered, the rope being held up for him by his corner men.

From the very start, the aggressor was Weathers; he never allowed the New Zealander to settle. The first round saw him on the back foot only once and the referee separated them when his opponent had backed into a corner. Throughout the rest of the fight there, Weathers was dominant. His opponent fought with great tenacity and would not go down under the wonderful barrage of punches landed by Weathers. Following the final bell, the decision was obvious to all present and there was no surprise at all as the referee brought the two together and announced the winner.

I was so delighted for my mate; he deserved the accolades. I did notice, however, that he was holding his injured hand and I decided to attend the dressing room to congratulate him.

On my arrival, Best, as the team's doctor, was gently removing Weathers' hand coverings. The right hand was severely bruised and obviously tender as he cringed in pain as the last of the bandages were removed.

'Broken again, I think,' Best announced in a fairly disinterested voice.

Having broken both hands previously, Weathers erupted in a tirade of invectives to which Best just shrugged his shoulders.

I went over to my injured friend and put an arm around his shoulders.

'You were bloody wonderful,' I exclaimed.

There was no response as he held his hand out to show me the mess that it was.

'I will send you for an x-ray, but I have no doubt you won't fight again here,' Best said in only a slightly more caring voice.

Weathers let out another line of unpleasant words and slumped onto the bench where all of his clothing and his gloves sat.

I sat down next to him and though I knew there was nothing to say, I wanted to give him any support I could, so I said, 'I will come to the hospital with you.'

He nodded resignedly.

Over an hour passed before we were transferred to the same hospital I had seen with Riefenstahl and her crew. We were taken to the x-ray department but were given no preferential treatment as most of these waiting were also athletes – athletes from several countries. This was obvious from the different languages they were using to communicate, or rather, not communicate, with the nurse at the reception desk.

The sign over her head said 'Willkommen' but the words she was uttering seemed to say anything else.

Two men were trying to explain their problems, one in French and the other in an African language of which I had no recognition. Speaking deliberately broken German, I asked the nurse if I may help and then asked the French speaking man what his problem was, in French. He explained that the athlete he had brought in had been taken for treatment almost an hour previous and that he wanted some kind of information as to his condition and whereabouts.

I explained to the nurse and she simply said in reply, 'You will simply have to wait.'

I explained this to the French official. He was obviously even more annoyed but after offering a few choice words, he moved away, finding a seat nearest to the entrance hall.

The second man I attempted to help had little English and no German. I could get a few words out of him in French and gleaned that his athlete had broken an arm and was in terrible pain.

I turned to the nurse and tried to explain the athlete was in severe pain but she dismissed me saying, 'You will just have to wait.'

I heard her mutter under her breath, 'Smelly foreigners.'

I had turned away but wheeled back to face her and demanded, 'What did you say?'

She raised an eyebrow and simply pointed at the 'Please wait' sign.

Then she broke her gaze, groaned and turned her back.

'So rude,' I exclaimed and turned to the other man and said, 'She said you must wait. Sorry. She is a very rude woman.'

Though I was speaking French, I could tell she understood what I had said as she shot me a glance of defiant rage. I moved with the man and after telling him I was a doctor from Australia, I asked if I could assist while they waited for treatment. He nodded and pointed to the man in question who was lying across three chairs just around the corner from where Weathers had seated himself.

I went to the man as his official informed him that I was a doctor and helping, while the 'croutes' were not.

I could see immediately see the broken bones of his lower leg. Though I knew he would need surgery, I also knew that he should have had the leg straightened. I got myself into position on the floor and, after telling the official to hold his friend's shoulders, I told him that it was necessary to extend the leg which would hurt but would give some reprieve from the pain when it was back in position.

The man nodded and explained to his friend. He looked me in the eye and nodded, closing his eyes in a pre-pain grimace. I took the lower leg and foot in my hands and applied quite some force. It was over in seconds and luckily his leg went back into a much better position.

He had groaned loudly and then gasped as the pain of the bones being out of place subsided somewhat. Though he kept his eyes shut, he said something to his friend under his breath several times. His friend related that he was thanking me.

I answered that he had been very brave and that it was the least I could do. I also told them that it should be splinted and apologised for not having anything around to use. Then, looking around, I noticed a pile of magazines on a table and though I knew they would not be perfect splints, I could see there was nothing else to use and so I grabbed several and then looked around for something to tie them with. The athlete's outer shirt was on a chair.

I reached for it and, helped by the other man, wrapped it around the impromptu splint. This was not a perfect job but I felt it would suffice. Shortly after, a doctor came bustling out of the theatre doors and guided by the nurse's finger, he moved to the man who I had just finished splinting.

'What is this?' he said loudly, pointing at the rough splint.

I stepped forward and said in German in an indignant voice, 'I was forced to extend the leg with no assistances being made available by your rude receptionist.'

He looked surprised at my ability to speak German fluently and glared at the receptionist who avoided eye contact.

'More than adequate,' he said, examining the bandages, then he turned to the woman and demanded that she get two men to assist in moving the patient. He turned back to me and asked, 'You are a medic?'

He raised his eyebrows as I answered.

'Doctor, actually.'

He nodded and I added, 'I am from Australia.'

He nodded again and asked if I would mind helping to get the man to a table in the treatment area. I moved back to Weathers to see him grimacing while holding his hand.

'I'll help get this bloke into the room. It may speed up the treatment line a little.'

Weathers said nothing but nodded understanding.

The doctor and two wardsmen arrived, having been called by the surly nurse. They transported the man on a stretcher to a treatment table in the casualty room.

The doctor began to unravel the shirt I had used on the splint.

'Sorry for any inconvenience,' he said to me in quite good English.

'No, I only tried to help. You obviously have quite a few people to deal with,' I answered now also in English, establishing our language of choice hence forth.

I stood, watching him as he assessed the injury and seeing that I had not left the room, he asked, 'Would you like to assist me?'

'Oh, sorry. I was day dreaming. Would you like me to leave?' I asked.

'Certainly not. You are a doctor and I would delight in your presence,' he answered in nicely spoken English though with the clumsiness which comes with knowledge of a language learned second hand or from a book.

He looked up and as I had not moved, he pointed to a door and said, 'You will find a spare white, er, smock in that room.'

The words were awkward but I understood and walked to the room.

A young nurse started as I entered.

'Who are you?' she asked, when she had gathered herself.

'Hello. I am to assist the doctor and need a gown and gloves,' I answered.

She looked a little disgruntled but pointed to a smaller room where sterile clothes waited.

She left, entering the theatre, and I moved into the smaller room and began to dress. There was a sink where I first washed my hands and as I turned the water, I heard some noise in another adjoining room. I moved to the open doorway and poked my head around the corner.

It was obviously a small ward. It housed six beds and they were all occupied. The room was all in darkness I could, however, see the stricken forms due to the small amount of light emitted from the room I had just left. I paused for a moment to allow my eyes to adjust to the lesser light and when I could eventually see fairly well, I wished that I had not.

The beds were filled with bodies in all manner of contraptions. The nearest man's head was encased in a monstrous-looking contraption which looked to be attached to his skull with bolts. What was this terrible place, some kind of torture chamber?

I moved slightly further into the room, pulling my gown on, and was appalled to see each bed filled with another hideously disfigured person. One was a woman, though her head had been shaved and obvious scars were visible – both of her arms were supported in spreader-looking devices. Were the arms being lengthened?

The man in the nearest bed suddenly opened his eyes and let out a muffled scream. He had obviously assumed I was another doctor, come to torture him and his roommates further.

I heard the voice of the doctor call to me and quickly rushed back through the small room, affixing a mask and some gloves. The doctor did not even look up but the nurse regarded me with suspicion. I felt physically ill but moved to the table where an incision had already been made. The patient seemed to have been made unconscious, by what means I was not sure, as there was no sign of tubes or needles.

'Would you like to hold the limb fast?' he asked, nodding to the nurse to give me her position. She looked annoyed and gave her head a little bobble as if she was put out, then moved away.

The doctor asked her to prepare some plaster bandages and she nodded and left the room through the door where I had just entered.

For several moments, I held the man's leg while the doctor operated. I could not but think of the tortured expression on the patient's face in that awful room. Why were they there? What had happened to them? I pondered these thoughts for several moments while still admiring the skills of the doctor.

'Place this man in the recovery ward for two hours then he can be released with crutches,' he ordered the nurse, and she wheeled the bed away.

When she had left, the doctor, who had removed his gloves, offered his hand.

'Dr Auersbach,' he said as I too removed my gloves and shook the proffered hand.

Looking into my eyes, he asked, 'You saw the people in the next room?'

I could not think of an answer. I had not expected the question.

'You came back so white, I thought I would have to treat you.'

I still said nothing.

'Don't worry, we have mutual friends.' He paused then added,

'That room is a torture chamber. Ritter and his cronies break people and then try different ways of putting them back together again. I can do nothing. They are just waiting for some mistake and I will be in there too.'

I knew I was gaping and wide eyed but could still say nothing.

'These nurses watch every move I make. Say nothing in front of them.'

I nodded, still astounded to silence.

'I am Jewish, you see. We are to be next.'

The woman returned, having deposited the man into a separate room, and Auersbach became silent. With blood still on his smock, he reached out his hands and received new gloves. He nodded to me and said, 'Bring this man's friend in.'

The woman condescendingly gave another bobble of her head, obviously annoyed at having to do what this lowly being said.

She walked out into the waiting area and Auersbach handed me another pair of gloves, as I put them on, he said, 'I have pictures of the torturing of the poor wretches, and I will—'

He stopped talking as the nurse re-entered with Weathers.

'Nurse, prepare the x-ray machine,' he ordered and as she left, entering yet another room, he quickly said, 'I will get the pictures to our friends. You must get them out of Germany to show the world—'

Again he halted as the woman entered.

Unwrapping the bandages on Weathers' hand, he ticked disapproval with what he saw.

'No. This is very badly broken.'

'Yes, Doctor,' I said in German so Weathers would not understand, then I continued, 'He will not accept what you say. He will still want to fight.'

Auersbach nodded and started to examine each bone. It was obvious that Weathers was in pain but he gritted his teeth and said nothing. As usual I was impressed by his bravery.

'Come,' Auersbach said in clear English and he led Weathers and I from the room. Now we were in the x-ray room and with practiced movements, the doctor positioned Weathers' hand and clicked a button. He repeated the process several times with the hand in different positions, then asked Weathers to wait in the other room.

Weathers obeyed and as soon as he had left, Auersbach whispered, 'One can't trust anyone.'

He nodded to make sure he was understood.

I had no doubts about Weathers but nodded to signify that I took his meaning. He continued in very low voice, 'There are evil men in our midst. The things they are doing in the name of racial purity are worse than murder. They drag Gypsies and others from the street and sterilise them. If they make any noise about it, they are killed along with their families.'

He paused and nodded, then continued, 'Even if one believed their so-called science, one could not sanction these terrible deeds. Deeds done by men and women who enjoy every minute of their work.'

Pulling a few levers and winding a handle, he started to say something else, but was interrupted by the nurse who entered the room and asked what she was to do for the patient.

'Splint and bandage the hand. It is badly broken but I will not try to set it. In a few days when I have the completed x-rays and it has lost the swelling, I will take a better look,' he answered, motioning to the woman to leave the room.

She sneered at me as she turned.

Auersbach leaned toward me and whispered, 'She suspects me of something, but she doesn't know what.'

Then he motioned to me to follow him back to the treatment room. As we entered, I saw the hand of Weathers, supported by a rounded wooden splint, being wrapped. It was obvious that she was not taking any care not to hurt her patient. Weathers glared at her but she denied him the pleasure of eye contact.

'Now listen, young man, your boxing days here in Germany are over. If you do not do as I say, you will never fight again.' His English was less than perfect but it was good enough to bring the hackles up on Weathers' neck.

'No. I will be ready to fight in two days, my next bout,' he assured the doctor.

'That would be foolish. You have a long life to look forward to and this is—'

Weathers raised his good hand. 'Thank you, Doctor, but my friend here will help me get ready for my fight.'

He stood and began to exit.

'But wait, there will need to be a daily dressing and possibly a plaster, and—' the old man reasoned but was again dismissed by Weathers who left the room.

Auersbach turned and raised his hands and shoulders in question.

'I will reason with him,' I said and followed my friend, saying as I exited, 'Thank you for your service, Doctor.'

Weathers said nothing as we left the main entrance and found that the car in which we had been brought to the hospital was waiting for us. I had no doubt that the driver was one of Dirlewanger's men. I was even sure I had seen him with Dirlewanger, in uniform. Tonight he was dressed, however, in Sevillian clothes.

I followed Weathers to the back seat and said thank you to the driver and he started the car and left the entrance to the hospital without asking where we were going. I assumed that he knew that we would be going directly back to our camp.

'You know—' I started, but was immediately shut down by my friend.

'I will fight. You will just have to give me painkillers or something to get me through it.

'But he is telling you the truth. You will do irreparable damage if—'

He interjected again. 'Don't you see? This is my one chance. I will never be anything without this.'

'That's not true. You can do anything,' I put in, but he was having none of it.

'I'm not you. I have no education; I have no trade save these,' he said, holding his hands up.

'You may not even have those if you do this,' I warned.

'Well, at least I will have a reason for being a failure,' he said determinedly.

I thought better of arguing with him in the car as I could see this was not an argument I was about to win.

We sat quietly all the way back to the camp and even on our arrival as I thanked the driver, we did not converse with each other. There was no purpose in my warning him further; he had decided that he would fight in two days and his next opponent was the favourite for his weight class: the man from Germany.

CHAPTER 15

The next day, I stayed at the camp with Weathers. I soaked his hand in hot water and then applied ice to help reduce the swelling. I also sought out some washing soda from the camp laundry, so I could use the crystals to draw out the fluid in an injured joint. I had gone to his room first thing in the morning and dressed the hand before we both went to the eatery for breakfast. Many of the team members were there preparing for the day. As we entered, the entire group clapped to welcome Weathers. None had seen him since his victory. Cain and others came and offered their hand. Weathers held his bandaged hand up and shook cross-handed with his left.

Several people asked if his hand was okay but Weathers deflected the questions, saying that I was just being cautious. I didn't disabuse any of them – this was his hand and I knew he wouldn't have wanted anyone knowing how bad it actually was.

We wished most of them farewell at the bus as they went out for another day of competition. Weathers even waved his injured hand nonchalantly.

We headed toward my room and on entering the hallway which led to it, we ran into Dirlewanger and one of his subordinates.

As we approached, he turned and said, 'Congratulations are in order, Mr Weathers,' and held out his hand as if to shake. Weathers nodded but did not offer his hand.

'Oh, yes. I forgot you have injured your hand. Pity, you would have had a real man to fight in your next bout.'

His lips snarled into the surly smug smile he always offered when he was showing, or trying to show, his superiority.

'There is no "would have,"' Weathers snarled back. 'Unless the German has thrown in the towel.'

'Oh, so you are still thinking of fighting, with one hand?' The bastard said, smirking knowingly at his companion.

'That's all I should need. He's only a German,' Weathers fired back. I could not have admired him anymore. He was a real 'man's man', so to speak. I gave him a slap on the back and we passed the disagreeable pair and entered my room.

Over his shoulder, Dirlewanger said sarcastically, 'You could get hurt if you fight with an injured paw.'

Weathers began to answer him but I pushed him through the door and closed it behind us.

It was obvious that we were not alone once the door was closed, as noises came from the bathroom. I crossed to the open door and startled a woman who was on her hands and knees, scrubbing the tiles on the floor.

'Oh, sorry,' she said in German. 'I thought you were out for the day.'

'That's alright, we will leave you to it,' I said as I moved back to Weathers and commented to him, 'The cleaners are in. We will have to do this in your room.'

He nodded and exited the door as I prepared a few bandages and my bag to take with me.

The hall was now empty; Dirlewanger and his lacky were nowhere to be seen. It was obvious he had staged the earlier meeting hoping to sneer at the pitiful loser he thought Weathers to be. Having no success with that, they slithered away and we saw nothing more of them for the rest of the day.

The hand looked terrible when I took the bandages off it. The bruising was just starting to come out and the swelling had been little reduced by the poultice I applied the evening prior, even though the bandages were wet.

'It looks bloody awful,' I said, not even thinking in medical terms.

'It feels even worse,' he answered.

I paused for a moment and thought, as I had through the night, what I was to say, how I was to manage him.

'Get the pitied look off your face. It is only one hand,' he blurted and I knew he was not to be reasoned with.

'I don't see how I am going to get the swelling down, even enough to get your glove on,' I countered.

'I know you will. I have more than twenty-four hours. It will be fine.'

I threw the bandages and padding into the bin. I didn't even consider their reuse after cleaning.

The hand was at least double its usual proportions and I really didn't think it would fit into a glove any time soon. I plunged it into a dish of iced water I had taken from the refrigerator, and we sat, neither of us saying anything for quite some time.

Throughout the day, I bathed the hand hot and cold and twice had to go to the kitchens to replenish my supply of ice.

In the early afternoon I removed it from its light coverings and looked at the injury. The swelling had subsided somewhat but the hand was obviously even more tender to the touch. I raised my eyebrows as I felt him flinch.

'I don't bloody care. I am going to fight,' he snapped before I even had a chance to comment.

'It is not something I want to argue about, but how do you think you will get past Best?'

This was the problem I had thought about. Best, as the senior team doctor, would have to say he was fit to fight and there was no way that was going to happen.

'I've thought of that. We will cause a diversion. Get him out of the way and you will have to take over as doctor.'

I hadn't thought of him as being as cunning as that. He knew I would not say no and he also knew there were enough people in the team who would help. I shrugged my shoulders. I didn't have an answer for the suggestion; I had thought I would be arguing the case of Best disallowing him and I playing the sad best friend.

By the evening the swelling had subsided somewhat, though the bruising had become even darker. I could see no chance of him gloving up and so I didn't broach the subject again.

On the return of the team members, Cain and Simons, along with Peter, came to Weathers' room looking for me.

We had spent hours bathing and icing and re-bathing the hand and it was in a bowl of ice water. Each came over to see the spectacle when they came in.

Comments were passed by each but Weathers only responded with 'it looks a lot worse than it is.'

Then he got up and entered the bathroom. We four sat and Cain waved his hands to get our attention.

'All is good,' he said and signalled, holding ten fingers up, then two more – we all understood him to mean twelve o'clock. Then he pointed toward the back of the camp. We each nodded understanding.

The time between the end of the evening meal at 7:30 and our meeting at the rear door of the complex seemed to take forever, but meet we did, Peter in his pyjamas. He wandered as had been planned through the door and headed slowly and via a circuits route toward the rear fence. This was a walk of perhaps only 100 feet if taken directly, and would normally take only a couple of minutes. Peter wandered this way and that, looking confused. We had hoped that the pretence would give anyone watching the idea that he was sleep-walking. He took around ten full minutes to reach the fence and then stood there for another couple minutes. Nothing happened.

No one came and there was no disturbance. The three of us who had been watching came out of the shadows which surrounded the rear entrance and walked quickly down the fenced area within a couple of yards of Peter.

I said loudly, 'Come on, mate. You have been sleep-walking.'

I walked over to him and took him by the hand, as did Cain and with Simons following us in, we re-entered the building and went directly to my room.

'Wonder why they didn't turn up?' Simons asked in a rhetorical way and none of us answered immediately.

In a measured voice, Cain said, 'No, that is surprising. Perhaps there was a problem.'

He had obviously decided that Simons need not know that there were those who doubted his loyalty and that he was being tested.

We talked for a few minutes further and they all departed and left me with my thoughts. This would mean that Jake was the only possible traitor.

Strangely, I still didn't really believe it. I thought it was so unlike him, but his test was still to come. We planned it to take place in two nights time as the boxing was to take up all of our time the next night.

I pondered things for several hours, trying to sleep, then when I eventually did drop off the alarm on my traveling clock sounded and to my surprise it was 8am.

I hurriedly showered and then made my way to the eatery for breakfast. Little cooked food was left in the service trays as most had finished eating and gone to collect bags and equipment for the day's outing. Around half of our male athletes left with events were to perform that day and our two remaining fighters late in the afternoon.

Most of the men decided to go to the main stadium and arrange transport to go to the boxing after lunch. Weathers and I tagged along, knowing that we would need to leave the stadium earlier than everyone else so that he could prepare. Our other fighter, Dan Mathews, decided he would go directly to the fight centre as he was to fight at 2pm.

We wished Dan good luck and said that we would be there for his bout.

I hadn't had time to talk in any real way to Weathers and as the bus door closed, he came and sat with me. Best sat only two seats ahead and had not acknowledged me on my entering, in his usual unpleasant way.

Cain and Simons sat directly between us and both nodded knowingly as I sat down.

Weathers leaned toward me and whispered, 'It is all arranged. One of the runners is going to feign a back injury after his event and get Best to accompany him to hospital.'

I shrugged in answer, I could not bear to tell my mate that there was no way he would be able to fight, even if he got rid of Best.

Accordingly, the selected man fell to the ground, having run second to last in his heat. Best was on the infield and rushed to treat him; the man gave a grand performance and Best soon called for a stretcher to be brought.

As the man was removed from the stadium, he was applauded for his bravery, Best came to me and said that it appeared to be a serious spinal injury and that he would have to go with the ambulance to the hospital.

I nodded as he said, 'You will need to be in the corner for our man at the boxing, until I get there that is. I will try to be back in time.'

Weathers and I immediately left for the boxing and in the taxi, I took the dressing from his injured hand and gave it the once over. It was not as swollen as it had been the previous evening but the bruising was extensive.

'Can you even make a fist?' I asked incredulously.

Surely, he could see how ridiculous it would be for him to fight.

Gritting his teeth, he closed the hand as tightly as he could and then nodded as if he had proven his point.

'I don't see why you feel the need to fight. No one would think less of you if you pulled the pin,' I said.

'I would. I would never be able to hold my head up if I threw in the towel,' he answered, looking me in the eyes. 'I watched this guy's last fight and he is no "big puncher". He dances and he is good at that. I just need to keep out of his way and score more points than he does.'

'Are you listening to yourself? How are you supposed to score without throwing punches?' I asked.

'I have a perfectly good jab and that will do most of the work. When I have to hit him with my right, I only need to land the glove to gain points. I don't need to knock him out, just out point him.'

He had obviously practiced this answer as he had the words ready and didn't pause to think as he usually did.

I put a light dressing on the hand and, on arrival, walked to the special competitor's entrance. Standing near the door was Dirlewanger and his cronies.

I was surprised to see him and he stepped forward, offering his hand and saying, 'You look tired. Had a long night?'

I had thought of not shaking his paw but force of habit led me to take the offer.

He did the same to Weathers and they clinched for a moment. I could tell the German was testing my friend and hated him more than ever. Weathers, to his credit, held the grasp and gave no quarter. I turned with my mate and went to enter the building and, having the gaze of that awful piece of work, I tripped up the step. Weathers grabbed me and I regained my balance.

Dirlewanger said sarcastically, 'Watch your step. We wouldn't want to see you get hurt, at least not before the fight.'

His entourage laughed uproariously.

I felt foolish and could feel my face blushing. I wanted to turn and tell him what a slug I thought him, but Weathers pulled me by the arm and we were inside before I could react.

'What did he say?' Weathers asked after we had gained the changing rooms.

'Oh, nothing worth repeating,' I snarled.

'He got you to lose your rag, though,' Weathers said, obviously trying to get me to tell him what the mug had said.

'He said to be careful. He didn't want us to get hurt, at least not until the fight,' I answered, knowing full well that he was right and still feeling foolish.

Dan Mathews exited the showers and greeted us. As he had his hand bandages secured by one of the team strappers, he asked where Best was.

'Well, one of our blokes hurt his back and had to go to the hospital,' I answered a little sheepishly.

'Is it bad?' he questioned.

In answer, I just shook my head.

Weathers had begun to take off his street clothes and said, without turning his back, 'I think he will have a miraculous recovery.'

Dan looked quizzically at him but he still didn't turn to engage the younger man.

Dan watched Weathers for a moment and then asked, 'What are you getting ready for? I thought you were not fighting?'

'You don't think I would let that kraut off that easy, do you?' Weathers answered, still not looking at him.

Dan paused for a moment and, raising his eyebrows, said admiringly, 'That takes a lot of guts.'

Weathers didn't answer and his aloofness impressed the three of us.

After a few quiet minutes, Dan's name was called and as he stood bouncing in the corner of the room, Weathers walked over to intercept him and clapped him on the back, saying, 'Knock his block off.'

Dan beamed with pride; his idol had wished him well. He nodded, understanding, and he, the strapper and I left Weathers still getting ready.

☙

I have no real knowledge of the technical terms of the fight game, but it was obvious from the first few flurries that Dan was simply going to be out-punched by his slightly taller and obviously stronger opponent.

The dark-skinned man was representing Turkey and he seemed to be incredibly well built – his muscles were incredibly well defined. In fact, he looked over-developed in his shoulder and neck muscles. This size made his movements somewhat more difficult and he was slightly slower than Dan. This seemed the only thing keeping our man in the fight, for when the Turk caught up his punches were almost lethal. Several times he caught Dan with a thundering right hook and each time the lad stumbled but did not go down. I admired his tenacity and hoped that he wouldn't get hurt too badly.

I had little time to look around during this first round but I was aware that Dirlewanger and his crew entered part the way through and took up their reserved ringside seats.

At the bell for the first to end, the Turk was well ahead on points. In our corner Dan was wet down and towelled off by the strapper and was told to keep out of reach and move his feet. This seemed to be excellent advice as Dan moved quickly around the surface perused by the slower man. Around halfway through the second round, Dan parried a hook and as his opponent followed through, Dan caught him with a glancing blow to the side of the head and the Turk fell.

He was off balance and sprang back to his feet, though the referee gave him a standing count. This seemed to spur the man into an even wilder mood and he attacked Dan's body unmercifully, and by the end of the round he had re-established his dominance. I moved as close as I could to Dan's corner to let him know that I was there. I shouted a few words of support.

Once again in the corner, the strapper repeated his previous instructions, 'Move your feet, move your feet, move and dodge. He is tiring but you will have to get a TKO to win.'

Dan nodded. He had no words. He seemed close to exhaustion and I thought it was not probable that he could last another round.

This thought only showed how little I knew about the fight game as Dan danced around the 'square circle' with greater dexterity and the Turk seemed to lumber after him. His wild barrage of roundhouse and uppercut punches rarely connected and when they did, they hit the faster hands of our man.

With about a minute to go, Dan again deflected a huge right hook and as the bigger man followed through, Dan again caught him on the right side of head and the Turk was again on the canvas.

Again, he got back to his feet and though it was slower than the first time, he now unleashed a wild flurry in a combination I thought would see Dan fall. Again, he caught most of the blows with his hands and several times found a way through his opponent's guard, as he got too close with short sharp jabs.

As the bell rang, both men embraced and Dan came back to his corner and fell to his stool, exhausted.

'You did so well, mate,' I consoled him as I had no doubt that the Turk had held sway throughout the bout and must surely gain a large points victory. This again showed how little I knew of the sport as when the two returned to the centre, the referee, taking both of their hands, held Dan's hand aloft.

At least half of the crowd booed – like me, they thought the Turk to be the superior. The rest of the crowd clapped. Obviously they were the more enlightened watchers, having seen more of Dan's jabs landing and therefore gaining more points than the wilder punches of the big man. Also, he was felled twice. I thought the first time was a slip but obviously those judging did not.

Dan bounced up and down with the delight these pugilists showed when they gained a great victory. The Turk, to his credit, took the hand of the victor and they again embraced.

I helped separate the ropes for Dan to exit and we made our way back to the dressing room with his back slapped heartily by many of the crowd.

As we entered the room, the noise died down and I said to Dan, 'Wow, that was wonderful. I thought he would have had enough points.'

'No chance. He hardly landed a punch in the last round. I was as confident as I could be,' he answered.

'Yes, you were terrific, but he looked so menacing,' I said, not thinking how ignorant my comment was to a trained eye.

'Yeah, some of his punches even hurt through my hands and arms but he didn't get many through,' Dan said and then the voice of Weathers, who was sitting on the opposite side of the room from the entrance, said, 'I judged it fifty-six to forty-eight. You did a great job. All of that thuggery is as nothing. The points from your jab alone would have beaten him.'

He got to his feet and strode over to Dan and gave him a hug.

The younger man beamed with pride – compliments from his hero. This was as good as it got.

I turned to Weathers, and he held out his injured hand. It looked so bruised that I still thought we would have trouble getting his glove on. I nodded, and moved to the box of bandages and selected several. Then I began to wrap the mangled hand as tightly as I dared.

'I think you will have to do better than that,' he said, looking at me and the strapper pushed past me and took over. There was no doubt he was much better equipped to the task than I was, and soon Weathers was gloved and ready.

We heard the crowd cheer as the fight now on concluded and after a few minutes Weathers was called to the ring. He went between the ropes and there was a mild-mannered response from the audience but when his opponent was announced, the home crowd roared. It was deafening.

I could only just hear the strapper speaking to Weathers.

'Keep your hands up and move, move, move,' he said and though I knew he had much more knowledge than I did, I added, 'Keep that hand out of the way.'

Weathers didn't even acknowledge either of us he was in his own world and simply glared at his opponent.

The referee moved to the centre and called the two to him. Soon the required instructions were given and as the fighters touched hands, they returned to their corners and the bell sounded. The first clash saw both men come in and feign blows, looking for an opening. Neither found one.

The first real punch was landed by Weathers, a jab. The German replied with a well-constructed combination left right left, but none of his punches landed. This was the way throughout the first round. Weathers would land a jab or two and a flurry would come back at him.

Without doubt, the fighter was waiting for a huge right, an upper cut or a hook and was surprised when none came. This uncertainty would, I thought, have given the points to Weathers.

As he sat down, our man breathed heavily. He was obviously in pain but as usual, he was hiding that from all and sundry.

Our strapper chanted to him, 'Keep moving, keep moving. He hasn't worked it out yet. He is still waiting for you to throw your right.'

I said nothing as I thought anything I could add would be of little use.

Just prior to the end of the break, I noticed Dirlewanger speak to the strapper in the German corner and that man then moved to his fighter and whispered something into his ear. The man nodded knowingly and the bell sounded.

On the first clinch, the German pushed forward and though he landed no blows, he cornered Weathers who landed two nice jabs.

The German's hands pushed forward and he dragged down on Weathers' injured right. He flinched and drew back into the corner. The German threw several big right hands. One connected with Weathers' head and the follow-up left jabs smashed into his defending right hand.

The pain was obvious to all present and Weathers reeled and tried to protect the injury. His opponent gave no quarter and more punches were landed. By the end of the round, the German had piled on so many points that it seemed impossible for him to lose.

Back in the corner, I tried to convince Weathers to concede so that no further and more extensive damage was done to the hand.

Weathers towelled his face down, looked at me and simply said, 'NO!' and handed the towel to his corner man, shaking his head.

The man understood and nodded. He had effectively been instructed not to throw the towel in, and it was certain that he was not going to let me near it.

The final round started with Weathers charging at his opponent and landing three consecutive left jabs, then he feigned to throw a big right hook but actually used the positioning of the German to land a left uppercut. There was little power in the punches but they were all point scoring and it seemed that he may still pull off a miraculous victory.

Several clinches ensued and the third saw the German again drag at Weathers' injured right. This again put Weathers in great pain and though the action was booed by the majority of the crowd, the referee took no action and several more unanswered blows saw Weathers' guard trying to defend his head and punch after punch seemed to land only on his right hand. Eventually his injured hand dropped unintentionally from his face and the German took full toll, landing blow after blow on Weathers' now unprotected head. I thought he must go down but that was not in his mind. He sprung away from the ropes and landed another left jab and followed it up with a right hook which, when it landed, did him more damage than his opponent.

Luckily the German started to tire and he landed only a few more punches before the bell sounded and they both retired to their respective corners.

It was very obvious to all present that Weathers was the more talented fighter but the German had landed far more blows and was certain to be the victor.

I undid the lacing of the glove on my friend's hand, knowing he was in terrible pain. He shook me off and stood, and returned to the centre of the ring to have the referee declare the winner.

As the official raised the German's hand, I noticed Dirlewanger opposite. He was smirking directly at me, not even watching the boxers who embraced, the German patting our man on the back. It seemed to be a condescending act to me but the crowd applauded wildly.

Weathers was clapped from the ring and many further slaps on the back followed as we made our way to the changing rooms. Once there, I, without speaking, tried to remove the right glove but the swelling was so extensive that the task was impossible.

A few moments later, the strapper, having rummaged through his bag, came up with a small pair of medical scissors and handed them to me.

I began to cut the glove's last laces and then, as it was still obvious that that was not going to be enough to allow it to be removed, I made a small cut in the lower part of the palm below the laces.

Still the swelling was too great to allow it to be removed, and I dreaded to think what I would see when it was cleared. I made another cut and Weathers, feeling that I was wasting time, simply dragged the offending glove off. It was obvious how much this hurt and he closed his eyes in a grimace.

'My God,' I exclaimed, forgetting all the training I had been given in not expressing any kind of horror at the first sight of a wound.

The middle finger's joint of the hand was shattered in such a way as to shorten the finger and overlap it into the palm of the hand. I knew that this would have to be re-positioned and that was not the only obvious trauma. The pointer finger was also broken and it sat at a strange angle towards the middle finger, drawn in by that dislocation.

'Mate, I have to relocate the middle finger and then I can see what else is needed,' I warned, knowing that it was going to be terribly painful.

Clenching his teeth, he said, 'just get on with it,' and again closed his eyes in a tight grimace.

I positioned the strapper at his elbow and told him to hold fast, then grasping the finger tightly, I gave Weathers a moment to soak up the pain and ready himself.

'Now, don't move,' I told him and began to drag the finger away from the palm. He let out a muffled scream and the finger was roughly back in alignment. Again, he amazed me with his bravery as he opened his eyes and looked at the swollen bruised and battered hand. There were no more expressions of pain nor the histrionics I had seen from so many patients with perhaps less reason than he had.

I had to get him to grasp a bandage in the palm of the injured hand and then using this as a support, a kind of splint if you will, I wrapped the hand in three roller bandages. Then I put the arm into a sling which supported the arm to the front of the chest and held the fingers aloft.

'We will need to go to the hospital for x-rays,' I said, thinking he would place himself in my charge.

'Not tonight,' he said and stared at me as if to make sure he was not denied.

I raised my eyebrows and thought how I could get my way, but after a moment of contemplation, I realised he was not about to agree to anything other than going back to camp.

'I will agree if, and only if, you allow me to give you a needle to help with the pain,' I insisted.

He glared back into my eyes as though I had given him some terrible news, but realising that I was going to dig my toes in on this point, he relented and simply nodded assent.

As I prepared to insert the jab, Dan burst into the room. He was now dressed in his civilian clothes, having dressed specially to go into the crowd to watch his idol's bout.

'Bloody hell, that was a fight,' he blurted and, being behind Weathers and not seeing the sling and bandages, gave the bigger man a rap on the back.

'Hoy,' I yelled and Weathers grimaced as the needle was jerked from my grasp while still protruding from his shoulder. I righted my grasp and emptied the morphine into it as Dan realised what he had done and began to apologise for his indiscretion.

Weathers just held up his hand and his younger devotee ceased and became silent as if commanded.

Then as if he could no longer hold his admiration in, he again blurted, 'What a fight.'

He waited for a moment and then seeing no reaction, he added, 'Damn bravest thing I ever saw.'

'I lost,' Weathers growled, becoming annoyed.

'But you would have beaten him if you—' he started then was silenced as Weathers interjected.

'He won, he did nothing outside the rules. He won.'

This was meant to silence the Dan but he didn't take the warning and continued his praise, 'Bloody bravest thing I ever saw.'

'Enough. He needs some quiet time to take the drugs on board,' I interjected knowing that Weathers was not one to take a compliment well.

The younger man, seeing my intent, fell silent and nodded,

understanding he should close his mouth.

We prepared to leave and as we walked from the building, we were met by a crowd of well-wishers. There must have been at least 50 of them and many were not in Australian uniforms. They gave a loud cheer when Weathers nodded and tried to hurry on, but there was no curbing their enthusiasm and they surrounded us expressing their admiration in several languages.

Two men in what looked to be medical uniforms pushed through the crowd and one said in very poor English, 'We have an ambulance waiting.'

I knew his face; he was one of the men from the resistance. I nodded, and whispered to Weathers that I knew who they were and we must go with them.

He understood and followed with Dan at his heels. The strapper had disappeared into the crowd with the first aid bag and my personal bag and as I couldn't see him, just the three of us got into the back of the ambulance.

I lay Weathers, who was starting to feel the drugs taking effect, on the bed and sat of a bench seat at his side. Dan crammed in beside me. I couldn't see how to dismiss him without saying too much so I just pretended he was not there.

The vehicle started to move off and though it was fairly slow at first, due to the numbers of people on the streets, it soon was traveling quite quickly away from the stadium.

Both the driver, whom I had recognised, and his off-sider who now sat in the front with him were speaking to each other in German and though I could only just hear them, I made out some words which I thought were 'we are being followed.'

CHAPTER 16

Soon after I heard the words of our driver, I noticed an increase in our speed. We moved from side to side as we dodged traffic. I could see nothing but bright lights through the rear window.

Weathers had become somewhat drowsy and a bit incoherent but even he had the presence of mind to ask what was happening. Dan seemed to be completely bewildered by the pace of our vehicle.

'What the hell is going on?' he asked.

I had a good idea what was going on, but just shrugged my shoulders.

We raced through the streets in a frantic dash to get away and the tail seemed to drop back somewhat as we rounded several sharp corners, and eventually there was no sign of other cars as we found the back ally of some large Government building. There were no street lights and only one other car in the street.

The passenger in the front jumped out and ran to the other vehicle starting it and our driver opening our rear door said, 'We change cars here. Ronja has pictures for you.'

I exited the vehicle and helped Dan who was lifting Weathers from the bed. We reached the second car and fed the shaky Weathers onto the middle of the back seat. I got in beside him and Dan walked around the back of the car and sat on his other side. The two men had jumped into the front seat and we were soon moving again.

As we slowly exited the dark street, we noticed that several cars were positioned blocking the road to the right. Some expletives were expressed by both the off-sider and the driver as he swung the wheel to the left but as we neared the end of that block two further cars drove out, blocking our way. One had a spot light which now shone in through the front window that powerfully that we were all blinded. Our driver began to back away but another car had moved in close behind us.

'Say nothing,' the driver said, turning to me and then began to roll down his window as a uniformed man with gun drawn approached.

'Out of the car, all of you,' he demanded. His German was harsh and authoritarian sounding.

Our driver said in answer, 'We are taking this man to the hospital.'

'Get out!' the soldier growled threateningly.

The driver obeyed and as several more soldiers approached with rifles pointing at all of us, we had no other alternative than to follow the instructions.

For a few moments there seemed to be a stalemate as we all just stood looking toward the great light, caught there like rabbits.

We heard the slow approach of deliberate footsteps and through the light appeared Dirlewanger – Dirlewanger with his revolver drawn.

He approached the driver and demanded in German, 'Papers!'

The driver moved as if to go back to the car but before he could take a full step, Dirlewanger had pointed his gun at the man's head and fired.

The man dropped.

'What the hell are you doing?' I roared in my own tongue, not having time to think of the German words for the same.

'Ah yes, Mr Heam. No need to thank us for rescuing you from these terrible insurgents,' Dirlewanger said in practiced and slow English.

The man was dead at my feet. I had seen dead bodies before and had indeed seen people die, in a hospital bed or on an operating table, but this man had just been executed in front of me.

I felt sick and Dan piped up.

'They were taking us to the hospital. We are Australians.'

'I know exactly who you are!' the Nazi said, moving to the second man and pointing his gun directly at his head, he again demanded, 'Papers.'

This time he spoke in English.

The man slowly put his hand into his breast pocket to comply but before he could take out the documents, Dirlewanger again fired and the man immediately dropped.

'What the hell are you doing, you bloody lunatic?' I roared in disgust.

'Oh, just saving you and your friends from these kidnappers, shall we say,' he answered in a measured voice but again in English.

'You bloody animal,' Dan blurted.

Tears had filled his eyes. This was a complete surprise to him. He had none of the background Weathers and I did of Dirlewanger.

We all stood for a moment and then the murderer pointed at the fallen men with his gun and several soldiers rushed up and dragged their bodies away.

'No need to thank me,' Dirlewanger snarled, this time in German.

'Get in your car. One of my men will drive you back to the safety of your camp,' he added in English.

'Everyone will hear of this, you bloody murderer,' Weathers said, the shots having seemed to revive him.

'No, no, no need. We don't want to be thought of as heroes. We need to keep all of our visitors safe.' Dirlewanger smiled back with that horrible sinister smirk. Then he signalled with his gun toward the car.

I wanted to wipe that awful smirk from his face and clenched my fists, but he held all the cards, and the gun.

'Come now, Mr Heam. You would not want to be thought as a supporter of these enemies of the German people.'

He waved the luger in my face, and added, 'We will get you home safely. I'm sure Mr Jones and the other Australian officials will want to thank us for saving you.'

He signalled to several of his troop, to move us on, and as we piled into the back of the car, two climbed into the front and the car was soon tearing off again, with the Dirlewanger staff car in front and several other vehicles behind.

Dan sat, bewildered. What had just happened? Had we been kidnapped and if so, who was our saviour? This violent uniformed man?

'What is this all about?' he stammered.

'This the true face of the Nazis,' I said. 'There is much you don't know, leave it for now. I will explain later.'

Not a single word was uttered by the two soldiers in the front seat until we reached the camps front gates when one told us to get out.

We obeyed, both of us still supporting Weathers. Jones, Cain and several other officials and several of the rowing team rushed forward to support us and gathered us.

'What is the meaning of this?' Jones demanded.

'Oh, yes. I thought you would want to thank me in person,' Dirlewanger said in English, attempting what he must have thought to be a cockney accent.

He sounded ridiculous and Jones was somewhat taken aback, but managed to ask, 'What are you talking about?'

'Yes, we have saved your three men,' the German answered, bowing at the waist, then added, 'They were kidnapped by insurgents. But they are unharmed.'

He presented Jones with an open hand and not knowing any better, Jones took it and they shook.

'That man's a bloody murderer!' Dan blurted, not understanding how Jones could take the other's hand.

'What are you talking about?' Jones stammered, not knowing whether to continue the grasp.

'He murdered them in front of us,' Dan answered, a little out of control.

'Oh, no. Your man misunderstands – they were both going for guns and I protected your "athletes,"' Dirlewanger answered.

Jones broke the grip of the German and said in a strong voice, 'The Government and, indeed, your Führer will hear of this.'

'Oh, thank you, sir. I am sure he will have us rewarded handsomely,' Dirlewanger answered and turned and re-entered his car.

Dan and I were left open-mouthed, gaping after him in disbelief. The gall of the man. Was life this worthless in Germany? In hindsight that was a ridiculous thing to think.

I turned to Jones as the car passed out of our sight and said, 'That bastard needs to be held accountable.'

Jones shook his head.

'I don't think we will have much luck with that, but who were the men who kidnapped you?' he queried.

'We weren't in any danger from them. It's the German government we need to be careful of,' I answered, trying to change the subject and was saved by the now-riled Dan.

'The bloody man just killed them. Shot them in front of us. Not a qualm, not a care in the world. It's not bloody right. He can't just do that,' he complained.

'I agree that it should not happen in these days and times, but I fear that this kind of behaviour is too evident under this regime,' Jones stated eloquently and continued after a measured moment, 'I will complain but I am sure it will do him more good than harm.'

Dan was keen to push the point but I, with the assistance of

Cain, ushered he and Weathers into the building.

'Your room?' Cain asked and, receiving my nodded affirmation, he led the way, holding Dan's elbow.

Once in the room, we placed Weathers on the couch and moved to the bathroom, leaving Dan staring after us. This must have all seemed very strange.

When the tap at the basin had been turned on full, Cain asked, 'What the hell happened?'

'Two of Ronja's men came to get us, dressed as ambulance men. She must have information to get to us, and have thought this would be a way of communicating with us without being rumbled,' I answered, then, as I saw that Cain had understood, I continued.

'Dan is the real problem. He will tell the story to all and sundry and I'm not sure what we should tell him.'

Cain nodded, obviously thinking the point over, then said, 'We will have to tell him everything I suppose, and hope he will agree to keep quiet – at least about us.'

I shrugged, not having a better idea and then said, 'Should we get him in then?'

Cain nodded and rose from his interim position on the edge of the bathtub. He walked to the open door and signalled to Dan who entered frowning. It was not every day he was moved around like a pawn – at least not in bathrooms, anyway.

I leaned against the basin, the water still running, and Cain, sitting back on the bath edge, signalled for Dan to sit next to him. The much-younger man looked surprised but obeyed.

I pointed to the tap.

'The place is bugged,' I said and then started the long explanation.

Dan, looking like a schoolboy, sat quietly for the most, but occasionally he would let out an expletive in disbelief or sheer frustration. Several times I had to put my finger to my lips to quiet him.

I concluded by saying 'the best thing you can do is say as little as possible about tonight. Keep fighting and training and leave it all to us.'

He looked at me and said 'I can be trusted' in a half-questioning, half-certain voice.

'We know you can, but you are the screen, like the rest of the team – covering up anything we have to do,' assured Cain.

Dan took a moment to take things in. He was not a quick thinker at all, but I liked and admired his spirit.

He eventually nodded then said, 'I will be there if I am needed.'

'Good man,' I said as Cain gave him a slap on the back, then realising that I sounded somewhat condescending, I added, 'We really are depending on you.'

Returning to Weathers, who had fallen asleep where he had been deposited, Cain said, 'I think we should all stay here tonight. Jones will want to interview each of you.'

We two nodded; Weathers did not stir. It was obvious that he was very susceptible to the action of the drug I had given him. I sat next to him and took his pulse, while watching my half hunter pocket watch.

'How is he?' Cain asked and added, 'I haven't even heard how he is?'

'Well, his hand is a terrible mess, but he felt he had to fight and I think it was one of the bravest things I have ever seen,' I answered.

'Yes, I watched from the rear of the seated area. I got in even though I didn't have a ticket; I had my ID and they just allowed me to go through. I was pretty surprised actually,' Cain answered. He paused and turned to Dan again and said, 'Bloody good fight by you too, mate.'

Dan beamed. This was another man he looked up to.

'Do you think you can win the next one?' Cain asked.

'Well, I always think I can win – that has been drummed into me by my father. He's my coach back home.' He paused, looking to select his words carefully and not sound boastful, knowing that is one thing Australians can't stand.

'The next guy is a better puncher than me and it will come down to whether I can out-box him.'

Not being really privy to the terms fighters used, I gathered that he meant whether he could out-manoeuvre the other man.

'That would be the best thing for Australia and the team: if you keep winning, or at least put up as good a show as you did today,' Cain said, putting a hand on Dan's shoulder.

The boy just nodded. There was a lot to go through in what he had just heard. After we re-entered the main room, he sat down in the lounge chair and I noticed his eyes darting back and forth as his mind tried to catch up.

Cain sat down cross-legged on the rug in the middle of the floor.

Dan suddenly asked, 'Who did you say that German was?'

Both Cain and I lifted a finger to our lips and the boy remembered that he was supposed to remain silent.

'Oh, sorry,' he blurted, again not thinking.

'Just keep calm and things will be alight,' Cain counselled and we all sat for a few moments silent, each processing the events.

My concentration was interrupted by a business-like rap on the door. I got up to answer it and found Jones quite red-faced.

'I have tried to get through to the hierarchy, but no one wants to talk tonight,' he said, and waited for a response from one of us.

I could think of nothing to say and that is exactly what I said.

'No, no. We must work things out here. This is all going to blow up in our faces and our team will be disgraced if they, for instance, threw us out of the country or worse: if they decided to charge one of you with something,' Cain said.

Dan glared at me. I am sure he didn't know just who to blame.

'I understand why you are worried, but what can we do about it?' I asked unsurely.

Cain pondered for a few moments and then said, 'What if we just complain about the kidnap.'

'Like hell,' Dan said and then continued, 'That animal needs to be stopped. He executed them with no reason.'

Cain shrugged his shoulders. I think we were all a bit at a loss to know what the Germans would do if we tried to take any action.

'It's not right,' Dan said and this seemed to rile Cain a little. He responded curtly.

'You are too young to understand what could happen.'

At this Dan became red in the face and held himself back, taking a couple of deep breaths. Obviously he had been trained to take deep breaths before he went on the attack.

He looked fit to burst and eventually he said, 'Two men are dead. We can't be worried about how things will be received by the bloody Germans.'

I admired him now even more than at the conclusion of his fight, but I said, 'Let's all just calm down for a moment, take a moment and think what we should do, then we can discuss it rationally.'

Cain put a hand on the young man's knee, and just nodded as Dan shot him a look which I read to say, 'I won't be silenced,' but he had great respect for Cain and stayed silent with difficulty.

I thought of the two men falling and couldn't get rid of the sight of that bastard's smile, that smug satisfied smile, that 'I dare you to do something' smile. I felt sick to the stomach, but I couldn't think of anything to do that would do him any harm. He had all the cards. If we complained, we would be the ungrateful hostages who were saved.

I knew that there would be no way of getting our story into German papers. We had no proof. There were no bodies if they decided to deny the killings. Yes, sure, we could put forward three witnesses, but he had a dozen soldiers who would swear to anything he told them to.

I shook my head and then said, 'We will have to tell our full story when we get out of Germany. When we are safe at home.'

'It's not about our bloody safety, he murdered them,' Dan said and I thought suddenly, 'oh God, they could be listening to every word we are saying.'

I waved my hands and put a finger up to my lips to silence him and pointed around the room. Both he and Cain nodded their understanding.

I walked over to my suitcase and took out a writing pad and sat down at the table and wrote, 'We need to keep any action we intend to take from them.'

They both moved and took up a chair at the table.

Cain took the pen and wrote, 'We can't really do anything which will work and they could really have us kidnapped or disappeared if they liked.'

'I think we will be alright if we stay in groups in full view. But if we cross this maniac, there is no telling what he will do,' he concluded and we all nodded understanding.

❧

The next night, we had set up the test of Jake and carried out the same work leading up to the late-night wandering of Peter. Jake had found out though, supposedly by accident. Cain and I made sure he heard the information as he sat with his back to Cain at the next dinner table. Peter and Weathers had found their way to sit with him so they could gauge his reaction, if any. After the meal, we four retired to my room and discussed, in writing, how Jake had reacted.

'He was sure to have heard you talking,' Peter assured us, then added, 'He showed no reaction at all.'

We all waited quietly in my room for the allotted rendezvous time of midnight and as we left the room and started down the hall, we heard someone walking from the other direction. There was no time to return to our rooms. Not having an idea what to do, we all just stood there like shags on a rock. The footsteps neared the corner and Jake appeared.

'I don't know what you lot are up to, but count me in,' he said quietly.

I couldn't think of a single word to say and was only saved by the quick thinking of Cain, who whispered, 'Keep quiet then.'

Signalling for the boy to fall in behind Peter and Weathers, Cain turned to me and raised his eyebrows.

I nodded back and all I could do was to shrug my shoulders as a sign of 'what next?'

We proceeded to the rear entrance of the building and Peter moved to the front. We all waited and looked around to make sure that there were no other late-night prowlers.

Cain put his hand out to stop Jake and when the coast seemed clear, Peter walked out into the middle of the yard. Waiting for a short time, he then moved to the fence which bounded the tennis courts and carried on to the rear fence of the compound. The air seemed thick. It was quite warm and there was hardly a sound to be heard, save the chirping of several crickets.

Peter wandered around for a few minutes more and then when he was sure that there was no one stirring, returned to us and we all re-entered the building and moved silently to my room.

Once inside Jake questioned, 'What the hell was that all about?'

Cain put a finger up to his mouth and signalled for the boy to follow him into the bathroom. We heard the tap being turned on and realised that Cain was filling him in on the events of our tour of Germany thus far.

When they re-entered the room, Jake looked at us as we sat in a semi-circle and looked bewildered. He shrugged his shoulders as if to say 'is this for real?' and we each nodded.

I took a notepad and wrote, 'We have to be sure of everyone who we deal with.'

I handed it to him and he scrawled, 'Why did you need to test me?'

I quickly answered, 'That bastard Dirlewanger has been hanging around and both you and Simons had been seen near him in the shops, at the training stadium.'

He took the pad again and wrote, 'We didn't even speak to him, he spoke to us and neither of us even acknowledged him. Well, at least the first time. The second time, Simons had gone into the back room and when I heard the Nazi speak, I followed and Simons had his back to him and did not answer him. Anyway, Simons doesn't even speak German.'

He pushed the paper back across the small table and raised his eyebrows. He was not impressed with having been thought a traitor.

I quickly scrawled, 'We didn't really think either of you were on their side, but we needed to be sure. We have seen some terrible things here. Everyone who we have trusted and allowed into our "inner circle" has been tested, and the Germans still seem to know what we are about to do.'

He still looked incredulous so I added, 'We have a leak and we need to find and "plug" it.'

He nodded, though he still looked perplexed.

Peter took the paper and wrote, 'We trust you now, mate.'

He gave the younger man a pat on the shoulder.

Jake was still a little unsure in his look but nodded.

I took the pad again and wrote, 'It seems that the walls have ears around here.' I added on regaining the paper, 'We have seen what he did to the people in the square on that first day and we saw him kill cold-bloodedly the other night. We can't be careful enough.'

He read and nodded understanding.

I said out loud, 'Well I s'pose' we should all get to bed,' and raised my eyebrows to solicit his understanding and he nodded and all of us stood and shook hands with him, as we made our way to the door. The four of them exited and I closed the door as quietly as I could.

Looking at the clock, I noticed that it was nearly 1:30am. I hurriedly got ready and took to the bed to sleep. I can't say that I slept soundly – so many things were whirling through my mind: the incredulous look on Jake's face when he had been told of the night's mission, the thousands of raised hands at the main stadium, the two men being murdered and, in the background, the face of Dirlewanger. Always the face of that smug bastard.

CHAPTER 17

The next morning, the men were transported to the training stadium. For some reason we were in a different bus and were taking a different route. Noticing this shortly after the corner where we usually turned to travel to the women's camp, I stood and asked the driver where we were going.

He replied in very poor English, 'Go training.'

Yes, another different driver, and I hadn't even noticed.

'Why are we not picking the women up?' I asked.

'They have bus,' he answered.

'Why are they not traveling with us?' I asked. The only thing running through my mind was that this was eating into my time with Berta.

'Yes,' the driver answered.

What the hell did that 'yes' mean?

I looked around and the majority of the team were looking at me and I realised I was making myself look like a love-sick fool. In truth, that was what I was feeling. I wanted to spend every waking moment with Berta. I could feel my face blushing and noticed that even Best had a smirk on his face.

After returning to my seat, I turned to speak to Jones, who sat as he usually did in one of the middle seats.

'What's going on?' I asked loudly, and detected some hidden snickers from several different directions and felt myself blush even further. I didn't like the feeling that everyone else was laughing at me, and I was determined not to allow it to worry me unduly. They were just jealous, poor fools.

Jones stood up and said loudly, 'The team management have decided that we will travel on different buses. It is more efficient and gets us to and fro quicker.'

A few boos were detected as he continued. 'We are trying to be better organised and this was a logical step. The Germans were not pleased about what happened the other night and somehow blame us. They will be watching us like hawks from now on.'

I glanced at Cain, Peter and Weathers and raised my eyebrows knowingly.

When we arrived at the stadium, Cain got the message around that the members of the of the team 'in the know' all meet at 10am on the far side of the track to discuss the situation as it stands.

I have to admit I was floundering; I had no idea how we were going to get in contact with the underground, nor had I any thought of what was the next step.

I knew I was considered the leader of the group, but it seemed to me that the better choice would have been Cain. He had much practice in the directing of men and I thought him to be, overall, more impressive.

As the last of the group arrived, Jake neared us. Cain began to speak.

'We are in a fairly difficult spot. We are now being watched most of the time and it is hard to see how we can help the victims of this awful regime. We have added Jake and Simons here to our number – both were tested as they had been in contact with the Nazis through Dirlewanger. Most of you know who he is and what he is capable of.'

'If you aren't aware, O'Calahan here is about to inform you.' He waved to me and stepped back a little.

I hadn't expected the light to shine on me quite as quickly and starkly as this but I had thought long and hard of what to say if I needed to speak.

'No doubt you are all aware something happened the other night.' I paused, expecting to see the nodding heads and they appeared.

'Weathers, Dan and I were still at the boxing stadium and were picked up by two of the men we had met from the underground. They came in an ambulance pretending to be taking us to the hospital so Weathers could be treated. Dirlewanger and his crew were aware and ready to intercept us. There was nowhere to run, and when we were stopped, I thought they would be taken away and we would be chucked out of the country. I had no idea that they would be gunned down in front of us. They were unarmed and …'

At that moment, Berta and Vadoma arrived at the gathering.

'Men, both Berta and Vadoma are part of this,' I said and went back to my spiel.

'The team management complained but rather than punishing the murderer, they heralded him as some sort of hero, saying how he had saved us from the terrible insurgents.'

I waited for a moment to allow them all to catch up and then added, 'We must get evidence of how badly the Roma and Sinti and even those with mental problems are being treated. I have seen it up close at the hospital. There are wards dedicated to practicing new treatments on these people and people are picked off the street and sterilised or killed if they are in one of these minority groups.'

Again, I paused. This was a lot to take in, if one hadn't heard of it before.

'There is a large part of the population who are just treated like slaves. They are seen as having little worth to the country and are literally being eradicated. As you probably know, there have been rumours of this and many countries wanted to take the games from the Germans, or boycott the games. They were probably right. How sick I felt when I saw how many of the foreign athletes, including us, raised our hands in the terrible salute. I feel we *have* given them legitimacy by having the world see the good things happening in Germany, while the murders and injustices are swept under the carpet.'

Several of the listeners shook their heads, remembering that salute at the Games' grand opening. Most right-thinking people would later be so terribly upset by the salute they gave.

'I feel sick at heart that we are unable to expose their terrible excesses now, but I hope that when we return home we may be able to show the evil and let the world deal with these bastards.'

I welled up, remembering how the two men were killed in front of us and had to pause a moment to collect myself, then I continued.

'We must make this happen, or this terrible injustice will only grow.' I had no idea how prophetic I was being.

There was a pause. No one wanted to follow up on what I had said; it was too awful to contemplate.

Cain finally broke the silence.

'My men and I were drawn into this. We did not come here knowing how bad things here were. Already we have seen how little liberty and life seems to count here. We can make a difference if we tell the world when we get home. I am here to warn you all against talking about these things while in Germany. They could silence anyone of us and blame the so-called "insurgents". We need to be careful – we need to stick together and so I suggest that no one goes anywhere without another of this group.'

He took a long pause and a deep breath.

'I believe O'Calahan here should be looked up to as a leader. He has already seen so much and has been trained for this kind of thing for most of his life. I intend to give him my total support and suggest that if you are unable to do the same, you just keep out of the way so as to not get hurt.'

He looked around those gathered and waited for comment; there was none.

'Well, do we have your support?' he asked and received affirmation from the entire group.

I decided to add to the comments.

'I have been prepared for this for a long time, as have Weathers, Nagel, Berta and Vadoma, though we didn't know why we had been trained until around six months ago. We all have Roma or Sinti blood, and so have a further reason to see this through. If anyone here feels that they don't want to risk involvement, they will be treated without prejudice and so if there is a problem and you want out, please let us know now.'

I looked around the circle. They all seemed calm, several shaking their heads to show that they weren't going anywhere.

'I can't tell you how much this support means to me and how much we can do to help the plight of the downtrodden if we stick together,' I said in gratitude.

Cain added, 'Speak to no one, and trust no one outside this group. Our cause, and perhaps lives, depend on that.'

Everyone nodded agreement and Cain continued, 'Hopefully the underground movement will be able to get some proof to us to take home so the world can really see what these bastards are doing in the name of the German people. I'm sure that most of them would not support this if they knew it was happening.'

'What are we to do next?' Berta asked, looking to me for an answer. She was positioned next to me and so I turned to address her directly.

'We must sit and wait. We have no power at this stage with Dirlewanger watching our every move.'

'That is not good enough. We need to be doing something,' Vadoma said and continued, 'When you were at the hospital and when the chase was taking place, did you get any proof?'

'No, none. I had not carried any camera or anything, not having anticipated any problem at the venue,' I answered untruthfully.

I had picked up on something in her question – not in what

she said but, in the way she said it. I was still not sure of her. She worried me.

'It would be good if we can meet again tomorrow but as there are events which some of our team are performing in, it may have to be at the stadium,' I concluded.

Cain added, 'Be careful, everyone.' And the group went about their business.

I was left standing with Cain, Berta and Vadoma and as Cain left, Berta said to Vadoma, 'I will spend the morning with Robert, and I will help you train this afternoon.'

Vadoma lingered for a short time and then excused herself, realising that she was a third wheel.

'I don't trust her,' I said quietly.

'Why?' Berta replied and stood opposite me with a questioning look on her face.

'I'm not sure. I just think when she asks questions like that last one, that there is something of the interrogator about her,' I answered.

'I feel the same, but she has given me no real reason to feel that way. What shall we do?' she replied.

'I will think about that. Meet me just before the busses leave and I will have worked something out. Make sure she is with you.'

I had in my mind a way of judging whether she was really one of us, but I thought I had better check if Cain thought it a good idea. She nodded her acquiescence.

Together, hand-in-hand, we wandered to the far end of the training ground and took seats in the front of the small stand watching the male runners as they prepared for their upcoming races.

I had something else on my mind.

'I hope when we get through all this, we will still be able to see each other?' I said, feeling fairly foolish.

'There is no doubt about that,' she reassured, smiling up at me.

I loved her. I couldn't really believe it; there had been other interests in my life but none as all-consuming as this. I felt like a small boy. I was so unaccustomed to falling head over heels. It was actually not the nicest of feelings. I was delighted she seemed to feel the same way. I would rather this trip have been just about us.

Knowing that we must part and get on with our individual days I bent forward and gave her a light kiss on the cheek.

Later in the day we moved camp to the main stadium and watched Vadoma compete and though her last throw was an Australian record, she too was eliminated from competition.

The last of our ladies was a middle-distance runner and she too was eliminated. That left the team with only three men still in contention and none of our women. It was very disappointing but no more than could be expected from such a small team.

Australia were, still, very much, a developing country in the sporting world. Of course, we could match it with anyone in cricket, rugby or rugby league – these were our main sports, and though we had individual champions in other sports, we were a long way behind where we wanted to be.

With this in mind, we bid farewell to the women as they boarded their bus and then after a little wait, loaded onto a different, somewhat older and smaller bus than those we had become accustomed to. We were no longer traveling first class. The mood was sombre. There was so much riding on the last few competitors.

In two days, Matthew Hunt, who we all called Matt, was due to compete in the triple jump. The remaining members of our team in contention were: Leonard Cook, a welterweight who was to face a Polish fighter, who was favourite to win the event, and Dan, who was against the winner of the bout between another Polish fighter and the favourite in the middleweight division, a German.

Both of these boxers were to be our last competitors of the games in three days' time. The team were clinging to these three men, everywhere they went, they were shadowed by most of the team and officials.

Matt commented that he had never been so popular and that most of the team hadn't even known his name prior to his previous win. Unfortunately, he was almost correct. He was such an unassuming man and though he did enter into the spirit of things, on the passage from Australia, I had trouble remembering for which sport he was preparing.

His previous bout had been fought the day after Dan's and had been conducted in the late afternoon. Most of the team were already at their respective camps and only a few witnessed his success.

Weathers and I had gone to Matt's room after dinner to congratulate him on his wonderful win. Dan was already there and Cain came in later. I'm sure Matt must have known that we all felt guilty for missing his triumph.

☙

We had two days until the next event and we were determined to try to shake our Dirlewanger tales, so to speak.

Virtually the entire team decided to meet in the centre of the main business district of Berlin and to visit nearly every shop. It was time to buy all of the usual souvenirs, to take home for friends and loved ones. The previous evening Peter, Cain and I had determined to split up into several small groups and to go in all different directions once our two busses rendezvoused.

I was to go with Berta, Matt with Weathers, Cain with Nesbitt and Jake with Vadoma. We had not made specific plans and were generally meant to take different directions and see if anyone, or everyone, was followed.

Almost immediately Berta and I picked out a figure following us. We didn't even need to turn around, we simply looked across the street and saw the reflection in the shop windows.

We walked miles and at no time did the man get any closer than around 20 yards. We walked for hours and crossed paths with each of the other three groups several times.

Berta and I entered shop after shop. It must have been driving our friendly follower mad. Eventually, we decided to go into a dress shop and after the man had a quick look into the display window and saw us looking back, he crossed the street and positioned himself to have a perfect view of the doors. Berta thought of a plan and whispered to me while trying on an extremely gaudy hat.

'I wonder if this place has a back door?'

I caught her drift and asked the young lady behind the counter if there were a rear entrance as 'my wife and I are trying to avoid some pesky relative.'

The woman nodded and used her eyes to indicate which direction the door would be found.

I thanked her and passed a couple of coins to her for the assistance.

'Oh, that is not necessary,' she said but did not attempt to hand the money back.

'I insist,' I told her and we quickly exited, walked a block further down from the one we were on, and turned into the first street which crossed the one we had started on.

We followed the path to the corner and peeked around to see Dirlewanger's man still standing across from the shop he thought us to still be in.

Quickly, we crossed the road and walked right past him. For a moment he didn't even notice us as he was so intently staring across the street.

'Oh, I did love that hat,' Berta said, and the man almost jumped.

'It was the most hideous hat I have ever seen,' I said, seeing in my peripheral vision the tail had again become attached.

We walked another couple of blocks and found a coffee house where we decided to have morning tea. Sitting in the table furthest from the front door, we ordered tea and scones, and sat happily eating them. The game of follow the leader took a break for around 15 minutes. Just as we were about to leave, Vadoma and Jake entered, obviously having had the same idea as us. We had stood and walked to the counter to pay but now we decided to go back to our table and ordered another pot of tea. Vadoma and Jake ordered what they wanted and we all sat at the same table we had just left.

Jake sat next to me and the two women sat with their backs to the door.

'Did you make anyone out?' Jake asked quietly.

'Yes, that is our man just across the street, reading his newspaper. We have led him a merry dance. What about you?'

'Yes, but we haven't seen him for at least an hour. He followed us into a small art gallery but didn't come out when we did,' Vadoma answered quietly, leaning forward as if to keep what she was saying between the four of us.

'That's a bit strange, where was this gallery?' Berta asked.

'Two blocks down on this side, that way,' Jake answered, pointing to the right of the shop, the opposite way to the direction we had come.

'There were a couple of rooms in the gallery, so we separated and the goon followed Vadoma,' Jake said.

'Did you see him following you?' I asked her.

'Oh yes,' she answered me, smiling. Smiling was not one of her usual traits and I could see why, she had a very unpleasant mouth. The overbite was noticeable. I rebuked myself for being so unkind.

'Well, when we leave here, we will go back that way and you go the other way,' I suggested and made a nod in the direction I meant. They both nodded.

We spent around a quarter of an hour with them and then I said that Berta and I would leave and they should give us a few minutes so we could get out of sight before they also went about their business.

As Berta and I exited, the man tailing us found a reason to look into the window he had been ignoring for the last 45 minutes. He was obviously watching our reflection, so he knew which way to go.

He almost kept pace with us as we walked to the end of the block and crossed the busy road after waiting for a horse and cart to pass. It was unusual to see many horses in the main part of Berlin at this time, though there were still mounted police which we noticed every now and then.

As we arrived on the footpath of the next block, we were startled by a screaming woman who had fallen to her knees in front of the gallery we were headed toward. We hurried toward the disturbance and Berta immediately knelt beside the distraught young woman.

She was ranting about death and pointing toward the entrance, her babbling was a little incoherent. I and two other men followed her directions and after having a quick look in the first display room, and finding nothing, I crossed the hall and entered another. This time the reason for her distress was very evident. Laying in the corner of the room was a well-dressed man with the bloodied handle of a knife protruding from his chest. I moved to him and, though I thought it to be evident that he was dead, tried to take his pulse. It was absent.

What the hell was going on now? Before I could stand, another pair of well-dressed legs approached me, I looked up.

'What have you done now, Heam?' the snarling countenance of Dirlewanger demanded.

'Robert O'Calahan,' I corrected, and stood so as not to be intimidated by him leering over me. He seemed to notice the body for the first time, and then glared at me again.

'I was just passing and a woman came out screaming,' I answered with the dire position I was in rushing through my mind.

'You always seem to be where trouble is,' he accused, and on gaining no response he stepped closer and, changing to English, he added, 'You will pay for this.'

Before I could reply, Berta had burst into the room and on seeing the body, recoiled a little.

'The lady said there is a dead man in here. She keeps crying murder, murder. You must come and treat her,' she demanded, grabbing my arm.

I followed her from the room and on reaching the distraught woman, I found that another young woman had knelt down and was caring for her. It took me only a moment to know that it was Dr Sophie Ehrhardt. Dr Robert Ritter's right hand 'man'.

Berta realised who the woman was even quicker than I and held my arm tight, saying, 'It looks as though things are under control here.'

She began to drag me away. I thought for a moment and then held my ground and said, 'I am a doctor. May I help?'

I spoke in German to be sure she understood me, though I knew from reading her profile back in Australia that she had perfect English and French and a smattering of other languages.

Dirlewanger, full of his usual bullying bravado, had obviously been appraised of the happenings and now knew that I could not have had anything to do with the murder.

'Why would we need your help?' he again spoke in English.

Before I could answer, a hand on my shoulder turned me around. It was that of Vadoma.

'Come away,' she ordered. I didn't move, thinking to become known to Dr Ehrhardt.

The crowd parted with a few screams from women on the footpath as two men carried the body from the building and lay it on the back seat of Dirlewanger's staff car.

Jake, who had walked up behind us said, shocked, 'That is the bloke who was following us.'

Vadoma dragged on my arm even harder and Berta also directed me away from the incident. They moved me to the corner which we had crossed only a few minutes earlier.

'We should get out of here. We don't need any misunderstandings,' Vadoma said and continued to drag me by the arm.

Her strength was impressive and with Jake following and Berta attached to my other arm, we left the site. Seeing that we were leaving, Dirlewanger said loudly, 'There will be questions to be answered later.'

CHAPTER 18

Everything was a blur. What the hell was going on? I couldn't get my head around it. Who had killed that man? Jake and Vadoma didn't mention anything happening to their follower in the gallery, but was it one of them who killed him, and if so, why?

We re-entered the coffee shop and took our usual table. The waiter came over to seat us and looked bemused. How strange he must have thought us, coming in and out and drinking more and more coffee.

Berta ordered four more cups and we sat. I cupped my head in my hands with my elbows on the table. I felt like my brain would explode.

Thinking for a moment, I asked, 'You are sure that that was the man who was following you?'

'Yes, positive,' Jake answered, nodding, and was joined by Vadoma, who gave a short and definite nod of agreement.

'And he was alright when you left the gallery?' I asked.

Both nodded an answer.

'And he was alright when you left him?' I continued.

'Of course,' Jake answered and Vadoma nodded, though she looked a little uncertain and obviously wanted to clarify something.

'Well, what?' I asked, leaning in to extenuate the fact that we should speak quietly.

'I was in the first room. I did not see him after he followed Jake into the back room,' she answered.

'I didn't see him in the second room,' Jake said, frowning.

'That's strange. I wonder what happened?' Berta said and we all sat quietly thinking.

I was thinking 'which one of them killed the man and why?'

We walked in pairs, separately, to the bus and it seemed that neither Berta or I knew what to say. Eventually, as we neared the vehicle, I whispered into Berta's ear, 'Be careful, I think she is a killer,' referring to Vadoma.

She turned and looked me in the eye and said, 'It might have been Jake?'

I nodded slowly, and trying to understand what had happened, I proffered, 'But why? I don't understand why. It doesn't make sense.'

She nodded and then shook her head, it being obvious by the look on her face that she had no idea either.

We arrived at the open bus first and entered, but instead of sitting near the front, I walked right to the rear. I thought we would need the ability to talk to all of our group some individually and also together to see if anyone could enlighten us as to a reason for the killing.

Cain and Nesbitt were the first to follow us on board and they saw Berta and I sitting hand-in-hand on the back seat. They began to sit near the front. I gave a little whistle and Cain turned and saw me beckoning. They both came and sat in the seat just in front of us.

'I thought you two might like some time,' he said, smiling.

'Oh Christ, there is no time for that,' I blurted and continued, 'The man following Vadoma and Jake was killed. We had a run-in with Dirlewanger.'

'What the hell are you talking about?' Cain asked, shaking his head disbelievingly.

'It's just as I said – I think one of them killed the man following them.'

I knew I wasn't explaining myself very well. In fact, I was babbling.

'That doesn't make any sense,' Nesbitt said.

'I know, but someone killed him – stabbed him – and they knew what they were doing. It was only a small knife, with a folding blade, but it was positioned where it would have gone right into his heart,' I answered.

'Shit, did anyone get arrested?' Cain asked.

'No, no. By the time the body was found they had come and had tea with us.' I paused, trying to get my words in order, and noticed Peter and Dan getting into the bus and after signalling them, they joined us and we had to go through the whole story again.

We all sat silently for a short time and looked to each of their faces to see if any flash of inspiration would come. I saw none.

'We will have to question each of them, separately,' Cain said. Everyone seemed to nod as one and Cain added, 'Where are they?'

'Well, they should not be far behind us,' I answered and the nods around me again fell in understanding. This buoyed me to some extent; at least *we* were all playing from the same sheet.

'Berta and Vadoma will need to come back to our camp to have treatment,' Cain suggested and raised his eyebrows to solicit a response.

'Yes, they are both so distraught, having seen a dead body for the first time,' I agreed and turned to Berta and gained her consent with a nod.

A few minutes later, Vadoma and Jake came up the front steps. They saw us and though other people had boarded and were still boarding, they came directly to where we sat.

'What's the verdict?' Jake asked. He always went right to the point when he was being serious.

'Vadoma and Berta will come back to our camp and we will interview both of you separately,' I said and realising that it sounded like a proclamation, I added, 'There may be something you saw or heard which will help us determine what happened.'

'You can't bloody think we had anything to do with it?' Jake blurted.

'No, no, nothing like that, but it is surprising what things one will remember if they are telling the story alone. There is no one to fill in any gaps. that is why we almost always interview people separately,' Cain said. He always sounded so professional and confident even when he was not giving the whole truth.

Vadoma sat down. She seemed a little more upset than when I had seen her after the murder.

Berta noticed and asked 'are you alright?'

'I haven't seen a dead body before,' she said and Berta placed an arm around her shoulders as she loosed a few tears.

Jake also sat down and he too showed an uncertainty and a little despair in his expression.

I gave him a pat on the back and thought if either were guilty of the murder, they were certainly playing the part well.

When Jones eventually boarded the bus, he came and told us he had spoken to Dirlewanger and that he had demanded to interview the four of us who were present at the *incident.*

'What the hell did you tell him?' blurted Jake.

'There seemed no way to put him off, but I did say that we would be amenable to his request tomorrow morning after the ladies got over the shock. He didn't want to agree to that, but I got a bit loud and there were lots of people around and I think he thought he was losing face, so he agreed.' He paused and then added, 'I think the women should stay with us tonight, they can have your room,' he said, looking directly at me.

I nodded and said, 'We had already decided that.'

The rest of the team had joined the bus except Best. Jones told us that he had some work to do at the training stadium and that he was being brought back to the camp later in the evening. I found this a little suspicious but he was one of the most diligent, perhaps obsessive, notetakers I had ever seen, he seemed to be able to turn a sprained ankle into a short story.

We arrived back at our home base just as the sun was dropping below the horizon. Jones told the ladies to have a shower as there would be questions after dinner when they felt a little calmer. He then instructed me to come directly to his quarters.

'Well, I would, but I will need to tidy my rooms for the ladies,' I answered.

'Shall we say fifteen minutes then?' This was his of speaking when a question became an ultimatum. I simply nodded.

As Vadoma, Berta, Cain and I walked to my room, it became clear that Jake wanted to go with us.

Cain, realising that was not what he really wanted, said,

'Give the ladies a few minutes to settle and grab a shower yourself and then come back. Jones will want to question you as well.'

Jake looked a little disappointed but nodded his agreement and left us without saying another word. I felt sorry for him. The little bit of psychology I had taken when at university made me think that his big personality was a cover for his stature; he was quite a short man. I wished he had never become involved. Vadoma, on the other hand, I found harder to like.

I didn't think she would have killed the man. What would she gain from that? I had no doubt, though, that she was physically capable of doing the deed.

We entered my room and I moved to pack a few things into my smaller case, just enough to get through to the morning. I removed my large case from the dressing table, if one could call it that – it really was an old table with a mirror on the wall behind it – and placed it behind the door out of the way.

Vadoma took her handbag and went to the bathroom.

'I think there are extra towels in the press near the shower,' I told her and she replied with a very quiet 'thank you'.

I did like her better like this. She seemed more feminine somehow.

Berta whispered to me, 'Do we ask her what she saw here or wait until Jones comes?'

She held her head on the side as if trying to ponder the situation.

'Perhaps you could ask her what she saw. I could go in to the other room to change?'

I'm not sure if I was giving an instruction or asking a question, but she nodded.

After a few minutes, Vadoma re-entered and sat down at the table and started sorting her handbag – a task, it seemed to me, she did at the drop of a hat.

'I'll go and change,' I said and moved to the bathroom with my bag. When I re-entered the room after about ten minutes, I noticed that both women were sitting on the couch looking quite sullen.

'Vadoma has something to tell you,' Berta said and took her chance to use the bathroom.

I sat down next to Vadoma expectantly. Was she about to tell me what she had done? I wasn't sure I would believe anything she said but determined to hear her out.

'Well, I, um, don't think there is anything to it, you understand, but, well, Jake went back into the bookshop after we had come out onto the street. He just said "wait a minute" and went back in. I wouldn't have thought anything about it, but he took a couple of minutes. He didn't tell any of you when we were questioned, and he did go back into the other room, the one where the man was killed. I saw him from the footpath. He came out carrying a small book.'

I was surprised by her admission and also by her dithering, almost rambling, way of speaking. She was never effusive; I had always known her to give very short and concise answers.

She put her head down and after a short pause, she said quietly, 'Why would he lie?'

She gave a little shrug of her shoulders. It seemed as if she were going to cry.

'I'm sure there is nothing to make of it. He must have seen the book and gone back to get it,' I tried to reassure her.

'Yes, but he came out without going to the counter,' she said and lifted her eyes to meet mine. The usual strength and purposefulness, confidence, one would always see in her expression was not there.

I may have just been a sap, but I felt sorry for her. She really looked bewildered.

'Well, we will get the whole story shortly,' I reassured her.

She didn't look reassured in the slightest. She shrugged her shoulders and giving a little sigh, dropped her head to break eye contact.

We sat quietly, and I wished Berta would hurry back. She didn't.

It seemed like an interminable amount of time before she quietly re-entered and looking at me, she raised her eyebrows questioningly.

I shrugged and then thought I would say nothing, suddenly remembering that the whole conversation with Vadoma had probably been listened to. I had forgotten to whisper and she had simply followed my lead. I felt like a fool.

I signalled for Berta to come and sit between us and then whispered, 'We have just had our whole conversation out loud. I forgot and now that bloody Dirlewanger will have heard the whole thing.'

I ran my hand down my face and held it on my chin, thinking that I certainly wasn't any good at all this subterfuge at all.

Berta shrugged her shoulders again and then said very quietly, 'They will ask the same questions when they grill us anyway.'

I nodded my head but still felt like a fool. Here I was, having spent weeks whispering so no one could know what we were talking about, and the first real event where we could have trouble explaining ourselves and I blabbed to the whole world.

A couple of minutes passed with me mulling over my stupidity and then there was a solid knock on the door. I got up and answered it. Cain and Jones were waiting along with Jake. I stood back and allowed them all to enter, then checked the hallway. It was empty so I closed the door.

'We don't need to beat around the bush. I will just ask you all what happened today and then I will report back to the Germans. Perhaps they won't demand to question you,' Jones instructed in his well-thought-out way.

'Explain what happened,' he added and looked at Jake.

'Nothing really. We were in the bookshop, that is, Vadoma and I, and our "tail" followed us and then, when we moved on to the coffee shop, he didn't follow us. We were a bit surprised but we noticed the other German at a shop window opposite, and I thought he might be picking us up,' Jake answered in his usual babbling way. His sentences never seemed to end.

'And from you?' Jones said, looking to Vadoma.

'Well, yes, as Jake said, but I didn't even realise we had lost the man following us until Jake mentioned it,' she answered.

'And you?' Jones asked, looking at me.

'We were in the coffee shop. The man following us was at a window opposite when Vadoma and Jake came in. I paid our bill and left a generous tip.

'When we left the café, there was a commotion outside the bookshop and Berta and I made our way to the front door. The woman shopkeeper was talking loudly about death – she was speaking so quickly that I was only getting a few words in each sentence.

'I went inside with another man, and found the murdered Nazi with a knife sticking out of his chest. He was very much dead,' I answered.

Jones thought for a moment, then turned to Berta and again nodded.

'Well, I don't think I can add anything,' she answered.

'If there is nothing else, I will report all of this to that buffoon Dirlewanger and he shouldn't even need to question you,' Jones said reassuringly.

He got up to leave and then as if having a second thought, he turned to Cain and added, 'Perhaps you would like to come as an extra representative.'

Cain shot me a questioning look and I nodded. Having Cain join the meeting would let us have an exact account of the proceedings.

I had been surprised that Jones hadn't asked more questions, but thought that he may have been thinking the less he knew the less he had to report.

Jake, who had been silent, sat down next to Vadoma and put his hand on her shoulder and said, 'It will all be okay.'

I thought, 'he doesn't know what I know,' but I decided not bring up the accusation Vadoma had made. I couldn't think of how I would bring it up, so I just sat mute.

After a few minutes of everyone sitting around being introspective, Berta asked if we should all play cards, to take our minds off the day's events.

Vadoma immediately said, 'No, I don't think that is proper.'

She could be quite the curmudgeon when in the mood.

Another silence gripped us. I thought how awkward we all were with each other. I supposed that we just didn't know each other well enough to know how to proceed with any meaningful discourse.

We waited and waited. It seemed that Cain and Jones were taking forever.

The 40 minutes which had passed truly seemed like hours, then the pair re-entered my room and Jones quickly dragged one of the dining chairs from the table to face Vadoma, Jake and Berta, who were on the couch. I understood that he wanted the rest of us to be facing him so I moved and sat on the armrest next to Berta. Cain brought another chair and sat by Jones, who launched into a tirade about our much-hated enemy, Dirlewanger.

'The bloody man wants everyone who was there to come and speak to him. I told him everything and he still demands to interview you all,' he said.

'I told him that I would not allow there to be interrogations of any of our team's members, unless you were all there. I also demanded two impartial team management representatives from the Great Britain and American teams. I thought that might call his bluff but he didn't even argue. They will come and get us as soon as they have arranged everything.'

Jones was quite impressive when he launched into one of his diatribes.

For a moment no one could think of anything positive to say, then Cain broke the silence, asking, 'Is there anything else any of you can think of that is relative and needs talking about?'

Most of us shook our heads but Vadoma just stared at Jones. I thought how strange it was to be so far away from home and in such danger. I did believe that Jones was trying everything he could to keep us safe. Adding the representatives from the USA and Great Britain seemed like a master stroke: each had far more athletes at the games and naturally were far bigger players on the international stage.

I knew that Cain would have told me if things were mentioned in their meeting with Dirlewanger which seemed dangerous. Though we had not spoken separately, his demeanour told me that he thought there was nothing to worry about.

We waited almost an hour before we were summonsed to go to the room allotted to host our interrogation. Dutifully, we followed the man who had been sent for us. I recognised him as the driver of our car on the night Dirlewanger murdered the two members of the underground. His expression did nothing to dispel the feeling of hate which emanated from him.

Jones entered first and greeted the American and Great Britain managers and as I entered along with Berta, Vadoma, Jake and Cain, I noticed that Dirlewanger and two other officials sat behind a long meeting table and it was obvious that the chairs which had been positioned opposite them was where we were expected to sit.

Initially there were only five chairs, but when the man who had brought us to the meeting realised that was not going to be enough, he moved to the far end of the room and gathered three extra and placed them behind the original chair positions.

Jones and the two invited officials took up the front row and Jones signalled to Vadoma and Jake to join them. I sat in the second row between Berta and Cain. I felt that this was orchestrated by Jones, to show that I was not anyone other than a team doctor and therefore under his direction. I couldn't help but be impressed by his actions as a tactician.

'Surely there is no need for all of these people,' Dirlewanger said gruffly.

'Surely there is little need for this meeting at all,' Jones fired back, making it perfectly clear that he was not going to be dominated or silenced by his opponent.

'This is a matter of German's sovereignty. We have been attacked by someone and we have a right to know who carried this murder out,' the man to Dirlewanger's left said in fairly good English, though his pompous way of speaking gave away his nationality.

'So, the man killed was a German citizen then?' Jones quickly replied, delighted that the second man had spoken, not just being a mouthpiece for his senior.

'Not just a German citizen; he was a member of the Führer's Security Service,' the man blurted and received a withering glare from Dirlewanger.

'And, why was this "operative" following my people?' Jones challenged.

The man went to speak but was halted by Dirlewanger as he

grabbed the man's arm, and realising that he had passed his station in the world, the man fell silent.

'We did not say he was following your people. You must realise that we have many people out in the public to protect our visitors, for your safety, you might say,' the shrewder Nazi answered.

Here, the American manager sat forward, and looking Dirlewanger in the eye, demanded, 'Do you mean to tell me our athletes are being followed?'

His accent was southern sounding but less broad and I thought he must have been educated in either the north or perhaps even in England.

'No one has said anything about following. We have operatives out in the general populous to protect all of the visitors to our great country.' Dirlewanger's gruffness grew as he sat forward, glaring at the American as if daring him to continue.

The American was up to the task and, showing his disgust, also sat forward and fired back. 'We will take this to the Olympic Committee, and see what they think of the athletes being followed all over the place.'

'Great Britain supports this action. We will call for a meeting of the delegates as soon as tomorrow morning,' the British delegate interrupted in an educated upper-class accent.

'You seem to be missing the point. A German has been murdered.' Dirlewanger snarled back; it was obvious he was itching for a physical confrontation. He was clever – perhaps even sly, one may say – but he was no diplomat.

'We are not missing any point. You are saying that our team members are at risk when out in public in your capital, Berlin,' Jones said with his eyes widening to a full stare as he sat forward to intimidate.

Dirlewanger was on the back foot but had enough presence of mind to calmly say, 'We have not said anything about safety. The point is that a man was murdered and we wish to question these people to see if they saw anything.'

'It seems to me that you are not questioning but accusing. Your whole attitude has been accusatory,' Jones said. His hands had gone to his hips and he seemed to swell in his seat in anger.

The Nazi seemed to change tacts now, seeing that he was not going to intimidate the men before him.

'Oh, no, you misunderstand. We only wish to get to the truth – the truth about what has happened to this man,' he said, smiling.

When Dirlewanger smiled he was even more detestable; it was such a fake piece of theatrics.

'So, none of our people are under suspicion then?' Jones demanded.

'No. No one has been accused of anything,' he answered, gritting his teeth.

'Then I see no reason for us being here,' the American answered and stood as if to leave. I also stood. I would have loved to leave without questions even being asked.

'You misunderstand. I intend to ask these people if they noticed anything suspicious,' Dirlewanger said slowly as if he were trying to be understood by lesser beings.

I suddenly felt confident enough to say something,

'I certainly saw something suspicious. Miss Smith was followed for most of the day by a very ugly man – a man who looked a lot like you,' I said and pointed at Dirlewanger's off-sider.

The man took a deep breath and turned a dark shade of purple. He was not the man I had mentioned but he comprehended English well enough to understand the insult.

'Good, I shall ask you about your involvement,' Dirlewanger said, looking smug as though he had tricked me into talking.

Actually, I was keen to talk. There was a lot I wanted to say. I nodded.

'Where were you when the man was killed?' he asked.

'As I don't know when the man was murdered, I can't answer,'

I said, feeling like I had scored the first point of some linguistic contest.

Sizing me up, the German said, 'When did you know that the man was dead?'

'When I took his pulse,' I answered. Point two.

'How did you get to hear he was where he was?' he fired back, obviously not enjoying the verbal games he was playing in his second language.

'I went to aid a woman who was calling for help,' I answered, raising my eyebrows as if to say 'got anything else?'

'Ah, yes. The hero to the rescue again.' He sneered.

'Just trying to help, when none of your men did,' I answered, considering I was certainly up to the stoush with this bully of a man.

'And you?' he said, turning his gaze to Jake.

'And me what?' Jake said, smiling.

This seemed to enrage Dirlewanger. He raised his voice and demanded, 'You will stop playing these games and answer the question.'

'What is the question?' Jake countered, also raising his voice.

'When did you see the man first?' Dirlewanger calmed himself and asked, again leaning forward as if to solicit an answer.

'Oh, that is easy. I saw him when he first started following Vadoma and I. Not a very good spy. He would turn away and gaze in another direction if we looked at him. It all seemed a bit silly really,' Jake answered with a smile.

'You people treat this like a joke. How dare you. The man is dead. This is not funny.' The Nazi again began to talk in at a much higher volume.

Jake had a bit of fight in him and it seemed as if he was ready to take the aggressor on.

'Not funny. The whole thing is a farce, following us around popping in and out of shadows. Not funny at all,' he said calmly but not breaking eye contact.

The German stayed sitting forward and raised one eyebrow. He was not used to people answering him back, challenging him, and he obviously didn't like it.

'We have people on the streets, to protect all of the athletes,' he said, curling one side of his top lip. It really did make him look even more unpleasant, though that was difficult.

Suddenly the English representative jumped to his feet. 'Why would we need protecting? I thought Germany was supposed to be a friendly place and that all Germans followed their Fuhrer,' he said and Dirlewanger, looking surprised at the suddenness of the other's movement, also stood.

'There are always trouble makers in any country,' he answered, again trying to sound calm.

Now the American got to his feet and took the cudgel. 'If what you are saying is true, none of us are safe in this country. Is that what you are saying?' he demanded, his voice loud and brash.

'I said nothing of the sort.' Dirlewanger backpedalled.

The American ignored him and continued. 'I will talk to the international community of competitors, the country leaders who are here. If we are not safe, we must simply get ourselves out of here.'

The threat seemed to stun Dirlewanger; this was not the direction he had seen the interrogation going. He knew that his position was on the line if Hitler's 'games for the world' were interrupted.

Reseating himself, he said, 'Your safety is not in question. We simply needed to hear what your people saw to assist the enquiry in to this man's death.'

Neither the American nor the Englishman took their seats and Jones joined them with his hands on his hips.

He turned to his colleagues in turn and then said, 'Gentlemen, I think we will need to have some guarantees – guarantees from the Führer himself that our people are safe. This is not acceptable.'

The other two blustered and all three talked over each other, being very negative, though each was almost incomprehensible and, of course, that was the intention.

'Gentlemen, gentlemen, there is no danger. There is no need for this fear.' Dirlewanger now began to backpedal even harder, fearing he had less control over these 'visitors' than he had thought.

'Well, I think we are in need of a meeting with at least Goring. He is your direct superior, is he not?' Jones said loudly and with a strength which was growing.

'Really, gentlemen, I assure you that is not necessary.' Dirlewanger cringed and looked uneasy in his seat.

'Well, I think it is, if there are gangsters running around all over the place,' the American said. He also seemed to be growing in confidence if that was even possible.

'These are not gangsters – they are a threat to our racial hygiene. They are imposters and they will be controlled,' the German said pointedly, looking directly at me.

I understood the implication and wondered if he were about to divulge my family history. He did not.

Everyone paused for a moment. I am sure the three politicians on our side were waiting for this malevolent bastard to say too much. I could almost hear the clock ticking; it was one of the longest pauses I ever remember. The awkward silence seemed to go on for ever, though it was probably less than a minute.

Jones broke the silence, demanding that the German let me and all of the athletes go so proper negotiations could begin to save the games.

This was another stroke of genius from Jones, turning the discussion away from us and directing the spotlight back on Dirlewanger.

Suddenly seeming to realise that he was no match for the three wily, older, and more practiced negotiators, he said, 'You may all go.'

He looked down and waved his hand to dismiss us.

We all stood. I was delighted with the outcome and I could feel the collective sigh from everyone else. Everyone, that is, except the Englishman.

He continued to stare at Dirlewanger and said loudly, 'I should think so. I have never been treated like this anywhere in the world. I think I shall speak to Hitler personally. *He* has always treated me with proper etiquette.'

The German didn't look up, fumbling with the papers on the desk in front of him, and waved a hand again. I enjoyed watching him squirm; it was a delight.

The Englishman finished as he turned by saying, 'Well, I never.'

This catch-all type of comment was his stock and trade. He was the consummate politician: say much and sound like you are in control of the situation without actually saying anything.

We were led from the room by Jones and we all walked directly to the meeting room where the management of our team held meetings fairly regularly.

On entering, Jones moved to the table and simply said 'sit,' and signalled with both hands.

'First, let me show my appreciation to our two good friends Mark Pratt from the Great Britain team and James Addler from the US.'

He used the two men's names for the first time as an introduction. Cain and I stood and shook hands and then Jake, as if led by us, did the same.

'Thank you both for assisting. I'm sure you made the unpleasant meeting less so,' I said.

'Any chance to have a go at that Dirlewanger, count me in,' Addler drawled and as he did, he leaned his chair backward and dropped his head under the table, returning moments later with a small listening device he had removed from one of its legs. He placed the device in the middle of the ash tray; one of three running down the centre of the table, proving that, like all other rooms, we were being spied upon.

The American held the ash tray up and displayed it to everyone, then placing it back on the table, he pointed in several different directions to indicate these devices may be anywhere.

Everyone nodded as if it were commanded; we all knew the score on these things. We had found so many in our rooms and in the eatery.

The American sat back in his chair and produced a cigar from a pouch in his top jacket pocket. He snipped the end off it with a round clipping device which hung from the same chain as his pocket watch. After taking a cigarette lighter from another pocket, he lit the cigar and offered the pouch to all present. No one took him up on his offer. He then held the lighter under the bug, melting it into the ash tray.

His actions brought silence to the room and for a few moments we all sat just watching him as the enormous plumes of smoke poured from his mouth.

Pratt, the Englishman, waved his hand, indicating that a dialogue should be maintained and then asked, 'None of you saw what happened to the murdered man, I suppose?'

Jones immediately answered 'certainly not' and pointed to me to indicate that I should speak.

I was taken by surprise and babbled a little, saying, 'No, no, only that he was following us earlier in the day.'

Seeing that he expected more, I gathered my thoughts and added, 'One of them was following us – that is, Miss Smith and I – as well. Um, it was a bit stupid, really – one man picked up each of our groups when we separated. It was so obvious. If they are Germany's best spies, we have nothing to worry about.' I threw the insult in just to annoy Dirlewanger who I was sure was listening, somewhere.

'I don't know what their game is. One has been noticeable

everywhere I go as well,' Pratt added and then indicated with both hands that everyone should add their own comments.

Berta quickly supported my comments, saying, 'Yes, we had a bit of a laugh when we moved into one shop or another and could see them in the reflections of the windows.'

'The dead man got so close to me in the bookshop that I could have touched him. Vadoma and I were surprised when he didn't follow us out of the shop and to the coffee shop,' Jake added and looked to Vadoma for confirmation.

She dropped her eyes and did not say anything.

This made me feel really uncomfortable and I quickly commented, 'There is no need to follow us, surely?'

Jones immediately took the chance to take control of the conversation again. 'Well, there seems to be something going on. What about those two men who were killed after picking you up the other night? Do you think they intended you any harm?' he questioned, waving his hand in a gesture to indicate that I elaborate.

'Well, I don't think so. They just seemed to be medical men to me,' I answered, not really sure what he wanted me to say.

'What is this about people being killed?' Pratt asked and sat forward as if that may assist him to hear the answer quicker.

'Oh yes, I haven't seen you since that incident. Two men picked up Robert and a couple of our boxers in an ambulance and they were stopped by Dirlewanger. And he executed them both, saying they were insurgents of some sort.'

'Why the hell didn't anyone know? I mean, is anyone safe around here?' blustered Addler.

'We let the Olympic Committee know and they were supposed to inform all of the teams. I didn't know you didn't know,' Jones answered almost getting himself tongue-tied.

'We were not told either,' Pratt added, looking indignant.

'I don't know why – it was not as though we were keeping it

from the world. In fact, I know your ambassador was in the know. He was at the follow-up meeting.'

'Son of a bitch!' Addler said with his cheeks reddening as he began to get worked up. Then, remembering himself, he added 'excuse me, ladies' and became even more red if that was possible.

Berta said, 'I understand. Why was it kept secret, I wonder?'

'I certainly can't see a good reason,' Pratt added in his most pompous voice.

'I can't see the Germans boasting about this one – not one of their better efforts on the world stage,' Jones mused.

'Boasting, boasting. I'm going to have someone's guts for garters.' The American continued to get agitated. He seemed almost ready to burst.

The Englishman, though markedly calmer, said, 'I understand your ire. There must have been some deal done above our pay scale.'

'Bloody diplomats!' was the next outburst from the American which he followed with another apology. He sat for a moment and then added, 'All I really need to know now is if one of your team were involved?'

'Not in any way,' Jones reassured him.

I saw Vadoma shift in her chair and I wondered if she were going to say something. Then she seemed to have second thoughts and settled again.

'Well, I'm sure this is late enough for all of us,' Pratt said, standing and preparing to don his hat.

Everyone took his lead and Jones said loudly, 'Thank you both for all the assistance. I'm sure this is not the last thing we will have to deal with while we are here.'

He shook the American's hand and then the Englishman's.

'We did have him on the run, like old times,' Addler said in a very loud voice, making sure anyone listening would hear.

'Indeed,' Prat added, also raising his voice for effect.

Jones excused himself and left with them. They were quite a formidable team.

I wondered if I should say something but failed to before Cain said, 'I think we should all get some sleep. I think we will all need to have our wits about us over the next couple of days.'

Everyone started to head off to their respective rooms and I noticed Jake lingering with Vadoma. He obviously wanted to speak to her; it seemed even more obvious that she had no such need.

The rest of us left the room. I waited just outside the door, hoping to hear their conversation and Berta, realising my intent, stood with me.

We could hear that they were speaking but could not make out the words until Vadoma's voice became raised as she said accusingly, 'Why didn't you tell them you went back into the shop?'

'I didn't even think of it, and I didn't think it was of any importance anyway,' Jake answered.

'I will not lie for you or anyone else,' she said, her voice becoming harder.

'Don't let a little thing like that come between us,' Jake pleaded.

'There is no us!' she scolded and I heard her walking toward the doorway. Berta and I rushed to the closest corridor and ducked down it, hoping she would not see us in her flight. She almost ran past the corner and certainly didn't notice we were there. She was quickly followed by Jake, who repeated her name twice in a pleading tone.

They were both gone and now Berta and I, looking at each other, realised that she would reach our room before us and would wonder why we were not there. I remembered only I had the key. We headed toward the corridor but before we could get there another figure rushed past. It was Dirlewanger.

We paused for a moment and then headed toward our rooms. On reaching our corridor, I could see Vadoma leaning against our door and it was not difficult to see she had been crying.

As we neared, I apologised. 'Oh, sorry. I forgot I have the only key.'

She gave no answer and as Berta tried to place an arm around her, she shied away. Berta did not try again.

We all entered and nothing was said until Berta, stopping at her door, said, 'Have a good night.'

She closed the door behind them before I could answer.

'Have a good night.' The words echoed in my mind well into the early hours of the morning.

Having a good night couldn't be further from the truth. I was a ball of nerves – I kept seeing the two men murdered by Dirlewanger and the victim in the bookshop; I kept thinking what if Jake was the one who murdered the man in the bookshop. Why had he hidden that he had gone back into the shop? What the hell was I doing here? Were there going to be reprisals or even arrests?

I knew I really wasn't the right man to be doing this; I had too many thoughts rushing around my brain and in a way, I wished I'd never seen bloody Germany.

The thought that it could have been Vadoma who killed the man ran through my mind but I couldn't think of a plausible reason for that to be true. What could she hope to gain from this? Nothing.

I was still running it through my mind, trying to put things together, when the alarm let me know I had wasted most of the night. I had probably slept as much as two hours, though it seemed more like ten minutes. I rose and headed toward the bathroom. The door was shut and I could just make out the sound of the hand basin tap running. I sat on the suitably placed chair and dozed for several more minutes.

The bathroom door opening startled me back to the waking world and I was confronted by Vadoma. She never looked pretty, but this morning she had an air of vulnerability about her and it softened her harshness. She did not seem the hard-faced, never-smiling Vadoma I was so used to.

'Are you well?' I asked in the clumsy way I'd always found myself speaking around her. She intimidated me – I'm sure that is what it was: a strong woman who never seemed to be happy.

'Yes, thank you,' she answered, her eyes looking away to break contact. We passed and I entered the bathroom and soon stood under the shower. The warm water revived me somewhat and I stood for some time just letting it pour onto my head and over my face. This was going to be a long day.

After drying myself, I realised that I had not brought my day clothes in with me as I was used to being alone. Thinking what an idiot I was, I had to redress in the pyjamas I had peeled off and simply let fall to the wet floor. At least my robe which I had hung on the back of the door was dry, so I quickly tied it and re-entered the main room.

'Nice look,' Berta said from the couch and I could feel my face blush.

'Yes, I forgot my clothes,' I answered feeling foolish for even explaining.

I went to my luggage and took the clothes I needed and re-entered the bathroom and changed.

On my return to the main room, I found Berta still sitting patiently where she had been minutes earlier. It was obvious she must have showered earlier as she was in her clothes from the previous day, not having her baggage at our camp. I still thought she looked beautiful and found myself staring. Realising she was watching me, I glanced away, embarrassed at my gawkiness. God, I felt pathetic and juvenile around her. She smiled.

'No Vadoma then?' I asked.

'No, she has already gone. She said she was going to meet us in the canteen,' she answered, then added, 'What do you make of all that happened yesterday?'

'I don't know. I feel so uneasy around Vadoma, but it was Jake who lied about going back into the shop. What do you think?' I answered her question with a question.

'I can't bring myself to look either of them in the eye. To be totally honest, I wish I wasn't even here,' she answered, sounding depressed.

'Oh God, if you weren't here I think I would crack up,' I said honestly, though I felt like a fool.

'I better hang around then,' she said and, taking my hand, led the way to the door.

Entering the meal room, we saw many of our teammates but not Vadoma or Jake. I considered this fortuitous as we would be able to discuss the events of the previous evening with Cain, Peter and Weathers. Not surprisingly, the three were sitting at the table furthest from the door. Cain motioned for us to join them and we complied with the usual greetings.

'Well, we have been talking about yesterday's events and it is hard for us to agree on anything,' Cain said in a less controlled and more questioning voice than usual.

'I just can't believe it was Jake, but he was the one who lied,' I answered uncertainly.

'But he didn't lie. He just forgot to mention going back into the bookshop.' Weathers defended Jake though it seemed from his tone that he was trying to convince himself as much as anybody else.

'Pretty big thing to forget, when someone has been killed,' Peter said.

We all sat, thinking. We were totally undecided but what happened next did nothing to make things easier.

Jake entered and, coming straight up to us, blurted, 'That bloody German is outside questioning Vadoma.'

'Like hell he is,' Cain said and quickly got to his feet.

I joined him and the two of us walked purposefully to the door.

Once outside we could see Vadoma. She was talking to someone out of sight at the next corridor corner.

We quickly walked toward her and as she noticed us, she said loudly, 'No, leave me alone!'

Dirlewanger stepped into view as we strode up and said, 'But I just wanted to ask a few questions?'

'Get the hell out of here. You got your answers last night!' Cain said very loudly, obviously making sure that everyone in the halls heard what he was saying.

'But I got no answers at all last night,' the smug German said, sneering as only he could.

From behind us, another very loud voice said 'what is the meaning of this?' and quickly we were joined by Jones, and he too meant everyone in the vicinity to hear him.

Glaring at Dirlewanger, he took a deep breath and demanded, 'Just what do you think you are doing?'

'Just having a simple conversation, not a problem at all,' he answered dismissively.

'If you don't stop harassing my team members I will be forced to seek your removal, and I know that all of our allied countries would support such an action.' Jones' voice almost came to a roar.

'Such emotional language, but what would anyone expect?' the German deflected.

'Right, out of it. All of you,' Jones instructed us and waved a hand toward the breakfast room, his face blushed deep red as he understood the inference.

'And you! You will kindly refrain from interfering with any of my people. You will approach me before even saying hello, do I make myself clear?' he said, stepping toward his adversary.

'No need for such hysterical comments. Do you remember where you are?' Dirlewanger returned.

'Is that some sort of threat?' Jones demanded.

'I assure you there is no need to get so upset.' The Nazi snarled back.

'Upset? Upset? You haven't seen upset. I will call your ambassador this morning and we will see who is upset,' threatened Jones and turned, almost running into Cain who had not moved from his side. He regained his composure and ushered all of us away, leaving Dirlewanger glowering after us.

Once in the canteen, Vadoma and Jones joined us. He was still red faced and I thought what a great candidate he was for a heart attack. The room was much nicer than the one at the men's camp. The tables were all set with tablecloths bordered with swastikas and even the flower vase on each held four flags. It was all a little over the top.

'What did he want, my dear?' he said, directing his question toward Vadoma.

'He just wanted me to tell him what I knew about Jake re-entering the shop. I refused to answer him and he became threatening,' she answered and took a deep breath and briefly glanced at Jake and then her eyes cast down to the floor.

'Bloody cheek. Well, no one is to talk to him without me being present, is that understood?' Jones demanded.

We all nodded our agreement. Jones could sometimes make one feel that they were before the principal at school.

A waiter arrived with a pad and pencil ready to take our orders and we each gave our requests.

The rest of the talk was basic, with each of us trying to think of something interesting to say, but each in turn failing.

Jones finished his meal and stood. 'Please excuse me. I have some important people to ring prior to catching the bus to the stadium.'

Some words were found but I just nodded. He had done a good job but I thought there would be a better time to thank him.

Again, there was an awkward silence and eventually I broke it, asking, 'What do we have to watch today?'

Weathers answered, reminding us that this was crunch day. All of our last team members were competing at the stadium except for the Dan – the last of our boxers – that night.

'Whoever he fights, he will give them a tough time of it,' Weathers said, proud of his team mate.

During our whole time at the table, I noticed several furtive glances between Vadoma and Jake. It was obvious that neither could find the courage to speak or test how the other was feeling. I stood and gave some feeble excuse to disappear and was accompanied by Berta, Cain, Weathers and Peter, and we left the two together to sort things out.

Later when we were loading onto the bus, it was obvious that they had certainly not worked things out. Neither spoke and Vadoma sat on her own in the second to front seat where I usually sat, and Jake passed us without comment and moved to the rear where he took up his usual position, though it was clear that he was not his usual bubbly self.

Berta, entering on my arm, sat down next to Vadoma. I assumed the seat behind but wished she had sat with me.

Peter came onboard and sat with me and as the rest of the members boarded, there was an air of excitement, almost like the opening day of the Games. Everyone determined to show undying support of our last few athletes.

Enormous crowds greeted us as we arrived as close as we could get to the stadium, but rather than where we usually unloaded, we found ourselves getting off the bus some three or four streets further from the main entrance. Seeing the massive crowds of people, Jones stood and moved to the front door and waited until the excitement died down a little.

'Listen up,' he said, raising his hand to gain full attention. 'This crowd is unprecedented. I want you all to stay together, link arms three or four abreast and keep in contact with the group in front of you,' he instructed and after thinking for a moment, he added, 'We have seen some very violent things here in Berlin and I don't want anyone to be alone at any time.'

He paused again for effect and then added, 'Am I understood?'

Mutterings with a tone of agreement came from all quarters and he stepped out of the aisle, allowing the throng to start to unload. The police rowing team were among the first to unload. They stood as a group like a guard of honour to allow the rest of us go egress unmolested.

The day was warm but not perhaps as hot as previous days and we assumed our positions in our usual part of the seating.

Events went fairly quickly against our endeavours on the track with everyone fairly convincingly bowing out of their respective completions. That was until the triple jump competition where the wonderfully built Matthew Hunt showed why he was one of the team's favourites as he fought through the rounds. At one time it looked as though Australia would take home a gold medal but, though Matt broke his one personal best distance twice, he was relegated to a very creditable third.

Yes, at last our team had gained a medal – a bronze medal, though from the greeting Matt got when he eventually took his place on the podium, one would have thought he had taken the gold. We were so proud of him.

We all left the stadium with boisterous enthusiasm as it seemed did the huge throng of people. There were only a few days left before the closing ceremony, and I knew there was little time left for us to make ground on the main purpose for my inclusion in the team. We had made some ground, but everything we had gained in the way of evidence of the Nazis' brutality was of a witness-based kind, therefore it was what we would say versus what they would say.

I knew that there would be little ground gained without real, hard evidence. I thought of the things we had seen, the cruelty the animus, but I knew I simply had not done my job and it was beginning to ware on me. I decided to hold a war council, of kinds, when we got back to the camp. There would be little time between that and leaving for the last night of boxing. I didn't think for a moment about not attending. I just couldn't do that to Dan. I had become so impressed by the young man.

Once on our bus, I called Cain and Weathers over to join Peter and I. I had deliberately moved several seats further back than usual and left Berta to sit in our usual position with Vadoma.

I did not ask Dan, Nesbitt or Jake to join us and I think it was understood that we wanted privacy, as none of the rest of the team came anywhere near us once we had begun to travel.

When we stopped at the entrance to the women's camp, Berta turned and waved to me, saying, 'See you tonight at the boxing.'

I nodded and waved back. I wanted to go with her, I wanted her to be safe, I wanted to spend the rest of my life with her. But now I had a duty, and it had to take precedence.

'Well, I am sure you all know why I asked you to sit together?' I said in what was a rhetorical question. They all nodded and I continued, 'We need to get in contact with Ronja or someone from the resistance.'

'Yes, I have been giving that some thought,' Cain said and then after a short pause, he continued, 'Tonight is really going to be our best chance. What if you and I were to slip out of the boxing stadium and try to find someone? It is likely they will be looking for us to make contact, if it is at all possible.'

As usual Cain's sentence was thought provoking and long winded and it took me a short time to process what he was proposing.

When I understood, I mused, 'I suppose you are right but what about the others? How do we keep them from noticing us as we disappear?'

'Well, I was thinking we would go to assist with Dan's preparations. You know, getting his gloves on, et cetera,' he answered.

'I don't suppose Best will like that. He will want to be in charge,' I said, thinking through the idea.

'We won't see Best, he will be in with Dan. We will just tell the others we are going to help and go out the athlete's door,' Cain proposed. He, as usual, had thought through his plan well enough to answer any questions.

'Sounds good but I should probably come too?' Weathers suggested.

'I think you should go with Dan. He will be looking for you more than anyone else. He looks up to you, and if anyone can help him win, it's you,' I answered.

'What about me?' Peter asked.

'You will need to keep an eye on Vadoma and Jake. Neither of them can know where we have gone,' Cain instructed, and Peter, to his credit, nodded his agreement.

'That's good. I still don't think we can trust either of them,' I added. Everyone nodded and I then thought of another problem. Vadoma had been instructed on how to secrete rolls of film and other pieces of evidence about her person. She was the one prepared to transport any important material through customs.

'Oh, Vadoma can't know if we do get anything to take home. She is supposed to transport any evidence we get through customs,' I said.

'We can give her some canisters of film and tell her that it is the evidence. That way she won't suspect anything,' Cain said, thinking on his feet, so to speak. I really found him impressive. He could have easily been picked to run this project; he had a lot more ideas than I did.

I suggested that we meet together for a meal that night to make final arrangements. We all knew that this may be the last chance we would have to get the evidence.

The rest of the trip home was not eventful, but I did notice several times that Jake was watching everything I did. Was he observing us for the Germans? I had no idea and I felt sorry that I could not bring myself to trust him anymore.

Later we sat at the dinner table and as usual were served by German table staff. I noticed that our usual attendants were not in the room and two other men were serving. I didn't like the look of either of them.

'More bloody Nazis' I thought to myself and I noticed that they were also being watched by Cain, who, after a short time raised his eyebrows to me knowingly and I gave a little nod. What little game was Dirlewanger playing now?

As we finished the first course, one of these men came and started to clear our table. As he reached to take my plate, I felt something drop into my lap. I quickly looked down and saw a piece of paper tightly folded and I quickly covered it with my napkin, then slipped it into my pocket. The man didn't change his demeanour and did not even look at me.

There was a dessert wagon being circulated by the other man and I thought I would take the chance to go to the toilet and read the message. I excused myself, and once in the toilet, took up a cubical.

Written on the page, I saw 'Must see you. I will be at the opening ceremony. I will find you.'

And it was signed 'Ronja'.

Luckily, I had a pen in my top pocket and I quickly wrote on the reverse, 'Cain and I were going to get out of the boxing stadium tonight, to try to make contact.'

As I finished writing, I heard the door to the bathroom open and someone walked in. Thinking it may have been Ronja's messenger, I quickly stood and opened the door.

I was confronted by Jake.

He looked very serious; his frown almost divided his forehead in two and he was red faced.

'I don't understand why you have all decided to exclude me from everything,' he blurted.

I was so taken aback that I found no immediate words.

'I didn't do anything to that German in the shop,' he continued indignantly.

'No, no. I never thought you did,' I stuttered clumsily. I really was a terrible liar. I was not deceiving him for a minute.

'If either of us did him in, the other would know about it. I only walked back into the shop for a few seconds. Vadoma was in the other room for longer than me but I'm sure you don't suspect her?' He was obviously upset. He didn't like the way we were speaking about things and leaving him out.

'Come on, old man, I don't suspect you of anything,' I lied and added, 'Why do you think you are being excluded?'

'I see the way you and Cain and Weathers and Nagel always huddle together, glancing around you to see of anyone is taking notice,' he fired back.

'Well, sorry if that seems the case but I have known Peter all my life and Weathers is one of my best friends,' I said calmly, knowing that what I said would not placate him for a moment.

I moved to my right to use the hand basin but he stepped to block me.

'I didn't do anything,' he insisted again.

'What the hell are you getting so worked up about?' I said, raising my voice.

I stepped past him and washed my hands.

'Honestly, it's not fair,' he mumbled, sounding like he was fighting back tears.

I turned and wiped my hands on a hanging towel.

'What can I do to help?' I asked, not knowing what else to say.

'God, damn it. Stop making me an outcast,' he said.

I looked into his eyes and I thought for a moment. I may be a bad judge but I believed him.

'We are going to the boxing tonight. Come and sit with us. Does that help?' I suggested and then thought what a gullible fool I was.

If he was working for the Nazis, the last place I would want him to be sitting was with us at the boxing, right in the middle of things. Then I suddenly had the thought – a memory of something my father used to say: 'Keep your friends close and your enemies even closer.'

I was thinking of all of this as I took a comb from my jacket pocket and ran it through my hair. I turned to look him in the eye and offered my hand. He took it and we shook.

'Okay, that seems fair. You know I would never do anything to hurt anyone,' he said in a lower and more calm voice. I nodded and we walked back to the meal area together.

As I sat down, and Jake went back to his own table, I said very quietly, 'Jake just confronted me over his exclusion from our group. He seemed genuinely upset.'

'What did you tell him?' Peter asked.

'I didn't know what to say so I said everything was alright and he should sit with us at the boxing tonight,' I answered, not sure what they would think of the suggestion.

Almost as if he had read my mind, Cain said, 'Not a bad idea, keeping him close so we can watch him.'

I nodded agreement. I felt vindicated to some extent but I could feel Jake's eyes boring into the back of my head. I knew If I looked around, he would be looking at me, so I resisted the inclination.

'What if we sit down and watch the first bout tonight? I think Dan's fight is second or third. Then you can go to help Jake get ready,' I suggested, looking to Weathers.

'Sounds good,' he agreed.

'I will go with you, but slip out, and the rest of you can watch Jake?' I said uncertainly. They all nodded.

'I got a note from the waiter – er, he is one of Ronja's men. I have written one back but I don't have any way of getting a note I have written to him, so he can give it to her.'

I thought for a moment, realising how confusing the sentence I had just uttered was.

'When he comes over, I will knock our plates off the table,' Cain said, stacking all of our used plates together near the edge of the table. 'When he gets down on the floor to clean them up, I will get down to help him and pass on the note. Then no one can suspect you,' he concluded.

I passed the note on to him under the table.

As our waiter neared with a jug of water, Cain placed his elbows on the table and turned to me. Then as he turned back, he knocked the plates and cutlery on to the floor.

'Bloody hell.' He swore and immediately got down to clean up the mess. The waiter followed suit and soon everything was in the man's hands and he was heading back to the kitchen. I saw no transfer of a note and thought it had not happened and I shrugged to Cain questioningly.

He gave a very slight nod of assurance and I felt I could relax at least a little. The people around me were more than capable.

The waiter again appeared and headed back to our table with the water jug. I watched him closely as he filled our glasses and found that he gave no indication that he had got the note.

'Sorry for the mess,' I uttered in poorly spoken German. He did not even look at me but gave one nod to acknowledge that he understood, then moved to the next table and continued to offer his water.

The four of us sat for a few more moments, wasting time and talking about the day's events. I admired the waiter and thought him very brave. He was risking his life, everything, just to give us a note and at no time did he even look in my direction.

CHAPTER 19

The afternoon and early evening seemed to take forever to pass. I sat, trying to read in my room as the time to get on the bus neared. I was so nervous.

About a quarter of an hour early, I began to wander down to the main entrance. I just couldn't contain myself any longer.

As I rounded the corner and the waiting area came into view, I was surprised to see Jake sitting on one of the benches. It seemed obvious to me that he couldn't wait any longer either.

I casually walked over to him and sat down. 'You're early.'

'So are you,' he answered, showing little in his expression.

'I couldn't stand the suspense. This is going to be a hell of a fight,' I added, nodding.

'Yes, it's about our last big chance,' he said, returning my nod. He paused for a moment, then added, 'Do you think Dan can win it?'

'Well, I did see the other guy fight the other day and he looks the real deal, but Dan has a big heart. Anything can happen once you get inside that square circle,' I commented, hoping that he not see through the thin veil of my hollow small talk.

There came an awkward silence which lasted about a minute, which seemed like an hour. I was delighted when Nesbitt walked up and started to talk to us.

'Ready for the big fight?' he asked and it was obvious that this was a conversation starter.

'It's gunna be great,' Jake said and I nodded.

We discussed the fight and the weather as one does when one can't think of anything else to say. Nesbitt was no conversationalist at the best of times and Jake and I were feeling quite awkward. It wasn't until Weathers and Dan arrived that normal communications were resumed.

I shook hands with Dan and wished him well and the others followed my lead. Dan looked fairly uncertain; he was young and had never fought a bout as highly rated as the one he was now preparing for.

It became a feature of the night that Weathers, the more experienced fighter, stuck close to Dan, continually telling him that he would be okay.

Dan nodded and his nerves were obviously being tested. He replied to this and the many other comments made about his chances with a sombre 'yep' and would look away, usually to gain sucker from his idol, Weathers.

When I entered the bus, Jake followed and sat down next to me. This was certainly not what I wanted. Each of the others in my immediate circle gave us space – they knew we were heading toward the women's camp. Everyone knew that Berta and I were an item, and they allowed us our space.

As if suddenly realising that fact, Jake said, 'Oh, I will move when Berta arrives.'

'No need,' I answered, saying exactly the opposite to what I felt.

When we arrived at the front gates, I was surprised to see Dirlewanger seated, facing the entrance road, in his staff car. He was well dressed and looked immaculate in his smart uniform. I could have thumped him there and then.

'Look at that smug bastard,' Jake said and his comment was met by a mumbled chorus of agreement.

Berta and Vadoma were the first to load and Jake stood to

concede his seat. To my delight, she took the offer and simply said, 'Thank you.'

Jake stood for a moment, looking to Vadoma, who passed him without speaking and moved to the middle seats and sat nearest to the aisle, leaving the window seat vacant.

Jake noticed her action and as he turned in that general direction, she placed her bag on the unoccupied seat. I saw him raise his eyebrows and take a seat two behind us. His dejected look spoke loudly.

I reflected for a few moments – should I move back and sit with him? I really didn't want to, but I felt sorry for him.

When the silence was broken it was by Berta. 'It will work itself out,' she said, trying to placate me.

'I know, I know, but it is so unpleasant suspecting everyone,' I answered quietly.

'I don't think there is a reason for us to suspect anyone. I don't. Neither had anything to gain by harming the man,' she reassured.

I shrugged my shoulders. I had nothing else to say.

Berta took my hand. I think she realised how impotent I thought myself. I felt so inept; I was not the man to be running this show.

✿

We seated ourselves near an aisle on the dressing room side of the ring. From there we could see everything and also give Dan a pat on the back when he entered to the roar of the crowd. Berta sat in the last seat and I next. Jake made his way to me and sat on my other side. Cain and Peter were next and then came Nesbitt and Vadoma. The gang were all here except Weathers and naturally Dan. They had retired to the dressing rooms with Best as we entered, everyone wishing Dan the best of luck.

The program for the night's fights was circulated. The first featured another Polish fighter and finished in the second round as he flattened his much less skilled opponent.

Dan's fight was scheduled fourth – later than I had expected and I began to feel that I should get out and go to see if the message had got through to Ronja. I waited until the next pair of boxers and their entourage passed us and entered the ring. Bending over to Berta's ear, I said fairly loudly, 'I'm going to go and see if all is okay with Dan.'

She nodded and stood to let me out to the aisle. The seats were very close together and as I gained the walkway, I turned to see Cain who gave me a nod to indicate that he would follow me.

I reached the change room corridor and passed the entrance as I walked to the external door. It was closed and only had an opening mechanism on the inside. It was meant only to be used as a fire door. I pressed the par and the door opened with some difficulty, making quite a noise.

As I waited a moment to see if I were to be challenged, I heard the roar of the crowd as the next bout began.

I stepped out and closed the door so the latch did not catch. I turned to move and was immediately confronted by a German soldier with his rifle raised, saying, 'Halt!'

'Oh, God. You startled me!' I exclaimed, trying to think of what to say.

'What are you doing here?' he demanded in confident German; though it was obvious he was young, he sounded very sure of himself.

'Oh, I came out for a smoke. I don't like to smoke in the change rooms,' I blurted in German, trying to think of the cover story I had hatched earlier to cover my exit if I was stopped. I had borrowed a cheroot case from Peter.

'You are not supposed to come out this door!' he said loudly.

'Sorry, but …' I started fumbling for my cigarette case in my jacket pocket, but was interrupted by Cain who had obviously heard my discovery from inside. He burst out the door and pushed violently between us, taking a few further steps and began to dry-retch, bending double.

Both I and the soldier were startled and he moved again, this time to challenge Cain. As he neared, Cain actually vomited. I didn't see how he achieved the feat but thought he must have put his hand down his throat.

The young German took a step back and swore.

'What is wrong with him?' he asked me and I simply shrugged my shoulders.

'You must go back inside,' he demanded of Cain, who began a whole new round of heaving. Moving a few feet, he slumped to a sitting position on the running board of a staff car, the nearest in the carpark.

I faltered for a moment, undecided whether to go to his side or to go back whence I had come.

The young soldier also looked perplexed and stood thinking for a few seconds, then as if enlightened, he said, 'I will get some help, a medic,' and hurried off toward the front of the building.

When he was out of sight, Cain said, 'Quick, you will need to go alone and I will say you were needed back inside.'

I understood his plan and moved as quickly as I could to the rear of the building and disappeared around the corner. Passing along the rear wall, I made my way to the far corner and peeked around to see if there were any other guards in sight. There were not and so I quickly walked between the first and second car nearest to me and continued several rows further until I could see the nearest road and take my bearings.

I had no idea where or even if I was going to meet someone. I had no plan on which direction to take.

Waiting for a few seconds, I decided that the brightest lights visible were probably those of the main part of the city and headed in that general direction.

On reaching the last row of cars, I saw that only a garden bed of about 20 feet or so width separated me from the footpath. I looked in both directions to see if anyone was watching and, seeing no one, I darted through the shin-deep flowers and started walking along the path.

After a minute or so, I passed a car parked on the edge of the opposite side of the road. Moments later, its motor started and it moved in the same direction I was going. It moved slowly and I thought I must be discovered.

Slowly, the driver's window wound down and though I could see no one inside, there was a quiet but distinct whistle. I walked a little further, not sure if they were friend or foe. The whistle came again and this time it had a slightly more urgent tone.

I bit the bullet, and walked across the road toward it. As I neared, the rear door opened and, seeing the friendly face of Ronja, I jumped in and the car moved off fairly quickly.

'Put your head down. There is a patrol car we are about to pass,' the driver said in strong English. I noted that there was no accent.

I did as I was told and actually slid off the seat and onto the floor, bottom first. It was unlikely that I would be seen there and after a set of lights were visible passing us in the direction, Ronja said, 'You can get up now.'

I obeyed.

'What do you have for me?' I questioned.

'I have bad tidings. You have been betrayed,' she said in the over-formal tone Germans seem to have when speaking in English.

'What do you mean?' I asked, wide eyed.

'The man killed in the bookshop was one of ours,' she answered with an urgency in her voice.

My reply was not very succinct. 'What?'

'Yes, he was one of mine. Which one of your people killed him?' she asked, the urgency still in her voice as she turned her head to see if we were being followed.

'I – I don't know,' I mumbled, still trying to grasp what was happening.

'Well, we had people watching and he was to approach one of you in private, during the day. He followed two of your people into the shop but did not come back out,' she blurted, and though she spoke quite good English, it was a little difficult to understand her at speed.

'But why, why kill him?' I fired back. Strangely, I felt as though I was defending my people.

'I'm not sure but no one else was seen entering the shop and then he was dead,' she answered, paused and then added, 'Did you recognise the knife?'

I shook my head. I still had doubts about who I thought was guilty. I wanted it to be Vadoma; I simply liked Jake more. I also wondered if Vadoma would have the strength to kill the man while stifling his screams.

'We have no intelligence on either of them. What do you know about them?' she asked.

Though the interior of the car was dark, I could see her expression: it was serious. She looked over her shoulder again to make sure that we were not being followed.

'Well, Vadoma is supposed to be the person who smuggles out anything you get to us. She is from a Sinti family and was part of our original group,' I mused for a moment, then said, 'I really know nothing about Jake but he is certainly more likable than Vadoma.'

She looked at me strangely and I defended what I had said.

'I know that is not the way to handle things, who I like best, but I have no intention of allowing either to be involved in our future plans. I thought of telling Vadoma that we had failed to find any evidence and then try to smuggle the films, or whatever, back in to Australia myself.'

Ronja nodded and then asked, 'Do you really suspect her?'

'Well, no, not really. What possible reason could she have?' I rejoined her question with a question.

'There are lots of bad people out there, but I can see no real reason either. Perhaps she was recognised.' She seemed to be almost thinking out loud.

We sat looking at each other, thinking for a moment, then our eyes were drawn to a sound from behind the car. The sound of a siren.

CHAPTER 20

Ronja produced a pistol from her bag and checked it. 'Pull over.'

We sat for a moment, awaiting the inevitable. We had been discovered. The whining sound came nearer and nearer, and thoughts of the terrible night when Dirlewanger had killed the two men in front of me rushed to my mind.

The sound grew louder and more threatening. Our driver had pulled almost all the way off the road into a driveway and the flashing lights met our gaze. But wait, they were not stopping.

The vehicle, some sort of rescue van which I had never seen before, raced past us, and though words on the side were evident, I was unable to read them.

I dropped my head and took an extravagant deep breath. We were safe – well, at least for now.

Ronja slowly and methodically re-stowed her gun and seemed barely perturbed by the event. I, on the other hand, could feel the beads of sweat ready to drip from my eyebrows. I drew the back of my hand across my forehead and exhaled.

'Well, what do you think of the man?' Ronja said, continuing on our discussion as though nothing at all had happened.

'No, I have no reason to think he did anything either. This is all too strange,' I concluded.

'You will need to be careful, as you say, and keep them both at arm's length,' she warned.

She produced a package, wrapped in brown paper from within

her inner jacket pocket. It looked light.

'These are films of the atrocities – at least the ones we have been able to catch on film. They must get back to our people in the rest of the world. Or no one will believe what is happening here,' she said, holding out the bag.

As I took it, I said, 'I understand,' and she nodded her approval.

Suddenly, another emergency vehicle was approaching from our rear.

Sitting in the rear seat, I could see flashing lights behind us.

'Turn around when you can,' Ronja instructed the driver, who I could see nodding.

The vehicle passed and soon we had affected a U-turn and were heading back toward the stadium.

Stopping closer to the main entrance than where they had picked me up, but not so as to be noticed, I began to get out.

'Wait a bit,' Ronja said calmly and I waited. There was no doubt as to who was in charge when she was around. I did admire her; her unflappable, determined spirit was extraordinary to me.

'I think I had better come with you,' she instructed, as usual dictating the next steps to be taken.

'Come with me, but how?' I questioned.

From the same pocket she had returned her revolver to, she took out an envelope and from inside it a handful of tickets – tickets to many events of the Games. Fumbling through them, she picked out two which were for the evening boxing events.

She handed them to me, saying, 'These should do.'

I took the offering and looked at them, thinking that her resourcefulness, or perhaps her preparedness, was impressive.

'Well, why do you think you should come?' I questioned as we both alighted from the same door.

Taking my arm, she said, 'Less questions for a young couple arriving than for you returning.'

I nodded and smiled. She was right. She seemed to think of

everything, but as she later told me, in her position it was imperative to be well prepared if you wanted to live.

Walking into the grand entrance, I handed the tickets to a young lady who was positioned near the only open door. This was to allow all of the other 'Welcomers' to go about other duties. The woman checked my ticket and handed it back to me.

As we came to the entrance to the seated area, I could see that the combatants in the ring included Dan.

The opponent was finishing a combination and though Dan had covered up well, the last blow had effect and knocked him onto the ropes.

I stood for a moment and watched as he regained his equilibrium and landed a left of his own.

I was already engrossed and wandered down the aisle, but when I reached our row there was no Berta or Cain, no Jake and no Vadoma. I looked around me, thinking I may see them – a puerile thought as the venue was full of writhing loud masses.

Noticing me from further along our row, Nesbitt signalled to me and made his way to the aisle.

'They went with Jones. Cain took sick again and they have taken him to the hospital,' he said loudly and then, seeing that I was still a bit surprised, he added, 'They said I should wait and tell you where they had gone.'

He was almost drowned out by another swelling of the tumult as Dan took several more blows. His opponent was getting on top. I could see on the opposite side of the ring that Weathers and Peter were attending the corner Dan returned to as the end of round bell sounded.

I nodded to Nesbitt and began to make my way through the now-seated majority, and on reaching Peter, he said, 'Thank God you are alright at least.'

'What's going on?' I queried.

'Cain took ill and Best was called to attend him. He was livid with you for not being able to be found.' He was obviously a little flustered but after a few seconds he continued, 'Best was required to go to the hospital with him and Berta went too I think.'

He paused again.

'I had to take Best's position here. You better take over,' he concluded.

I nodded and he began to depart in the direction of our seats, then he turned and came back to me. 'Bloody hell. Jake and Vadoma are gone too. I'll go and see if I can find out where they are.'

Thinking for a moment, I said, 'Be careful.'

He nodded and left heading toward the changing rooms.

Now, for a few seconds, I was distracted as Dan and Weathers took my attention.

'… you need to keep out of the way of his left and don't drop your hands,' Weathers was saying as he towelled the younger man's face.

'He's so bloody quick.' Dan gasped.

'Yeah, but don't get caught up in trying to guess what he is going to do. Be ready all the time for his left, and cover up. Your left is the weapon which can hurt him: right jab, right jab and left hook – it's the only way you can get at him,' Weathers instructed.

He was impressive in this sort of situation. He seemed to thrive on confrontation.

'You can do it, mate,' I added and it was obvious that I was totally uneducated in the sport.

The last round started and I noticed from the adjacent corner that Dirlewanger and his crowd were in attendance in what were almost religiously their reserved seats. Dirlewanger, as usual, was watching me.

Our eye contact was brief and it was I who was first to look away as a flurry of punches enlivened the crowd – their cheering was near fever pitch. As I looked away, I noticed that Ronja was just a row behind the German. She too was standing, clapping. I wondered what her intent was but the fight held my attention for several more seconds and when I looked back she was nowhere to be seen.

I wondered if I had imagined the whole thing. Why would she go so near the man she hated so much. Then the thought crossed my mind; she had that Luger in her jacket pocket.

Imagination – how ridiculous. As if she was going to take him out there and then, with hundreds of witnesses.

At the next clinch in the ring, Dan clung to his opponent, trying to halt the relentless barrage inflicted on him. It worked for a moment but as the referee separated them, Dan was caught by a ferocious right hook and was felled.

At a four count, Dan had regathered himself and was ready to resume. The referee tested his hands and the bout continued.

Weathers continued to yell encouragement and instructions, most memorably telling his young friend to keep his hands up.

Dan was absorbing a huge amount of punishment and I thought he must fall again but he toughed it out and, on the bell, landed the last punch of the fight: a well-placed left upper-cut to his opponent's jaw. Though it would have been a scoring blow, it held little venom.

The expected raising of his opponent's hand by the official drew a roar from the wild onlookers and the two fighters embraced in centre ring. Soon, Dan, as graciously as he could, made his way to our corner, leaving the victor to accept his well-deserved accolades.

Dan dropped onto his seat and we began to towel him down and Weathers gave him water. Spitting the water out into a bucket provided, it was obvious to detect quite a bit of bleeding from his lower lip. As I moved to place a towel over the wound to stem the flow, he mumbled 'Sorry.'

It was directed at Weathers who immediately returned, 'There is nothing to be sorry for. You did a great job.' He paused for just a moment, their eyes meeting, then he concluded, 'We all meet a better man on the night, sometime.'

I thought this was tough love but it did seem to placate the young man somewhat and he nodded.

Soon we had him back on his feet and out of the ring and as we headed to the change rooms, I noticed Ronja near the aisle in one of the last seats. She was watching us retire without making eye contact. It seemed to me that she was trying not to draw attention to herself.

I quickly looked to my two companions, and though they were both keenly headed out of the noise-ridden room, I could see that Weathers had noticed Ronja and he flashed me a knowing look to which I did not react.

Entering the rooms to a somewhat muffled roar from the crowd, Weathers instructed, 'cold shower,' and, nodding, Dan turned to the left and went into the shower area.

'You saw her?' Weathers questioned.

'Yes, I have spent the evening with her,' I answered.

Raising his eyebrows, he said, 'I thought you must be out of the area when Best was looking for you. Boy, was he pissed!'

'Isn't he always?' I answered and he gave a little scoffing laugh, and returned, 'Anything happen?'

'Well, only one thing. The man killed in the bookshop was one of Ronja's men, acting as a double agent sort of thing. She thinks either Jake or Vadoma must have been recognised by him and killed him so he couldn't expose them,' I answered and Weathers' eyes widened as he said, 'Bloody hell.'

'Yes, I don't really know how we can trust either of them,' I muttered almost under my breath as I noticed another boxer entering the main door. I added quietly, 'And now, they are both missing from their seats.'

Weathers said no more, not even looking around to see who had entered. He had understood my action of lowering my voice.

Shortly, Dan came, dripping, from the shower area and then dried off with a towel thrown to him by Weathers. As he finished, he wrapped the towel around his waist and sat down on one of the benches and put his head down.

Weathers gave him a rap on the back and said, 'You did well. There will be other fights.'

'Yeah, he was just too good,' the young man answered, not looking up.

'You did well, mate; do I need to fix that lip?' I questioned.

'No, it's stopped bleeding. It wasn't much,' he mumbled but still didn't look up.

I turned to Weathers, hoping he would have some more words of consolation, but he remained silent and I thought of the old maxim 'Better to remain silent and be thought a fool than speak out and remove all doubt.'

We remained silent until the young man, obviously feeling awkward, asked, 'What happened to Best?'

'Cain was taken ill and had to go to the hospital and Best went with him,' Weathers answered.

'Cain, again?' Dan said and looked up to get my conformation. I nodded and he gave a grunt of understanding.

I wanted to go to the hospital. Why had Cain let the charade go that far? I wondered if he had thought to contact the doctor I had spent time with, but I thought that unlikely – there was no guarantee that the man would even be working, and he didn't know Cain.

I knew Cain wasn't really sick, so what was going on?

I went into one of my spirals of doubts. Bloody hell, I wasn't up to this.

What to do next? I was out of ideas. I sat down on the same bench as Dan and also put my head down to think.

After what seemed an eternity, the silence was again broken by Weathers.

'We'd better go to see Nesbitt and see what he knows?' he said in what was more a question than a plan.

'Yes, that sounds the best course,' I answered, trying to sound convinced. I was not, still I doubted everything. I even questioned in my own mind as to the trustworthiness of Nesbitt. I knew that was unfair but once I had a doubt about a person, I seldom fully trusted them again.

We waited for Dan to dress and I treated and taped his right eyebrow which had a small cut that, though very minor, refused to stop bleeding. As we re-joined the row of team members there was a spontaneous outbreak of applause, with everyone wanting to congratulate Dan for his spirited effort. There could have been little more noise from the group if he had actually won the gold medal.

Nesbitt shook his hand and then turned to me and coming close, he whispered into my ear, 'Cain is okay. Berta and Vadoma went to see him with Best when he was taken ill.'

I nodded and he continued, 'He sent Vadoma back with a message to stay calm and he would see us back at the camp. Berta and Best went with him to the hospital.'

He stepped back a little as if he were gauging my understanding. I nodded.

Though there were several more fights on the card, the group decided to get our bus back to the camp, missing the crowded departure of previous nights.

As we headed toward the main exit, I noticed Dirlewanger and two of his cronies exit their seats and follow us out. Before they caught us up, Nesbitt again whispered into my ear.

'I don't know where Vadoma and Jake are. She went to the ladies' shortly after she had given me the message from Cain, and Jake followed her saying he was going to get a drink.'

'Well, that is inconvenient. What do we do, wait for them?' I asked rhetorically.

Nesbitt shrugged his shoulders but after a short moment of thought, said, 'No, I don't think we can. Surely they would have told us if they were going to take off. Perhaps we could ask for an announcement to be put over the PA.'

No sooner had he said this, Dirlewanger and his men were in front of us.

'Not waiting to see the rest of the events won by the superior German fighters, Mr Heam?' he said in his smug, sneering way.

'Mr O'Calahan,' I returned bluntly.

'Oh, yes. It is as if I forget,' he said, feigning misunderstanding, in a broken English which he certainly did not need to use.

I went to push past him but was halted by Nesbitt who took my arm and said, 'Perhaps you could assist us, Oberführer. We are wishing to leave but can't find two of our people?'

'I see,' the German answered.

'Yes, we are missing Jake Pankhurst and Vadoma, err, I've forgotten her name?' He turned to me to gain information.

'Vadoma Codona, and Jake Pankhurst,' I said, addressing him instead of the Nazi.

'I'm here!' called Jake from the throng gathering behind us and held his hand up to be seen.

'Good, have you seen Vadoma?' Nesbitt asked loudly.

Jake, who pushed his way to us, shook his head.

'Well, we will all gather directly outside the main doors and I will see if I can have an announcement put over to find Vadoma,' I instructed.

The rest of the team began to follow the instruction but Jake and Nesbitt stayed at my side as I neared the hat stand in the foyer.

The young lady attendant asked for ticket numbers in a precise German voice and then repeated the same in English, then she began to repeat in French but, raising my hand, I halted her well-practiced patter.

'We need to have an announcement put over for a member of

our team. We need Vadoma Codona to meet the Australian team at the main entrance. Do you understand?' I instructed.

The woman stood, looking at me, and it was obvious that she did not.

I repeated what I had said in deliberately poor German. This gained the response I was looking for and she moved to the far end of the counter and made the announcement, in German, and then she tried to do the same in English fairly unsuccessfully. The result created a feeling of mirth and some amusement for the crowd members who spoke English.

Our group stood just outside the main doors, waiting, and soon Vadoma appeared.

She looked somewhat flustered and as she came near, she said to me, 'I must speak to you, urgently.'

I responded with a nod and then she walked away from the group and turning away from me, she said quietly, 'I saw Jake with that German. You know, Dirlewanger.'

I raised my eyebrows, stunned. This was not what I had expected and though her gaze was not on me and indeed seemed to be far away, there were a few tears. This was also not what I expected from Vadoma.

'Okay, I will keep an eye on him. He has attached himself to me and I will make sure nothing important passes his way,' I said. This seemed to paint a clearer picture of what our 'friend' Jake was up to. I still didn't want to believe it, but there it was.

Re-joining the team, I commented that Vadoma was feeling a little under the weather and I escorted her to the bus. She clung to my arm and I felt an unsureness in her which I did not recognise.

This may well have been getting to her as much as it was to me.

Once on the bus I deposited her about half way along the seats and went to the seat I usually sat in. Jake had assumed the window seat and I sat down next to him.

He nodded and then whispered, leaning in to me as he had a

habit of doing, 'I followed Vadoma and she met with a German. They exchanged pieces of paper. I didn't want to believe it but I think she is a spy.'

Though he was speaking quietly, the last word was louder and I whispered back. 'Not so loud, she will hear you.'

He nodded and went on. 'What are we going to do?'

'I don't think there is anything we can do, but I will keep her out of important meetings,' I returned, becoming more and more confused by the minute. Here we were in a 'he said, she said' situation.

I wanted to believe him more than her but I knew I could no longer trust either of them. The fact that Cain and Berta, two of my greatest confidants, were unavailable was making things worse in my mind. Oh God, how I wished everything was alright.

CHAPTER 21

I was pacing, and nothing I could do was going to ease my distress.

Peter and Weathers had retired to my room with me when we had returned to the camp, and now they both sat, trying to belay my fears.

I was most worried about Berta. I knew that wasn't a good thing to admit, and I hadn't said it out to my two companions.

'They will be alright. Best is with them and Jones was going to go back to the city to find them at the hospital to help if there was a problem,' Peter said reassuringly.

'Yes, I'm sure it will all be okay,' I answered, trying to sound like I believed what I was saying. I did not succeed.

'Sit down, you're making me dizzy,' Weathers demanded.

He was sitting on the mat in front of the couch. He had a habit of getting on the floor if the weather was hot. I obeyed his direction and sat down on the couch.

'I have to tell you both something,' I started, then after I was certain they were listening I remembered that the room was probably bugged. 'I'll tell you both when I get back from the toilet,' I concluded and signalled for them to follow me.

We entered the bathroom and I immediately flushed the toilet and ran the tap. I had a quick look around the room and felt under the edges of the basin cabinet, the underside of the windowsill and around the door. They both watched me, probably wondering if the whole thing had made even more paranoid than usual.

Peter joined the search and fumbled with each of the drawers in the basin's cabinet.

We found nothing but Weathers, who stood and groped the edges of the mirror, backed away and sat down on the edge of the bathtub, holding up a small piece of technology. I was surprised at how compact it looked on the palm of his hand.

Peter pointed at the toilet and Weathers, understanding, dropped the device in and flushed. All three of us watched as the water settled and Peter smiled as he realised it was gone.

'What is going on now?' he asked.

I answered by whispering the events of the night with the statement by first Vadoma and then by Jake.

Weathers gave a little whistle as the predicament became clear to him.

'Bloody hell, we can't trust either of them,' Peter said, shaking his head with incredulity.

'Well, that is really no different. We haven't been trusting them since the bookshop.' Weathers pointed out. We all nodded, looking at our feet, each trying to think of something sensible to add. Nothing came and after a few moments I again flushed the toilet and washed my hands.

Re-entering the main room, all three of us sat at the table and I took out the notepad and began to ponder what to write. I was just about to put pen to paper when there was a loud knock on the door. We had not expected it and I jumped, startled. It was a very rude awakening that our silence was not that of the rest of the world.

Peter was nearest the entrance and quickly rose and opened the door to reveal Cain. Peter took his hand and ushered him into the room followed by Best and Jones.

Weathers and I stood and met each with a handshake.

'Good to see you, old mate,' Weathers said, also clapping Cain on the back.

'And where the hell were you?' Best fired at me.

'Well, I had not been feeling well either and went outside to be sick. I wandered around for a short while and my stomach settled. Probably the night air,' I explained. The answer had been rehearsed in my mind since I had been told that Best was on the war path.

'Bloody nonsense. The night air!' he said mockingly.

'Nonetheless, I did feel better after about fifteen minutes and was surprised to find what had happened when I came back inside,' I explained.

'You really need to be more careful,' Jones put in calmly.

'Yes, yes I know, but one doesn't always act sensibly when about to throw up,' I blurted, a little annoyed that Best was questioning my bogus claims.

'Well, good. All that is settled then. You should all get some sleep,' Jones said in his fatherly voice. He put a hand to Best's shoulder and ushered him back to the door.

Best was annoyed and muttered 'bloody incompetent' and other muffled words as he was literally pushed out the door.

Jones had done his part getting that pompous jackass out of the way and Peter closed the door at their backs.

'Oh, shit, I was sick,' Cain muttered and as he did, he shook his head to show that he was not telling the truth.

'Yes, I felt ill as well. Must be the poor food we are eating here,' I added hoping the insult got through to whoever was listening.

We all sat down at the table, each understanding that there was a lot to write and Jones took the pen first.

'I was given two rolls of film.' He wrote and, opening his shirt, he felt his right armpit with his left hand and, after a ripping noise, produced the films, wrapped in tape which he later told us the doctor had tapped there so it would not be noticed when he left the hospital.

Now he added, 'I thought the nurse saw him do it, but she didn't comment. He seemed a little worried as I left.'

Taking the pad, I asked, 'what's on the film, do you know?'

Cain shook his head and took the paper again writing, 'He asked after you and I said to him quietly that I was working with you and he produced the films and placed them under my arm and taped them there just in time as the woman came back to us.'

His pen paused, then went on. 'She looked at me strangely as I redressed. The doctor told me I would be right to leave.'

I nodded understanding.

Again, he took a little time thinking what he needed to tell me next. 'I was met by Berta, Jones and Best who had been made to stay in the waiting room. Best was pissed off to say the least.'

I took the paper and wrote, 'Where are the films and what are we to do with them, now that we can't use Vadoma?'

No sooner than I had finished, he had taken back the pen and was writing.

'I will keep them on me, then if they come after you at least we will have them to use as evidence.'

I nodded and Weathers and Peter followed suit.

So many thoughts ran through my mind, but it really seemed an incoherent mess, I could think of nothing more to say.

'I think I should stay here with you tonight, if that is okay. Just in case I get sick again?' Cain asked.

'Sounds like a good idea,' Peter commented and then, thinking, added, 'I will go and get your clothes and let your men know that you are alright.'

'Yeah, just bring my smaller bag. That's all I will need tonight.' Cain answered.

I was still mute and was thinking of his last written comments.

'If they come after you' was troubling me. Why would they come after me, I thought. Oh, I supposed he may have been speaking metaphorically – or was it a real possibility?

I was still deep in thought when Weathers said that he would go with Peter and would see us in the morning. They left.

Cain and I sat on the couch, neither of having anything to add, but after a short while I regained my composure and asked if he would like a cup of tea or something.

'Got anything harder?' he asked.

'I do have a bottle of red wine. German wine I brought the other day in town,' I answered.

'Beggars can't be choosers,' he said and I went into the other room to get the bottle.

Returning, I noticed that he had found two tumblers. Not what one usually drank wine from but it seemed certain that he was not about to let that stop him. Finding a small cork remover in a drawer in the kitchenette, I quickly had the bottle opened and was pouring a little in each glass.

'You've got to be joking?' he quipped as he took the bottle and filled his glass.

'Your evening out hasn't stopped your thirst then?' I commented with a smile.

'It wouldn't be right to waste it, even if it is only cheap German rubbish,' he commented, and I thought how Dirlewanger would be seething if he were listening.

I took a sip and then said, 'You're right, it is rubbish.'

Actually, it was quite a nice wine. I had spent more than usual as I was going to have it with Berta if I got the chance.

'Yes, like most unsophisticated drops, it's a little more like vinegar than wine,' he said, giving a little laugh.

Our condescending wine comments were interrupted by a knock and Peter entered with Cain's baggage.

'Thanks, mate,' Cain commented and gave a little salute with his glass.

'Like to join us?' I asked also raising my drink.

'I thought you would never ask,' Weathers answered and sank into the armchair opposite us.

I got up and after going through the limited crockery under the sink, I pulled out the only other style of drinking vessel available: a teacup. I poured my wine into the cup and washed my glass, refilled it for Weathers, and returned to my seat.

As I handed over the glass, he commented, 'classy,' in a sarcastic voice.

I laughed and raised my own cup to show just how classy.

It didn't take the two of them long to polish the bottle off, though it really wasn't a bad drop. I didn't have any more. All I really wanted was a long sleep and after a few minutes I left them to it and found my bed.

CHAPTER 22

The next morning when I got up, I found Weathers and Cain asleep where I had left them. The evening tipple had obviously knocked the both out where they sat and I mused over whether I should wake them or let them sleep. In the end, I decided to leave them and went in to have my shower.

I had just stepped into the cubicle when the door opened and Weathers said, 'Sorry, old mate, but I'm busting.'

He moved to the toilet and lifted the seat and proceeded to drain the previous night's swill.

I continued with my own ablutions and he washed his hands and left, apologising on the way.

Soon, the door opened again and Cain entered to repeat the same process.

'What is this, a bloody highway?' I asked.

These blokes seemed not to understand privacy.

'Well, you filled us with your cheap German wine.' He laughed and then as he left, added, 'Sorry, mate. I will get out of your hair.'

When I exited the bathroom, they had both gone to their own rooms to get ready for the day. I prepared myself and headed to the meal room. I was surprised how hungry I felt. I was sure that my two 'drinking mates' would not feel the same.

I was surprised to find Cain and Nesbitt at the usual table – Cain with a huge helping of bacon and eggs. He devoured his food with little or no effect from the previous night. I took a smaller plate of food and sat with them.

'We should be able to settle into a quieter day today. There are no more events with our guys involved,' Cain said; I think he was just trying to make conversation.

Nesbitt and I just nodded and after an awkward pause, Cain leaned in and whispered, 'I have filled Nesbitt in on the happenings. We may need him.'

I nodded and he continued. 'Are you planning to go into the city today?'

'Yes, I have to de-camp from the training rooms and will need to bring my gear back here,' I answered.

'Good, I think we should come with you. Had you planned to meet anyone?' he asked in full voice and gave me a knowing wink.

'Well, I was hoping to catch up with Berta but I haven't set anything up yet.' As I answered, I noticed a change in his face and realised that he was not talking about Berta.

'Oh, I see what you mean,' I continued, understanding that he was talking about Ronja or the resistance. 'Uh, no, we have not set up any more meetings. She can get hold of me more easily than I can get her, so I think I have to leave the ball in her court.'

Cain nodded and Nesbitt said in a low tone, 'Probably contact you at the closing ceremony.'

We all nodded.

As the team all seemed to be headed in different directions, Jones had arranged with camp management to have several cars available rather than the usual bus. Cain, Nesbitt, Peter and I piled into the first of these and asked to be taken to the training ground where I quickly got my equipment together and the four of us carried it back and placed it into the boot of the car.

I asked the driver to take us to the café we usually frequented and to take my equipment back to the camp. We also dismissed him for the day, saying we would find our way home in the evening.

We entered the café and took our usual seats at the rear table.

Each of us ordered a coffee and we sat for some time and I think everyone knew I was hoping Berta would turn up.

I ordered a second coffee and had started to drink it when Peter said, 'So, you're going to sit here all day waiting,' and gave me a knowing smile.

'Well, what's wrong with that?' I said rhetorically.

'Good. You stay here. I want to go and have a good look at the area where that man was killed the other day. Where was the body when you got there?' Cain asked.

'It, that is, he, was against the front wall in the left half of the building, at the far end,' I answered and then thinking about his request, I added, 'What do you think you will find there?'

'Nothing, nothing at all, but it is always a good thing to see the scene of the crime,' he answered, nodding as if to enquire if I understood.

'Always the policeman, hey?' I concluded and he and Nesbitt left Peter and I sitting as they paid and walked out. At the door, Cain turned and said, 'We will meet you back here,' and left.

We sat for another 20 minutes or so and they returned and re-joined us, both ordering another coffee. Once they were served, Cain began to ask questions.

'What height do you think the dead man was?' he asked.

'Well, I think he was about my height, around six foot or so. I didn't see him standing though,' I answered, wondering where he was going with the enquiry.

'Yes, I think he could have had his back to the attacker. I think he would have had to be surprised by his assailant. Did the knife penetrate on an upward or downward trajectory?' he continued my deposition, leaving nothing to chance.

'Oh, definitely downwards,' I answered, remembering the wound and the position of the body.

'Was he right in the corner?' he continued.

'Ah, no, about ten feet from the actual corner, or the book shelves at that end,' I answered trying to give every detail I could remember.

'I think that the evidence shows that he was jumped from behind someone coming out from that last aisle. The two things that worry me are the downward angle of the knife and the strength needed to commit the crime.' He paused for a moment and looked around at our faces, gauging whether we were understanding him or not. 'Jake is simply not tall enough to be the killer, and I can't imagine either of them as strong enough to do it,' he concluded.

As we each thought about his theory, we each in turn glanced at him, wanting to say something which would add to the tale, but none of us found anything to add.

After a pause, Nesbitt said, 'I think she would be strong enough, especially if she has been trained for this sort of thing.'

'Oh, she has been well trained. We were all well trained,' Peter said. As usual, he seemed willing to accept the idea of Vadoma being guilty while having no thought of Jake's involvement.

'We were shown basic self-defence but this is an attack – an attack with the possibility of only one outcome. We were not taught how to attack someone,' I said. 'Sorry, that sounded as if I were telling you off. I am not certain of anything; I don't think I could just do that in some bookshop somewhere, do you?'

'No, I don't think I could and I don't really think she could, but the guy was done in, and someone did it,' he answered and I thought his reasoning was sound. I nodded.

'We don't really know if someone else was there,' Nesbitt put in, his tone seemed to be soliciting a response.

'No, nothing is set in stone but I think Jake just can't have done it. He simply is not tall enough,' Cain mused out loud.

We all sat for a moment longer and it seemed that none of us had anything else pertinent to say. Eventually Nesbitt broke the silence, saying, 'I believe she could have done it.'

That noticeably raised eyebrows in the circle but no one responded.

The conversation was cut short as Berta and Vadoma entered the shop. I was delighted to see her though I tried to curb my boyish enthusiasm, just giving a little wave to indicate that they should join us.

Berta smiled back but Vadoma was her usual stoic self. She neither seemed pleased to see all of us, nor disappointed.

'Speak of the devil,' Nesbitt said quietly.

As the two women approached, we all stood and greeted them. It seemed so silly for me to only notice Berta as we all re-seated ourselves.

'What have you guys been up to?' she asked, flirting with her eyes.

'Oh, I had to clear my things out and have them sent back to the camp,' I answered, fumbling for words.

Loquacious as ever, Berta began a monologue about their morning and how they had been shopping for souvenirs. I hardly heard a word but watched her unceasingly.

As we paid and left the shop Berta fell in alongside me and took my arm. I couldn't have been happier. I also couldn't believe she had chosen me from the many Adonises from whom she could have had her pick. She was so beautiful and she had a mind. A mind probably more developed in many ways than mine.

Vadoma took no one's hand and none was offered, though Cain did hold the door courteously. If she was a viper in our midst, she gave no one a real reason to jump back, and certainly no reason to get closer.

I hated all of these thoughts rushing through my mind, but there was no controlling the thought every time I saw her: 'don't trust her.'

It was a very pleasant afternoon. We wandered around in the bustling streets. So many of the visitors were, like us, enjoying our last day of freedom in Berlin. The feeling in the throng was happy; everyone seemed determined to have a good time. I was a bit over the crowds – the noise bothered me. I just wanted to be alone with Berta.

At around three in the afternoon, we all decided to take taxis and return to camp to ready ourselves for the Games' highlight: the closing ceremony.

As we parted, Berta gave me a little kiss on the cheek and everyone beamed as we went our different directions.

❧

We had been ordered to wear our team blazers to the ceremony. I was very proud of my own blazer but it had always been a little tight fitting and so as usual I had carried it to the bus over my arm. We were dropped a few blocks from the actual stadium where we had usually been deposited and as the bus was unable to get any closer, it was determined that we would have to take our luck in finding it later in the evening.

Disembarking, I failed to notice that I had left my jacket on the back of the seat. As soon as we neared the stadium, I realised my mistake and told Jones I would quickly return, find the bus and pick it up.

He shook his head in that way older people do when their next words were going to be a disparaging remark about young people, and, or, the state of the world today.

I just raised my hand and rushed off before he could get the words of condemnation out.

It was hard going, walking against the tide of thousands headed to the main stadium. Faces beamed everywhere, only frowning when they met someone heading the wrong direction.

I found the bus only a short distance from where we had left it. The driver was trying to make a right turn to head to a quieter street to park. From what I could see there were no quieter streets; there was literally a seething mass everywhere one looked.

I tapped on the door and it took a few moments for the driver to even notice me. When he did, he shook his head to indicate he was not going to open the door. I pointed toward my seat and tapped again. He glared down at me and then seemed to recognise me and the door swung inward. I quickly explained that I had left my coat and rushed back to get it.

Getting off again while I hauled on the offending piece of clothing, I left him with a farewell and he continued to try to get around the corner.

One didn't have any real hope of adjusting one's direction once in the masses and I was forced to enter through one of the side doors on the opposite side of the entrance area.

People were gathered up like lambs being led to the slaughter and there was simply no real chance of getting to where I was headed, aisle 136.

I decided to give up and backed in next to one of the pylons which supported the outer wall and simply stood as the world seemed to pass me by.

I stood for almost 20 minutes and just as I thought there was a lull in the onslaught, and began to leave my safe harbour, I saw Jake.

He was making his way to the right side of the area near the entrance doors. He was heading in the wrong direction; he should have been going left. Now with all my might, I headed after him.

He crossed through the crowd, passing opening after opening, and was on several occasions almost unwittingly pushed inside. I, too, had to fight for every yard, but soon the entrances were behind me, and I could make more easily my way in following him.

Jake did not look around; he headed quickly to a corridor which was marked 'staff only'. It seemed, as I gained its end, to be a hall used to take rubbish from the stadium. Jake was now out of sight and I quickly ducked down the hall. There were several halls on either side.

At the first right and left, I glanced in both directions and saw no one and I could hear nothing. I walked past a stairwell where a large garbage skip was housed, and then to another cross corridor. On nearing its corner I could hear talking from the left side and decided to stop and try to understand what was being said.

'No, I don't think they suspect you at all,' I heard in a woman's voice – a voice I thought I knew.

'You have both done well, but I would like the films recovered. The traitor who supplied them will not betray us again.'

It was Dirlewanger and Vadoma.

Oh, what fools we had been. They were working together. We had suspected one or the other but had never thought it could have been both of them. I felt heartbroken that Jake was one of them. I had still believed in him, or at least had wanted to.

Dirlewanger continued, 'You will both return to Australia and continue your work. Do not risk being discovered. If you are at risk, lay low and let our Australian friends deal with Heam and his idiots.'

He paused to hear their agreeable responses and then continued, 'Now, get back to your roles so you won't be found out.'

I heard him start to walk and I suddenly realised I would be found out. I turned and ran as quietly as I was able.

I realised that I was not going to make the main thoroughfare and so rushed into the stairwell and quickly hid as well as I could behind the garbage skip.

I thought I would be discovered. I was not completely hidden. I could hear his footsteps as he quickly passed, then a moment later, more steps and someone else passed. I could not see who but thought from the light tread that it may be Vadoma. Then a third set of steps.

I waited what must have been two or three minutes. I wanted them all to be clear of the area before I moved.

Eventually, I gave in to my need to get out of there and stood and pushed past the rubbish trolley but as I stepped into the corridor,

I was confronted by a charging Vadoma, a knife in her hand raised to strike.

I instinctively stepped backwards and tripped, falling heavily on my back. Before I could move, I heard two muffled *thwock*ing sounds and Vadoma fell on top of me. It took me a moment to realise that she was not moving.

I looked to the hall from where she had come and was confronted by the sight of Ronja, a pistol raised and a slight wisp of smoke coming from its silencer.

It took me a few seconds to push the corpse from me. I was horrified.

Oh God, what had I become involved in? Ronja, placing her weapon into the inside of her jacket, began to help me to my feet.

'Quickly!' she exclaimed and, taking one of Vadoma's legs, began to haul her body into the stairwell. I did not help I was standing aghast.

'Quickly, help me!' she ordered more loudly as she began to remove Vadoma's team blazer. I was just dumbfounded.

'Now!' she yelled, and that spurred me into action. Having removed the jacket, she was searching for any form of identification. She removed a small wallet from the inner pocket of the blazer, then she grabbed the small handbag she had been carrying and slipped it over her arm.

I had knelt but not done anything else. I was still trying to take the event in.

'We can hide her in the garbage skip,' Ronja barked at me and started groping with one of the dead arms.

I understood and though I was horrified at placing her in a garbage bin, I helped drag the corpse to a sitting position against the wall, and then we struggled to lift her and turn her upper body over the edge of the receptacle. We lifted her legs and she toppled into the garbage and, without missing a beat, Ronja pulled out several pieces of newspaper from the bin and began to clean the blood from the floor and the wall as best she could. Lots was left behind but at least there were no pools.

It seemed as though she did this sort of thing all the time. I was still on my knees and she was covering the body with waste. Soon there wasn't a sign that anything had happened.

'Pull yourself together,' she said and slapped me across the face.

I was shocked. It didn't hurt much, though I put a hand to my cheek as if that would soothe it.

'What the hell do we do now?' I asked and I could feel my jaw drop as I gaped at her.

'I will need to become her,' she said, pointing at the skip and picking up the team blazer. She took a long look at it. There were two small holes in the back just below shoulder height; there was no evident blood on the outside and only a small amount on the inner lining which she quickly wiped with another piece of paper.

I was surprised that there was not more blood on it, but as she had fallen face down it must have been the exit wounds in her chest that did most of the bleeding and formed the pools.

'What the hell are you talking about?' I blurted.

'If they find the body they will have us. We just need to get you all on your train tomorrow and you will need to have the whole team,' she said, obviously planning things through as she went. She was quicker thinking than I was but she had not considered that Jake was also the enemy.

'But Jake would put us in as soon as he saw you,' I warned.

'Jake, what has he got to do with it?' she asked, pulling the team blazer on over her own. Finding that it was too tight, she removed it again and then took off her own black jacket to allow it to fit better.

She then put the blazer back on. It was larger than she would have bought for herself but, overall, not oversized enough to cause people to notice.

'Oh, you didn't see him. He was in the meeting with Dirlewanger and her,' I explained. I found it hard to use Vadoma's name.

'We will need to get me on that train without him seeing me, then,' she said.

'I can't see how,' I said, bewildered by the whole situation.

'No, neither can I,' she admitted, removing the blazer again and folding it over her arm. 'Come, we need to get out of here before we are discovered.'

I followed her to the end of the corridor and we walked out into the now much reduced crowd.

'You go, and be as normal as you can. I will get back to you when we have set a plan,' she instructed and vanished quickly.

Immediately I had questions, but with no one to answer them, I decided to take her order and run with it; after all, I could hardly do anything else and she had saved my life.

That thought suddenly came to mind – yes, she had saved my life and yes, Vadoma was dead.

CHAPTER 23

On finding where our team were sitting, I stood for a few moments trying to compose myself. I still felt so dumbfounded. I just stood there and looked at them from about a dozen rows behind. Settled as much as I could be, I decided to bite the bullet and join them.

Berta had saved me a seat on the aisle and took the next herself. She had also saved another seat to her left and only I knew it would not be filled.

Cain, Nesbitt, Peter and Weathers with his acolyte Dan were to her left again and then, as if nothing was wrong, Jake. Bloody hell, I still couldn't believe he was working for Dirlewanger.

I sat down next to Berta and she leaned over and gave me a peck on the cheek. This gave me the opportunity to speak quietly.

'The shit's hit the fan. Don't react but Jake and Vadoma are both with the Germans.'

'What do you mean?' she said in a whisper, staying close to me in a greeting embrace.

'I caught them with him, and Vadoma tried to kill me with a knife but Ronja shot her,' I blurted.

'What? Calm down,' she whispered.

I tried to pull myself together, and thinking more about what I wanted her to know, said, 'They were both in it together. When they left, I had hidden behind a garbage trolley and Vadoma was the last to leave. I don't know how, but she must have seen me and came back with a knife drawn, and Ronja shot her just as she was going to do me in, just like that guy in the bookshop.' I realised I was babbling but was so worked up I could not control myself.

'Was Ronja with you?' she asked, not really seeming to understand what I was saying.

'No, not exactly. She had brought me back and we had separated at the front doors and I saw Jake going down this corridor and followed him,' I explained and leaned away from her, putting on a fake smile so as to not excite Jake's interest. I really was quite poor at deception. It was not something I had really practiced and I felt Jake's eyes watching me carefully.

I gave a little laugh and changed the subject, saying something about getting lost.

Everyone who could hear me laughed and even Jake gave me a smile with an expression which I'm sure was meant to imply 'that was just like me.'

Berta and I sat back and looked to the events which were unfolding in the stadium in front of us; there were, it seemed, thousands of swastika flags and banners everywhere. Flashing bulbs of cameras rippled across the gathered thousands as each new happening took their attention, but I just couldn't think of anything else: Vadoma was dead and Jake was a Nazi.

I'm sure I was betraying my thoughts and Cain looked at me. He knew something had happened; I was sure he knew. He spoke to Nesbitt, who announced he was going for drinks. Several of the group offered to help and soon he and two other rowers had taken orders and were getting ready for the fight to get to the shop.

I think Jake thought something was happening and offered to help.

'I don't think we need four of us to go,' Nesbitt said and one of his men sat back down and Jake, Nesbitt and the other man began to shimmy their way along the row toward me.

As Jake neared, he asked if I was alright and I nodded and smiled, feeling so false and out of my depth.

'I could do with a bottle of something,' I answered and began to get my wallet out.

'No need for that. You can get me back later,' he said and shuffled past and the three of them were gone.

'What the hell is going on?' Cain asked, leaning over the top of Berta so he could hear my answer.

'It's Jake and Vadoma. They are both Nazis. I saw them meeting with Dirlewanger.'

Peter could hear what I said but Weathers frowned, obviously not making out the words, but I dare not speak louder.

'Perhaps it was all a coincidence,' Peter said and turned and whispered something to Weathers.

'No. I could hear what they were saying and each were reporting to him, saying that they were both suspected but that it was more Vadoma who we thought was one of them,' I blurted and the crowd became very loud around us, people jumping up and down with excitement.

In the next lull, I explained what had happened to Vadoma and how Ronja had dealt with her. They all stared at me with their mouths open.

Cain was the first to come out of the shock. 'What are we to do now? Everyone will miss Vadoma.'

'Well, Ronja took her team uniform and I think she is going to try to fill the hole, you know, be there without really being seen, at least till we get out of Germany. You will have to help with that,' I added, looking to Berta, then I continued, 'We will need to control Jake. I have no idea how. We all looked from one face to another, trying to find a plan. Cain, as usual, was lost in his own mind – he almost seemed to leave one when he was deep in thought. A minute or so passed then he said, 'We need some beer. We need a lot of beer.'

On their return, the three handed out bottles of ginger ale, telling us that there was nothing else other than beer and that it was impossible to get near the two bars. Obviously too many of the crowd didn't like ginger ale.

This gave Cain the reason to break formation and, away from the rest of us, he took Weathers with him saying that he would not be drinking that rubbish when there was good German beer to be had.

Berta and I took the drink offered by Jake and I wondered if it were wise to take opened bottles of anything from him now that I knew who he really was. We both took sips and I expressed my distaste for the rubbish. Berta said 'well, it's better than nothing' as she took a second, longer, swig.

Jake sat down next to her, assuming Cain's seat.

'Thanks, Jake,' she said, showing her gratitude, and I nodded while taking a swig with a smile. Even she was better at this deceiving caper than I was.

After around 15 minutes, Weathers and Cain returned to us, Weathers carrying a wooden crate which contained a dozen bottles of beer – apparently, from what Weathers told us later, Cain bribed one of the waiters, telling him that he wanted to shout the German rowing team to congratulate them on their victory.

There was only one German who was actually going to be drinking any of the beer, and that was going to be Jake.

Cain had ordered Weathers to challenge everyone to a drinking competition. Cain declined saying that he only wanted a quiet one with travel ahead the next day.

Several others were taunted and then Jake, those first challenged received a withering glare from Cain and each understood that they were to have only a small amount.

Jake also refused the challenge but Weathers knew that he should be able to dare the young man to join him even if it were only one bottle.

'What are you, some sort of prude? Have a drink, man.' Weathers sneered at him and Jake, wanting to fit in and keep his cover intact, agreed, taking the bottle offered.

Taking a small swig, he was again chided by Weathers who wanted to get him into the 'competition'.

Weathers was appealing to his base instincts, and he was even more convinced that he should take the brash Australian on when Weathers commented that he drank like a German Fraulein.

Weathers chugged a large portion of one bottle and Jake, in answer, took down a whole bottle.

Most of the lights in the stadium dimmed and columns of light blazed into the zenith, looking for all the world as if they were holding some great unseen roof. There was an intake of breath from the masses which was extremely audible followed by a great cheer as the representative flags from each competing country marched.

A visual tsunami of flashing camera bulbs swept across the crowd, with even Berta using her camera. It was most impressive, though I was very doubtful that any flash photograph could accurately depict the spectacle. Weathers and Jake began their second bottle; each seemed to be ignoring the ceremony all together.

Speeches were made. I don't think I really heard any of them as I was running a marathon in my mind. How could I see the woman killed and then really concentrate, or even think of anything else?

I did hear the last few words as the Olympic flame began to die down and noted that one of them was Tokyo. I didn't take in any other information but thought it to have been prefaced with the words, 'the next Olympiad will be held in Tokyo'.

How pathetic I felt – people were hugging each other jumping up and down and cheering. It must have been obvious to everyone and I found my eyes meeting those of Jake, and in a moment, I felt he must read the fear and loathing in my expression. Berta saw what was happening and, grabbing my head, pulled my face down to hers and kissed me passionately. To some extent, this broke my morbid train of thought and I gave in to her whiles totally.

Jake and Weathers were on their third bottle each of the amber and when our kiss ended, I could see that Jake had other things on his mind. He was no longer interested in my demeanour.

The party raged for almost an hour, athletes from all countries mixing and making new friends, medal winners were fated to loud cheers as they joined another group. I couldn't have cared less. I was in the arms of the woman I loved.

Eventually things started to move out of the arena and into the streets but Berta and I stayed where we were talking in low tones and kissing. She was the tonic I needed; she brought me back from the edge of despair. When we realised that most of the crowd had spilled out and we were among the last to leave, we too got up and, arm-in-arm, headed toward the exits.

Cain had waited for us near the stairs which brought us down into the main foyer, so to speak.

'I have sent the rest off to find their way home. Ronja found me and she has a car waiting to take you and her back to your camp,' he said, looking to Berta.

'But everyone will know it's not Vadoma in a heartbeat,' Berta answered.

'Yes, well, we thought you could say she had had a fall and you had to bandage her face?' Cain said uncertainly, looking to me for some sort of indication of what I thought.

'I can't see that working, well, not for long at least,' I said.

The worry must have been writ across my face as he quickly added, 'It only needs to work tonight, to get her back into the women's camp.'

I nodded but still was unsure what he meant. He realised and continued, 'You will need to go with them, be the doctor, and in the morning Berta can go for breakfast and tell everyone that Vadoma has a badly broken nose and is feeling very embarrassed and needs to be left alone until she feels better.' He paused for a short time and watched our faces, then continued, 'You two can bundle her onto the bus and from there onto the train. Once we get out of the city, we can keep her in one of the compartments and keep everyone away from her.'

I thought for a moment and then asked, 'But how do we get past the border check, and why does she need to come with us at all?'

'We will have her bandaged up and, being supported by her doctor, they won't ask us to take the bandages off and we will clue Jones up, so he can make a lot of noise if necessary.' He paused and nodded to ensure I was following him, then explained further. 'If we have the wrong number of team members, there would be an enquiry immediately and they would realise Vadoma was gone. We need to get out of the country before they cotton on. Ronja also has film footage of the atrocities and many documents – she wants to deliver them herself, first to the Australian security community and then to the United States Ambassador.'

I nodded. I could see the difficulty this would cause if we were missing a member, but I still had doubts about us carrying it off with our own team.

'Doc, you need to get your head around this. It's going to depend on you. It won't work without you,' he warned, frowning at me and I could do nothing other than nod.

Berta took my hand. 'We will make it work,' she reassured Cain and I understood she was saying that she was there with me.

The three of us left through the front left side of the doors as directed by Cain. There we were met by a man I knew to be one of Ronja's men. We followed him for a short while, though not making it obvious that we were doing so. Cain wished us luck and told me that he would bring my luggage from the men's camp the next morning. Then he merged with the crowd and was gone.

We followed the man at a distance of a few meters and only got close to him when he neared a car and opened the rear door for us. I entered first and was confronted by a heavily bandaged Ronja, or at least Vadoma as I would have to remember to call her. Berta got in and the man closed the door behind her and entered the front passenger seat.

'Do you really think this is going to work?' I asked and as we moved off.

Ronja answered, 'Only you can pull it off. We will have little or no questioning from our own, but the border may be a little harder,' she answered. She was prepared at least.

'When we arrive back at the women's camp, we will need to stay in the room Berta and Vadoma shared. Cain will take care of things at the men's and will prepare Jones for the fight,' she instructed then her eyes, between the bandages, looked me up and down and she added, 'Are you up to this?'

I nodded, perhaps trying to convince myself, then a thought came to me, 'What will happen when they find the body?' I asked.

'They won't. Two of my men were on the arena's staff and I directed them to get rid of it. It is already under way,' she reassured me.

I felt a little sick and thought of the 'it' they were getting rid of. I knew she had to be callous but 'it' had been a person. Once again I thought of the maxim – better to remain silent and be thought a fool than to speak out and remove all doubt.

The car pulled up at the camp gates and I got out and quickly walked up to the guard station at the main entrance. A young man I had not seen before sat with his feet up on the desk. I tapped on the service window and, startled, he jumped to attention. When he realised it was not one of his superiors, he slowly regained his composure and opened the door and asked, 'What do you want?'

'I am the Australian team doctor and I have an injured member of the team in the car out the front. Can you find a wheelchair?'

'Yes, well, we have one in the medical room,' he said and pointed to the room just down the hall on the opposite side.

I began to walk in that direction but he said 'halt!' in a surprisingly loud voice.

'I will need to see some identification,' he added as I turned to face him. I frowned disapprovingly and dragged my wallet out and showed my Games identity card, then I turned again and as I did, he repeated 'halt!' this time in a much less forceful voice.

I turned again and, scowling at him, I said, 'Oberführer Dirlewanger will not be delighted if I tell him you held us up!'

'Yes, er, but the room is locked. You will need the key,' he said quietly and turned to his little room and, reaching around the doorway, he retrieved the key. Handing it to me, he added, 'I'm sure the Oberführer need not know?'

I understood that the statement was rhetorical. I quickly moved to the room and recovered the chair and then, having a second thought, I went to the supply cupboard and took as many bandages as I could carry.

The young guard gave me a nod as I passed him and then asked if I would like assistance. I said that I was alright and with Berta made quite a fuss about getting Ronja/Vadoma into the chair. We began to move into the front hall and I was again confronted by the young man.

'Sorry, sir, but I will need to see the identification of the two ladies.' He sounded apologetic rather than confrontational and I only wanted to get the three of us out of view of any prying eyes.

I nodded and Berta showed the two cards. Ticking the two names off the list he had produced, he again took my identification and added my number to the bottom. We were in.

Settling in to Berta's room, Ronja was soon out of the chair and had placed a dining chair under the door handle. 'We don't need any uninvited guests,' she explained and began to unwrap the mask of bandages, revealing a perfectly undamaged face. Her hair was, however, particularly dishevelled. She went into the bathroom to straighten up and take a shower, and Berta and I got our chance to talk at last.

I sat down on the couch and motioned to her to join me which she did. Taking her hand, I spluttered in a whisper 'God, this is all too much.'

She leaned in and gave me a kiss on the cheek, then whispered, 'You know, I was kind of fond of Vadoma. Strange, isn't it? Even though I know what she was I am still a little sad that she is gone.'

'You mean dead,' I whispered back and immediately thought how callus the comment was. 'Oh, sorry,' I continued, 'It's just the shock of all of this.

Shedding a single tear, she asked, 'Did she suffer?'

'No. There was no time for that and she didn't see it coming,' I reassured her clumsily.

'I need to work on my bedside manner,' I thought as another tear tracked its way down her cheek.

We sat for a while in an embrace until Ronja came back into the room.

'It's still bleeding,' she said, waving a hand in a circular motion to solicit response.

'You poor thing,' Berta said loudly as Ronja moved around the room obviously looking for listening devices, running fingers along edges, looking under the dining table and around the large mirror, which, along with two small paintings, were the only decorations on any wall.

'I can give you some sleeping pills if you need them or some pain killers?' I stumbled over my words and she shot me a glance which seemed to say 'pull yourself together, man'.

'Yes, I think I would like to sleep,' she said and we went through the charade of me pretending to hand her some pills and her taking them.

Berta went to the cupboard and took a cup and filled it with water, and handed it to Ronja, saying, 'Here's some water.'

The pretence over, she kept searching the room until she waved a hand to bring us both to her next to the back of the main entrance door. There, where the dado rail met the doorframe, sat a very small and hard-to-notice listening device.

She pointed to the device and then whispered into Berta's ear.

Berta nodded and moved to the bathroom and returned, handing Ronja a small bottle of fingernail polish.

'Well, I think I will go to bed,' Ronja said with the accompanying circular hand motion.

'Me too, but first I'll take a shower,' Berta answered, then added, turning to me, 'Would you like a blanket from one of the beds?'

'No, no, I think I will be fine,' I answered and sat back down on the couch knowing that that is exactly where I was going to spend the night.

Ronja turned to go to the bedroom and I noticed her hair had been pulled up in to a bun under a towel. She looked quite a bit taller than usual.

Berta also left the room and I was left with my thoughts. Not a good place to be at that moment – they kept returning to the killing of Vadoma. The blood – well, really, the lack of blood, when I thought about it. I would have thought it would be a lot bloodier. What a strange thing to think; I was a doctor and I was thinking about blood, about there not being enough blood. I could see her face as she fell, that lifeless face.

'I'm so pathetic,' I thought.

Mired in my own pit of depression, eventually I fell asleep, but the dreams were no easier. People being shot and being chased and running. I felt like a little fish in a very big pond.

CHAPTER 24

I woke the next morning, though there was some doubt in my mind as to whether it was morning or if it was still the middle of the night. Certainly, there was no sunlight yet visible through the room's only light source: a small sky-light. My head ached, looking down at my watch, I could see that it displayed five o'clock. God, why would I wake so early? I switched the bedside lamp on and walked into the bathroom and prepared the shower. True, I didn't have fresh clothes to change into but I still needed a shower. I closed the door and went about my business, the hot water felt soothing and I stood for some time just letting the deluge cover my head and face.

I dressed and re-entered the main room to find Berta sitting at the table waiting for me. I sat down, obviously looking dishevelled, and feeling only a little better, she had some clothes sitting on her lap along with a brush, a tube of toothpaste and toothbrush.

Taking the brush, she started to do my hair. I didn't resist as I had not used a comb and knew how messy I must look. I reached for the toothpaste and squeezed a small amount onto a finger and ran it across my top and then bottom teeth. Swirling the strongly mint flavoured concoction around in my mouth, I realised that I had not thought things through: there was nowhere to spit the remanence.

I sat for a moment and then swallowed.

'Oh, yuck,' Berta said but did not stop brushing.

'It all goes down the drain eventually,' I said wiping my mouth with the back of my hand.

'Gross,' she exclaimed and leaned away from me to inspect the job she had done on my hair.

'You'll do,' she said, getting up to go have her own shower. 'You might want to wake Vadoma up and change her wounds,' she concluded closing the door behind her.

I walked over and tapped on the bedroom door. There was an almost immediate answer.

'I won't be a moment,' Ronja's voice said and only a few seconds later, the door opened and she stood before me, a clump of unravelled bandages in her hand. I took the bandages as she offered them and then walked back to the couch. Soon I was preparing her for the day's disguise. I used one of the unravelled bandages after rewinding it and then two more of the new ones I had purloined from the camp infirmary. I left an opening for her nose but made sure that even this was covered by a hanging edge which allowed air flow but still hid the face from any possible prying eyes.

Ronja was quite a bit shorter than Vadoma had been and so had stuffed her shoes to make herself just a little taller, and she made that preparation again with pieces of rolled up newspaper.

'If you both support me and I lean forward, no one will realise I am so short,' she mumbled and I nodded my understanding. Naturally the eyeholes I had left were looking down to where she was fixing Ronja's shoes. She stopped and looked up to see if I was agreeing with her.

'Oh, sorry. Yes, I will get everyone to stay at a distance,' I said. 'I will spread the word, at breakfast. If you stay here we can bring you back some food.'

'Just a couple of bananas. They would be easy to mash, if I needed them to be mashed.' She seemed to think of everything way before I did.

Re-entering the room, Berta smiled at us on our seat. 'You've already got it done then?'

'Yes, and I thought it best that I wear these clothes,' she answered, generally waving both hands toward the sides of her body to indicate the said clothes. Everything had come from Vadoma's wardrobe and though the lack of size would reveal that they were certainly too large for the wearer, she had chosen the tightest-fitting and darkest clothes available, knowing that if anyone was looking at her, she would be either be in the wheelchair, leaning on both Berta and I or sitting on the bus.

It was now around 6am and knowing that the eatery would be opening, Berta and I began to walk out the door to eat. As we left the room, we noticed a guard at the end of the hall and he noticed us.

Berta halted a moment and then whispered, 'Bring back some food. I better stay here.'

I nodded and then she added loudly, 'Damn, I've forgotten something. I will follow you down.'

'Okay,' I answered, understanding what she meant, and continued as she ducked back into the room. I wandered down the ten yards of the hall and the guard gave me a smug, somewhat sly look as if to indicate something inappropriate had taken place. I wanted to say something, feeling a little indignant, but I thought better of it and just nodded indifferently in his direction.

As I neared the food hall, I was met by Jones. 'What the hell is going on?' he demanded, taking my arm. I could tell he had been waiting to see me and that he was quite worked up. This was not his usual demeanour and it betrayed the usually calm exterior he showed to the world.

I took his arm and gently led him to the far side of the hall, 'Keep your cool, things have happened,' I answered, knowing that the likelihood of some listening device in the hallway was fairly unlikely.

'I bloody know that is Miss Vadoma, alright?' he said.

'Well, no, not at all,' I answered and on seeing just the surprise in his eyes, I continued, 'You knew we were here for other things that the Games?' I asked rhetorically.

He nodded. 'We found out that both Vadoma and Jake are German spies who were put in place to ensure we would not complete our mission.' His eyes widened and he glanced around to make sure we were alone.

I leaned in to him and whispered, 'She is dead. She tried to kill me and Ronja shot her.' I paused – it was obvious that, though he had seen action in previous conflicts, was a situation he understood and had prepared for.

'This is about life and death now,' I added.

'Well, the Germans will know and it will be out and how do you hope to defend your actions?' he demanded, though this time he whispered.

'No, we have a replacement and the body has been disposed of.' Again, I paused and could see he was having trouble understanding what I was saying.

'Look, we have Ronja in Berta's room and she is acting the part of Vadoma. We have floated the story that she had a fall when drunk and she has bandages covering her face. Also Weathers and Cain had Jake really drunk; I'm not sure what they had in mind'

'Yes, they have drugged him with sleeping pills. I saw them all this morning at our camp,' he answered then added, 'I can't believe you think this is going to work.'

'Well, surely they won't ask to see Vadoma's face if she is with a doctor. I don't know what we can do with Jake but we certainly can't let him loose. He would report to Dirlewanger and we would be undone,' I answered.

'Bloody troublemakers, the lot of you,' he said, sounding more put out that he may have to lie about something than there being a dead person.

'We are here to show to the world what this bastard is doing to the Roma and the Sinti and the handicapped,' I said angrily then got hold of myself, knowing that I needed this man. If I insulted him, he may wash his hands of the whole affair. 'I'm sorry I didn't mean to take it out on you. I am just a beginner at all of this.'

'Yes, well, what do they expect? Sending a lot of amateurs in to do work that people like me should be doing, bloody ridiculous,' he blurted indignantly.

'I'm sorry. Perhaps that is why you were selected to be on the team's management,' I said, unwittingly sowing the seeds of doubt in his mind. His face hanged; he was thinking.

'Could we, arrr, get Jake taken away by this resistance group?' he asked, then thinking further. 'No, no they would be noticed if they contacted us. Let me think.'

'How long could you keep him senseless?' he asked, looking up and to his left, as though searching for some inspiration from on high. I wasn't sure he was even including me in his thoughts.

'It is always dangerous to drug people for any length of time, but it can be done. I have some strong hallucinogens in my bag. I could just keep him on the edge,' I answered.

'Yes, yes, that seems the best thing to try. Now, you haven't said how you know that they are both spies, and what this is all about,' he said as an instruction rather than a query.

'I followed Vadoma to a secret meeting with Dirlewanger at the stadium and I could hear them – all three of them, as Jake was with them,' I answered and as he prepared to ask his next question, I added, 'Their meeting broke. I was hiding behind a garbage trolley which was under the stairs nearby. I heard the three of them pass, one at a time, going back to the public areas of the arena and after a few moments I came out of hiding and was confronted by a mad woman with a knife. I had never seen her like that. She was unhinged.'

His eyes widened and he looked shocked.

'Then just as she was going to bump me off, she fell – the thud of a bullet hitting her from a silenced gun. I had met Ronja early in the night and she must have seen me entering the service corridor and came to see what I was doing. Bloody hell – the shock, the blood. I was dumbfounded. She had to push me around to get me to help with the body and she took Vadoma's uniform so the body would not be easy to identify. Then she sent me to the stand to find the others and keep up the pretence that nothing had happened.' I was babbling now, everything filling one sentence, a droning monologue, which surprisingly he seemed to be understanding.

Nodding slowly, he put one hand on my shoulder. 'Pull yourself together, man,' he said quietly, and I could tell that he was not being aggressive with the comment, he was being supportive.

'I'm alright, it's just the shock of it all,' I reassured.

He nodded. 'Let's eat. We will need every bit of strength we can muster today,' he said and turned my shoulder toward the dining room entrance. I followed him.

On arriving back at Berta's room, I knocked quietly and Jones and I entered. Berta, having opened the door, greeted Jones with a nod.

'Good morning,' he said and then added, 'Where is she?'

Berta walked to the bathroom door and knocked. Ronja, understanding that she was safe, entered, looking like a mummy from some long-lost tomb of Egypt.

'What are you planning to do?' Jones asked, completely dispensing with the niceties, as was his way.

'Good morning to you too,' she answered. It was difficult to gain much of her demeanour without facial expressions, but he seemed to understand the rebuke.

'Oh, yes, good morning,' he answered.

'None of this was supposed to happen, but Robert here was not able to defend himself,' she explained and then quickly added, 'I had no alternative and thought the only thing to do was taking her place.'

'Bloody amateurs. Should never have happened if professionals had been used,' Jones blustered.

'Well, we don't have that luxury, do we?' Ronja fired back.

'No, no, I suppose not,' he mumbled uncertainly.

'Our pleas for help have fallen on deaf ears. No country has come to help us, so we have learned to help ourselves.' The bandages muffled her voice but did nothing to hide her contempt.

It was obvious that he felt the jibe deeply. He nodded, looking down, thinking for the right words. 'Well, everyone knows what this lot are – bastards, but no one is able or, it seems, bold enough to do anything about them,' he said.

'You can do something about it. I have film footage, photographs and recordings of victim statements. I have lists of the perpetrators, the infiltrators and of our people who are in the middle of their apparatus. You must help us,' she almost ordered.

Jones, not a man to be told what to do, stood, looking at her but said nothing.

'Will you help us?' I pleaded.

'You are all part of my Olympic team. My duty is to defend you, and your evidence will be presented to the Government once back in Australia, I guarantee that,' he said in his most stately voice, the last part of the sentence directed to Ronja.

Ronja nodded back at him and once again my doubts surfaced – she looked like some kind of puppet in her bandages. This would never fly. We wouldn't get past the first border crossing.

Oh God, what the hell was I doing in the middle of this?

CHAPTER 25

The time grew near to our departure. I sat quietly with the two women in their room; Berta was holding my hand. I was startled and jumped when the loud rap on door came, even though it had been expected.

Jones had seen most of the women's team board the bus. He had given a lecture to all not to approach Vadoma as she was too upset to talk to anyone and he had stowed his own luggage in the appropriate area at the rear of the vehicle. Now he had come to escort us to board.

Berta supported Vadoma/Ronja, holding her arm and Ronja played the part, keeping her head down and staggering a little as she came in sight of the team members. I carried their baggage and quickly stowed it and helped the driver to close the rear door.

Jones had positioned himself in the front seat on the passenger side of the bus, had placed Berta and Ronja in the seat directly behind him and pointed to the seat behind that, indicating that he wanted me to sit there. To be as protected as possible, Ronja was seated at the window with Berta on the aisle.

Soon we were on our way to pick up the men at our camp and I became a little less apprehensive. No one had challenged us in any way. Really, no one showed the slightest interest in the team and it was obvious that the camp staff I did see looked delighted to see the back of us.

On our arrival at the men's camp, Jones alighted the bus quickly and entered the main gateway building. I thought it safe enough to also exit, though I did not enter the buildings.

When Jones returned, he was alongside Cain and Best, who stepped to either side of the main doorway. Members of the team then filed out all loaded with their own luggage and that of Best and Cain and I also noticed that Nesbitt was carrying my large bag and with some difficulty, my medical case.

Nesbitt took a moment and placed the luggage on the ground to shake my hand. I was a little surprised but realised as our palms met that he was actually surreptitiously handing me a note.

As I loaded my bag, I glanced at it. 'Dirlewanger is in the gatehouse. Need a diversion to allow us to load Jake.'

I whispered 'okay', crumpled the paper and stuffed it into my pocket. Not sure what was needed, I went to the building and there found Jones in a fairly amiable discussion with the Nazi.

'Ah yes, Mr *O'Calahan*, come to thank us for our hospitality, no doubt?' he said sarcastically and deliberately stumbled over my surname.

'I wouldn't think there was much to thank you for, *Dirlewanger*,' I answered, meeting his surliness with my own. I positioned myself so to look at me, he was turned away from the loading passengers and Cain, seeing this, waved two of his men to bring the barely stumbling Jake through to load.

'I would have thought you would be grateful for our hospitality,' he said sarcastically.

'If this is what you call hospitality,' I said pointedly and then, seeing Jake and his entourage had loaded, I placed a hand on Jones' shoulder and began to leave.

He took my lead and followed me out of the gatehouse with the self-centred pig of a man looking on with that stupid smile.

On gaining my seat, Jones signalled for the door to be closed and he began a count.

He sat down when satisfied all numbers were correct.

As our bus departed, a feeling of relief washed over me. It was to be premature as suddenly Best arrived at the side of my seat and demanded, 'What the hell is your game?'

I paused for a moment and then answered, 'What do you mean?'

I answered in quieter tones than he had used.

'Bloody cheek,' he said even louder and stood with hands on both hips.

I prepared myself for a reply, but to no avail as Jones stood and motioning to his seat. He said, 'Sit down, Best!'

This was not a request, and before Best could reply Jones followed up with, 'I said *sit down.*'

Like a chastened school boy, Best sat and Jones in turn sat next to him.

I stood and moved to the stairwell in front of them and turned to look Best in the eye, but before I could say anything, Jones said, 'All of this is above your pay scale.'

He removed his wallet from his blazer pocket and flashed a security card. This was something I had not seen before and I was surprised that he was still an active operative.

'O'Calahan here is undercover. You need to speak quietly.' He paused, perhaps expecting Best to say something, but no reply came. Best just looked dumbfounded.

'You need to be told nothing, and you certainly need to keep out of his way,' Jones said in little more than a whisper and nodded to me.

'But the woman—' he began but his query was stifled by the raising of Jones' hand.

'You will do as you are told and you will leave Miss Codona's care to O'Calahan, am I understood?' he ordered and pointedly nodded raising his eyebrows as if he was soliciting a reply. Best nodded.

'You will also notice that Mr Pankhurst is being silenced. He is not part of the team and is being chemically muted. This I will leave in your hands. He must not be able to speak as we go through the border or when we board the train or ship. Can you do that?' he concluded and I must admit I was impressed with his strength of purpose.

Best nodded then turned to me and asked, 'What have you given him?'

'Nothing. I was not present, but Cain and his men gave him some sleeping pills with quite a lot of grog,' I answered.

'Oh, that is not very good. It's quite dangerous,' he blurted, staring at Jones.

'He is expendable, do you understand?' Jones said, his authority seeming unquestionable and Best nodded, wide-eyed.

Jones didn't give him another moment but rose and nodded sideways to indicate that Best was dismissed. He got to his feet and slunk away like a dog with its tail between its legs. I was at least somewhat pleased and smiled at Jones. He did not smile back but in turn gave me the same dismissal.

I returned to my seat and Berta turned and asked, 'Is everything alright?'

I nodded and gave her a little smile. She beamed back at me. It almost seemed that she was enjoying the intrigue. I wasn't, and I felt a churning in my stomach which just wouldn't go away – the beginning of a self-diagnosed ulcer, no doubt.

About 30 minutes saw us close to the railway station. Several extra platforms had been constructed expressly to accommodate 'the foreigners'.

Our train was the second on the list to depart and we quickly readied ourselves for leaving the bus and porters met us and transported our luggage to the train on large flatbed trollies. I moved to the back of the bus and gathered my medical bag; I knew I would need it at some stage. Best had had the same idea and we stood next to each other at the back of the vehicle. He looked at me as if he were going to say something, then thinking better of it, he retrieved his bag and pushed past me on his way to assist with the unloading of Jake.

I walked back to the front door and assisted first Ronja and then Berta to disembark. Ronja clutched a small bag tightly to her and I understood why.

German porters were everywhere. They had been well tutored in the handling of people if not the handling of luggage which seemed to be of secondary importance as they threw bags one on top of another uncaringly.

It seemed as though we were being herded toward the train, and though these men were not part of the army, the operation was conducted with the ominous shadows of many a well-armed soldier at the perimeters.

The train we boarded was even more luxurious than the one we had arrived on and we were conducted to four and six berth compartments. Best took the first four-person one and shepherded Berta, who was supporting Ronja, and myself inside.

He was obviously intending to be our number four, but he went about his business loading the next room with Jake, who was practically carried onboard, and Cain, Nesbitt, Weathers, Peter and Best. After these people were right where he wanted them, he seemed to lose interest and moved the waiting throng, giving each a small push from our compartment door.

'Is everyone alright?' he asked and on received affirmation from the three of us, he moved down the carriage behind the last team member.

'Oh, I thought we would never get through that crowd,' Berta said, giving a little pant to express her relief.

'I got a little attention from one of the soldiers. He seemed interested in a person whose face was covered. Did you see him? He started toward us and was run into by a woman and man,' she asked.

'I saw the woman knocked over and the German being all

apologetic. But I didn't notice him before that,' I answered.

'That was lucky then,' Berta said and whistled, indicating how close it may have been.

'No luck at all. They were just two of the seven of my people I saw at the station. The first of the porters was one of mine,' Ronja answered and Berta gave another whistle.

'Wow, your people really know what they're doing,' Berta commented.

'When you have been so badly treated as a people for so long, you learn how to make some things happen.' She paused for a moment then added, 'The day we first met and you protected me from Dirlewanger and his men, there were three of my people with guns ready to react. They backed off when you intervened.'

Berta and I looked at each other surprised, wide-eyed.

'You stopped a bloodbath that day,' she added.

'Typical of me to blunder into a gunfight without even giving it a second thought,' I admitted, feeling a bit of a fool.

'Not at all, I thought you quite chivalrous,' Ronja answered.

'Yes, me too,' Berta added, sitting down in a window seat. Ronja took the seat opposite facing her.

'Not chivalrous at all, but I couldn't just stand there while a man hit a woman,' I said, remembering how that bastard had struck the seemingly helpless Ronja.

'The very meaning of chivalrous,' Ronja answered.

'And bravery,' Berta added.

'Bravery – well, I haven't acted very bravely since,' I said, feeling a bit foolish for enjoying the praise.

Once I was onboard, I found my seat next to Berta and she gave me a little kiss on the cheek. I could feel the blushing of my cheeks. I loved it though; nothing could spoil my mood with her by my side.

It took Jones about another ten minutes until he was satisfied that all of our team were where they could be found as needed and then he returned and closed our door and sat down opposite me.

'All in order,' he commented and I took it to be a rhetorical statement. Berta, on the other hand, thought it to be the beginning of a conversation.

'Good, how are they doing with Jake?' she asked.

'Well under control,' he stated. Obviously he had no intention of reporting his actions to anyone. 'The next hurdle is the border crossing. If we get through that we are pretty much home,' he stated, removing his blazer and rolling it up to use as a pillow. 'Better get some sleep. It will be harrowing to get through unscathed.'

He placed the makeshift pillow against the compartment wall and put his head against it to keep it in place and closed his eyes. This was an instruction – not very subtle but we all understood the action.

It was a long train journey and it seemed all the longer now that things were so tense. I dozed eventually and, not knowing how long I had been out of things, I started as the clattering carriage came to a halt. On opening my eyes, I noticed that Jones was gone and the compartment door was open. I could hear raised voices on the platform, which I could hardly see through the windows as the low sun hit each from its low angle.

There were people moving and a platform sign, which I couldn't make out. I heard the door we had entered through thrust open and muffled voices. After a few moments, I could hear Jones say forcefully, 'Show me to your commanding officer!' and then loudly complaining as he was led across the platform to a building.

I understood why he was being so loud. He was warning us that we had reached the border. I stood and moved to the door. Sticking my head out, I looked left then right and saw Cain at the next door doing the same.

'Here we go!' he said and I nodded.

Several minutes passed and eventually Jones came around, followed by three serious-looking soldiers.

'I have shown these men all of our passports but they still demand to see every passenger,' Jones said.

I glanced back into the compartment Berta was sitting with her handbag opened on her lap and Ronja was moving the less tight part of her face bandage and I saw her place something into her mouth.

Pushing past Jones, the officer among the soldiers confronted me and told me to step aside.

In German, I protested. 'This woman is very badly injured and can't be disturbed.'

He glared at me and raised one eyebrow, then pushed me out of the way and entered.

My first thought was that Vadoma must have been discovered and now the bastards were coming for Ronja.

The man demanded Berta's papers and, holding one of the many passports his second-in-charge held, he compared her to it and nodded. Turning to me, he held the passport handed to him and stumbled over the name O'Calahan then nodded again.

Now, he moved to Ronja and turned back to me. He demanded, 'Show her face.'

'She is Vadoma Codona. She has been very badly injured and the bandages may not be removed,' I said and coming from the door, Jones attempted to intervene but was simply pushed aside.

'I am ordered to see every passenger,' the officious cur said and moved toward Ronja.

I was in the best position to step in front of him and as I did, I shouted, 'I am her doctor and she must not be interfered with!'

The third of the soldiers with gun drawn pushed me into my seat. I resisted, and tried to get back up, I was met by his revolver. There was nothing I could do.

Jones was shouting threats about how the man would be in great trouble with his superiors for this terrible affront. Surprisingly, my German was better than his and I could hear how much he was struggling with the words.

The officer knelt on one knee in front of Ronja and she retreated with her upper body until she could move no more. He took one side of the bandages and began to pull at them somewhat carelessly.

The first tie gave way and the bandage came loose and revealed Ronja's lips. Suddenly a mouthful of blood burst from her lips and as she coughed, an amount sprayed onto the German. His revulsion was evident and he smeared his face with his first attempts to rid himself of the blood.

I took the opportunity to get up and push them both aside. 'My God, what have you done?' I roared as I replaced the bandage over her lips. 'If you have ruptured the stiches – you will pay for this, you bloody fool!'

He regained his composure a little as he stood and took a handkerchief from his pocket and wiped his face.

'I was simply trying to do my duty,' he said uncertainly.

'Get out, you bloody fool. Berta, please get my bag,' I spoke urgently and Berta got up and rushed to get my bag down from the baggage rack. I held the bandage to Ronja's mouth and some of the blood oozed over my fingers.

'What do you need, doctor?' she asked.

'Some gauze pads,' I answered hurriedly and then, changing my mind. 'No, there is too much blood. Give me that hand towel.'

As Berta and I played at doctors and nurses, Jones took up the cudgel and roared furiously at the man in both poor German and loud, if not rude, English. 'I will have your stripes for this. Good God man, I will complain to the Olympics committee. Bloody fool, this is an international outrage.'

The German backed away. No doubt he was shocked but he didn't look as intimidated as Jones had expected.

I had a thought and wheeled around and said, 'Jones, this is outrageous. Demand to be taken to a phone and ring your friend Oberführer Dirlewanger, he will deal with this fool!'

Jones caught on immediately and, placing his finger in the middle of the man's chest, he demanded, 'Take me to a phone.'

The desired effect was evident on the young officer's face. It was obvious that he, like most Germans, knew the reputation of Dirlewanger.

Backing to the door of the compartment, he stammered, 'I'm sure that is not necessary. My apologies,' and he disappeared and headed toward the next compartment.

Jones was not one to miss an opportunity and he rushed after the man. I heard him say, 'How dare you walk away from me …'

He continued to rant but the words from that point became inaudible.

We could still hear raised voices and I think the man felt that discretion was the better part of valour and left his men to count the rest of the team. He quickly retreated from the carriage with Jones in pursuit, his loud haranguing continued out of the carriage.

Soon, the rest of the team had been accounted for and the soldiers dismounted. Jones had to hurry as the train was waved off and started to move.

I had hovered around Ronja, pretending to move bandages so the lie seemed credible. As we began to move, I sat down, letting out a whistle and said, 'God, that was close.'

Ronja lifted the bandage at her mouth and spat a small package into one of her hands. It became evident that, seeing the troupers entering the train, she had taken a fake blood pack. Berta handed her the towel she had used as a soak and cleaned the small portion of her face which could be seen.

'I hope that is the last I see of those terrible Germans,' Berta said and then realising her faux pas, she quickly added, 'The soldiers, I mean.'

'None taken,' said Ronja, and even though her face was covered I could tell she was smiling. I could also see that her hands were trembling.

When Jones came back into the cabin, he looked very pleased with himself. Ronja blurted out a strained appreciation in English.

'All in a day's work,' he answered, smiling broadly. He always seemed to resort to a glib saying when basking in praise.

Taking up station at the door, he said, 'Now we just need to get on that bloody ship.'

CHAPTER 26

Many times, during the walk from the train to the bus which was to take us to the ship, we saw Italian soldiers and several times German ones, and thought they all gave Ronja a second look due to her strange look, none interfered with our progress.

Boarding was also a simple thing: a single purser was stationed at the top of the gangway and was simply counting passengers in a very broad Mancunian accent. He didn't even comment when Ronja passed with Berta and I supported her. In fact, he only made one comment and that was when Weathers and Cain, followed by us, virtually dragged Jake aboard.

'What's all this?' he demanded, stepping between both groups.

'Can't hold his grog,' answered Weathers and pushed past the purser, not wanting to have any other questions asked.

Jones was quickly on hand to change the subject by asking, 'What is your name, man?'

The man turned away from the struggling threesome and looked to where the Jones' comment had come.

'There is no need to worry about the team. Everyone is very tired and some worse for wear, but they are all here,' Jones instructed.

The man gave a little shrug of his shoulders, remembering Jones's long windedness from the journey over, nodded and went back to counting heads.

We had made it. We were safe. I couldn't believe how lucky we had been.

Behind us, the New Zealand team began to board and I noticed several soldiers on the dock. They were heavily armed. They formed a row, all facing the ship, and it was then that I could see that there were six of them. They were in a uniform I had never seen before and I could not even have said what nationality they were.

They made no movement toward the ship or the boarding passengers. I was relieved but then I thought what a pointless exercise, a show of some sort of superiority, some fascist display meant to show the world who they were dealing with. My skin crawled and I was on edge, at least until the ship pulled away from the quay.

We stayed on deck, Berta and I, while the rest of our party, led by Jones, arranged and rearranged cabins to suit our changed retinue.

There was some cheering from another national team who were waiting to board their ship home. I could not tell which country they were from, or perhaps I was more interested in the company I was with – either way I spent no time waving. We were away.

Jones had relinquished his cabin in favour of Berta, Ronja and I. It was the only cabin which had two rooms – a bedroom and a large lounge/dining area. This would have usually been reserved for the most regal of dignitaries.

My luggage had been placed on the table near a lounge which was meant to be my berth for the trip. It was only just large enough to accommodate me if I were in the foetal position.

'You need to be nearby, if things kick off,' Jones had said as he pointed to the bags. 'You will need to keep the pretence up throughout,' he added, pointing again, to Ronja.

I nodded. I was not delighted and knew that my sleeping arrangements were going to be less than perfect, but I was close to Berta, so it couldn't be more perfect.

Jones left us and the two women retired to their room. We were all exhausted. It had not been a particularly long trip but it was as stressful.

I tried to position myself with any amount of comfort but it was impossible. If I lay stretched out with my legs over the arm of the couch, my lower hip was immediately over stretched and uncomfortable and laying on my back with both legs over the arm was not even a little uncomfortable. I had never been able to sleep on my back. I tried the foetal position but my knees and much of my upper legs hung over the edge, and I would have, no doubt, fallen off in the middle of the night.

I bit the bullet and, placing the one blanket I had on the floor, I lay down and was soon sound asleep.

Some hours had passed before a loud knocking wakened me and I sat up. The knock came again but before I could move Berta had entered and unlocked and opened the cabin door. Standing there were Jones and Best.

'Please come in,' she said in a somewhat redundant way as the two had already passed her.

'Best says that it is unsafe to keep the bastard drugged now we are on the ship,' Jones blurted and as I got up off the floor, he went on. 'I told him it doesn't matter as he is only a spy, but—'

Best interrupted. 'Ridiculous, of course it bloody matters. You can't just go around killing people.'

It was obvious that this argument had been going on for some time. They were both red in the face and looked flustered.

'Well?' Jones said and glared at me over his glasses as if I would settle the argument.

'Well, what Best says is true. It is dangerous,' I answered, but seeing the look on Jones' face, I added, 'Jones is in charge of things and I will be guided by what he says.'

'Do no harm, do no bloody harm!' Best said and directed his vehemence at me.

'Yes, yes, I know, but he is an enemy and how would we keep him silent if we don't have him, well, drugged?' I asked, knowing how feeble and undecided I sounded.

'I won't bloody do it. Do you hear me? I won't bloody do it,' Best said, raising his voice to a volume where people several cabins in each direction would have heard him.

'I don't think I have the knowledge to keep him out of things for very long and it is a long trip,' I admitted to them both as a way of trying to calm both of their tempers. It had the opposite effect, both turned their backs on me and faced each other down angrily.

'Gentlemen, you need to lower your voices or get out,' Berta said, stepping between them. They both showed surprise at being spoken to like two small school boys, and for a moment they remained silent.

'Sorry Miss, but this does not concern you,' Jones said and continued to glare at Best over his glasses which had become steamed up due to his excitement.

'Well, if it doesn't concern me, you may both leave my room,' Berta answered strongly, and God I admired her more than ever.

The two combatants were silenced, then Jones said in an apologetic tone, 'Oh, yes, sorry. We must not be so rude.' He continued to glare at Best.

Best glared back and it was evident that the argument was far from over.

There was a short silence and then Best turned and exiting the cabin, said, 'I won't bloody do it!' and was gone.

Jones, obviously not expecting this, was silent for a few moments. He was not used to people not doing what he said.

'Well, give me an alternative?' he finally uttered, turning to me.

'Perhaps we could post a guard with him?' I proffered.

I didn't think this was a workable thing on a ship of this size. If he were to yell out, people would hear and come to his aid.

'If you are determined, I will go and get Cain. He would be best placed to keep him under lock and key.' It was obvious he was thinking things through as he spoke, and when he finished, he walked out without soliciting any further comment from me.

'Please, come again,' Berta said sarcastically as she closed the door and Jones' voice, though muffled, could be heard to say 'get out of my way' to some unsuspecting passer-by.

Berta and I were joined by Ronja, and I began to re-apply her bandages. Those I removed I placed into a paper bag which the new bandages had been taken from. This was to be washed with some urgency as these were the last taken from the camp infirmary.

As I completed the shroud and Ronja became Vadoma, the cabin door was once again under assault. Berta came from her room and opened the door after assuring herself that the visitors were Jones and Cain.

'Your idea. You tell him,' Jones said abruptly.

'Morning, Cain,' I said and then began to inform him about the earlier discussions.

When I concluded, he said, 'We can put him under guard, but it will be hard to keep him quiet.'

Moving to the bathroom door, he surveyed it and then the bedroom. 'If we were to move him to this room there would only be the one cabin next to his. So, I mean, swap your cabins around and keep at least one guard on him all the time. We could tie his hands but this would be hard to maintain for days on end,' he explained, then gaining no affirmation from any of us, he added, 'Do you get what I'm saying?'

'Yes, you're saying it can't be done,' Jones said bluntly.

'No, no, it can be done and if we have to, we will do it, but it won't be easy. It will take a huge effort from my men and that may not be enough. We may have to use Weathers and Nagel and even yourselves to do it twenty-four hours a day all the way back to Australia,' he explained.

'Well, it seems as though you are all going to be on duty for most of the trip. I will make some excuse to the captain and our purser as to Pankhurst's malady,' Jones said and as he turned, he added, 'Don't cock it up.' Then, as he was facing Berta, he concluded with a mumbled 'oh, excuse my language.'

He left and went to the next cabin to arrange the transfer.

Berta came to my side and said in a doubting tone, 'He could be dangerous once he knows what is going on.'

'That's very much the case. We will have to keep our wits about us,' Cain answered.

Ronja, who had sat quietly through all of the discussions until now, spoke, 'I want to be there when he is *enlightened* about his position.'

Neither I nor Cain could think of anything to say in answer and Berta, recognising that, said, 'You should maintain your disguise. He may be dangerous,'

'I could take care of him if I need to,' Ronja answered and none of us doubted her sincerity. After all, she had shown no compunction in disposing of Vadoma when the necessity arose.

Cain just nodded in her direction. He must have felt as I did, that she was not a woman to be easily dissuaded about anything.

The women both gathered their belongings as I did and soon the transfer was under way. Jake was carried in and placed in the room where Ronja and Berta had slept. He was still out cold and was accompanied by Best.

'He's your problem when he wakes up,' Best said in his usual surly tone.

I just raised my eyebrows. I was totally over his condescending attitude and the way he treated everyone.

'Yes, well, if you can't handle it, I will step in,' I said in as dismissive a voice as I could muster.

He sneered at me and then turned but as he was passing through the door, I heard him say in no way disguising his distaste, 'Bloody cheek.'

I felt as though I had finally got the better of him at his own game and from then on, I found myself standing up to blusterous bullies if challenged.

Food service had been arranged by Jones and our waiter delivered a large three-tiered trolley, absolutely packed.

Berta and I ate heartily. Ronja, on the other hand, had a small bowl of something which I would call bird seed and a cup of tea. We each drank our hot tea together and though there was little conversation, I think we were all happy. I am sure Ronja was feeling a loss of sorts having to leave her place of birth and indeed her leading role in the resistance to the bloody-minded Nazis.

We sat for some time quietly and soon the door was knocked again. This time Nesbitt had come to fetch me to come with him the interview of the awakening Jake.

In a semi-recumbent position as I entered the room, Jake snarled at me indignantly. 'What the hell is this all about?'

He looked unwell and uncertain.

'You can drop the charade now. I followed you to your rendezvous with Dirlewanger.'

His face turned even whiter, and though it seemed he decided to tough out the story he had been peddling to us all along, the guilt was evident in his eyes.

'I don't know what you mean?' he muttered back at me.

'Oh, I think you have an idea. Vadoma certainly knows what I am talking about,' I said sealing my gaze on his ever-paling face.

He knew the ride was over but he still wasn't sure where his stop was.

'What has she to do with it?' he asked, knowing I had exposed him.

'Well, nothing now,' I answered, not wishing to tell him any further information on Vadoma.

'Where am I being taken to?' he fired back, almost dismissing the defence he had conducted and then added 'I demand to see whoever is in charge.'

'For all your needs I am in charge of you until you are handed over to the Australian intelligence community, and you can think yourself lucky that you will be at least alive.' I wanted to sound as though I was truly in charge but he didn't buy it for a minute.

'Ha, you in charge. That's rich.' He scoffed.

'Well he's not the one in chains.' Nesbitt scowled back and I could see that he was annoyed that Jake would try to continue the charade.

'You will be charged with crimes against Australia and you may be hanged,' I said with a completely blank face.

'Germany will protest. It will never happen,' he answered. His bearing seemed to change and he assumed an air of superiority.

Now it was easier for me; I realised that I really didn't like this man or feel sorry for him anymore.

'Oh, but you are an Australian citizen. The Germans will have no part to play,' I said and sounded even more surly than I intended.

'I am a German. I have never renounced my heritage or the heritage of my country,' he said proudly.

'That's not what your passport says,' I fired back at him and was not at all surprised that he tried to jump up and take a swing at me but his efforts were negated as his legs were also tied.

'You will pay for this.' He snarled like a junk yard dog on a leash.

'Perhaps, but that won't help you,' I said curtly and turned my back and walked out, followed by Nesbitt.

'You handled that pretty well,' he said as he closed the door behind him, then added, 'I am to stay with him for the first watch. Cain is preparing a roster of who will be with him and he said he will bring it to you when he has finished.'

'Thanks,' I said and wandered back to our cabin. I knew that Cain would have things in hand and with Jones covering the possible backlash from the captain regarding the room changes or the isolation of our two prisoners, I felt more confident than I had for some weeks.

ဢ

It was near to mid-day before Cain paid me a visit and he came with Jones and Peter. Answering the door, I let them in and both Berta and Ronja stood to leave the room.

'Ladies, I'm sorry to put you out, but there is a lot of work to do.' Jones apologised and dipped his cap even though he wasn't wearing one.

'I assure you *we* are both capable of anything you are,' Ronja said in poor English and sounding a little peeved, but they both crossed and entered their room.

'Damnable cheek, it's getting hard to know who are the men and who are the women,' he said in an exasperated but quiet voice.

I could see no point in arguing with him – he was of the old guard, and though I knew what Ronja said was correct, I also knew that he was in no way interested in what I thought.

I saw Cain smile at Peter and I thought they were both probably thinking the same thing.

'You attended to him this morning?' Jones questioned.

'Jake? Yes, I saw him,' I answered

'What do you think? Can he be kept safe, quiet?' he stumbled over the word 'safe' and cleared his throat before repeating, 'quiet?'

'I am not really the person you should ask for that kind of information,' I answered and gave a little nod to Cain.

'Well?' Jones asked, turning to face Cain.

'Obviously the answer is no,' Cain answered, then seeing the displeasure on Jones' face, he added, 'Nothing short of a bullet will keep him quiet, but I don't think he will escape easily,'

'What do you mean exactly?' Jones pushed.

'I'm sure that he will not remain quiet if he knows there is someone nearby who may help him,' Cain answered quietly and calmly.

'Yes, that is what I thought,' pondered Jones and turned his gaze back to me, as if looking for a solution.

'We could report to the captain that, ah, he has had a breakdown due to over indulgence in alcohol and his failing to medal at the games. That would give us a cover story in case he is overheard by someone – you know, shouting.' I was surprised at the idea as it came out of my own mouth. I hadn't really thought it through and it developed as I aired it.

'Just so we can lay it on thick, tell him that it needs to be hushed up so the team will not be shamed,' Jones said in his usual way, making one feel as though it were his idea all the time.

'I'll go with you to see the captain,' Cain suggested.

'No, I think it should be the doctor, in case there is a need to sprout some medical mumbo-jumbo,' Jones said, looking to me.

I nodded and Cain responded the same way.

Jones seemed to have a talent for knowing where everyone was at all times and he led us to the bridge. The captain was giving out instructions and his last words were of interest to everyone.

'Keep an eye on the other ship,' he ordered. Then, noticing that we had entered his wheel-house, he muttered, 'May I help you gentlemen?'

'Yes, indeed, we need to speak to you and your head purser in private,' Jones answered. He sounded as though he was giving an order as he often did, and the visual effect on the captain was obvious. He was incensed.

'I'm trying to run a ship here,' he said as he glowered back at us.

Jones stepped forward, taking some identification from his pocket and flashed it in the captain's face. The man glanced at it and gave a begrudging nod, then he signalled to the purser to follow and the four of us left the bridge and followed the captain to his cabin.

I marvelled at the lack of grandeur of his rooms, looking little better than the smallest of rooms one would have expected to be his home.

He noticed me looking around.

'Yes, I'm here to work. Not have some pleasure cruise,' he said.

A small table stood to where a couch may have been expected to be, and he quickly ushered us to it and all four of us sat.

'What the hell do you lot want?' he asked, obviously not impressed with us taking up his time.

'We have a man on board named, er, Jake Pankhurst. He has been placed into my cabin,' Jones said, looking to the purser questioningly.

'Why yes, sir, I was informed,' the man answered.

'He took too much alcohol and he's around the bend,' Jones informed the two men, who looked at each other and then to me for some form of conformation.

'Yes, he was so drunk that I think he had alcoholic poisoning. He was found unconscious and when we revived him, he became paranoid, very unstable, one minute lucid the next ranting like a man possessed,' I answered, then seeing the look of incredulity on both of their faces, I added, 'I think it has caused brain damage, and I can't tell if it will be permanent or not.'

'So, what do you want from us?' the captain asked, spreading his hands upturned in a questioning gesture. He thought for a while then added, 'I could send for the ship's doctor. He is just a regular doctor, wouldn't know much about brain damage, I wouldn't think, though,' he offered.

'Oh no, nothing like that,' Jones answered and then continued quickly, 'Sometimes he is shouting and we were just letting you know that he is not right. Sometimes it sounds like he is being tortured or something.'

The captain raised his eyebrows but said nothing and Jones continued, 'I have given up my room with the intent that he will not bother other passengers. This would be such a terrible scandal if it got out, you know, one of ours being such a bad loser, and drinking to excess.'

Jones was babbling, and I wasn't sure the captain was believing everything he was saying, but after a few moments where he was possibly trying to see how this could affect his own status, he said, 'As long as it doesn't upset the other passengers, it is none of my business. Why did you want to see the purser?'

'Meals will need to be sent down to his cabin and there will be at least two people with him during the day and one at night,' Jones said turning to the purser, but before he could answer, the captain asked, 'Is he dangerous?'

'No, not to others but we fear he will take his own life if he were to get out,' I answered, not feeling particularly good about lying to anyone.

Both ship's officers seemed to take it all in their stride, and we turned to leave but the captain, suddenly remembering, asked, 'Oh, one thing, Jones. We are being followed by a frigate. It looks British – a bit hard to tell. She is staying just in sight of us, but displays no flags. We have been sending radio messages since early this morning but no one answers. Do you know anything about that?'

'No, but if it were British, it would surely be flying the ensign,' Jones answered in his usual dogmatic tone.

'Yes, well, we will keep an eye on it,' the captain answered and nodded. It was obvious that he thought he was not being told the whole story. He turned away and we left the room.

Once outside on deck, Jones stopped and strained to see the ship mentioned. I looked in the same direction, trying to see whatever there was to see. Eventually, we both picked out a shape and though we couldn't really see it in any definition, it obviously was a large ship.

'What is that all about?' I asked. I felt sure he would know.

'Not at all sure. Not one of ours, though, I don't think.' He shrugged his shoulders and began to walk away.

I was quite surprised at his seeming lack of interest.

'Well, is that all you have to say?' I asked.

He halted and turned back to me, looked once again in the

general direction of the ship and answered, 'That is not something I can do anything about. It may be a show of strength, it may be a bluff, but whatever it is, must be dismissed as a threat until it threatens us in some way.'

I thought of the word parables and knew that it was a perfect way to describe the way Jones spoke. He was so much more highly educated than I so decided to stay silent until he had something he wished for my input on.

During the next two days, the guarding exercise continued and on the horizon behind us, there was always a visible presence. There was really no point in watching and wondering nor fearing the veiled threat if that is what it was – that didn't stop me from wondering and looking in that direction every time I came on deck or looked out a porthole.

I informed the rest of our inner circle and many eyes watched for a change of status or a hint of intent. The only thing we knew for sure was that it was there.

CHAPTER 27

Though Jake was no longer playing the game of charades and had dropped the pretence of who he really was, he did seem less worried and less nervous. In fact, his demeanour was puzzling to me. Was he resigned to the fact that he would be imprisoned or worse? Was he just being stoic? Or was it something else?

On the third day, I entered to do my usual daily inspection of his condition and the status of his incarceration. He was standing, looking out of the porthole and there seemed to be a look of knowing on his face. It bothered me and what bothered me even more was that the man watching him, Weathers, was indeed not watching him.

'Why is he able to stand?' I asked.

'Well, it's not as though he is going anywhere,' Weathers answered, turning to look at Jake.

'That's not the point. He's dangerous,' I scolded.

'He's still got his hands tied and we have a kind of a deal. I let him stand and he doesn't try to escape,' Weathers said, obviously a little annoyed by my tone.

We had never had a moment where I had thought to tell him what to do before, but here I thought I must insist.

'Sorry, no. That is not good enough. Please retie him,' I instructed.

Weathers' face changed. He gave Jake a death stare. He was not amused but began to retie Jake's legs.

'Thanks,' I said but he only gave a small bow acquiescing while showing his displeasure.

I turned my gaze to Jake. He was glaring at me with a loathing in his eyes that was palpable.

'Do you need anything?' I asked as Weathers finished securing his legs.

'Not from you,' he answered in a surly tone.

I shook my head. I didn't understand where his hatred came from, nor could I see why he acted so superior. After all, he was a prisoner and a traitor from my point of view.

'Please yourself,' I answered and walked out.

When I came on deck, I took a while to locate the small shadow on the horizon, but it was still there and seemed as threatening as if it were alongside with its guns ready to open fire.

I decided to follow up on the discussion with Weathers and walked off to Cain's cabin. Opening the door, he stuck out a hand and shook mine. We moved to the centre of the room. Nesbitt was at the table, engrossed in a game of patience, and another man sat on the couch, reading.

'Did you know that Weathers was allowing Jake to have no leg ties?' I asked.

'No, but where is he going to go?' he asked calmly.

'That is not the point. He could do something – you know, hurt someone,' I answered, wishing I didn't find it necessary to cause such a furore over this.

'Okay, I will tell everyone,' Cain said in a reassuring tone.

I was delighted that he had taken me seriously, that allowed me to drop the matter and concentrate on the many other pressing matters.

We both sat down at the table and watched the cards moving about. Nesbitt seemed to be just wanting time to waste time. Cain eventually spoke.

'Who is on watch next?' he asked,

Responding quickly, Nesbitt answered, 'I think it is Nagel,' while searching for the piece of paper on which the 'roster' was written. He recovered it under some papers on the far end of the table. He looked at it and said, 'Yes, it's Nagel. He is on from mid-day.'

'I think you'd better get everyone together so we can go through our rules again,' Cain instructed, and, nodding, Nesbitt stood and left us.

A few minutes passed, then at fairly regular intervals the others joined us. When everyone was present, Cain started by thanking them all for their assistance.

'Some have been allowing the prisoner to walk about. That is simply not to happen. We don't know what he is capable of and he must be kept secured at all times and he should have two people guarding when he goes to the toilet.' He paused to watch everyone nodding agreement and then continued, 'This is for everyone's safety and for his too.'

Everyone present showed some form of agreement and the main thread of the gathering was completed. I decided to give everyone a pat on the back for all of their work and so I began to speak, a little weakly at first but I did gain some momentum.

'I wanted to thank you all. This has been an amazing trip. It would have been wonderful if only the sports we came for had seen us give our best, but you have all given so much more.' I paused for effect. 'I know many of you have questions you would like answered, but still you have shown your belief in your country and have rallied to protect the unprotected.'

I realised that I was sounding a bit corny and so I changed tack a little. 'This has been an eye opener for all of us, and I couldn't have had better people around me. Thank you all and stay safe and strong. Australia isn't that far away,' I concluded.

All present gave a little clap. I knew that I had done nothing to answer any of their questions, but it seemed not as important as the feeling of team spirit.

Jones and Cain then spoke and added to my thanks. Cain also gave out several more jobs and asked for some assistance in the afternoon between prisoner-watching duty and the 'evening shift' as he called them. Several hands shot up and, as usual, the first of these was Nesbitt's.

It made me feel even more proud of what we had done and were still doing. Indeed, it brought a lump to my throat and I was glad I had already spoken.

Jones then effectively dismissed all of us, always the military man, with the parting words, 'You should all get as much rest as you can while you are not working. This must be, and will be, run like a special op's mission – secrecy is paramount and you will all only be given the information you need, on a need-to-know basis. Am I understood?' he concluded and it was obvious that his instructions were of less significance to most than the word of Cain or even myself. Everyone nodded dutifully and we left to go about our own days.

I left and went to our cabin, and met with Berta and Ronja. I gave them a quick recap of the meeting. Both nodded, but I could see that they both felt left out. They had both been vital to the mission so far and I knew that they should have been involved in the discussions.

'Really, it was just about the shifts and how they are to look after Jake,' I said, knowing that this would not placate their thoughts of gender bias.

'Was anything said about the ship that is following us?' Ronja asked.

'No, no one seems to know anything,' I answered and, feeling their disappointment, in my head I made myself a promise that they would not sit outside any other meeting.

Late that afternoon I took Berta on a walk around the deck and we stopped at the hand rail nearest to where our cabin was, and just watched the other ship.

'Who do you think is looking back?' Berta said at length.

'No idea. It's not as though it would be one of ours. We haven't notified anyone. I don't see what the Germans would hope to gain if it's them. Let's face it, they don't really care who knows what they are doing. I wonder if we haven't all wasted our time,' I mused.

'No, don't say that. Someone needs to stand up to those bastards,' she said, taking a long hard look at me.

I did feel a little ashamed; that was the first time I had ever heard her swear, and though I knew what I had said was what most of us were feeling, I should not have said it even under my breath.

'I do hope you are right,' I offered and took her hand.

The evening breeze was not that strong but it was a little cool and she snuggled in close to me. I felt like the luckiest man alive.

'I love you,' I blurted and immediately felt like an idiot.

'Well, it's about time you said so.' She laughed, looking up into my eyes.

I couldn't find any other words and just gaped at her.

'I love you too. I love the way you say "well" at the start of most sentences, I love how you drop into that vacant look when you feel uncertain. God, I even like your hair,' she joked.

'My hair? What's wrong with my hair?' I asked rhetorically, knowing full well that it was fairly unkempt.

She stood on her tippy toes and kissed me as if to stop me from talking. Oh God was I head over heels. I held her tight to me, hoping that I would never have to let her go.

We stayed in the embrace for several minutes, but as is often the case, the moment of bliss was broken in upon by some shouting. There was the sound of men yelling and soon the door nearest to us burst open and Peter came running out, closely followed by Nesbitt.

'What the hell is going on?' I questioned and he answered quickly.

'He's out!'

CHAPTER 28

A search of the ship was commenced. The following was related to me later by Cain and Ronja.

Cain had entered the protected cabin and had come face-to-face with Jake who held a knife.

Weathers was laying on the ground bleeding. Cain said he could see blood on the ground in a pool but not the wound it had come from.

Jake waved the knife toward the bathroom and Cain understood that he was to enter. On doing so, the door was closed and jammed shut. Cain couldn't tell how but when he tried to open it, he found it immovable.

Hearing the cabin door open and close, he presumed that Jake had left and began to shout. It appeared to him that no one could hear him.

Ronja had heard the commotion but thought it much like the times previously, when Jake had been ranting. She took little notice, then her door had burst open and Jake entered.

'Vadoma, quick, we haven't got long.' He panted.

As she was sitting on the chair on the opposite side on the table, she didn't move but started to write a note.

'What is happening? I can't speak,' she wrote.

Jake took up the pad and read, then said suspiciously, 'What the hell have they done to you?'

'I was beaten,' she wrote when she retrieved the pad. 'How did you get out?'

He seemed to be suspecting that this was not Vadoma. She didn't know why.

'Get up,' he ordered.

Ronja knew the game was up if she stood, her stature being so much shorter than the real Vadoma.

She began to write a new note, but he grabbed the pen and pad and threw them across the room, shouting, 'I said get up!'

Ronja stood and he immediately realised that his suspicions were correct – this was not his accomplice.

'Who the hell are you?' he asked in a much softer tone.

Suddenly, the bandaged face spoke and it startled him.

'Vadoma is dead and your little game is up,' Ronja said.

There was no further discussion. He lunged at her and, though she was able to grab his knife-wielding hand, the blade entered her abdomen and was quickly withdrawn for another thrust.

She fell to the floor and saw Jake's shoes exit the door. She soon became unconscious.

❧

Our people ran up and down the deck looking for the escapee but to no avail. I ran to the rear of the deck and Berta followed me. We could see no one, save a few New Zealanders gathered at the stern rails, taking in the air.

They were below us, though a good 20 yards further to the stern. I turned and began to run back toward where I had started but Berta let out a yell and though I couldn't make out what she said, her tone was urgent. I turned and ran back to her.

Immediately, she pointed to Jake who was threatening the three startled men. They backed away from him as he neared the rail.

'Stop him,' I shouted but none of them were close enough nor ready to throw themselves at some madman.

Jake mounted the rail and suddenly Weathers and Peter ran up. He waved the knife at them and they too saw no chance to accost him without great risk. Turning away from the ever-growing crowd, he leapt into the air and dived in to the water. Though I only saw the top of his leap, he looked like a champion diver.

I could not see him as he hit the water but as we moved on, he was visible, breaking the surface. A cry of 'man overboard' was heard and repeated, and two safety rings were tossed overboard. Neither of the rings landed with in 50 yards of the now bobbing head of Jake. I felt the ship respond to the calls and we seemed to slow, though we were now at least 300 yards further away.

I knew nothing about ships but it seemed evident that the engines had been put in full reverse to stop forward momentum. The captain or whoever was in charge of the bridge was unable to see the body to have some sign of where they would need to turn to come back around.

Soon an officer arrived at the rail and quickly relayed some co-ordinates. His shouted messages were soon going back and forward.

Jake's head was now very hard to make out and I tried to keep it in sight while taking in everything that was happening.

I heard shouts of 'there' and 'over there!' and many other garbled shouted instructions. Really, it was a shambles. No one seemed to know what was happening though I give credit to crew who were trying to rescue the 'man overboard' through all of the uninformed and untrained shouting passengers.

Slowly, we turned, but the body in the water seemed to become further and further away and was now nearly impossible to locate.

Around 15 minutes slowly crept by as we were manoeuvred skilfully back to the point where Jake had last been seen. Everyone, seeming to move as one, headed toward the front of the ship.

The decks were now full of people and all were straining to see something, anything. All were silent until someone from behind me shouted 'there' and repeated 'over there'. All heads seemed to be turned to port as if directed by some unseen control. Many more shouts of 'there, he's over there' were uttered.

I couldn't help but think that each person who made out the shape in the water thought that they were the only person aboard who could see it, and each were trying to be heard as the shouts became louder.

An officer now standing at the prow of the ship came into view as I, with so many others, made my way to the rail nearest to the action. Movement on deck suddenly caught my attention as members of the crew prepared, uncovered and readied a life boat to lower. The process seemed to take forever and the drifting body and the ship were soon several hundred yards apart again.

Obviously, this was not something which had been practiced enough. One of the crew fell hard onto the deck as the boat moved as it was winched. The man was quickly to his feet and though he moved to recover his position, it was obvious that he had taken quite a blow to the head and he stumbled, being caught by Best and several other men.

Best immediately began to treat the man and Nesbitt, who was near the lifeboat, soon took one of the guide ropes and stopped the swinging movement. The small boat cleared the side of the ship and three men wearing life jackets quickly boarded while a fourth, without any safety equipment, took the place of the fallen man.

As the lowering of the boat began, shouts broke out among the onlookers as the water, around ten yards further away from us than Jake, seemed to boil.

A woman screamed and Berta took my arm. Her hands were shaking.

What the hell was going on? Was this a whale? No animal could surely cause such a large disturbance. I remember thinking terrible thoughts of sharks and what terrible fate was about to be meted out to the man who I once thought of as a friend.

A few hair-raising moments, which seemed to be an eternity, passed then, as though fired out of some invisible cannon, the water was broken by the turret of a submarine.

The crowd gasped as one and one voice said, 'Bloody hell!'

Quickly, figures appeared on the deck of the sub and a rope was tossed in the direction of the now-swimming Jake. The scene seemed to be too unbelievable to be true. What the hell was really going on?

Visibly, many of the German crew were armed and all weapons seemed to be trained on our ship.

'Bloody hell!' the voice, which I now recognised to be that of Jones, repeated.

Everyone stood, not knowing whether to run, and where they were going to run anyway.

Catching the rope, Jake was quickly pulled to the side of the now fully surfaced U-boat. The crew were dressed in German naval uniforms but their vessel had no identifying markings. I knew this was against international law but that didn't really surprise me as nearly everything the Germans were doing at the moment seemed to be against international norms or usual practices expected by all civilised countries.

Jake, once on the deck, was moved to the base of the turret where he saluted an officer, possibly the captain above. The officer spoke, though it was simply too far away to hear what he said, then Jake answered, obviously giving his report.

The officer barked some order to the crew who all trained their weapons on our ship. There was a ripple of disbelief in the form of gasps and our captain, who had arrived on deck near Jones, asked loudly, 'What the hell have you gotten us into?'

Jones, in answer, held a hand up to silence the outburst and the captain, though ready for a fight, said no more.

Suddenly there was the sound of five short blasts of a ships horn which came from the stern of our ship. We all turned to see the frigate, which had been tailing us for several days, bearing down on the confrontation. It seemed that the Germans saw it too and we could all see it bore the insignias of the British navy.

The ship had been in front of us when we were headed back to try to save Jake, then had been to our port rear as we turned and drifted when the submarine appeared. Now she was only around half a mile from us and obviously was steaming to intercept.

There was no movement from anyone on our ship at first and none of the crew on the sub moved, though it was obvious that their attention was now on the frigate and all heads were turned in her general direction. She let out another five sharp blasts of her air horn.

There was no doubt of her intention. She looked to ram the other vessel.

The Germans knew that what they had done could be termed an act of war but as they were not flying a flag, the British ship had the right to treat her as a pirate vessel and had the right to fire on her. Indeed, that would have been the likely outcome if they had not been so near to our vessel.

The Germans blinked first and suddenly men were scrambling in the direction of the turret and loading as quickly as was possible as the sub began to move forward and slowly submerge.

The last crew member disappeared just moments before the sub was completely under water and the frigate was alongside us just moments late. She slowed to drift there only around 150 yards away.

Though virtually no one on our ship really knew what had just happened, there came a spontaneous cheer and wild waving toward the British. We all joined in, except the captain and Jones who quickly moved to the bridge to make radio contact. Soon both vessels turned in unison and we resumed our original course.

Only a few of the British crew were on deck and visible to us. Obviously they were still at battle stations – of the few we did see, only two did acknowledge our cheers and the spontaneous singing of 'Rule Britannia'. After all, they had come to our aid and though both Australians and New Zealanders liked nothing better than getting one over on the mother country on the sporting field, both countries recognised Britain as the leader of the Commonwealth since the Statute of Westminster just a few years earlier in 1931.

This revelry continued as Berta I and tried to make our way to our cabin. We were challenged by several New Zealanders asking what was going on, and why one of our team members had defected. I was more worried about other things and brushed them off, shrugging my shoulders.

When we reached our corridor, we could see several people gathered at the doorway to the room where Jake had escaped from. As I neared, they all parted and allowed me to enter.

Cain was leaning over Weathers and Best was treating him.

I dropped to my knees. 'How bad is he?' I asked.

'Hard to tell. Internal bleeding, not sure how extensive. I will need to operate. He's lost a lot of blood though,' he answered. 'We need to get him on the table, and someone get my bag and the ship's surgeon.'

As men went off to obey the orders given, there suddenly came a chilling scream. I knew the voice; it was Berta. She had carried on to our cabin and discovered Ronja in a bad way. Blood was everywhere.

I responded to her cry and, reaching her side, I could see how bad things were.

Cain had followed me and, seeing the blood, called back to Best. 'There's a woman down in here. She may be worse than Weathers.'

It was as if he had forgotten I was also a doctor.

I immediately began to treat Ronja, seeing that she had two separate wounds to her abdomen. She was unconscious.

'O'Calahan, can you deal with that?' Best yelled back and I shouted an answer in reply.

'Yes, but she has lost even more blood.'

'Triage practices, where do I need to be?' he shouted back.

'You need to be here,' I called and soon he was at my side

relieving me of the patient.

'Get to the other casualty,' he said calmly and I obeyed.

Almost at the same time as I bent down to Weathers, the ship's doctor appeared and I told him to report to Best, he being the most experienced doctor.

Just a few moments later, he returned and took control of Weathers' treatment.

'We will have to operate here to stop the bleeding,' he instructed and I nodded, knowing that he too had far more experience than I did.

Soon, the little round-faced man had extended one of the wounds in Weathers abdomen and was busily finding the damaged areas. He went to work and I assisted doing the role usually completed by a theatre nurse.

When the major part of the operation was completed, he instructed me to 'close' and left, obviously going back to the other operation being conducted by Best.

I was a fair hand at stitching up wounds, but these two wounds were fairly extensive and it took me some minutes to complete. Two sailors instructed by the purser soon arrived with a folding stretcher and loaded Weathers to take him to the infirmary. I followed them, my sleeves still pulled up and my hands and forearms covered in Weathers' blood. Members of the crew had set up lines to hold the throngs of passengers back until the areas affected were cleaned.

As we passed through, they all stepped to one side and allowed us passage. All remained silent save one of the New Zealanders who asked what was going on.

'This is not the time or place,' I answered and he nodded, and like everyone else cleared the way.

I knew there would need to be some spin put on this by Jones and I had no intention of trying to work out what that spin was.

Once I had arranged Weathers' position on one of the four treatment bunks, I pulled up a chair and sat taking his pulse every few minutes. I knew this was not of any real help but I hoped my friend knew I was there offering comfort.

Around what I thought to be midnight I heard a light knock on the door and Berta entered.

'They have set up a large table in our room for Ronja. She had a second bleed and they had to open her up again. I helped—' she started to explain but the emotion got the better of her and she broke down in tears. Though I sat and she stood, I took her hand and drew her close to me.

'There, there, she is with the best men. The old bloke is bloody brilliant,' I reassured her.

She rested the side of her face on my head and I just hugged for some time. God, she was wonderful.

Several minutes passed until there was another knock on the door. It seemed we could never be alone.

'Come in,' I said and Jones, Cain and Peter entered. Berta stepped to my side.

'How is she?' I asked, fearing the worst.

'Still uncertain, but Best is doing a fine job,' Jones answered, his usual formal tone dropped for the moment.

'We need to talk,' Peter said and Berta went to leave.

'No, I'm not having Berta excluded any more. She is as much a part of this as any of us,' I insisted.

'Fine with me,' Cain supported and Peter immediately nodded his consent. Jones, seeing that he was outnumbered, begrudgingly added a single nod.

'Alright, what is so important, now?' I questioned. a little annoyed at being interrupted.

'I have been thinking about what has happened. Someone else has to be involved. There had to be someone there to help Jake escape and the radio room was ransacked while the operator was absent,' Peter answered.

'But how can a radio room be unattended?' I questioned.

'Yes, strange how the man was taken ill just before all this kicked off,' Cain answered.

I shook my head, not really taking in everything that was being said, and wondering if any of this sounded like normal life. It didn't, but, then, nothing about this trip seemed normal.

'Well, what do you want to do about it?' I asked.

'Weathers is the most likely to have seen something. It would take more than Jake to have overpowered him. I think we need to have a guard on him through the night, or at least until he wakes and tells us anything he can,' Jones answered.

'Well, I'm not going anywhere,' I answered.

'That's just what we thought you would say, but one of us will be staying with you,' Cain instructed.

It was clear that they had decided as a group that they would just tell me what to do and I would accept their plan. I did; I had no reason to go against anything they said.

Jones produced a pistol and handed it to Cain.

'Where the hell did you get that?' I asked, knowing that the couple of guns we had were jettisoned before we started boarding.

'The captain has been of great assistance, now that he knows who is really in charge of the ship,' Jones answered me and gave a little smile.

My eyes widened as he smirked, pleased with himself. Cain took the pistol and looked it over. It was similar to those issued to police in New South Wales. He nodded and placed it in his pants pocket.

'I will be on the bridge if I'm needed,' Jones said and left with Peter closing the door behind him. Cain came and sat on the floor with his back against the wall directly opposite the only room entrance.

'God, you don't have to sit down there,' I said, but before I could offer an alternative, he broke in.

'I am quite comfortable here and this is the best vantage point in the room,' he said.

'If you say so,' I said but threw him a pillow from one of the other beds.

Berta and I sat holding hands and we all tried to think of things to say. Nothing much came and Berta and I soon fell asleep.

It must have been almost dawn when I was awakened by a scratching sound. Cain was at the side of the door and as he looked back toward myself and Berta, he placed a finger to his mouth to tell us to be silent.

We just sat there. The sound came again. I think someone was trying to get one of us to open the door and then take us by surprise.

Cain had no intention of falling for that one and remained where he was. The scratch came once more and then there was nothing.

When the coast seemed clear, Cain, with my assistance, moved the couch, which was connected to the wall by a small bracket he had to break and placed it in front of the door. This was never going to stop a determined attacker, but it would slow anyone down. Cain returned to his position and Berta and I both sat on chairs alongside Weathers' bunk.

I know it was probably obsessive of me, but I had been racking my brain before drifting off to sleep, trying to make some sense of who the supposed third conspirator might be. We were back there, suspecting almost everyone, but try as I might, I couldn't find another person who had not done everything asked of them.

I now quietly broached that subject with Cain.

'Who do you suspect?' I asked, sensing that he was getting very tired as well, he having stayed awake throughout.

'No, I can't think of anyone,' he answered, looking across at me. The intrigue seemed to give him a second wind. 'What about you?' he asked.

I shrugged. 'The only other people we saw with Dirlewanger were Nesbitt and Best and I really don't suspect either of them,' I answered and after thinking for a short while he said, 'No, neither do I.'

'I don't like Best. I don't trust him. He always looks at you in an unpleasant way,' Berta said.

We both considered her opinion but I still had no real reason to suspect him. Just because he didn't approve of me doesn't mean he was a Nazi.

'I guess he just doesn't see my inner beauty?' I half-joked.

Berta smiled a little but her eyes were still darting from side to side in the way they always did when she was pondering something.

'Well, I have to be Best's alibi. He was with me treating Ronja when Weathers was jumped and he could not have got to the radio room as he was never out of those two rooms. I was there all night until I came here,' Cain explained.

'It could be anybody. One of the crew, one of the New Zealanders, even?' Berta proffered, not really looking convinced.

'I don't really think it can be any of those. They haven't been involved with us enough. I think it has to be a member of our team.' He paused for a moment, then added, 'I wish I didn't think that.'

I had nothing to say and so just shrugged my shoulders.

'And who is to care for Ronja?' Berta questioned.

'I was hoping you would stay with her while Best gets some sleep this morning. I can ask Peter to stay with you both if that helps,' he answered her.

'Oh, yes, sure,' she said, a little surprised at his idea.

I soon went back to sleep and only woke when Berta shook my shoulder and said quietly, 'he's awake.'

Cain was standing at my right side and I could see he was helping Weathers take a sip from a glass of water. Weathers put his head back down, looking exhausted and gave a loud blowing sound as he closed his eyes.

'Oh good,' I said as he opened his eyes and looked up at me, nodding.

'Do you know what happened to you?' Cain asked.

Weathers shook his head. 'No, I was hit from behind and I can't remember anything else.'

'How do you feel?' I asked.

'Like I just finished the twentieth round of a prize fight,' he answered, opening and closing his eyes slowly.

'You were stabbed,' I said and a strange look came across his face, then he raised one eyebrow and gave a single nod.

'I don't remember that, but what happened to Jake?' he asked in a rather confused way.

'He escaped, after he hit you,' Cain said.

'No, no, I don't think that's right,' Weathers answered with a puzzled look on his face, then he added, 'I was looking at Jake when I was hit.'

'Yes, that was what we were most worried about. You didn't see who hit you?' Cain half-asked and half-told Weathers as he put his head on one side.

'Ah, no, I can't remember if I saw anyone. I was just hit.' Weathers struggled to answer.

He needed to rest and recover. I thought that telling him about Ronja, and Jake's escape, could wait until later.

'I think that is enough for now,' I said in my most doctorly voice.

Cain and Berta took the hint and Berta left us for her duties with Ronja while Cain resumed his position on the floor.

The rest of the day passed uneventfully and at around 7pm, I resumed my position at Weathers' side, having had around four hours of sleep in the afternoon. I had checked Ronja's condition just prior to my evening vigil and it seemed from the ship's doctor's report that she would most likely have a full recovery, though, she was not yet out of the woods.

I was pleased to hear that information and knew I could pass on better news when Weathers was more intent on finding out what had happened.

The next few days seemed to drag by. Weathers showed great powers of recovery and Ronja was now finally taking soft foods. Neither had any further information which would help us to discover who our traitor was and still we placed overnight guards on both of them.

I saw Berta only in passing and realised how much she meant to me. I couldn't, even for a short time, stop thinking about her. I wanted to take up where we left off on deck that fateful night when Jake had escaped. Duty kept us apart for almost five days until Weathers was back on his feet and wanted to see Ronja, to see with his own eyes that she was recovering.

I went with him to the other treatment room and there we found Ronja sitting in a lounge chair, having her feet washed by Berta.

'Oh, sorry,' I said, turning as if to leave.

'No, it's alright. Come in,' she said, obviously not embarrassed by our presence.

Weathers walked over to her and took her hand. 'I am so sorry.'

'You have nothing to be sorry for,' she told him and smiled, the first time she had done so since the stabbing.

Berta finished by drying Ronja's feet and then beckoned for me to follow her from the room.

'We will give them a few minutes. They can help each other get through this better than we can,' she said and I knew that she was right.

Over the next week or so the two patients grew ever closer and it certainly seemed to me that they were meant to be together.

CHAPTER 29

On our arrival back in Brisbane, members from Queensland disembarked to the fanfare usually reserved for an all-conquering team of the day. Streamers flew and the cheers went up as individuals were announced as they disembarked.

Almost before the gang planks were emptied of the disembarking athletes and officials, they were filled by the many members of the secret services and the Government.

Those of us involved in the 'events' were ushered to the room which Jake had been imprisoned in and one at a time we were taken before the inquisition, starting with Jones then Best. One by one those before us entered and were then shown to an empty room at the end of their evidence.

I was third last to be followed by Berta and last, Ronja.

As I entered, I could see that Jones had joined the panel and was sitting to the right end of the seats. A long table had been placed between us and it was covered by large amounts of paperwork. One of the nameless heads was taking notes.

'Mr O'Calahan, you are not compelled to speak to us without council,' the man in the middle of the group said, I thought a little loudly for the size of the room. 'Are you willing to answer some questions?' he asked.

Jones gave me a little nod.

'Yes, certainly,' I answered, feeling somewhat unsure of myself.

The same man continued. 'What was your part in this event?'

'I was the team's second doctor,' I answered.

'And did you have a second role?' he continued.

I was uncertain how to answer and so shook my head.

'Isn't it correct that you were indeed the leader of a renegade group of some kind?' he persisted, hardly allowing me to prepare an answer.

'I am no leader,' I answered, hoping he would not push that point.

'Our intel leads us to believe otherwise,' he said, his eyes boring into me. 'What is this group?'

'We were all members of the Australian Olympic team,' I answered.

'So, you are not all members of the Roma-Sinti, ah, alliance?' he pushed.

'We are certainly not all members of anything,' I answered, staring back at him.

'I put to you, that you were a member of this group and that you were conducting an unauthorised spying effort,' he said, sounding smug and arrogant.

I thought for a moment and then said nothing, but shifted in my chair. I wondered if this was about to be a face-saving effort. Had the Germans complained?

'Well?' he continued.

'While in Germany we did collect a large amount of evidence which should see the Germans held accountable for the atrocities they are committing,' I answered, trying to sound as strong as could.

Jones had told us to answer the questions and to give any information other than information about the Roma/Sinti involvement.

'Would you have us believe you all acted out of the goodness of your hearts?' he persisted.

'Out of a sense of patriotism and what is wrong and what is

right,' I answered and was now feeling that I was ready for this pompous bag of wind.

There was a moment of silence, then he asked, 'And how many members of the team did not return home in this service to patriotism?'

'Two members of the Australian team, Vadoma Codona and Jake Pankhurst, did not return with the team,' I answered confidently.

'The boarding records of the vessel show that all team members boarded to come home to Australia,' he pestered.

'That is correct. Pankhurst defected at sea and Codona was replaced by a German citizen, Ronja von Esser,' I answered truthfully.

'What do you mean replaced?' he asked, leaning forward, his arms on the table.

'Codona did not arrive to depart and Miss von Esser was needed to bring the proof of the atrocities to the world,' I said, trying to sound confident.

That confidence was dinted by his next question.

'And who made that decision?'

I thought for a moment and then, not wanting to implicate any of the others, I answered, 'I did.'

'Oh, you did of your own volition?' he said mockingly.

'Yes, that is correct,' I answered shakily.

'I put it to you that that is not correct?' he pushed.

'I was asked to answer questions. I was not told you were going to be a puppet of the Nazis,' I answered, then as he faltered, I added, 'If that is your intent, I am finished answering you any further.'

I thought what I had said was fairly strong and Jones gave a little smile which reassured me.

I made as if to stand and the man next to Jones said, 'Please stay seated. We are certainly not trying to implicate you in anything and we certainly do not answer to the Nazis.'

I repositioned myself and gave a nod. I was not sure if they were all working for the same agency, and so I looked to Jones to see if he had any questions. He took the lead.

'You have no knowledge of what happened to Miss Codona?' he asked.

He had primed us to answer this question in the negative so we would not implicate Ronja in Vadoma's death.

The first man shifted in his chair and asked, 'Do you understand that there are a number of charges which could be brought against you?'

He sat even further forward in his attempt to intimidate me.

I had readied an answer but before I was able to proffer it, the man sitting next to Jones said, looking to his right, 'I think I've had enough of this.'

The three other men looked annoyed and the one in the lead position said, 'We are to be allowed to question the prisoners.'

This took me by surprise and I quickly protested. 'I was not aware I was a prisoner and so if I am being accused of something, I demand a lawyer.'

The man sitting alongside Jones intervened. 'That is enough. These people are not prisoners and need not have answer any questions in the first place. You are dismissed,' he ordered.

The man in the centre turned bright red and looked as though he could explode. His companions began to stand which seemed to enrage him even more.

Jones and his compatriot stared the man down but he was not finished. 'You have no right to throw us out of this investigation,' he said in a rather loud voice.

The little man seated next to Jones looked in firm control. He did not blush and he was obviously of a higher rank than the others.

'Oh, I think you know that is not correct. Now get out,' he ordered, pointing to the door. 'Ring your superior and he will tell you I am correct. Now, get out!'

The two men who had remained silent got their bags and walked quickly to the door the now-purple spokesman, it seemed, was going to go further but the little man who had retained his composure throughout, glared at him and then dismissed him with a withering burst.

'You have no standing here. You were allowed to stay as a curtesy and nothing more. This is a matter of national importance and you are just a little beat cop, who will be lucky to hold that position. I will be speaking to your superiors and to the Prime Minister about this and your name will be front and centre. Your impertinence will be aired. Now, get out.' He raised his voice for the last two words and the now-embarrassed and bewildered-looking man began to fumble with his papers.

'You can leave your papers and I will have them destroyed,' the little man ordered.

Finally, the other realised he was in a tenuous position and, grabbing his case, he quickly stormed out. His two offsiders had left well before him when they realised they were being directed by a higher authority. The door was closed.

'Now, O'Calahan, Jones has filled me in as to the 'events,' shall we say. He has insisted that you be present during the discussion with the two ladies.' As the little man said this, he had pointed to the door and Jones left, returning with Berta and Ronja, who were seated either side of me then Jones resumed his seat.

The little man began by introducing himself. 'My name is Rosenberg. I wish to ask just a few questions. Please do not feel pressured.' For the first time he smiled and it was the most ingenuous thing I had seen him do.

In my peripheral view right, I noted that Berta nodded.

'Now, I have heard enough from your friends about the events. I only need to see if there is anything you need to add.' He paused and nodded to the two women, then continued. 'I fear that what I have been told about Vadoma Codona is not the whole truth?'

'It was a necessary evil. She was about to kill Robert and so I shot her,' Ronja said strongly.

'I see. Do all German ladies carry a shooter?' Rosenberg asked with a smile.

'Only those in danger of their lives,' Ronja answered and stared unblinkingly into his eyes.

'And, of whom are you afraid?' he continued.

'Of no one when I have a Luger.'

This produced an even more pronounced smile on the man's face.

'I understand. You work for who?'

'I am a freedom fighter and I fight for my people: the Roma and for the Sinti and for all the so-called inferiors being eradicated in Germany,' she said powerfully.

'Eradicated?' Rosenberg questioned.

'My people are being taken off the street and sterilised, or worse, against their will. If they speak out, they are mysteriously found dead, like my father and so many others, or they disappear,' she answered.

The emotion in her voice was very touching.

He asked no further questions but nodded to indicate that she could continue if she wished.

'I was about to be taken when your wonderful team stepped in and stopped the devil, Dirlewanger. He is just one of the evil ones we have been harassed by.' She took a long breath to calm herself then continued. 'I have proof of the many terrible things they are doing in the name of racial purity. People with a mental disability are simply killed. Homosexuals are usually killed or sometimes castrated and left on the streets. The hospitals are all experimenting on those who are in their way. Robert Ritter is the architect in charge of our most tortured people.'

Again, her imperfect English let her down.

I smiled at Berta and she rolled her eyes. There was no doubt that Rosenberg was flirting with Ronja. The only one who seemed not to notice was Ronja.

'I have this package,' she said, taking a thick envelope from her inside coat pocket.

Now I understood why she was wearing such a heavy coat in what were quite warm conditions. She handed the package to the little man who took it and placed it on the table in front of him.

He showed no intent to open the package and again nodded for her to continue.

'You will find photographs taken in several German hospitals showing the grotesque operations which are being performed by these animals. Also, the lists of the many who have been killed or have simply not come home to their families.' The last words stuck in her throat and she dropped her head, her hair fell across her face.

'There are pictures of many who have been killed, including my own family.'

She broke down and Berta put an arm around her and they turned to each other in a sombre embrace. It was clear that Ronja would not be able to go on immediately and so Rosenberg turned his attention to Berta.

'And how do you fit into all of this?' he questioned.

Berta turned only her head to him and said, 'I was recruited at the same time as the rest of the team. I, too, am Roma.'

Rosenberg did not ask any further questions, but launched into a diatribe which, it seemed, he had rehearsed, for the sentences seemed too perfect to have been ad-lib.

'All of what you say is already known by the international community. Your pictures and information will be of assistance at some stage in the future,' he said, looking from one to the next of, as if judging our facial responses.

'I have to tell you, though, that the current governments of Australia, England and America are loath to upset this Hitler. No one has the guts to call him out. Everyone knows that getting into another war with the Hun is politically suicide.' He again paused. It almost seemed that he expected some kind of affirmation.

'He builds the army to numbers outlawed and the navy and air force have such large numbers of planes that they may even be a threat to British air superiority.

'Still, our allies sit on their hands, though the sabres are rattling loudly in the wings. This is going to be, it is as certain as it can be, there is no doubt. We will see a widespread conflict which will probably involve most of Europe.' He paused.

Though none of us knew how prophetic his words were, we did not doubt that Hitler's regime must be stopped.

Seeing the look of betrayal on Ronja's face and the likelihood that we would all protest this inaction, he raised his hand to command silence.

'I do understand your position. I, too, have relatives in Germany in several Jewish enclaves in the country and they are also in the sights of the Nazis.' He paused, also showing some emotion in his voice.

'I have been tasked with putting together an intelligence operational collective to serve the Australian Government. They are not going to be caught out as they were in the great war, completely unprepared.'

I glanced across at Berta and Ronja and both had turned back to face Rosenberg, who after letting that sliver of information sink in, added, 'I would like to have this in hand quickly. I think things will move at pace after this spectacle which was the Nazi Olympics.

'I would like to offer you, Mr O'Calahan, and your team positions in which you can serve your country and the downtrodden in Germany and Europe in general. What say you?' he concluded.

We all looked dumbfounded. Jones gave an air of disgust, rolling his eyes. The rest of us glanced uncertainly at each other. We gave no answer. I, for one, thought that all of this was over. I wanted nothing more than to go back to being an average every day doctor.

I was shocked when Berta finally answered. 'I will help in whatever capacity you wish.'

I raised my eyebrows looking at her in surprise.

She nodded and, as I would have followed her anywhere, I added, 'I don't know how I would be able to help but I am at your command.'

I felt and sounded like a fool but continued to look at the two women. For quite some time, Ronja sat, unsure if she was being offered the same burden. Then she sat forward and looked purposefully into Rosenberg's eyes. Jones had sat looking uncomfortable; he was part of the establishment being discussed.

'If I am to be considered, I would wish to setup an escape route for the Germans under threat,' she said uncertainly.

'Oh, indeed, you will be a crucial part of the team. A team led by Jones here. You would all answer to him and he would report to me. I am answerable to the Prime Minister directly. You will have all the assistance we can offer.'

The look of satisfaction beamed from Ronja's face. Jones' countenance had changed his self-importance sated.

Rosenberg turned his focus back to me.

'You will be head of operations in the field, does that meet with your approval?' he asked.

I was, to say the least, dumbfounded. What the hell did I know about running anything?

'Do I understand you have misgivings?' he asked quickly.

'Well, yes. Frankly, I have no training in how to run anything,' I answered honestly.

'Oh, you will have plenty of training. Though, the best training you could have is holding things together under fire as you did at the Olympics,' he reassured.

'I think you have been misled. I was mostly doing what other people told me,' I answered.

'That is not what the others I have interviewed think. They all speak of you as their leader – that is except Doctor Best, but he will just be going back to his practice and will not be involved any further,' he reassured and on seeing that there was still some doubt in my eyes, he added, 'You think someone else is a leader among the group?'

'Well, yes. I think Cain would be a perfect leader if he is to stay involved?'

I knew I was dithering but I really wasn't sure I wanted to continue in this field. I really didn't believe I had the guts to do it. I wanted out, but there was Berta, eyebrows raised nodding in expectance. I would have walked over broken glass.

'Cain will be offered a position, along with Nesbitt. They will be the strong arm, both being trained by the police. Nagel is also in our considerations if you want him,' he concluded and then seeing the continued uncertainty written large across my face, he added, 'Is there anything else?'

'Yes. I would not be involved if Weathers was to be left out,' I answered.

'There is something of a cloud hanging over that young man. His uncle was a traitor, and collaborator. Someone in your group was in league with Pankhurst. How else would he have gotten away?' he said.

'No, it is not possible. He was wounded very badly and nearly died. If he is a traitor, then I want no part of this whole thing,' I answered, raising my voice and showing that I at least had some backbone and loyalty.

Rosenberg smiled a little. 'I would have been surprised if you had said anything else. I am sure he is with us, but there are others who are very unsure,' he said, turning his head on one side and raising his eyebrows, questioning.

'I don't give a damn what others think. I have seen him under fire and he is without doubt one of the best among us,' I answered, feeling annoyed that others would cast aspersions on one of my greatest friends.

'Be calm, no need to get upset. It is nice to hear that from you, though. I have seen him fight and he is a talent – homegrown, so to speak,' he said, gesturing with his hands to calm me.

'You will all be rigorously investigated which is a natural course when one is being selected as an operative,' he answered in a stilted way as though he thought I may be upset by what he was proposing.

'I would expect nothing less,' I answered bluntly, though I was a little annoyed that any of our team could come under question after the way all had risked their lives in Germany.

℘

Things moved very quickly from that point and we were all in training within weeks. We were to be known as '1936' and were all involved in the 'intelligence community' for the rest of our working lives and beyond.

I considered myself the luckiest man alive when my wonderful Berta consented to be my wife and lifelong partner, we married in January of 1937.

To this day, I have never loved another more.

Ronja later married Peter. Yes, I too was surprised.

I had always been of the opinion that she would choose Weathers, but he was adamant that they were just friends when I asked him how he felt about the marriage. Peter and I were each other's best man and Weathers was a groomsman at both weddings.

1936 operations conducted covert missions throughout the terrible madness which was the Second World War. Later in 1940, we would again be pitted against Dirlewanger and his cronies. It was only then that we discovered our last traitor.

We continued throughout the Cold War and conflicts in Korea and Vietnam. Though most of us are gone now in 1986, we technically have never been disbanded and are to this day current operatives.

1936 was the start of a life time of service. None of us ever felt the hurt of the betrayals our conflict in Berlin. We were somewhat hardened by the terrible events and things we saw at that time, but the one thing we always had to come back to was our total belief in each other and the knowledge that we were helping to make the differences we wanted to make where possible.

I often look back on our time in Germany and sometimes I feel that it was all for nothing So much pain could have been halted if the international community had taken some form of action.

Soon after our Olympics, the vitriol and violence was redirected, turned from the Roma and Sinti to the Jewish communities of Europe, with the resulting holocaust seen by the world.

I have often wondered what would have happened if the information we had gained and that of the many other sources had been heeded and acted upon by world governments.

1936 lives on.

Shawline Publishing Group Pty Ltd
www.shawlinepublishing.com.au